D1547424

DEVIL MAY CARE
SINNER TAKE ALL
WADE MILLER
Introduction by Nicholas Litchfield

STARK
HOUSE

Stark House Press • Eureka California

DEVIL MAY CARE / SINNER TAKE ALL

Published by Stark House Press
1315 H Street
Eureka, CA 95501, USA
griffinskye3@sbcglobal.net
www.starkhousepress.com

ISBN: 978-1-951473-06-8

Book design by Mark Shepard, shepgraphics.com
Cover design by Jeff Vorzimmer, ¡caliente!design, Austin, Texas
Proofreading by Bill Kelly
Cover art by Sam Cherry

First Stark House Press Edition: September 2020

DEVIL MAY CARE

Biggo Venn doesn't want to admit it but he's getting too old for the mercenary soldier routine. Still, when an old friend comes to him with a small job down in Mexico that's got an easy $20,000 payoff, he agrees to make the contact. Seems simple enough. But the small town of Ensenada is a lot more treacherous than he bargains for. First there's Jinny, the deceitful blonde with an itch for his traveling cash; Len Hardesty, a long-time rival and soldier for hire who just happens to appear whenever he's least wanted; and Pabla, the sweetest vision he can imagine, and possibly the most dangerous. When the bodies start piling up, Biggo knows he's in for the fight of his life.

SINNER TAKE ALL

They want him dead. General Gayoso knows that the only way to assassinate Bruno Lazar is to get the reclusive rebel out in the open. So he has Lazar's best friend poisoned, and hires Jack Cox, a down-at-heel American sharpshooter, to plan Lazar's murder at the funeral they know he will attend. The plan is brilliant in its simplicity. But it doesn't take into account the mixed emotions of Lazar's protégé, Dorlisa Von Ritter, who precedes him to Tijuana to make sure the way is safe. Nor does it take into account Cox's fatal sense of conscience. Gayoso is not a man to be thwarted, but even he cannot know what will happen when the assassin and the protégé fall in love.

THE REMORSEFUL MERCENARY AND THE RELUCTANT ASSASSIN
by Nicholas Litchfield

Much has been said of the successful writing team of Robert Allison Wade (1920–2012) and H. Bill Miller (1920–1961), who became inseparable friends when they were twelve years old and went on to co-author notable thrillers, mysteries, and detective stories throughout the late 1940s to the early '60s. It was a remarkably fertile collaboration that produced thirty-three novels and a dozen or so short stories.

To date, their books have sold more than fifteen million copies worldwide and have been translated into at least eighteen languages. Nine of these have been adapted to screen, including two made-for-TV movies, and *Badge of Evil*, a novel published in 1956 under their Whit Masterson pseudonym, which became the basis of the Orson Welles directed film noir masterpiece *Touch of Evil* starring Welles, Charlton Heston, and Janet Leigh. Around the same time, their short story "Invitation to an Accident" was nominated for the Mystery Writers of America's Edgar Allan Poe Award.

Surprisingly, despite of their vast canon of work and the solid impression they made on the crime, mystery, and thriller genres, the Wade-Miller literary partnership spanned a comparatively short period. Commencing in 1946 with the detective tale *Deadly Weapon*, it ended in 1961 with the premature death of Bill Miller, aged forty-one.

Robert Wade, who received the Life Achievement Award from the Private Eye Writers of America in 1988, continued to pen successful noir novels and police procedurals, occasionally writing under his own name but mostly using pen names, including the Whit Masterson one. Singly or in collaboration, he authored forty-six novels (thirty-three with Miller and thirteen on his own), with his final book appearing in 1979. He also wrote plays, teleplays, and film scripts. Between 1977 until 2011, he dedicated his time to writing mystery reviews for the *San Diego Union-Tribune.*

An enlightening interview with him can be found in the *San Diego Reader.* In a 1993 article, reporter John Brizzolara asks the burning question: "Why use pseudonyms? Why not just Robert Wade and William Miller?" Wade responds, "First of all, publishers didn't and possibly still don't believe that a joint name on a book is commercial." He explains that they were advised to drop the "and" from Wade and Miller and, subsequently, sold their first book. Their prolific output and Farrar, Strauss & Co.'s hesitancy about committing to further books right away compelled the duo to seek other options. The concern about damaging relations with their first publisher led them to adopt various *nom de plumes*, such as Whit Masterson, Dale Wilmer, and Will Daemer when placing work elsewhere.

Devil May Care, the opener in this Stark House collection, was a Fawcett Gold Medal original from June 1950. Four years earlier, *Deadly Weapon*, the pair's triumphant debut, garnered rave reviews, and in the ensuing years, they hammered out a whole slew of popular titles in rapid succession. Most featured enduring series character Max Thursday, who is an alcoholic ex-cop turned private investigator. *Guilty Bystander*, the novel that introduced him, was adapted into a motion picture of the same title.

According to journalist Bruce Eder, demand for the pair's work was so great that actor and producer James Cagney "requested that Wade Miller author a book that he could film and star in, and the result was *Devil May Care*, containing the character of Biggo Venn, written especially for Cagney." In 1955, Edwin Schallert, the drama editor of the *Los Angeles Times*, mentioned in his long-running column that TV writer-producer Eugene Solow was packaging the story as a feature film with Frank Sinatra and Gary Cooper in co-starring roles. Possibly, Robert Mitchum might have been an ideal choice for the central part, according to mystery critic Ted Fitzgerald of *Mystery*File*. Sadly, no movie version was ever made.

Set mainly in Mexico, this standalone is a somewhat unpredictable postwar adventure about a hard-edged former soldier of fortune, Biggo, who is enticed away from his public speaking engagements in Cleveland by his old comrade, Daniel Toevs, a veteran twenty years his senior, to travel to Ensenada, Mexico, and deliver a deathbed confession that will exonerate Tom Jaccalone, a deported racketeer. Once Jaccalone has overturned the deportation charge, he can legally re-enter the U.S., take revenge on the crook that framed him, and take back control of his rackets. In return for his efforts, Toevs promises Biggo a half share of the $20,000 paycheck.

Once in Mexico, things get complicated, and the seemingly straightforward job becomes a battle for survival. Biggo's contact—an innocent saloon owner named Zurico—is brutally murdered, and then a bargirl dupes Biggo and steals his luggage. Later, he falls in love, and then a rough acquaintance from his soldiering days turns up without warning and puts Biggo through the wringer. Shot at, beaten up, imprisoned, and hurt by a love rival, the bruised and battered hero, who carries Jaccalone's fate in his pocket, winds up caught between the lines of two enemy gangsters with no way of knowing which side is which. Ably buoyed by a gung-ho, devil-may-care attitude, the once formidable fighter—now a shadow of his former self—must rely on his wits to outmaneuver the opposition and come out on top.

Superior, stylish prose and thoughtful attention to character encourage the patient reader to excuse the harsh, unappetizing characters and pardon the measured opening and curiously winding narrative. The payoff is certainly worth it. This hot, sweaty, gritty tale of brutality and vengeance builds to a particularly tense and thrilling finale. And Biggo's strenuous evolution from the confident, selfish, unafraid, unapologetic brute at the start of the book, to the vulnerable, disillusioned, mournful, half-decent person he becomes is something to savor.

Secondary characters, like Jinny Wagner, the loyal yet mistreated love interest, Toevs, the jittery old rummy, and Pabla Ybarra y Calderón, the conceited temptress, leap off the page. And what can one say about Lew Hardesty? This "vigorous male animal," full of "strength and manhood" and slyness, who bears a restless, reckless "see-you-in-hell" look in his eyes, fully lives up to his fierce description. Younger, slenderer, taller, stronger, he's the perfect foil for the aging "old tiger" Biggo whose upper body is a hash of battle souvenirs and whose recent mistakes and defeats and humiliations puncture his pride and make him question his abilities.

If it weren't for Hardesty, the man with "a knack for showing up where he wasn't wanted," this yarn wouldn't have had the cruel, aching punch it needed. Rather than just a tougher, meaner version of Biggo, he is an illustration of what Biggo might have become if not for people like Toevs and Jinny to steer him back on the straight and narrow.

Distinctly different parallel themes crop up in the second tale in this collection, *Sinner Take All*, another Fawcett Gold Medal original, which was first published in August 1960. The suave American horse trainer, James Cox—a former military man who served in Korea— replaces the uncouth character Biggo from the earlier tale. Cox, a wanted man, sought by the U.S. government as a material witness against his shady employer, refused to rat on his friends and fled to Mexico during the court trial to escape a subpoena. Lured by a substantial bounty and the promise of citizenship, he accepts a cloak-and-dagger assignment to assassinate Bruno Lazar, a former senator, newspaper-owner, and cabinet minister. Lazar, whose anti-government publications threaten to cause an uprising, is regarded as a dangerous radical. The fierce General Gayoso, head of counter-intelligence, concocts a devious plan to eliminate him, which hinges on Cox taking down Lazar while the elderly cripple attends a friend's funeral in Tijuana.

As in *Devil May Care*, a couple of young, beautiful women divert the main character from his goal and add an element of romance to the proceedings. Here, it's a strong, intuitive widow—Lazar's faithful social secretary, Dorlisa Weber, née von Ritter—who captures the hero's affections. Odilia, Gayoso's junkie bondswoman, fills the role of manipulative seductress, competing for Cox's attention. As was the case in the previous story, a "love triangle" is formed, with Cox torn between duty and desire.

In lesser hands, the burgeoning romance between Cox and Dorlisa might have allowed *Sinner Take All* to become encumbered and slow, but the interesting, realistic interactions between the leads help strengthen characterizations and add emotional heft. Additionally an exemplary focus on pacing and structure, as well as deft use of multiple points of view, elevates the tale.

In a *New York Times* article in 1950 addressing concerns about the declining quality of new mysteries and the competing rise in popularity of science fiction, columnist Anthony Boucher lauded the work of Wade Miller as cause for celebration. Along with half a dozen other "Grand Old Hands," Boucher contended that Wade Miller were master craftsmen who had the ability to churn out exceptional, tried and tested mysteries "with just sufficient variation to put new life into the form."

Devil May Care and *Sinner Take All* showcase Wade and Miller's aptitude for first-rate drama and suspense, and their expertise in depicting tarnished, cynical men battling with their conscience. Rounded protagonists, enthralling physical duels, and sly, unanticipated narrative shifts keep these absorbing tales from seeming dull or commonplace. And while the reader might not empathize with or condone Biggo or Cox's behavior, they will certainly appreciate the complexity of character and accent on human conflict.

In print for the first time in many decades, these neglected, once popular novels are a welcome treat for lovers of tension-packed, hard-boiled suspense thrillers. These "Grand Old Hands" will have you turning the pages with glee, and eager to seek out more of their work.

—June 2020
Rochester, NY

....

Nicholas Litchfield is the founding editor of the literary magazine *Lowestoft Chronicle*, author of the suspense novel *Swampjack Virus*, and editor of nine literary anthologies. He has worked in various countries as a journalist, librarian, and media researcher and resides in western New York. Formerly, a book reviewer for the *Lancashire Post* and syndicated to twenty-five newspapers across the UK, he now writes for *Publishers Weekly* and regularly contributes to Colorado State University's literary journal *Colorado Review*. You can find him online at nicholaslitchfield.com.

DEVIL MAY CARE

● ●

WADE MILLER

CHAPTER ONE

SUNDAY, SEPTEMBER 10, 9:30 P.M.

He hurried out of the lighted foyer of the church into the cool night, hoping that the girl with the insolent red mouth had waited for him. He had amused himself during his lecture by staring at her meaningfully. And she had returned his gaze, the only one of the faces—the attentive, bored or blank faces—to which he'd paid any attention.

But the faces were gone now and so was the girl. The man with her, probably her husband, had taken her away. He stopped by the bulletin board on the lawn and swore to relieve his disappointment. The bulletin board was a glass-front case with white plastic letters set against black felt. Under the permanent heading of Northside Open Forum, it read: Biggo Venn—Soldier of Fortune—"What is India's Destiny?" Then tonight's date. Below that a reminder: Don't Forget The Picnic Sept. 17—Everybody Welcome.

It occurred to Biggo that maybe she'd thought he was too old. He didn't believe it. He looked about like any other healthy, husky man who wasn't young any longer and still hadn't gotten old. He had a habit of lying about his age, never admitting he had passed forty. Part of that was vanity but most of it was common sense: nobody wants an old soldier.

His body gave an impression of more strength than could be possible. He wasn't tall and his barrel chest and slightly bowed legs caused him to appear shorter than he was. In uniform—any uniform—his squareness seemed less awkward than now. But tonight, in Cleveland, he wore a double-breasted tropical suit and though it was well-cut it made him look a yard wide.

Except for his flattened nose he showed no visible scars. He had easy-going undistinguished features which enjoyed life while his squinting amber eyes priced it. There was some gray in his sand-colored shock of hair but it was hard to detect. He had big hands with sandy hair on their backs and big feet. His teeth were good except for a broken molar which showed when he laughed.

Biggo didn't laugh now. He had counted on the red-mouthed girl being there. Now the evening was just another speech, just another fifty dollars.

Somebody else laughed, behind him. A cigarette butt flipped against the glass case and sparked before it fell at Biggo's feet. A voice said, "Even if I wanted to know India's destiny I sure as hell wouldn't ask you."

Biggo wheeled and regarded the tall old man who stood in the glare from the church entrance. He said, "So you can read at last." Then he grinned and put out his hand. "What are you doing in Cleveland, Toevs?"

"What's wrong with Cleveland? A fellow has to come home someday."

"Haven't seen you since Marrakech."

"Last I saw of you was your backside running away from those French bayonets." Toevs looked at the glass sign-case and good-humoredly spat on it. "Soldier of fortune, huh?"

Biggo just grinned and glanced him over. He was glad to see Daniel Toevs but vaguely disturbed at the changes. A short time before, perhaps even so short a time as a year or two, Toevs had been a fierce and rugged man. But the long hard life had caught up with him. It had stolen away his stock in trade, his commanding air of strength. It had puffed Toevs' belly and narrowed his shoulders. It had bagged his clothes, caused his gray hair to need cutting, perfumed him with cheap rum and left him standing in Cleveland for Biggo to see. Biggo didn't like the idea but he grinned and said what he thought had happened to Toevs.

"The rope hasn't been made yet," the old man said. "Did you actually tell them you were a soldier of fortune?"

"It was free. You should have come in and learned something." In his mind, Biggo was estimating the touch that Toevs was obviously after. And in his mind, he shrugged. Money was only money and friends were friends, after all. It had been ten years since Marrakech.

Toevs must be deep in his sixties by now.

"Well," said Toevs, "I have a deal that is made for a soldier of fortune. So simple even a dumb mick could handle it. Even you could handle it, Biggo, I think." He was too anxious; it still looked like a touch. But talking to Toevs would make up for missing the girl. "All it involves is a run down to Mexico for a couple of days where you collect the money. No work at all. I've been waiting all week for you—I saw this sign and I said—"

"You bet. How much is it going to cost me?"

"For what, you son of a dog? This is a break for you. This is bigger profit than guns and a lot easier to transport. You thickheaded—"

Biggo laughed. "Let's get down to my hotel where the bottle is."

"Sure," said Toevs happily. "Just wait till I get rid of her and—"

"Her?" asked Biggo sharply. He followed the direction of Toevs' thumb and saw the girl on the corner near the streetlight. At first, he thought it was the red-mouthed girl, after all. But it wasn't; it was another girl. Biggo felt better. He cut across what the old man was saying with, "Never mind getting rid of her, Dan'l. Bring her along."

"Well," said Toevs doubtfully, "I don't know that we can talk with—" But Biggo was already walking toward her so he shrugged and tagged along.

Toevs made the introductions. Her name was Felice something. She was young, almost over-stacked, like a caricature of a girl. Her eyes had seen a lot and right now they were seeing Biggo. She held onto his hand after they had said hello. Biggo didn't mind. Felice's red hair was possibly dyed but the thrust of her breasts was real. She wore a cheap cloth coat which she left unbuttoned to show how tight was her jersey dress around her boyish hips.

"We're going up to my room for a drink," said Biggo, looking her up and down. "Want to come along, honey? You'll be safe."

"If I wanted to be safe, I'd join the YWCA," Felice said. She wiggled slightly. "Besides, I don't think anybody should drink alone, do you, Biggo?" They understood each other instantly and hotly.

Toevs was busy shouting down a cab. They rode to the downtown hotel where Biggo was registered, Felice squeezed in between the two big men. Her slim leg pressed against Biggo's thigh, rubbed occasionally. Her dime store perfume filled the cab and he thought it might be a pretty good evening at that.

If Toevs had anything special to talk about, he didn't bring it up in the taxi. His hands were nervous. He didn't relax any until the three of them were in Biggo's room and the door was locked behind them. He wandered around while Biggo stripped off coat and tie.

Felice shed her coat and kicked off her shoes. She bounced on the bed. Then she made herself comfortable and pulled down her skirt until it was only a little way above her knees. "Say, this is high class," she said. She liked the wallpaper.

Toevs said, "How'd you get into this public speaking business, Biggo?"

"Marking time, Dan'l. When I got out of the Caribbean—I was with that bunch that figured to light a fire under Trujillo—"

"Cuba kind of stopped you cold, didn't they?"

"Cuba—and that money from next door never did come." Felice was stretching out a nylon-sheathed leg, examining a run near the stocking top. Her toes pointed directly at Biggo. He got his eyes away with difficulty. "Some of the boys are still locked up down there. Paget and Sammy Winter, you knew them, didn't you? I was broke but I had something the comandante wanted so I bribed my way out and when I lit in New York I hooked up with this agent for a tour. Matter of C.O.D., two or three speeches a week."

"I think that's wonderful, simply wonderful," cooed Felice. "Do you make much money that way, Biggo?"

"Enough to have my fun." Biggo sat down at the writing desk and addressed an envelope. "Trouble is the agent gets twenty per cent." He put a ten-dollar bill in the envelope and sealed it and put it where neither of his guests could steal it. "Well, that's enough business."

He looked down at Felice. She arched her back, lidded her eyes briefly. "What I want is a little drinkie," she announced.

Biggo got out his bottle of bourbon and found glasses in the bathroom. He decided he couldn't stand much of the girl's voice. He wasn't interested in her conversation anyway. He asked Toevs, "What are you doing, Dan'l?"

Toevs had a drink first. "Well, I've been thinking about China."

Felice exclaimed over that and Biggo said fine and they all drank to China. Biggo wasn't fooled. China was just another way for Toevs to say he was going nowhere, had nowhere to go.

The girl picked up the small leatherbound Bible that was lying open on the other pillow. She said, "For goodness sakes, what's this doing here?" She thought it was funny. She looked at Biggo. "A church—and now this? You're a character, Biggo."

Toevs remembered. He laughed too. "I see you're still carrying the Good Book around with you. Looks like the same one you had then. Turned holy yet?"

Biggo kidded him. "Not a boy like me. That's for old goats with one foot in the grave, like you." Then he said seriously, "Good fighting in that book. Those Hebrews were tough ones when they had a decent command staff. Makes good reading."

Felice thought that was funny too but Toevs sighed. "Ah, we knew some tough ones, didn't we, Biggo?" In silence, he savored his memories as he did the whiskey. "How long's it been?"

"Since Marrakech? Ten years, I guess. Maybe less."

"Ten years?" said Felice as if it were the end of time. "Damn, that's—"

"Must have been less," said Toevs hurriedly. "Must have been because I'm still in mighty good shape. You can see that for yourself. This around the middle could come out in a hurry, if need be."

"You bet. You haven't changed a bit, Dan'l." Biggo was sorry he had kidded about one foot in the grave.

"Just because a man is coming into sixty doesn't mean I don't have a couple of wars left in me yet." Toevs was lying about his age but Biggo couldn't see correcting him. Especially with the girl there. "When I see some of the young fellows they're hiring to fight their wars these days ..." He shook his head dolefully.

They drank to something turning up. They talked about the old days and enlarged them. Toevs seemed in no hurry to mention his proposition now. He was acting important while he had the opportunity. Biggo didn't rush him. He sat on the bed and Felice curled up beside him with her head on his leg. He ran the tips of his fingers along her back. She was warm like an alley cat and she squirmed excitedly under his hand. He patted her idly and played with the fastener of her brassiere through the thin dress.

The two men drank to the foreign place names, liking the taste of them on their lips, more familiar than their home country to them. And eventually, Biggo told of a happening that was since Marrakech. It was a happening with a cruel and bloody ending.

"I still feel bad about those twenty Arabs," Biggo said. "I was responsible for them, Dan'l. He didn't have to do that to them."

"I didn't know him. Seen him since?"

"I heard he was down in Bolivia. I'll run across him some day and we'll settle it. It's one of those things that has to be settled."

Felice rolled over, shivering. "Aw, honey, they were only Arabs."

Toevs shrugged. "Fighting's fighting and it doesn't matter whether men are shot in cold blood or hot blood. They're just as dead either way."

"That's right, honey." Felice linked her arm behind Biggo's neck and began to pull him slowly down towards her. "Don't think about Arabs. Think about me."

Toevs cleared his throat. "Biggo, how you fixed for money?"

Biggo let himself be drawn closer to the painted young mouth in his lap and answered, "I can let you have some."

Toevs snorted with dignity. "You think I came all the way up here to listen to you gab so I could make a touch? I'm talking about some big easy money for you."

Felice was whispering to him, just barely moving her lips an inch away from his, "Kiss me, Biggo, kiss me." Her tongue beckoned insistently and her dress was disarrayed again.

"How about it?" Toevs demanded.

"I never turned it down yet," Biggo murmured, still not looking at the other man. He brushed over the open mouth briefly, teasing her. Toevs took his shoulder. "Come on, come on," he said impatiently. "This is important stuff, Biggo." Biggo raised up and Felice said something under her breath. She rolled off his leg and lay back on the bed, pouting. Toevs said to her, "Kid, we've got business to discuss. You wait for me somewhere, in the bathroom maybe. And run the water."

She met Biggo's eyes and shrugged. She swung off the bed with a display of nylon and bare flesh and the tailored edge of pink panties. She said, "Don't be too long," and strolled into the bathroom. She took another drink with her.

Biggo watched her trim buttocks twitch out of sight. He had to have Toevs repeat what he'd said.

The water started in the bathroom so the girl couldn't overhear but Toevs lowered his voice anyway. "Ever hear of Tom Jaccalone?"

Biggo thought about it and said no.

Toevs rummaged in his pocket for a newspaper clipping and handed it over silently. It was from an old newspaper but not very worn; Toevs had probably torn it from a library file somewhere.

Biggo looked at the picture of Tom Jaccalone who was coming out of a courtroom between two policemen. Jaccalone was a short bald fellow with a hook nose. At that time he had been going to prison on extortion charges. Before his fall he had been the controlling factor in most of the gambling in the Midwest. Before his rise he had been a Sicilian immigrant.

When Biggo tried to hand the clipping back, Toevs said cryptically, "Keep it."

"Why?"

"Let me tell you, Biggo. This Jaccalone served about two years in prison and then the government deported him to Sicily as an undesirable alien. Well, Sicily wasn't for him so he came back across the ocean and settled in Mexico, on a ranch in a southern part. He's been living there ever since. He's not easy to get in touch with."

Biggo said fine and had a drink and thought, but not about Jaccalone. "Say, did I ever tell you about the time this alcalde's wife in Yucatan—"

"No, listen to me. Jaccalone wants to get back in this country."

"Okay. I can bring him in. Anybody could. How much?"

Toevs shook his head. "But he wants to get back in legal. A lot of his money is tied up in his business here in the States. A fellow named Silver Magolnick is running Jaccalone's business up here now. He was

the second-in-command before Jaccalone got sent away." Toevs stuck
a thumb in his own chest. "Through me, Tom Jaccalone can come back
in legal. There's money in it, Biggo. You want some of it?"

"All depends." Biggo lay down where Felice had been lying; the
spread was still warm. "Keep talking, Dan'l. You're doing fine."

The story was simple. Jaccalone's prison term had been the result
of extortion charges brought by a pool hall owner named George G.
Noon. After the conviction, Noon had dropped out of sight. Silver
Magolnick had paid him enough for the frame-up so that he could live
as he had never lived before. Noon went through his money and his
health rapidly and ended up in a cheap rooming house in Gary where
Toevs had met him.

Toevs paused, stared, then said slowly, "Kind of odd what things will
prey on a man. With you it's those twenty Arabs. With George Noon,
it was one Sicilian—Jaccalone. You tell me why. Jaccalone's a son of
a dog ten times over. But he was still on Noon's conscience. Well, before
he died Noon wrote out a confession in his own hand. A regular legal
deathbed confession which I've got. Right here in my pocket, Biggo."

He leaned back proudly and poured as if he owned the bottle.

Biggo said, "The confession makes the conviction illegal. Which
makes the deportation illegal. Talk about the money."

"Twenty thousand dollars when this Noon paper is delivered. I
managed to contact Jaccalone by letter."

"Where do you deliver? And collect?"

"I picked Ensenada. Know where that is? South of San Diego,
California, about sixty-five miles across the border. I picked Ensenada
in case Jaccalone wanted to come himself. But he writes like he'll send
an agent. Ensenada is close enough to the border in case he tries any
fancy maneuvers."

"What if Magolnick tries any fancy maneuvers? I can't see how Noon
could write all this stuff down without using Magolnick's name a few
times. If I were Jaccalone, I'd kill Magolnick."

"That's right, but give him time. How's Magolnick going to know
about this little paper of mine?" Toevs said it almost pleadingly. "You
let Jaccalone worry about settling that later. Will you take this little
paper down to Ensenada, Biggo?"

"Why me?"

"You're my friend. Didn't we soldier together?"

Biggo laughed and the bed shook. "For twenty thousand dollars, you
don't have a friend in the world."

"You get a quarter-share."

Biggo laughed louder. "You shouldn't throw your money around like that." He got up off the bed and unlocked the hall door. "Dan'l, I don't want to take advantage of you in any way. Take your tart with you."

Toevs looked scared. "Just footwork is all this job is. All you have to do is go to Ensenada and collect some money. What's hard about that?"

"What's hard about sitting here in Cleveland waiting for me to come back? Jaccalone sounds like the kind who would as soon take the Noon paper off my cold dead body. Why should I run all the risk for a quarter-share?"

"But I got the confession and I set the whole thing up. And I set it up so there's no risk."

"Then finish the job yourself if it's so bloody simple." Biggo opened the door wide.

Toevs stared into the hall and asked, "Please close the door, Biggo." He had another quick one while the door was being shut. It calmed his hands. The old man said, "Look, I've got this friend in Ensenada. Named Zurico. Runs a saloon down there. He'll give you the lay of the land and he's already watching for the signal. The signal is anything connected with peacocks." He chuckled at the memory. Practically everybody knew the story of Toevs and the royal peacocks. A story of his younger days which involved a beautiful native woman and a good fight. A fine story which anybody would be proud to tell about himself and it had almost happened the way he always told it. "So the Jaccalone agent or agents will flash a peacock signal around somehow; that's up to them. Then all you have to do is pick your moment to trade. They don't know anything about you so you can make the trade and be out again with the money before they have time to renege or try anything. As you say, they're nothing more than gangsters but you'll run no risk."

Biggo stood by the door. He said, "Fifty-fifty."

Toevs' face screwed up. "Ah, give a man a break, Biggo. We soldiered together." Biggo opened the door again and Toevs said hastily, "All right. Fifty-fifty it is."

Biggo closed the door and came back and poured the last two drinks, taking the short one himself. He tossed the empty bottle into the corner angrily. He was somewhat shocked with Daniel Toevs. Ten years ago Toevs would have told him to go to hell before he split a simple deal like this down the middle. But Toevs had let part of himself wither away. He was afraid to go to Ensenada, afraid he would fumble and lose the chance at big money. Toevs had gotten old. The thought of that made the whiskey thicken in Biggo's mouth and he had a difficult time swallowing it. He was angry with himself for driving a hard bargain and angry with Toevs for letting him do it.

So he scowled down at the old man in the chair. "Okay. I'll leave tomorrow."

Toevs was holding up a folded paper to him. "This is it, Biggo. Take good care of it." He couldn't understand why Biggo should be angry. This made Biggo even angrier. Why did weakness always ask for a pushing around?

To make himself feel better, he took out his wallet. "You'll need some operating expenses. Deduct it later." He had five hundred dollars, more or less. He gave Toevs two hundred.

"No. I didn't come all the way up here for a touch," said Toevs. But his hands were shaking again.

Biggo scornfully quoted some Arabic profanity and Toevs laughed. Then Biggo said, "It's an investment, you dumb Dutchman. You put up that paper. I put up the money. Even-steven." This gave Toevs some of his pride back and it was the least he could do. Biggo felt sorry for him.

Toevs gave Biggo a Cleveland telephone number—apparently a bar—to call as soon as he arrived in Ensenada. There was always the possibility of further developments.

They were through talking now. Toevs was ready to go but he was hesitating, looking at the bathroom door closed against the sound of running water. Biggo couldn't see pushing the old man around any further; what's-her-name—Felice—was just another girl. He said, "Hell, take her along, Dan'l."

He threw open the door and steam came out. Feminine clothes were scattered carelessly on the floor. The tailored pink panties had worn threadbare around the elastic. Felice was stretched out in the tub, her hair up and her head back as she sipped luxuriously from the glass in her hand.

She turned off the tap and smiled sleepily at Biggo. "I hope you don't mind, honey. It feels so good." Her small breasts pointed at him through the suds and she wiggled. Some of the suds drifted away.

Toevs was gazing over Biggo's shoulder. The girl raised her bare knees and lathered them, refusing to look at him. After a minute, Toevs said, "Well, I guess she's figuring on staying, Biggo." He almost made it sound as if he didn't care.

Biggo closed the door and helped Toevs shrug it off. Toevs groped for his hand fervently as he left.

"You take good care of yourself, Biggo."

"I always have, Dan'l."

"You watch your step," Toevs said earnestly and shook hands again and walked carefully away down the hall. He looked even older than he was.

After Toevs had gone, Biggo wrote out a telegram that would cancel the rest of his lecture tour. That didn't break his heart. He read the confession of George G. Noon. It was everything Toevs had promised. It would certainly mean the end of Silver Magolnick. Biggo thought it was a very good thing that the present gambling boss didn't know the confession existed.

He got out his knife and slit open the paper binding inside the battered leather binding of the Bible. He slipped the Noon confession into the aperture and glued the bindings together again. Nothing showed.

Felice hadn't emerged yet. He undressed and lay on the bed, smoking. After a while he took up the Bible and opened it to First Kings. He began to read about the battle at Ramoth in Gilead, reconstructing the strategy from what he remembered of the land around there. He nodded approvingly and said aloud, "They were tough ones."

Felice was still making splashing sounds in the bathtub. Finally Biggo got tired of waiting and yelled for her until she came trotting out.

CHAPTER TWO

WEDNESDAY, SEPTEMBER 13, 2:00 P.M.

He arrived in Ensenada three days later by way of a twin-engine DC-3 operated by an unscheduled airline out of Los Angeles. As soon as the ship passed over San Diego and the border, Biggo kept one eye cocked at the thin black ribbon of road that wound along the coastline below. He memorized its curves from habit because he always liked to know the ways out of a place.

Except for the road he took little interest in the plane or the scenery. He could fly some himself and he had seen too many semi-arid shores like this one of Baja California, Republica de Mexico. So he spent his time balancing his expenses against what remained of his money. Plane fare, meals and a big night in Los Angeles (and what he had given Toevs) had pared his five hundred dollars down to a lean two hundred. Not much but enough. He didn't intend to live like a tourist and he did intend to close the deal as quickly as possible.

He sat behind a pair of honeymooners. They made Biggo uncomfortable although he thought the girl was a pert-looking trick. But he thought the man was hardly old enough to start shaving. Biggo would glower out the window, then glance back at them, refusing to admit he was envious. He didn't like the possessive way the young man clasped the girl's hand against her thigh. He wished now he'd brought the girl from Cleveland along with him, the way she had wanted. Try as he might, he couldn't remember her name.

They landed in Ensenada at two o'clock. The hot Mexican summer afternoon swept into the plane as soon as its door was opened. Biggo got out first and felt himself begin to sweat as he looked around. Near at hand was a crumbling adobe storehouse and across the unpaved airstrip was another shack and that was all. A few old planes, some flyable and some not, sat by the buildings. The airport was managed by two grinning Mexicans; their office was the front seat of a dilapidated Dodge.

Watching to see where the honeymoon couple would go, Biggo nearly forgot his suitcase in the plane. He hadn't been back long enough to get used to it or its weighty prospect of clean clothes. A musette bag was usually ample enough to carry his straight razor, Bible, ammunition and Beretta automatic. He climbed back into the plane to get it and emerged again looking more like a tourist.

His eyes were caught by a man in a black suit who was squatting in the shade under the wing of an old Stinson biplane. The man was looking at Biggo intently. He was cow-faced and redheaded. Biggo studied him for a minute. Since the man didn't produce a live peacock or anything like it, Biggo decided he was just a Mexican government agent inspecting the new arrivals. When Biggo looked at him again, the redheaded man was eyeing the cute honeymoon girl with the same intent stare.

Biggo found a cab for himself and told the driver, "Take me someplace where there's beer," and sank back into the seat. He lapsed into Spanish automatically. *"Hace mucho calor, no?"*

The airport was toward the southern rim of the foothills which ringed the broad curving bay where Ensenada nestled. To reach the town they drove north, coming upon houses immediately, just across the road from the airstrip. They stood on small lots, most of them, with no trace of grass or shrubbery. The streets were wide and dusty. Only the main highway leading through the business section was paved. A gang of street repairmen broke off their leisurely work to watch them roll by. Biggo looked away from the heat-shimmering hills and at the glinting ocean. He tapped the driver and asked about the big white building like a sultan's palace. It turned out to be the Riviera Pacífico, the tourist hotel and the town's pride. But, in its own oasis of palm trees and green growth, it held itself aloof from the town.

He was pleasantly surprised with Ensenada. Backed up against the northern rim of hills, looking out at the placid bay, it had for him a natural charm, peaceful and unhurried. The high sagebrush hills displayed rows of whitewashed boulders which spelled out boasts of local liquors and business houses. The business district was three blocks wide and five long. Biggo had the taxi drive up and down the main streets while he got the lay of the land.

He saw a lot of souvenir shops and bars for tourists but nothing like Tijuana or Juarez. This place wasn't a commercial tourist trap or a squalid native village. It was a middle-class Mexican city, a port town of some less than twenty thousand people. At the curb, new Cadillacs and Buicks parked next to ancient Ford trucks and once he spotted a burro-drawn cart. Shopkeepers lounged in shadowy doorways, contentedly surveying their world. The streets were almost deserted. It was hot. On one corner a group of Americans, with their parcels and cameras, glanced around for a new direction to wander.

Over it all hung the too-sweet smell, the old familiar smell. Not an unpleasant odor, certainly, but merely foreign. Biggo had smelled it in many corners of the world. Lower standard of living, that's all it was. Its ingredients were too numerous to classify.

Then he saw the painted sign that said ZURICO'S. He paid off the cab-driver and got out by the statue where the town petered out on the north end. He felt pretty good. Coming into Ensenada gave him a coming-home feeling and he couldn't understand why. This was another foreign country, wasn't it? As usual, he was the arriving stranger.

"I was born out of my time," Biggo said aloud. He had read that somewhere and the idea had stuck with him. He looked up at the calm face of the statue. Miguel Hidalgo y Costilla, the little priest who had stirred all Mexico to revolt nearly a century before. "Those were the days," Biggo told Hidalgo. "That's when I should have been living too."

Zurico's was saloon below and living quarters above. Its back-end loomed over the stone embarcadero and the sportfishing pier where a few men cast lazily. Hundreds of white seagulls soared overhead and hundreds more floated on the bay waters like wave-sparkle come to life. Small fishing craft and some larger tuna clippers bobbed on the incoming tide.

He forgot about Miguel Hidalgo. He squinted at the girl, the bare-armed American girl, who was going up the three steps into Zurico's. Her brown hair was shingled short and cool-looking. She wore a peasant blouse and skirt. Her arms and legs and neck were bare and white, seemingly soft to the touch. Biggo glimpsed quite a bit of her legs as she went up the steps. He picked up his suitcase and crossed the street.

He shoved through the swinging doors, and went around the curved screen that kept passers-by from looking into the long room. On one side of him was a bar with stools; on the other side were scarred tables and straight chairs. A stuffed wildcat snarled perpetually behind the bar, flanked by two calendars, out of date, which exhibited pictures of nude women. The floor was bare wood.

The two Mexicans sitting near the entrance screen calculated Biggo as he came in. The bartender was a young kid who probably should have been in school. The American girl was talking to a hatchetfaced Mexican dandy with sideburns at the far end of the bar. Biggo made the sixth person present.

The dandy with the sideburns stopped smirking and talking at the girl when he saw Biggo and went into a tiny backroom off the bar. The girl made a mouth after him as if she was mad about something. Then she looked at Biggo. Everybody was looking at Biggo.

He didn't mind. He dropped his suitcase with a thump, ordered a beer and drained it without taking the stein from his lips. He ordered another. The two Mexicans approached him, violin and guitar in their hands, and asked if he would like to hear some music. He shook his head but sent one of them out for the local newspapers. All this time he didn't pay any attention to the girl. She finally grew tired of waiting. She came and sat beside him at the bar.

"You a stranger in town?" she asked.

Biggo looked her over. She was not quite pretty and not getting any prettier in this place. Her face looked vaguely disappointed with the way things had gone. But there was nothing disappointing about her figure. Biggo decided she was built better than either of the two calendar women easy. And the cologne she wore wasn't too cheap. "My first trip," he said when he was finished looking.

"Think you'll like it?"

His eyes let her know what he was thinking. "I always have." She kept her red moist smile on anyway.

Her name was Jinny. She didn't bother to give a last name so he matched her. "Just call me Biggo."

"What kind of a name is that?"

He told her Irish. She suggested they move to a table. They did. He stopped buying beer and started ordering whiskey. But the kid bartender made up a fizzy concoction for her with a cherry in it.

So he asked how long she had worked there. She wilted a little and asked, "Oh God, does it show that much?"

She really wanted to know the truth. Biggo felt a bit sorry for her. He said, "Well, I can't imagine anybody coming in here just to drink with that mangy wildcat."

That made it all right with her pride in appearances. "It's a dump all right but Zurico has big ideas. He plans on dressing up the place and giving it some class. I'm the beginning, a sort of hostess."

The sideburned Mexican was watching them from the little cubbyhole behind the bar where he'd disappeared. "That Zurico?"

"That's his brother. Zurico's fat and short and not too hard to take. He's older too. He hasn't come in yet today." Biggo shrugged; that took care of business for the moment. Jinny said, "Smile or something, won't you, so hell-on-wheels will think I'm doing the job right?"

Biggo smiled and dropped his big hand on her knee. She jerked out from under. "Don't overdo it, pal."

The musician came back with the newspapers—two local ones—that Biggo had sent him for. He leafed through all the stories and ads for any mention of peacocks. No luck but perhaps the elder Zurico brother had seen the signal around town.

Jinny said nastily after he had ignored her for a few minutes, "Would you rather I went off and died or anything?"

"One thing at a time, honey. What are you doing tonight?"

"Why? Aren't there any good shows in town?"

"Where's a nice place to stay, then?"

Biggo found her bitterness and wisdom somewhat pathetic. She looked at his secondhand suitcase. "You can always get a suite out at Riviera Pacífico. They start at sixteen bucks a day."

"I'm down here incognito," Biggo said with a wink. It wasn't too far from the truth but he played it as a joke. "I don't want to be ostentatious about it, honey. Now where do you live?"

"But my seven big brothers don't have a spare bedroom. Sorry. Why don't you try the Hotel Comercial? Down the street two blocks. It's good."

Biggo could practically see the thoughts going through her head. She had him pigeonholed neatly: a husband off on the loose for a moment. He let her get a better view of his bankroll when he ordered the next round of drinks. It still looked impressive. She was friendlier. "What are you doing in Ensenada, anyway, Biggo?"

"Where's this Zurico fellow?"

"You going to buy the joint?"

"I might—if you come with the fixtures. I got a business proposition which Zurico might be interested in since he's going for so much class."

"He's his own bouncer. What are you selling, Biggo?"

"Peacocks," he said and watched her face. "Tell him I stopped by."

It didn't register. "He's running a bar, not a zoo. He even says it's a cocktail lounge. What are you talking about, anyway?"

"I raise them. Peacocks, I mean." He had the kid bring the bottle over to the table to avoid delays. Plane rides always made him thirsty.

Selling more drinks pleased Jinny. She said, "You're kidding me, aren't you? Nobody raises peacocks. Don't they just happen in a state of nature?"

"No. Haven't you ever had a peacock cocktail?" The sound of it amused Biggo and he repeated it. "A pea-cocktail. You know, an old-fashioned with a peacock feather in it." He was just rambling, feeling good. He had thought that perhaps the percentage girl might recognize something familiar in the peacock talk. But she hadn't. Evidently Zurico hadn't set his employees to watching for the peacock signal too.

Jinny laughed. He liked to see her laugh. She had a wide moist mouth that wasn't meant to be sullen; it was meant to be kissed. He decided to make sure about that tonight.

"A feather merchant," she said. "An honest-to-God feather merchant."

There was somebody shouting behind the saloon, on the edge of the bay. They had to raise their voices to talk. "Zurico could make fans and give them to the women customers. I got all sorts of ideas."

"Oh, I'll bet you have, Biggo."

"Simple case of supply and demand. I've got the feathers. If Zurico's got a heart in his body, he'll create a demand."

The shouting went on. The Mexican troubadours laid their instruments on the bar, the kid put down the glass he was drying, Zurico's brother popped out of his cubbyhole office—and suddenly they were gone. They disappeared through the back door of the saloon.

"Hey, what's the story?" Jinny wanted to know.

So did Biggo. He had caught a few of the shouted words and one of them was *muerto*. *Muerto*. Death.

He decided he'd better find out what was going on. He finished off his drink and picked up his suitcase. "Be seeing you, honey."

Jinny said, "Well, I like that!" and was still sitting at the table when he went through the back door and onto the stone embarcadero.

He stopped. Below him, below the pilings of the sport-fishing pier where a strip of sand hadn't yet been covered by the incoming tide, clustered a little group of men. There was Zurico's brother and the kid bartender and the musicians and some other men Biggo hadn't seen before. One still carried a fishing pole. Biggo looked where they were looking, at what lay at their feet.

It was the body of a man, his hands bound behind him. The brown business suit he wore was sodden with sand and salt water. He had evidently just been washed ashore or discovered in the shallows. It looked to Biggo as if the man had been shot through the head.

And when he realized that the dead man had, in life, been short and fat he began to notice whose voice made a keening sound that dominated the babble below. The voice kept repeating, "*Hermano mío!*" over and over. The mourner was the younger Zurico.

Biggo stared at the body harder. The sweaty handle of his suitcase turned cooler in his hand. Instinctively, he held the suitcase which contained the Bible a little closer against his legs, reassuringly. Because he had sighted the queer boutonniere strung through the lapel of the dead man's suit. Long and bedraggled, the peacock feather still gleamed blue and bronze under the bright sun.

Biggo grunted. A crowd was gathering on the embarcadero around him. He heard the clanging of a police truck. He began to sidle backwards gradually, letting people shove eagerly in front of him. When at last he was at the rear of the crowd, he turned casually and ambled away.

CHAPTER THREE

WEDNESDAY, SEPTEMBER 13, 4:30 P.M.

Zurico's dead body, as such, didn't bother Biggo. He had seen the dead often when he had known their first names and their whole lives. But the implications of the peacock feather did bother him.

He didn't think hard about it at first. Action came before contemplation—he counted this as one of his virtues—and he needed a base of operations. He walked two blocks south to the Hotel Comercial and signed the register as B. Venn, Los Angeles, California.

The hotel was tan stucco, clean, with an arcade that shaded the sidewalk in front. His window on the second floor overlooked the roof of the arcade and the main street, Avenida Ruiz. It was just a room, much like a thousand other rooms he had passed through and better than still another thousand.

Biggo flung his suitcase on the bed and unstrapped it and made sure the Bible was safe inside. It was, so he left it there and strapped the suitcase shut again. He didn't unpack. There were several reasons for not doing so but Biggo didn't analyze them. The action indicated was to call Daniel Toevs in Cleveland so he immediately went back downstairs to the lobby. There was no phone in his room.

The lobby was neat and bare with plate glass windows along Avenida Ruiz and a door at the rear open into a paved area. There was no phone booth but the manager let him use the instrument in his private office. Biggo gave the Ensenada operator the number, then went back upstairs. It would take time.

He opened the window and sat in it with his broad back to the street now cooled by long shadows. Biggo grunted at the suitcase on the bed. Then he said to it, "You know, something has gone pretty damn wrong."

A knock on the door and there stood the manager saying that Biggo's call had come through. Biggo said, "Quick service," and followed the manager downstairs. He laughed softly at the idea of Toevs haunting that bar phone in Cleveland for three days, waiting for news. It was past dinner time in Cleveland and he hoped Toevs was still sober. Perhaps he had already drunk up the two hundred dollars; Biggo hated waiting himself as much as anything.

He sat back in the farthest corner of the tiny office with the phone, watching the door, careful that nobody should overhear. The connection was perfect. Toevs sounded as if he were across the street instead of across the continent. "Why didn't you call me sooner?"

"I just got in this afternoon."

"You done anything yet, Biggo? You know what I mean."

"I had a drink."

"Ah, I get you." Toevs sounded cold sober but jumpy. "What'd Zurico have to say?"

"Not much of anything. He's dead. Somebody shot him through the head and stuck a peacock feather in his coat lapel."

Toevs was silent for a long time. At last he said, "Biggo, that boy's papa and I rode two wagonloads of black powder in to Villa."

"Well, that was bloody fine of you," Biggo snapped. "Make up your mind. Are you drunk or sober?"

"I'm all right. I just notice when people die, that's all. You still got the paper, Biggo? We can't afford to lose the paper."

"Don't worry about the paper. Worry about me. What's going on?"

Toevs didn't say anything. He husked his throat and it sounded as if he spit in Cleveland.

Biggo reached out with his foot and kicked the door to the manager's office shut. He growled into the receiver, "Talk up. Can you change the signal with Jaccalone?"

"No."

"Why not?"

"I've lost touch with him."

"Well, Dan'l, I can't say I like this peacock signal any longer. It's not much of a secret when Zurico floats ashore with a feather on his coat." He barked, "What's going on?"

"What I was afraid of happening," Toevs said uneasily. "Somehow Silver Magolnick found out. He doesn't want Jaccalone back in the States. He knows he's all through—even dead—if Jaccalone comes back to the States with that confession."

"Which leaves me where?"

"I guess about the same as before. Except that you'll have to watch out for whoever Magolnick has sent down there to stop the deal."

Biggo thought it over carefully. Then he said, "What do you mean— it's about the same? Zurico was shot before I even got to town. How'd Magolnick's man get here so much faster than I did, anyway? And how did he find out about the confession and Zurico and the peacock high sign?"

"Well, that's what I was going to tell you. Some fellows got me drunk and I talked my fool head off. I'm sorry, Biggo. It got back to Magolnick what's going on. I've been hiding out ever since."

"How much got out?"

"Most of the main stuff. Not your name though, Biggo. I haven't said a word about you. The only name Magolnick has got is mine."

Biggo sat down in the manager's chair and teetered back and forth. He scowled at the phone as he leaned over it. He said, "You hyena bastard, if I ever see you again I'll kill you."

"Ah, Biggo ..."

"You've been lying to me all along, Toevs. You're lying to me now."

"Swear to God, Biggo, I'm telling—"

"You drank my whiskey and called this a simple job. But this Magolnick knew all about it before I did, didn't he? That's the only way his man could get down here first. No wonder you were willing to give up fifty per cent before you'd come yourself, you stinking coward."

Toevs pleaded desperately. "Biggo, please listen to me. I was a marked man. I didn't dare go down there. But nobody knows about you."

"You weren't man enough to come down here yourself. You gave me a no-good password and hoped I wouldn't get shot quite as quick as you would be. And I'm not going to forget about this."

He slammed down the receiver and barged out of the office and up the stairs. He banged the door to his room behind him and said, "Biggo stupid, you should've known there'd be a catch in it. Isn't there a catch in everything?" He kicked a chair across the room and walked around kicking the other furniture while his anger boiled. He damned everybody and everything he could think of but it never entered his mind to quit a job he had started. Finally, he kicked the chair again and it lit upright where it had stood originally. He laughed at the sight.

Then he was all right again. He bounced down on the edge of the bed and put his head between his fists and tried to do some good thinking. He was caught between the lines of two enemy gangsters and he had no way of knowing which side was which. He could identify Tom Jaccalone from the old newspaper picture but Jaccalone undoubtedly wouldn't come to Ensenada himself. Neither would Magolnick. They would both send armed representatives.

Both agents would be looking for whoever carried the Noon confession. The Jaccalone agent would have money in his hand, the Magolnick agent would have a gun.

Biggo had been sitting still too long so he got up off the bed. "And all Biggo Venn has to do," he announced, "is to pick the right man to deal with." He furrowed his brow, not seeing any way he could know in advance. He saw himself worrying in the mirror and he told himself pityingly, "You be right the first time, you dumb ape. There'll only be that one first time." The dead Zurico was proof of that. Zurico had evidently overextended himself or had been decoyed by a false peacock signal.

He strode around the little room, occasionally swinging his fists at nothing. "But what's there for you to *do?*" he asked. At the end of fifteen minutes more he still couldn't work out any positive action. That was what he longed for: action. It was what he lived for, had been born for, that split second when the whole world was action. Something happened then, cleansing and worthwhile, in the height of battle. But even as he revelled in the thought, he remembered the interminable dreary days of waiting for action and then the emptiness of afterwards.

So this fight, if it could be called a fight, was no different from any other he had known.

"It's obvious. What you have to do is nothing at all." He stood in the center of the room, head down, squinting at the suitcase. "The Jaccalone man is not going to give any signals, not when he hears about Zurico wearing a feather. So you wait. Let them look for you. None of them knows Biggo Venn." He had this in his favor. Both Magolnick and Jaccalone were probably more anxious about the Noon confession than he was. They couldn't afford to wait and if they didn't, something interesting might happen which would change the present deadlock.

But how long could *he* afford to wait? Biggo got out his bankroll and counted it. Taxi fare and drinks with Zurico's drink-pusher had cut his capital down to $191. Still plenty for a short visit but certainly not enough for a siege. He grunted.

Then he winced and swore. He had forgotten about the Jinny girl. Feeling secure that afternoon, he had talked too much. Not too much for the situation as he had understood it then but too much for his necessary strategy now. He had kidded around about the peacock signal. If she remembered anything about him—and Biggo didn't doubt that she was thinking of him this minute—she would remember the peacock salesman, the "feather merchant" joke which had made her laugh that once.

Biggo laughed too, sarcastically. He could see her repeating her joke to every customer until at last it reached the wrong person. He swore at the girl and at Toevs some more but mostly at himself. Then he had his first idea of the day.

He muttered, "The only way to keep her from talking too much is to shut her up." And things suddenly didn't look so bad, having something like that to do.

CHAPTER FOUR

WEDNESDAY, SEPTEMBER 13, 8:00 P.M.

Zurico's was going full blast that night. Biggo found business-as-usual a little surprising. He had expected to find the saloon closed with crepe so he would have to search through other bars for the Jinny girl. But the proprietor's memory was being honored with a sort of hilarious wake. Or perhaps it was a celebration of the younger brother becoming boss. Biggo wasn't sure which.

The crowd was having a good time. It was mostly Mexican with only a sprinkling of Americans since this was the middle of the week. The two musicians were playing and some of the American couples were dancing while everybody watched. Jinny was working two unattached men, obviously tourists, at the far end of the bar. She drank soda water with cherries.

Except for the way she looked, she didn't seem to be especially fitted for her job, Biggo noticed. Too shy or too suspicious of the customers or something of the sort. But her luscious look made up for it. She wore a shiny black dress that showed off her white shoulders and part of her back. The dress came to her knees and she had on stockings tonight.

Biggo found a table in a corner, ordered a drink and tried to catch her eye. She knew he was there; he knew she was aware of him and perhaps a little scared of him too. What with a drink in his hand and his eyes on the silken sheen of her legs, Biggo found he wasn't quite so angry with Daniel Toevs. He could never stay angry very long anyway and he began to see some excuses for the old fellow. And the evening ahead—making sure Jinny forgot about the peacock talk—didn't shape up as such a bad job.

He had another drink and every now and then she'd look down the room at him and then she'd concentrate visibly on the two Americans for a while. Biggo waited. A boy came around with lottery tickets and was sent away and after that somebody tried to interest him in a concert two nights away. The music went on and so did the dancing. One of the tourist women, just drunk enough to think it was funny, asked him to dance. She carried a sombrero she had bought for her little girl at home. Biggo danced with her and then danced with her again. She was thirty and not quite hard and she kept saying that she was having the best time she had ever had in her whole life. Her husband finally took her away.

When Biggo went back to his table Jinny was sitting there. Her lower lip was sulky. "Well," she said.

"Well, well. Where you been?"

"I thought you were coming back to see me."

"Here I am."

"Didn't you wear yourself out, dancing?"

"No," he said. "Would you like to dance, honey?"

"No. Sit down. Why didn't you come over to the bar and rescue me?"

Biggo looked at the two unattached Americans. They were watching Jinny and him. They looked irritated. "You can handle fellows like that with both hands tied behind your back."

"Nobody's going to tie my hands behind my back."

Biggo sat down, gave the bartender a shout and ordered two straight shots. Jinny said she didn't like liquor straight.

"All that soda water isn't good for you. Shortens your sex life."

"I don't care."

"I do," he said. "I might be in town for a long time."

"As I said, nobody's going to tie my hands behind my back."

The whiskey came. Biggo looked at it approvingly, approving himself. He had figured out that the best way to keep Jinny shut up about the peacocks was to confuse her, obscure the peacock motif so she would remember him for other things. But he couldn't confuse her while she stayed sober. He said, "*Saha*," and tossed the drink off.

The Arabic toast meant nothing to her but she followed suit. Then she made a face. "That stuff is awful!"

"Well, I don't work here. You do."

"I haven't made up my mind yet. Did you know that Zurico was dead?"

"I didn't even know he was sick."

"You ought to be on the radio, feather merchant." Biggo was relieved. Evidently she hadn't seen the body with its feather decoration. At least, she gave no sign. He said, "I am, didn't I tell you? I'm in television."

"I thought you raised birds."

"No, I'm the man who draws the test patterns for all the different stations."

"You're nuts."

"I got into it because I know a fellow high up." Biggo ordered more drinks. "You'd be amazed how high he is up."

Jinny shook her head helplessly. "You're nuts."

"No, I just got a romantic nature."

"What man hasn't?" she said and drank grimly.

Zurico's brother was glowering at them from the bar. He motioned with his head at the girl, telling her to circulate among the other customers. Biggo grunted. "I see. Does he inherit you along with the saloon?"

"He thinks so." She started to get up. "Well, back to work."

"Sit down." He held onto her wrist and liked the feel of it. "I haven't told you my life story yet. It gets better later on. Like me. Mellow."

"Try not to leave scars, will you? And I don't think I'd believe your life story if I read it in the Bible."

"Well, I've got one of those too," Biggo said. He had left it—together with his gun—in his suitcase back at the Hotel Comercial. No reason it shouldn't be safe enough there at this stage of the game. "I'd be glad to show it to you."

"I've seen one, thanks." She wanted loose but he rather enjoyed the quiet struggle between them. "Oh, come on. Biggo—fun's fun but a girl has to eat."

"If that's all that's bothering you, let's go have dinner someplace."

Zurico's brother appeared by her elbow, his face threatening. He rattled his Spanish at her like a snake, "Get back to your job immediately and quit wasting time with this fool." He didn't think Biggo would understand. "Otherwise, go practice your trade on the street where it belongs."

Jinny said in English, "Don't talk to me like that, you greasy little—"

Zurico's brother slapped her sharply across the mouth. Without rising, Biggo planted his foot in the man's stomach and propelled him against the nearest empty table. Zurico's brother fell to the floor with a clatter of wood. The room came upon a silence all of a sudden, the music squealing away to nothing.

Zurico's brother got up, his face contorted in black lines. Biggo sat still and regarded him quizzically. Zurico's brother hesitated a moment, then sneered around at all the people watching and limped back to the bar. The music started again.

Dismally Jinny said, "Why'd you do that, anyway? That tore it for sure."

"Do you just let him slap you?"

"What's a slap more or less? Now I don't have a job."

"You've still got a dinner date."

"Yes." Her eyes were the same brown as her hair, Biggo noted now.

They gazed at him like a whipped dog but adding and subtracting seemed to be going on behind them. "You do owe me something, don't you?"

She went into the back room and got a black purse and they left, accompanied by looks from Zurico's brother. They ate in a clean little café around the corner, not too far from the jail. During the meal Biggo told her two more fantastic stories about his occupation and she laughed. Despite her protests, he kept filling her glass with tequila and proposing toasts to everything he could think of. She seemed to have forgotten about peacocks and feather merchants and he congratulated himself on obscuring his trail so well.

He bought more tequila to take back to the hotel. He winced when he thought of what the evening was doing to his bankroll but he counted it money spent in a good cause. Life insurance, he considered it.

When they were finally alone in his room, Jinny didn't sit down. She stood in the center of the room and slowly revolved, looking at the four walls so close. "What am I doing here?" she asked them.

"What are any of us doing here, honey?" Biggo moved his suitcase from the bed to the straight chair by the door. He rounded up glasses for the tequila.

"I should be back home in Scribner, Nebraska, that's where. No, I shouldn't." She was feeling the liquor. She held onto her purse and zipped it open and zipped it shut senselessly. "I ought to remember that there I was a happy little thing but I wasn't. I never have been. But, oh, what am I doing in Ensenada?"

"There is some corner of a foreign field that is forever Scribner, Nebraska," said Biggo and poured.

"I'm just no good, Biggo. I'm sorry but turn me inside out and I'd still be no good at all."

"What you need is a drink. And quit playing with that bloody pocketbook."

She simply held her hands apart and let the purse fall to the floor. "What I need," she said, "is a clean soul. I'm all dirty inside and whichever way I turn." But she settled for the drink. "God, that's vile."

"There's supposed to be salt and lemon go with it."

"Does it improve it any?"

"No." They sat on the bed together because there was nowhere else. "Nothing improves anything. That's my philosophy." Actually, Biggo was feeling pretty gay. What he dreaded most, when he admitted it, was an empty room. But the girl was here, even if she seemed somewhat detached, and so he wasn't alone. If he wasn't alone he couldn't be lonely. He shifted his knee so that it was against hers.

Jinny took the bottle in her lap and poured the next drink and the next in silence. More and more, as he gazed at her, the overhead light gleamed from the bare flesh of her shoulders and from the shiny black soft-looking arcs of her dress. And her mouth was another arc, red and tragic. He said after a while, "Quit watching me."

"I'm not watching you."

"You are." He shook his head which felt a little heavy. "You sit there looking like a stranger and you shouldn't be." He dropped his arm around her, over her shoulder, so that his fingers dangled idly inside the front of her dress.

She didn't breathe. She looked down at her bosom and the only movement was the slight motion of his hand. She said, "I don't even know your whole name. And here I sit on your bed and drink your liquor."

"Do you think people like us need introductions? We're both outsiders, Jinny. This is where we belong, wherever we happen to be. Nebraska is for people who aren't outsiders." For emphasis he pushed his knee against the pliant part of her leg and the dress tight across her lap sparkled up at him.

She shivered as his hand slid lower, persuasively. "I don't want to be an outsider, Biggo." Gently, she wriggled free and rose and wandered away with the bottle.

"No," he muttered and held out his hands toward her. "Outsiders have to stick together." He was abruptly very tired and he didn't know why. He hadn't done anything to make him tired. He wasn't that old, not yet. "We ought to form a union. A more perfect union."

From the center of the room her faint smile considered him. "All right," Jinny said. With one hand she lifted the edge of her dress. Expertly it peeled up her voluptuous body and somehow she got it off over her head without letting go of the tequila bottle.

Biggo leaned forward, watching. He felt his blood coming faster but the excitement seemed to increase his lethargy rather than surmount it. All she wore now were stockings and a sleek black girdle with lace edging and a brassiere that had no straps. She was the kind who went in for lingerie, he decided; the flimsy black lace of the brassiere didn't do much except decorate the lower curve of her breasts.

"What are you, Biggo? I mean what are you really?"

He tried to think. Her free hand went behind her and then she let the brassiere drift to the floor. It lay there, fragile and helpless, and his eyes moved from her high heels up the dark stockings to the startling white bands of her thighs where she was unfastening her garter straps. He remembered her question and said, "I don't know."

"Everybody knows what they are. I know what I am. I'm dirt. I've been told. But what are you?"

"I guess I'm a soldier, that's what I am."

A new triangle of white flesh appeared at her hip as she slowly unzipped the girdle. She wasn't bothering to remove her stockings. He stared where she stood clasping the bottle, her desirable self, flesh and lace, white and black. The overhead light licked over her and she dazzled as if on fire. She hurt his eyes. He shoved up to his feet, intending to go get the bottle or help Jinny disrobe, he couldn't remember which. He stretched wide his tremendous arms, seeking their strength. "I am the best soldier in the world, Jinny. Without exception."

She flickered a long distance away. He couldn't take the beginning step. His tongue thickened. "I am the best soldier and I am the tiredest soldier."

"Are you tired, Biggo? Are you?"

"I'm tired, Jinny. I'm tired of it all. I am tired of the whole goddamned world."

She was still watching him as he swayed back and forth. She watched him as he tried to join her and as the numbing weariness seized him. Why was she watching him like that? But he was too tired even to think about it or to feel the floor as he toppled forward.

CHAPTER FIVE

THURSDAY, SEPTEMBER 14, 9:00 A.M.

Biggo woke up. He was lying on the floor by the bed, his face breathing against the carpet, and his outstretched hand was hot from the sun that came through the window.

He staggered to his feet, groaning, and slumped at once on the edge of the bed. After he had squeezed his head a few times and practiced swallowing, he commenced to look around the room. He saw the half empty tequila bottle and the chair by the door. It was the chair by the door which started him thinking.

Last night he remembered putting his suitcase on the chair. But it wasn't there now. Biggo stood up and plodded into the bathroom to see if he had moved it in there. He hadn't. He drank several glasses of water, pulling off his tie so he could get them down. All the while he tried to remember.

When he did, when he noticed his wristwatch was no longer on his wrist, he dashed the glass into the bathtub and reached for his wallet. His hip pocket was also empty. "Jinny!" he roared.

She was gone, of course, as was everything he owned except the wrinkled white suit he had on. As the details came back painfully, he swore in a steady stream. He had been rolled. He had been doped and rolled by the very girl he had been so clever with. When he thought of how clever he had been he called himself names as well as her.

Finally he saw his unshaven wild-man self in the mirror and had to laugh. He rubbed the back of his neck which was stiff and said hoarsely, "She could have put me on the bed, damn her." He solemnly vowed never to let a woman pour again, not even any young drink-pushers whom he might be outwitting. She had cleaned him out, except for fifty-seven cents in his watch pocket. Well, he could remember being broke before. But it galled him that he could be made a fool of.

"By God," he said, "and I didn't even get to kiss her for it."

Then he stared with sick eyes at the empty chair and said again, slowly, "By God!"

His suitcase was gone and in the suitcase was his Bible. And hidden in the Bible was the Noon confession which meant twenty thousand dollars to him and Toevs.

His face flamed and his mouth snapped shut. Boiling, he slammed out of the room and down the hotel stairs. The street was already busy with the morning's housewives and as soon as Biggo reached it, he stalked toward Zurico's saloon. He muttered to himself all the way.

He shouldered through the swinging doors, nearly bowling over the kid bartender who had just unlocked them. The kid ran. Zurico's brother was adding up figures in his cubbyhole office. His gigolo face turned sullen as soon as he saw who the early visitor was but he bounced out in a hurry when Biggo yelled at him in Spanish.

"I don't know," he answered.

"Did she come back here last night?"

Zurico's brother wanted to tell Biggo to go to hell but he didn't dare. Instead, he stroked down a sideburn and said, "She resigned her position with me last night. That is all I know. With your permission, I am busy."

He said it with distasteful politeness and commenced to turn away but Biggo reached across the bar and took him by the necktie. "Now," asked Biggo, "what's her name?"

"Jinny."

"What else?" Biggo gave the necktie a jerk.

"Wagner." He pronounced it "Oohagner."

"Where does she live?"

"She has gone, señor. Please."

"You're hiding her, aren't you? You found out the work your brother was doing for his father's friend in the States and you set the girl to lying in wait for me, didn't you?"

Zurico's brother looked stupid, not understanding. He shook his head dumbly, nearly choked by the necktie. Biggo sighed. His suggestion didn't sound sensible even to him; he felt fairly positive the girl had robbed him on her own.

He said, "Well, don't let it happen again." He wanted to hit his victim but he had no good reason for doing it. So he mussed up the sleek hair a little and let go of the necktie so suddenly that Zurico's brother fell backwards against a stack of glasses and broke a couple. That made Biggo feel better. He stomped back out to the street.

There was one of the town's blue and white taxicabs parked nearby and the driver was getting a shine. Biggo led him over to the cab with only one shoe completed. The shoeshine boy followed after them, screeching epithets. Biggo scowled at him and he shut up.

They roared off toward the airport. Biggo didn't really analyze the situation. There were a bus and taxis and even private cars which could have taken the girl away but if she was still in Ensenada, which he doubted, he expected to find her at the airport. She had his money and he assumed that she would do what he would do under the circumstances. All he worried about was being too late.

He kicked the back of the seat, urging the driver to step on it. The driver laughed and looked around, anxious to share whatever the joke was. Biggo kicked the seat again to show him there was no joke about it. The driver saw his face and turned forward and bore down on the gas. Biggo chuckled and kicked the seat intermittently, watching the man's neck bounce. The cab went faster and faster.

They careened onto the airfield in a cloud of heavy dust. A plane was just taking off and it blew pebbles and twigs against the side of the taxi. But it wasn't a passenger plane, only a tiny Aeronca.

An old twin-engine Curtiss sat on the field near the adobe storehouse. Brown-faced mechanics swarmed around the starboard engine, giving the ship more than ever the appearance of an ailing bird. The pilots were sitting on boxes in the shade under its wings.

And Jinny was standing nearby, regarding the oncoming taxi helplessly. Biggo saw his suitcase on one side of her ankles and another suitcase, smaller and blue, on the other.

"I'm back in business," Biggo told the driver. "You'll even get your fare now." The driver took no chances and drove harder, skidding up beside the girl.

She waited for them, unable to think of anything else to do. She wore a green suit which was too hot for daytime. The ground around her was littered with cigarette butts. She had been waiting for quite a while. All the mechanics stopped work to gaze at the taxi.

Biggo got out and held the door open for the girl with a courtly gesture. She stood looking at him with no expression at all. Then she climbed into the back seat. Biggo picked up the two suitcases and tossed them into the cab after her, not caring where they landed. Jinny said nothing.

The driver looked at Biggo inquiringly. Biggo smiled and said fondly, "Let us return to town, my friend." The driver slowly understood that he had not offended his passenger. They left the airport.

Biggo gave Jinny the benefit of his smile.

She spoke her first words. "You go to hell, you big ox."

"What I like about you, honey, is that you're a lady to your fingertips. I like ladies. I like their pocketbooks." He took hers, opened it and dumped it in her lap. From the contents he selected his wristwatch and his wallet and an airplane ticket. He put on the watch and counted his money. It was down to $133. He inquired, "Should I turn you up and shake it out of you?"

"That's all there is. The airplane ticket cost about fifty bucks."

"Didn't you ever hear of the bloody bus? That only costs five."

"I wish I had taken the bus. You'd never have caught me then. I should have known nothing in this town would run right."

"That's a shame, the hard life you lead." Biggo unstrapped his suitcase on the floor and thrust an arm down into it, groping. He came up with the Bible and examined the binding. It was all right. He dropped the Bible in his coat pocket and fastened the suitcase.

They were nearly into the business section. Biggo told the driver, "Find a secluded spot and park the automobile for a moment."

Jinny was poking her belongings back into her purse. "You've got all my money. What else do you want—the clothes off my back?"

"You poor lady. So it was your money?"

"Yes, some of it. I only used what I had to of yours. I was going to send it back to you with whatever I got for the watch and the suitcase."

"Send it where? Care of the Ensenada poorhouse?"

"You're so witty," she said. "You ought to be on the stage. And don't tell me you are. That witty line of yours is coming out of my ears, did you know?"

"This will do," Biggo told the driver. The taxi stopped by a little park, presided over by an antique cannon and a statue with wings. Biggo took three dollars out of his wallet and passed it up to the driver. "Take a walk around the block. I would like privacy for a short while."

The driver seemed glad for an excuse to leave. He pocketed his keys and walked away swiftly, not looking back. Soon he was around the corner.

Jinny was watching Biggo stolidly. He took her by the shoulders and forced her to squeeze against his swelled chest. He could hear her swearing behind her tight lips. He began kissing her viciously across the mouth, kisses like blows.

Then he could feel the hopeful thought come into her head because she ceased being rigid. Her arm's trailed around him and she opened her mouth; she twisted softly against him.

She sighed and her closed eyelids trembled when he raised his head finally. It was all fake, Biggo knew. "That's part of what you owe me, after all," he murmured. Then he got what distance he could in the crowded seat and hit her face with the flat of his hand. It wasn't as hard as he could hit her or even as hard as he would have liked to hit her. But it had a good satisfying sound to his ears. "That's what I owe you," he said and hit her again. "Don't let me see you around this town anymore, honey."

Jinny didn't cry. She simply opened her eyes wide and sat there and took it. That made Biggo mad so he slapped her again just to see if she'd react. Her face got redder but she still didn't cry or duck.

He growled, "Oh, go to hell, anyway." He wasn't sure whether he was consigning the girl or himself or just what. But what he was doing had gone sour and he didn't even feel successful about getting his Bible back.

He got out of the cab and dragged his suitcase after him. Halfway down the block he looked back. Jinny still sat in the cab where he'd left her and from the set of her shoulders he knew she still wasn't crying.

CHAPTER SIX

THURSDAY, SEPTEMBER 14, 10:30 A.M.

Biggo plodded north along a quiet side street, cutting across to the business district. He wanted to go back to the hotel but only to get rid of the suitcase. He needed a shave but mostly he wanted something that would take the taste of loaded tequila out of his mouth. He could almost feel it coming out his sweat glands.

The Bible weighed heavily in his coat pocket and his wallet felt thin in his back pocket. $133. He got out the wildcat airplane ticket and read it. It was to San Francisco, good for thirty days. Absolutely No Refunds, it read in large letters. He put the ticket away again, feeling lousy.

"Why is everything going so bad for me?" he asked and the question sounded like Jinny Wagner so he didn't even try to answer it.

He passed a restaurant which was only a stucco house with a lawn in front and a low wall around it. There were umbrella tables on the lawn. The sign said Cuisine Française. A scattering of people sat at the tables, eating late breakfasts. The atmosphere was too happy and unburdened to please Biggo this morning. Those people aren't looking for peacocks, he thought as he got beyond the restaurant.

Something struck him in the back of the neck, sudden and startling. Biggo whirled around, scything the air with the suitcase. Then he saw the half grapefruit that lay on the sidewalk at his feet and he palmed the sticky pulp off his neck and coat collar. Somebody was laughing in the outdoor restaurant.

The man who laughed was at a table next to the wall. He had black hair and a mahogany tan and a neat mustache. He roared with joy, flashing all his white teeth, when Biggo discovered him.

"Well, *sahit!*" said Biggo and smiled thinly. He stood where he was on the sidewalk, spreading his feet a little. His arms came up, holding the heavy suitcase over his head. He hurled it like a boulder at the man who laughed. It crashed against his chest and he sprawled over backwards in his chair, upsetting the umbrella table as he fell.

Biggo vaulted the low wall. The other man was trying to struggle up from among the dishes and spilled food. Biggo planted a foot on his throat and looked down on him like a victorious gladiator. All he lacked was the sword.

"Say it," he commanded.

The fallen man was still grinning while his face purpled. Biggo's foot on his windpipe made it difficult to talk but he managed to croak, "*Ezzy yellallah.*"

It was a ritual between them.

"That's much better," said Biggo. He removed his foot and set up the overturned table and collected the dishes, none of which were broken. From the front door of the house, the Mexican woman who ran the restaurant regarded the scene with horror. The plump young waitress, her daughter, huddled close to her for protection. The other late breakfasters began eating more quickly so that they might depart.

The man on the grass got to his feet and brushed off his snappy sport clothes. He said, "The trouble with these places is that they let just anybody in."

Biggo took the crisp handkerchief out of the other man's breast pocket. He wiped the back of his neck. "Your aim's improving, Lew."

"I fired at the biggest thing about you. Your head."

Lew Hardesty was a vigorous male animal, at least ten years younger than Biggo. He was handsomer and slenderer and taller, built like a swimmer. A deep scar straggled down his right cheek. Only in his eyes was there anything remindful of Biggo Venn. A restless reckless see-you-in-hell look.

They set up the chairs and sat down. Hardesty called for more coffee. It was the mother who brought it. The waitress-daughter had disappeared. So had the customers. The mother stayed as far away from Biggo as she could.

Biggo growled, "I thought you were in Bolivia." Just because he had met one of his own kind made the outlook no brighter. Hardesty was a comrade but something less than a friend. Hardesty had a knack for showing up where he wasn't wanted.

"I was. Now I'm here."

"What happened?"

"Have you ever spent a summer in Bolivia? Very hot."

Biggo understood the old pattern. Hardesty had been on the wrong side, whichever side happened to be losing that year. "Yes, Lew, I was thinking about you only the other night."

"I love you too."

"I know that. I remember the time you let me go out after that tiger in the Malay with a jimmied gun."

Hardesty laughed. "That was a fine joke. Those man-killers are always old tigers, anyway. You've got more teeth than he had. Was that any worse than shipping me that opium in Transjordan? I sat in that mud jail for two months until one of your shells knocked out a wall."

Biggo laughed in turn. "That was the gunner's fault. He'd promised me a direct hit." They had been on different sides that season. Like Toevs and like himself, Lew Hardesty was one of the professionals who gravitated naturally toward the troubled places. Sometimes they fought together. Sometimes they fought each other. Today's enemy was the same soldier as tomorrow's ally.

"I really thought I had you spotted down in Bolivia. With the government, I mean."

Biggo shook his head.

"Too bad. I wonder who got my present for you?" Hardesty sipped his coffee and hitched his chair closer for the story. "We were pulling out of a little place called Cuernavaca. Not much there except one or two houses and a bully little bar. I figured you'd head there first thing when you got in. I wired up two charges under the counter with a bottle for the trigger. Oh, it was perfect, Biggo. I laughed about it all the way to the coast."

"I've been in the States since early this year."

"Sad, sad. Shame to waste a joke like that on a greaseball."

Biggo was thinking how different it was meeting Hardesty than it had been meeting Toevs. Hardesty still roved through the prime of life, just as Biggo did, full of strength and manhood. He had a disquieting thought: Had old Toevs felt the same way about him? Did old Toevs really believe his own lies about time not passing? Biggo swigged down coffee, rallying. "What are you doing in Baja California?"

"Waiting. I find I can't loaf properly in the States, what with the noise. Nobody seems to rest up there, you notice? I'm waiting for China to break."

Biggo laughed loudly.

So did Hardesty. Then, soberly, almost convincingly, "God's truth, Biggo. I'm expecting word from the Egyptian any day now. If you're free, I'll put in a good word for you. We might as well be on the same side for a change. You're not much fighting help but you're good for laughs."

"Like those twenty Arabs, Lew?"

Hardesty grinned. Then he quit it when he saw that Biggo had lost his humor. "We couldn't take prisoners, Biggo. We didn't have the water for it. I'm sorry they happened to be your pets, but—*c'est la guerre, camarade.*"

The carefree atmosphere between the two men had changed into something hard and dangerous. They sat regarding each other silently. Biggo's mind automatically segregated two solid facts from his swirling resentment. One was that his own Beretta lay deep within the strapped suitcase at his feet. The other was that Lew Hardesty never failed to carry his gun on his person. Even now the well-known pearl-handled Mauser would be hanging under Hardesty's arm, beneath the sport coat. Biggo realized he had carried the resentment so long that it was making him think in extremes, such as guns. So he didn't unlock his gaze but he shrugged, meaning not now.

Hardesty said slowly, "Any time it bothers you, Biggo …"

"All right. I'll let you know."

They were silent again for a moment. Then, as suddenly as it had happened, the tension was cleared off the table between them. Hardesty dug out cigarettes. They lit up. "And what brings you to Ensenada, Biggo, my boy?"

"Thought maybe I'd buy a little rancho, get close to the soil and the good life."

"Oh, ho, ho!" Hardesty said. "You working or playing?"

"When did you ever see me working, Lew?"

"Which means you are. What's up your sleeve, Biggo? Come on, I'm your old tentmate. You can tell me." His eyes were shrewd and calculating, as if he saw bags of gold heaped where Biggo sat. This was the other side of easy-going Lew Hardesty. "If there should be something afoot here in Baja, why, China can wait while I give you a helping hand. The governor getting big ideas? Like giving Alemán the heave-ho? Or are you organizing a William Walker?"

"Nothing's going on in Mexico that I've heard about." From way back, he knew Hardesty was a man who liked to cut himself in on another fellow's hard work. If there was an easy dollar to be made, Hardesty would know an easier way to make it. "I'm waiting for China too."

"Yeah," said Hardesty. "Oh, sure."

Biggo brought his Bible out of his pocket and slapped it on the table and put his hand on it. "Word of honor, Lew." The gesture amused him, waving twenty thousand dollars under Hardesty's nose.

"You still carrying that thing around?"

"Why not? I've gotten some fine tactics out of there." Biggo put the Bible away in his pocket.

Hardesty shrugged. "*Hay gustos y gustos*. I subsist on billets-doux myself." He winked and rolled up his eyes. "So I let you know what the Egyptian has to say. If and when I hear from him."

"Why wouldn't you?"

"He owes me money on the Bolivia thing." Suddenly Hardesty was morose. "When do we ever get paid in full?" he complained. "When don't they ever try to short us and cheat us and take our good blood on credit?"

It was rhetorical. "Yeah," Biggo agreed definitely.

"Dog robbers, all." Hardesty swallowed the dregs of his coffee. He was a little ashamed and angry, though not with Biggo. "Up and down. Always times when the going gets kind of rough, Biggo. Stinking life except for a few first-class fights. God, the jobs you have to stoop to, sometimes."

"Yeah." Biggo was thinking of his shorted lecture tour, the faces looking up at him, wanting to adventure through his broad strong body. He felt for his suitcase and made motions of getting up. "I'll probably see you around, Lew." He hoped not.

"Stand by. I'll give you a ride uptown in my car." Hardesty grinned to wipe out his morose moment.

"No, I want to shave and so forth."

There was some commotion in the stucco house that served the restaurant as a kitchen. Then the mother and daughter were coming across the lawn toward them. With the women were two men in baggy uniforms of drab green, heavily belted and carrying carbines at ready. Police. The daughter was pointing and the mother was spouting a fountain of Spanish.

"What's going on here?" Biggo said. They were all looking at him.

One of the policemen said in painful English, "You are required that you accompany with us—"

Biggo snapped, "Speak Spanish."

The policeman breathed gratefully. "You are under arrest for disturbing the peace, assaulting this foreign gentleman and destroying valuable property belonging to the Señora Lopez."

"Under arrest? You've lost your mind. I haven't done anything."

"Nevertheless, you will come with us," the policeman said firmly. The other policeman, staring at Biggo's unshaven and fierce face, leveled his carbine.

"Don't be silly. There is a misunderstanding. This man is a dear friend of mine. We were only joking. Nothing serious."

The policeman cocked an eyebrow. He turned politely to Hardesty. "Is this the truth, señor? Is this man your dear friend?"

Hardesty said, "I never saw him before in my life and I have an excellent memory for such faces. It is true, he struck me with his suitcase and threatened to murder me unless I bought him some breakfast. He belongs in solitary confinement, Capitán."

Biggo yelled at him, "You bastard, I'll carve your heart out for this!" The second policeman jabbed his carbine barrel into Biggo's back. The mother and daughter shrank away from the American's rage.

Hardesty, unappalled, waved his hand. "Take him away, Capitán."

The first policeman bowed to him and led the way. As Biggo tramped away up the street, the police guns pointed watchfully, he could hear Hardesty laughing at the joke. He thought that Hardesty would explode with laughter.

He shouted Arabic back over his shoulder, "May Allah stop your throat with camel dung!" With what dignity he could muster, his suitcase banging his legs, he stalked on toward the jail.

CHAPTER SEVEN

THURSDAY, SEPTEMBER 14, 11:30 A.M.

And there was other laughter that morning. As Biggo was marched through the narrow portal of the jail he heard a woman's bitter laugh from across the street. He didn't have time to look around and see who it was. And, at this glowering moment, he didn't give a particular damn whether it was Jinny Wagner or not.

The Ensenada *calabozo* was a small fortress, its walls about three feet thick and dingily stuccoed over. A perpendicular bulge up the façade eyed the street with gun ports. A sign told tourists not to photograph this building. Like Zurico's saloon, the jail presented its backside to the water. The bay smell was clean and fresh.

The chief of police was a gray-haired man with a bored intelligent face. His uniform was tightly tailored and Biggo felt like a tramp in contrast. The jefe laid aside his cigar and heard the charges without speaking.

When his subordinates were finished, the jefe asked them, "Is the señor drunk?"

Biggo said in Spanish, "I can answer for myself. The answer is no."

"Ah?" The jefe raised his eyebrows. "Do you deny the accusation, then?"

"Certainly I do. It was all a joke, that's all."

"A rather violent joke, I would say. Well, we shall see. In the meantime ..." Biggo gave the first name he thought of and the jefe made an entry in a ledger. "Are you an American, Señor Smith? You will wish, then, to consult with your nearest consul who is in Tijuana."

"Not particularly. All I wish is to pay my fine and get out of here."

"Ah?" the jefe observed again. "In time. Yes, in time."

They took his suitcase and his wallet. They commented on his carrying no identification. Then they removed the belt from his waist and the laces from his shoes. To prevent suicide, the jefe informed him gravely.

Biggo didn't resist. But he kept one fist clamped around his Bible. "I want to keep this by me."

The jefe examined it respectfully and handed it back. "Of course, señor. The regulations permit. Your other property will be kept safely for you until your departure."

"When will that be?"

"Shortly, shortly. The formalities must be observed. That is all." The jefe overcame a yawn by replacing his cigar in his mouth. "Justice. The law," he added.

The two policemen took Biggo down a cool corridor. They opened an iron gate and let him into a large whitewashed room with a concrete floor. It was the community cell for minor offenders. About twenty other men lounged around the room, all of them Mexicans. They reclined on *petates*, the woven mats which served the lower class as chair and bed. The prisoners looked at Biggo curiously.

Biggo regarded them indifferently. Being in jail was nothing new to him. He didn't know the names for these twenty brown faces but that was all he didn't know. This might have been Fez or Peshawar or— most recently—Havana. When he located a vacant *petate* he sat down on it cross-legged. Nobody spoke. It wasn't hostility but merely the native courtesy that withheld the direct question. They were wondering diligently who and what he was but he might be in here a month without being asked anything straight out.

Biggo slumped against the wall sullenly. He might be in here a month.

Seeing that Biggo was going to volunteer no information, the other prisoners went back to what they had been doing. Some slept. One group was gambling, racing little beetles they had captured. Most of the men did what Biggo did, sat and stared at the floor.

He stared and felt more bewildered than angry. He believed in luck but he never blamed it when it vanished. He could take it both ways, good luck and bad. When things went right that was as much luck as when they went wrong.

Biggo told himself it was just the turn of the wheel, this happening, just as it was last night's doctored liquor that was making him think stupid and depressing thoughts. Like whether he was slipping.

Yet he had accomplished nothing on this job except cut himself in on it. He had barely managed not to lose the Noon confession. "You been running like hell to stand still, Biggo," he growled to himself. "But you can't help it if you got curry for brains, can you? One thing, matters can't get much worse."

His wallet full of money was as good as gone. He knew native police. God only knew how long he would be in jail. He knew native justice; the hotter the weather, the slower it moved. And as soon as the jefe went through the suitcase, up would turn the Beretta automatic. Illegal possession of firearms, crime of crimes in any of the revolution countries.

Biggo sighed and wished he had a drink. He imagined a tall drink. He imagined having Hardesty here in front of him, bending over. His foot twitched involuntarily. He chuckled. The Mexican next to him smiled brightly.

Biggo played with the precious Bible a while. It beat thinking. Except that he still had the Noon confession, he wasn't any closer to the twenty thousand dollars than last Sunday night in Cleveland.

Something struck him funny and he said aloud, "What is India's destiny, huh?" He roared with laughter. He was wondering what the forum faces would think if they could see their adventurous hero now, broke and unshaven in this Mexican jail.

The prisoners watched him respectfully.

After a while the man next to him said, as if it had just occurred to him, "You laugh bravely." He was a scrawny beanpole, lantern-jawed, with a shiny, almost black, face. He wore overalls only and his ribs were obvious.

"Things are funny all over," Biggo said.

"Of course. A comedy," the Mexican said and grinned and scooted his *petate* closer. He introduced himself as Adolfo Huerta, who spoke no English.

"Call me Biggo."

Adolfo bowed gravely from his sitting position. "A treat to find a companion of your sort, Don Biggo, in such surroundings."

"You've been here before, then?"

"One has one's ruts." Adolfo shrugged. "Especially where women are concerned."

"Your wife?"

"And those of others."

"No Edens without forbidden fruit. They say that in the south, anyway."

"It's national," said Adolfo. "But it's a masculine proverb. Women refuse to agree with it. For example, my wife, Rosita. *Caray*, how she loves me, Don Biggo! But—" he indicated his *petate* "—here I am."

"I guess I'm here because of a woman too." Biggo was thinking of Jinny. If she hadn't stolen his suitcase, he might not have run into the joker Hardesty.

"I am not surprised," said Adolfo as a formal compliment.

"Nor I at your case," Biggo returned. "I only hope that your needs were satisfied, amigo. With me, the sky fell in first."

"My incident was satisfactory. I had decided to take a vacation with some companions somewhere, anywhere. A week, a month, who knows? My Rosita objected. What else could I do but beat her with a small stick? Otherwise, I might lose her respect as well as my own."

"Yet here you are."

Adolfo shrugged. "In the anger of the moment, Rosita forgot herself. By now she's repented. She wishes me home. When I decide that she has suffered enough, I'll return to her." He ignored the iron gate and the barred windows. "I'm not hard-hearted, Don Biggo."

Biggo liked his dark companion. Somehow he felt a little envious of him. Plainly shiftless, Adolfo was just as plainly happy, secure in his position as a failure. And he had his Rosita who wished him out of this jail. Who cared where Biggo Venn was?

They talked some more, mostly about women. Finally Adolfo said, "*Hasta luego*" and went to sleep. So did the other prisoners. It was siesta time. Biggo rolled up his mat and put it under his head and spread out on the floor. He stared at the ceiling. There was an American consul in Tijuana. But the consul wouldn't do anything for him unless Biggo established his identity. And the identity of Biggo Venn would be on an undesirable traveler bulletin somewhere in the consulate files. So the consul—Biggo detested the breed—probably wouldn't touch his case, anyway.

"Well, something will turn up," Biggo said confidently. He closed his eyes and slept immediately.

The evening meal was surprisingly good. Biggo would have enjoyed it no matter what; he hadn't eaten for twenty-four hours. He wolfed down the beans, scooping them up with the folded tortilla. When he had wiped his plate clean and chewed up the tough tortilla, he was still hungry.

The single electric bulb high in the ceiling looked puny as long as the sun slanted in. But when the sun had set, the bulb was sufficient to light the whitewashed room. One of the prisoners had a guitar. He played and another sang. The songs were not gay but they were not consciously sad, either. Just full of the peon's wistful wonder at the expressions of the life force. Biggo felt comradeship for the men. He felt more warmth in their presence, he admitted, than he had standing before the pale faces in American auditoriums.

Presently he took his Bible out of his pocket and rested back against the wall. He thumbed through the pages for a good story and settled for David.

Adolfo watched. "A wonderful gift, this reading."

"I guess it is at that." Biggo had never thought much about it.

"In your country, it is said that everyone, even the poor, can do reading. That's hard to believe, I find."

"It's true. Or as nearly true as anything is. Mexico's doing all right, though, Adolfo. Another ten or fifteen years ..."

Adolfo nodded. "My Doroteo, my first born, is already learning in the district school. But his father—" He pretended his head ached, all the while looking bemused at the Bible. "A wonderful gift, Don Biggo."

Biggo said, "Maybe you'd like for me to read to you." Adolfo grinned and hitched closer. Biggo began to read about David ben Jesse, the herdsman. He read slowly because it was awkward translating the poetry of the Old Testament into everyday Spanish. When he was stumped, he told it in his own words or described how the country and the crops were when he'd last been there.

Another prisoner joined them, then another. The singer stopped singing. The guitar player put his instrument away. Soon Biggo was ringed by an intent circle of faces. They showed no particular emotion but simply listened to how David went to court to play his guitar for King Saul ben Kish. They watched Biggo's lips as if afraid a word would be lost.

Their eyes brightened when he read about David the bandit chief and saddened at David, without a country, a mercenary in the pay of the Philistines. The guard came in to put out the light. He lingered with his finger on the switch. Finally he joined the listeners. The only sound in the room, cut off from the rest of the world, was the slow cadence of Biggo's voice. David the conquering hero became David the aging king. David, for all his wives, sought the warmth of a young girl as his days ran out.

When it was over no one spoke. There was only a little concluding sigh from the group, like an amen as they went slowly back to their own *petates*. The guard left them in darkness.

Adolfo murmured, "*Caray!*" in the gloom. "They were men in those days, Don Biggo."

CHAPTER EIGHT

FRIDAY, SEPTEMBER 15, 9:00 A.M.

The next day was just another one for Biggo. But to the Mexicans, guards and prisoners alike, it was special. Independence Day, the traditional Grito de Dolores. It recalled the turbulent times of 1810 when the soldier-priest Hidalgo had rung his church bells and led his countrymen against their Spanish overlords.

It was fiesta in Ensenada and throughout all Mexico. Shortly after breakfast the prisoners were routed out to take part. Adolfo explained to Biggo, "We have to show the queen of the fiesta how healthy and patriotic we are."

Biggo wasn't interested; he had just learned the jail served only two meals a day.

Since he was a foreigner he was allowed to remain in the cell. His only companion was a grizzled patriarch who sat silently at the far end of the room. The shouting from outside sounded as if the prisoners were playing soccer in the vacant lot beside the jail. Biggo listened a while, nursing his hunger. Then he sat down and leafed through his Bible. He stopped at the story of Jacob. He read drowsily. The air in the cell was thick and warm. The noise of the players made a lulling background. He nodded over Jacob's wrestling match with the angel.

Through his half-sleep, he could hear the prisoners returning to the cell. He grumbled lazily and let his head droop lower. Something rapped at the sole of his shoe. It startled him. He looked up.

At first, he couldn't understand. A vision in white stood over him, smiling down on him tenderly. Glimmers of light played around her head; she might have stepped out of the pages in his lap.

Awkwardly Biggo got to his feet. He felt grimy and apish suddenly.

She had a fine-boned face and the faintest tint of gold in her skin. Beneath the soft hollow of her throat the white Grecian robe began its descent over the points of her breasts and to the floor. The robe made her seem to float before him.

He licked his dry lips and squinted his eyes and grunted.

Her pink mouth continued to smile, amused. Beneath the black arches of her eyebrows she gazed at him with even darker eyes, the deep velvety color of blue-black petals. Biggo saw innocence there and behind that, fire. A tall lace *mantilla* bound by a rhinestone crown hid her hair.

She said in throaty Spanish, not moving her eyes, "Is this the señor of whom you spoke?" Biggo tried to think of an answer before he suddenly became aware of the crisp jefe standing beside the girl. He also became aware that he was gaping stupidly.

"This is the one, our queen," the jefe said. With his swagger stick he touched Biggo's wrist, the hand which held the Bible. "As you can see, *muy religioso*."

Biggo said, "Uh—excuse my bad manners, señorita. I had no idea that the world would send its most charming visitor to this place." The other prisoners had all filed in and were standing around the walls watching them.

The girl inclined her head, accepting his words. Her movements were regal and real. She was the most beautiful Mexican girl Biggo had ever seen, an ethereal combination of Spanish nobility and Aztec royalty. She was used to accepting homage as her due. She accepted Biggo's. She smiled again at him and floated on, followed by the jefe.

Biggo watched her talk with some of the other prisoners. He mopped the sweat off his face. Beside him, Adolfo muttered, "The queen of the fiesta, Don Biggo."

"What's her name?"

Adolfo shrugged.

The jefe rapped on the iron gate with his swagger stick. Everyone looked at him. He said, smiling, "This will not surprise you, I know. Our gracious queen of the fiesta of the Grito de Dolores will now exercise her royal prerogative."

To Biggo's surprise, the prisoners set up a shout, "*Olé!*" Adolfo clapped his hands and dusted off his overalls and laughed. Only Biggo—and the grizzled old man in the corner—held aloof from the general glee.

"What does all this mean?" he asked Adolfo over the uproar.

"She is going to liberate us, Don Biggo! We're free to leave the *calabozo!*" The "*Olé!*" cheer continued ringing against the walls.

"Well, what a bloody pleasure!" Biggo beamed, then asked suspiciously, "Everybody goes, you mean?"

"All the lesser criminals, such as you and I. See, already she has taken the keys."

With a low bow, the jefe had relinquished a ring of keys to the queen.

She carefully unlocked the gate and tugged at it until it swung wide. She said then, apparently a formula, "In the name of the father of our honor, Father Miguel Hidalgo y Costilla, I offer freedom to the oppressed and the unfortunate on this Day of Independence." There were *vivas* from the prisoners. They surged toward the gate. Biggo tried to keep an eye on the girl but she had gone out at the head of the procession. He put his Bible in his coat pocket. He noticed the silent old man still sitting in the corner. He asked Adolfo why.

"*Estuprador*," said Adolfo. "Now he is sorry for his major crime. Perhaps today only."

As Biggo went out, he gave the old fellow a bow of admiration. The rapist shrugged.

Biggo began wondering about his suitcase. Perhaps the jefe had never gotten around to searching it. Perhaps the gun had not been found.

Then he saw the jefe standing in his office door at the end of the corridor. The jefe scowled and motioned to him. Biggo shambled toward him, his spirits turning grim. The gun had been found. He clenched his fists. Now that he had gotten this far, he was ready to slug his way free.

He edged through the office door and the queen was seated beside the jefe's desk. When Biggo made a third, the office became crowded. The jefe was highly ceremonious. He said, "Señorita, may I present—" he hesitated wryly over the name "—Señor Juan Smith. Señor Smith, the queen of our fiesta, Señorita Pabla Ybarra y Calderón."

Biggo tried to figure out why all the formality. Not because of illegal firearms, surely. The girl let a slow smile blossom as he made the correct elegant reply to the introduction. She said to the jefe, "You see? He is not such a bad choice, I believe."

The jefe shrugged. He wasn't pleased about something.

Biggo said, "If I could have my suitcase and so forth—"

"Certainly. First, however, you have been signally honored, Señor Smith. Our queen has seen fit to choose you to represent all the freed prisoners in the parade which begins shortly." He added, with hope, "Do you have any objections to this?"

Biggo ran his hand over his jaw, heavy with two days' beard. Then he grinned at Pabla Ybarra. "If our queen doesn't, I don't know why I should."

"Excellent," said the jefe sourly. "Then all is arranged. While you are not of this country, Señorita Ybarra feels that you command certain religious qualities lacking in the other prisoners. For this reason ..."

Biggo didn't listen to how the honor had been thrust upon him. He was looking at the seated girl, the white robes sculptured over her body. He felt a throb of excitement in the pit of his stomach at the delicacy of her. He was ready to bet that her eyes had never looked on anything crude or dirty, such as himself. Yet she refreshed him, made him feel cleaner. He could see innocence written all over her. Pabla met his stare candidly. No coquetry; she was merely interested in him as a symbol, the freed unfortunate, as she herself was a symbol.

She rose in the silence and the white material changed shape. She carried a fan of carved ivory laced with white satin bows. She said, "Señores ..." making it both a suggestion and a command.

Biggo watched her go down the corridor, outlined against the light. The jefe gave him his belt and shoelaces. Biggo put them on. He picked his wallet up off the desk. The jefe lit his dead cigar and suggested they go outside. Biggo tried to count his money surreptitiously on the way. He grunted in disbelief; it looked like it was all there.

Outside in the brilliant September sun was a considerable swarm of people. The parade was forming at the jail. It included police, soldiers, sailors, cadets, school children, municipal employees and political groups. There was a navy band and a fishermen's union band and several neighborhood combinations. Among the cars lined up was a brand-new Ford flatbed truck festooned with flowers and crepe paper. Two thrones were mounted on the bed of the truck.

"Yes," said the jefe, "there is your place in the parade."

Pabla was already being helped up to her throne. Biggo saw her garment tauten around her behind for an instant and he got his eyes away and called himself a vicious damn fool. A policeman tossed his suitcase into the front seat. Biggo swung aboard the truck bed and sat beside the queen.

She glanced at him, then looked straight ahead. She raised her hand and the bands struck up, all of them at once. The sidewalk crowd gave a cheer. The Ford truck growled and the parade became a living thing, winding south. The streets were lined with people, natives and tourists. They shouted for the queen. She smiled and nodded for them.

At the first corner she said in English, graced by the faintest tang of accent, "They are cheering you as well as me, Señor Smith."

Biggo had been thinking what a perfect target he made, sitting on this ridiculous flower throne and being carted through the streets like a Roman emperor. If the wrong one of these anonymous cheering faces knew what he carried hidden in his pocket, in the Bible, this gala parade had might as well turn toward the cemetery.

The girl touched his balled fist. "Can't you give them at least a tiny smile? They deserve it, you know."

At that moment he saw Lew Hardesty standing beneath a flag-draped lamp post. Hardesty's mouth, under the suave mustache, dropped wide open. He looked like a caught fish. Biggo laughed happily.

"Very much better," Pabla said and patted his fist and went back to smiling at the spectators.

Biggo opened his hand and looked at the back of it, where it tingled under the coarse sandy hair. He looked at her profile against the sky and the store fronts. She became aware that he was watching her. She colored slightly, he thought.

When the fishermen's band behind them stopped for breath, she said, "You're an American, are you not?"

"More or less."

"I don't understand."

"I was born in the States. Since then I've just wandered around."

"Oh, and do you like wandering to Ensenada?" She didn't wait for an answer. "I do. The people are good and the air is sweet. Look!" She swept her arm around the horizon, from bay to mountains and back again. "Can you imagine disturbance or unhappiness in a setting such as that?"

Biggo could. But he didn't say so. He preferred Pabla's mood. "This isn't your home, then?"

"No," she said regretfully. "My family is of Mexico City. I rest here when I can. You know it is a great honor to be the fiesta queen and a foreigner." She rolled her eyes like a little girl recounting mischief. "Oh, some of the girls were very jealous of me, a foreigner. That is why I selected you to ride with me, because you are a foreigner too. And the very picture of religious study, martyred almost."

Biggo grunted.

Pabla added, "Except that you were falling asleep. But that will happen." Her amused smile danced away from him and out to the crowd and the band struck up again noisily.

The parade turned at the south edge of town and returned down Avenida Ruiz to the statue of Miguel Hidalgo. There Pabla alighted to decorate the statue with a wreath of flowers. She knelt for a moment's prayer and indicated that Biggo should kneel beside her. He did. With his side glance, over the curve of her bowed neck, he could see Zurico's saloon across the street. Zurico's brother leaned in the doorway. He gave no sign of recognizing Biggo. Biggo half-expected to see Jinny around until he remembered that he had made it pretty clear that she should leave town.

When the statue ceremony was over, the parade wound back through the city again, back to the southern fringes. The bands stopped playing. The military units were dismissed and everybody tromped in various directions, raising lots of dust.

The truck stopped. Biggo jumped off at once so he could help Pabla down. He placed his hands with care on both sides of her slim waist and lifted her down to the road as if she might break. She was light and warm to touch. She made him feel like the strongest man in the world.

He said, "What happens now?"

She indicated a Cadillac convertible sedan with its top down. A woman of about sixty dressed entirely in black sat in the back seat. "My duenna," Pabla said. She called, "Mamacita!" and waved. The old woman looked daggers at Biggo.

"Well, thanks for the ride, Pabla."

She took no notice of her given name. "I am driving south, Señor Smith."

"Thanks again. But I have to get back to town." He said suddenly, "Back there in the *calabozo*, when I first looked up and saw you, I thought you were an angel."

She laughed like rain on chimes. "Oh? But that was your first thought only. Since then you doubt?"

"Not necessarily. It's just that I never thought of an angel having black hair."

Her eyes lit up with amusement. She lifted her hands and unpinned the crown-and-*mantilla* headdress. She took it off. Above the darkness of her eyes and eyebrows her hair was the color of new gold. Freed of restraint, it fell to her shoulders, part of the sunlight.

Pabla said gravely, "There. An end to your doubts, señor."

Then she laughed again and picked up her skirts to run gracefully over to the Cadillac. She drove off without looking back. The duenna was leaning forward in the back seat, talking to her sternly.

Biggo stood in the road and watched the big car roll away from him. He saw something at his feet, a white satin bow from her fan. When he picked it up, it fell apart and became just a length of ribbon which his fingers had already soiled. Biggo put it away carefully in his wallet. Then he got his suitcase and trudged toward town.

CHAPTER NINE

FRIDAY, SEPTEMBER 15, 1:00 P.M.

The suitcase seemed lighter in his grasp and Biggo didn't mind the sweaty walk. Pabla Ybarra was something to think about. Once he patted lovingly the pocket that held his Bible, the thing that had made her notice him. "*Muy religioso*," he said and laughed because he felt good.

The parade had ended near the airstrip. It was a long hike back to the Hotel Comercial. But by the time Biggo reached the business part of Avenida Ruiz the parade crowd had mostly disappeared. The streets were lazy again. It was lunch time and after that, siesta. Biggo stopped in the first bar and had a beer and a beef sandwich. While he had his wallet out he counted his money carefully. Then he blessed the honesty of the jefe and the Ensenada police in general. It was all there, $133. He had another beer and another sandwich to celebrate. If anyone in the bar recognized him as the late symbol of freedom it wasn't mentioned.

He rambled on up Avenida Ruiz toward the hotel. The world looked great. "Bad luck's run out," he told himself. "Good luck's coming." Getting out of jail as fast as he had made him feel invulnerable. He still had the Bible and most of his money. He was free to wait out the peacock business. And, aside from that, he didn't doubt for a minute that he would manage to meet Pabla again.

Across the street from the Hotel Comercial a man loitered. Biggo looked at him again. It was the redheaded cow-faced man from the airfield, the one who had watched the incoming passengers. At the time Biggo hadn't thought too much about it. But that had been before Zurico's death.

Biggo stopped in the shade of the hotel arcade to tie his shoe. He studied Red. Red looked less innocent today; he began to look more like a fellow who might be mixed up in Biggo's affairs. And, from the size of him, he probably could take care of himself, name the weapon. As at the airport, he didn't pay any particular attention to Biggo. He was just there in the same black suit, lounging in front of a shoe store, doing nothing but existing. The Hotel Comercial was directly in his line of vision.

Biggo picked up his suitcase and went on into the big-windowed lobby. There was no one present except the manager. Biggo glanced past him at the rows of pigeonholes behind the counter, one for each room. From the pigeonhole labeled with his room number protruded a large brown envelope, so large it had to be folded double to enter the compartment.

Biggo understood what Red was waiting for. He didn't even pause. He said, *"Buenos días,"* to the puzzled manager and kept going through the lobby. The manager was trying to figure why B. Venn, who had registered two days before, had suddenly reappeared with his suitcase, looking like an incoming tramp. Biggo proceeded through the rear door and into the paved area behind the hotel. It opened onto an alley. He walked down the alley, one direction being as good as another.

Red had been waiting across the street to see who would claim the large brown envelope. He had been waiting to see who would claim the identity of B. Venn.

Biggo made animal noises in his throat. Ensenada wasn't so much his oyster as he had begun to think. He had a hunch he had just dodged Magolnick's assassin, the factor out to stop him at any cost. Somehow Red had narrowed the suspicious arrivals in Ensenada down to the mysterious B. Venn who had shown up two days ago and then disappeared.

"Maybe he's still on a routine check, still narrowing down," Biggo growled. "Maybe there's others still on his list."

Routine or not, he couldn't see himself going back to the Hotel Comercial. Not even if Red was the Jaccalone representative, with twenty thousand dollars in his pocket. He couldn't afford to trust either side; he didn't care for this role of sitting duck. The manager would remember—might have remembered aloud already—that his guest had made a telephone call to Cleveland. Red probably had a vague description of B. Venn, anyway.

B. Venn had to disappear again.

That might not be so easy, Biggo reflected. He came out of the alley and turned west. Two people in town knew him by name. But he had scared Jinny away and that left one, like a kid's game. Lew Hardesty was the kind who would be hard not to run into, especially in a little town like Ensenada. Hardesty would pawn Biggo's life for the price of a drink or maybe just for the joke of it; unless he thought he could make more by throwing in with Biggo. And Hardesty thought he was onto something, he had that gleam in his eye.

"Damned if I'll cut this thing three ways," Biggo announced to the seagulls. He had come to the embarcadero. He squinted out at the fishing craft, the pleasure boats, the rusty corvettes of the Mexican navy. "I got to move around where Lew isn't likely to be."

He looked north and saw motels on that edge of town. He decided they wouldn't do since Hardesty had a car and might be at a motel. He looked around at the hills themselves. He could always camp out for a few days; that sort of appealed to him. But it wouldn't solve anything to be out of touch with the town completely. And he might attract attention.

Biggo looked to the south. He began to rub his jaw, roughing up the bristles. His eyes took in the many-towered whiteness of the Riviera Pacífico, the million-dollar resort hotel. It was part of Ensenada and yet detached from it too.

"Yeah," he said. Out there he would be on a different social level from the middle-class Hotel Comercial. He would be out of Red's way and he doubted that Hardesty would come seeking Biggo Venn in a high-class tourist palace.

He counted his money again and it was $132. He sighed. That wasn't much for a hotel where the rates started at $16 a day. But maybe this deadlock wouldn't last too long; maybe something had already changed in either the Magolnick or Jaccalone factions. And he comforted himself by remembering that he hadn't had to pay a hotel bill in Ensenada yet. Who could tell how it might work out at the Riviera Pacífico?

He started to hunt for a cab before he realized again the shape he was in. He couldn't check into the Riviera Pacífico looking as if he had just gotten out of jail—whether it was true or not. He needed cleaning up.

Biggo walked back to the corner of Avenida Ruiz and peered around cautiously. Red was still at his post opposite the hotel. Biggo muttered, "You've got a wait ahead of you, amigo."

He made a detour so that he wouldn't pass before Red's eyes again. He spotted a barber shop and went in. As he set down the suitcase, he decided he was getting pretty tired of carrying it back and forth across town. And Biggo decided, when he did get a place to stay, the very first thing he would unpack was going to be his Beretta and some ammunition.

CHAPTER TEN

FRIDAY, SEPTEMBER 15, 2:00 P.M.

The barber had a brother who was a tailor. While Biggo had his hair cut, a blanket over his bare legs, the brother pressed his suit two doors away. A Mexican kid shined his shoes. He was the only customer in the shop.

He read through the newspapers for the past couple of days. He saw no news concerning peacocks except the murder of Zurico. The police hadn't made much of the feather on the body. They were rounding up the various town drunks who had been refused service by Zurico at one time or another.

During the hot towel part of the shave, Biggo fingered a crevice through the toweling so he could watch who passed along Avenida Ruiz. He didn't see Red or anybody else suspicious. He couldn't really believe anybody was dogging his trail that close but he had fleeting baseless worries which were unusual for him. The Bible was hot on his lap under the blanket. He wondered where the Jaccalone agent was at this moment. Probably in a hotel room around town, peeking out from behind the window blind. He would be stewing over Biggo's possible identity, just as Biggo was over his. "Find you as soon as I can, brother," Biggo murmured. But he didn't know how.

His suit came back from the tailor. Biggo got a clean shirt out of the suitcase and dressed in the back room. He looked quite different from the bum who had been let out of the *calabozo* that morning. The mirror gave him back a pleased grin.

While he was paying the barber $4.50 for the works (leaving his bankroll at $127 plus) he saw a late model Chevy pull up across the street. It was a maroon coupé with California plates. Lew Hardesty drove it. Biggo backed up so he wouldn't be seen.

But Hardesty wasn't looking his way. Hardesty was sizing up the girl who had just stepped out of La Posada, a neon-fronted American-style bar. The girl had generous curves under a too-warm green suit and she carried a small blue suitcase. She looked bedraggled.

At the sight of Jinny Wagner, something happened to Biggo's grin; he felt as if he'd swallowed it. He swore. "Señor?" the barber inquired politely.

"Forget it." Biggo knew as sure as fate what was going to happen next before his eyes. The last two people on earth he wanted to have meet.

It happened. Hardesty slid out of his coupé like a snake, spoke to the girl and took off his panama hat. She forced a smile and said something back. A hesitation later the pickup was accomplished and they both went into La Posada.

Biggo said, "I told that tart to leave town." He shook his head. He had to break that combination up. Jinny was too likely to tell her troubles to Hardesty. Hardesty had a nose for undercover business; if he couldn't get into Biggo's business, he'd do his best to spoil it.

"Got a phone?" Biggo asked. It was shown to him. He asked the barber to recommend a garage. Biggo got the number of Hussong's. He told the man who answered that his name was Hardesty and that his car was parked in front of La Posada. "No, I don't know what's wrong with it. That's why I called you. Also I've lost the keys. Get down with your tow car and haul it away as soon as you can."

"Perhaps we can find the trouble without—"

"Don't give me any arguments," Biggo said. He figured that if he was nasty the garage might charge Hardesty more. "Just come and take the damn thing away." He craned his neck and read off the license number.

"*Muy bien*. Our truck will—"

"I'll be in La Posada. Call me there the minute you find out what's wrong." He hung up. The barber was regarding him curiously. "Thanks for the phone," said Biggo and picked up his suitcase and hurried across the street. He lifted the Chevy's hood and raked his clawed hand over the engine. Wires broke loose in every direction. Biggo dropped the hood and saw the barber still watching him. He waved.

He sat down in a nearby doorway and waited patiently for five minutes until the tow truck from Hussong's arrived. Biggo could hear the mechanics speculating over the absence of the ignition key. But they had been told not to disturb the owner, a vile tempered American. At last they hoisted the front wheels of the coupé into the air and took Hardesty's automobile away.

Satisfied so far, Biggo caught up his suitcase and ambled into La Posada. It was cool and dim after the glare of the street. At first he couldn't see a thing. Then he could see two backs at the bar, Jinny and Hardesty, the only customers. He put on a big smile and strolled over.

"Small world," he said and gave Hardesty a friendly clap across the kidneys.

Hardesty's martini dribbled along the bar. "Too damn small, some days," he said. He had been playing with Jinny's hand but now he let go to dry the sleeve of his sport coat.

Jinny said faintly, "I thought you went to jail." She looked ready to be sick. She held a cracker halfway to her mouth, forgotten.

"Can't keep a good man down, honey."

"What's that got to do with you?"

"You know this fellow?" Hardesty asked Jinny. She didn't know what to say. Hardesty chewed his mustached lip suspiciously. "I just want to know what the set-up is, lady fair."

Biggo said, "We're old buddy-buddies," and sat down on the other side of Jinny. She edged away from him. The bruises on her face where Biggo had slapped her didn't show too much. She had powdered over them and the light was low. "What are we drinking, Lew?"

"Make it easy on yourself, Biggo, and don't start anything in front of the young lady. Go somewhere else. Go back to jail."

"They don't want me anymore."

"Then that makes it unanimous."

"An angel came down from heaven and turned me loose," said Biggo. "What do you think of that? If neither of you know what an angel is, it's something out of the Bible." He patted his pocket where it was.

"Here we go with that line again," said Jinny bitterly. There was a dish of cheese and crackers in front of her. She went back to eating the crackers as fast as she could cover them with cheese. "He thinks it's so witty. Get him to tell you about—"

"Martinis," Biggo ordered the bartender. "Make them dry."

"I don't want to drink with you," said Jinny. "I don't like one thing about you. You've got hair in your ears. You ought to be out in a field somewhere."

Hardesty patted her leg. "That sums it up, all right." He and Biggo looked at each other across Jinny's head. Biggo showed his teeth in a false smile. Hardesty's eyes flickered. "Move on, Biggo."

"I like it right here, Lew."

"No!" Jinny begged. "Please, no trouble. Let's let live and not have any trouble. I'm just a girl trying to get along."

The martinis came and she gave the bartender a pained smile. They drank. Jinny only sipped a little of her drink after she had eaten the olive. The crackers were all gone and she used the toothpick to eat the cheese straight. She turned her back on Biggo so she and Hardesty could talk softly.

Biggo leaned closer, not wanting to miss anything. It was just sweet talk and Hardesty was toying with the hem of her skirt. But she was working too hard at being picked up.

She swiveled around when she felt Biggo listening. "Oh, for God's sake, leave me alone!" she cried. "I'm tired of you lousing up my life, Biggo. What's so big about you, anyway? Nothing that I can see except your big mouth."

Hardesty applauded.

"Well, it's true. The other day, Lew, all he did was yap, yap, yap about some p—"

Biggo's elbow caught her in the stomach. All her wind gasped out and she bent forward on the bar. Hardesty slid off his stool and came around to see Biggo.

The phone rang.

Hardesty drawled, "I think it's about time you and I—"

The bartender called, "Is one of you gentlemen a Señor Hardesty?" He held up the telephone receiver.

Hardesty started to finish his remarks. Then he changed his mind and went to the phone. Biggo traded his empty glass for Jinny's nearly full one. He reclined his head on his fist and watched Hardesty's face. It slowly turned from incomprehension to astonishment and then to anger. Hardesty slammed down the receiver. Biggo laughed.

Hardesty understood. He came back and got his Panama and jammed it down on his head. He said, without much malice, "Oh, you son of a bitch, you," and went out, not giving Jinny a second glance.

She still had her forehead resting on the bar. Biggo tapped her shoulder. "Hey, kid, you all right?"

She raised her face and looked at him, eyes huge and watery. "I'm all right." She fell off the bar stool sideways, hitting another one on the way down.

Biggo picked her up off the floor. The bartender came out from behind the bar, chattering like a monkey. Jinny was breathing regularly but she was out cold. Biggo rocked her against his chest and muttered angrily, "The poor kid." He felt ashamed of himself. She looked younger now that she had passed out. She was as forlorn a sight as he'd seen for some time.

The bartender was chattering something about a doctor. Biggo shut him up. "Get her some food. She's hungry, that's what's the matter with her." He carried her over to a shadowy booth and propped her up in a corner. He unbuttoned the front of her green suit. He got some water from the bar tap and used his handkerchief to bathe her forehead. She opened her eyes and stared, getting him in focus.

He said, "I'm having them bring some food over."

"Thanks, I guess." She closed her eyes again and whimpered despairingly. "What makes me so obvious to you? I don't want to have anything to do with you."

"When did you eat last?"

"Oh, I don't know. I guess the last real meal was the one you bought me the other night. I haven't got any money."

"Zurico's brother wouldn't take you back, huh?" Biggo had already forgotten he had tried to run her out of town.

Without opening her eyes, Jinny passed her hand over her face. The water had washed away the powder, revealing the bruises and swelling. "I don't even look good enough for Zurico's. Thanks to you."

"I didn't ask you to give me the knockout drops, honey."

"All right, all right. Where's Lew?" Her eyes popped open, panicky. "Oh, God, did he leave? Did you get rid of him too, Biggo?"

"He left."

She slumped. "Thanks again."

"For what?"

"For nothing, you dumb elephant! For scaring off the only real live meal ticket I've seen in the last couple days, that's what!" She flattened her hands over her face. When she took them down again, she looked frightened. She asked him, as if he were someone new, "What am I going to do, Biggo?"

The food came, Mexican fare from the restaurant next door. Jinny wolfed it down hurriedly, apparently afraid he might take it away from her. Biggo smoked a cigarette and watched her. He was considering a stray idea.

He said, "That's a good question. What are you going to do, honey?"

"I don't know," she said sullenly. "Maybe I'll go to the police. They'd probably send me back to the States." She added with a flash of venom, "Maybe they'd like to know what you were doing with that gun. The one in your suitcase."

Biggo grunted. She could be dangerous, all right. "What do you think I was doing with it?"

"Well, I don't know." She hadn't gotten that far. She remembered something. "Zurico was shot, wasn't he?"

"So was Lincoln. Doesn't mean a thing."

"Wait a minute, wait a minute." Her forehead wrinkled and she thought as she tried to get some more food off the empty plate. Jinny said slowly, "I read that when Zurico was found, there was a feather, a peacock feather. And that first day you came into his bar, you kept talking about ..." Her eyes got excited and she sat up straight.

Biggo smiled amiably. He gazed at her and blew smoke in her face. "Suits me," he said. "Let's go to the police."

She was easy to bluff. A second later she dropped her eyes. "I don't know," she said vaguely.

Biggo said, "How'd you like a job? One with not much work to it. Good food. Nice place to stay, pleasant surroundings, good company."

"You kidding, Biggo?"

"No."

"Do you really have connections like that? What do I have to do?"

"Pretend you're my wife for a few days."

"Not a chance," she said flatly. "I'd rather go to the police. I'd rather keep on bumming drinks and eating free crackers."

"Don't kid yourself. This is just a business deal and nothing more." He had it all worked out in his mind. Red would be watching for a lone man at a middle-class hotel. But Biggo, under a new name, was going to turn into a married man at a high-class hotel. Reminded of a couple more selling points, he said, "Then, in a few days, I'll give you that airplane ticket to Frisco. I just need a wife for a little while out at the Riviera Pacífico."

The airplane ticket sounded good to her, Biggo could tell. So did the Riviera Pacífico. She rolled the name on her tongue. She hesitated. "Just business. No monkey business? I don't trust you a bit, Biggo."

All at once, with that idea, they were eying each other like two animals. He was conscious that their knees were warm together under the table and so was she because she swung hers away with a rasp of hosiery against his pants legs. And she discovered that the front of her suit was open. She buttoned it quickly but all that did was confirm the fullness of her breasts.

The animal feeling vanished. She said between her teeth, "You know where you can go."

He snorted. "You bet, honey. But nobody's asking you to trust me. You're old enough to know when to scream."

Biggo cussed her out mentally. Her figure hadn't caused his original idea. Neither had sympathy. All he wanted was to use her as a mask. At the same time he could keep an eye on her, see that she didn't talk about him to anyone. And, when the time came, she might come in handy as trap bait. He might have her walk the trail ahead of him, let her spring the deadfalls instead of himself.

"Yes," Jinny said a moment later. "I guess I know when to scream."

"Well, how about it?"

"I guess so. I don't have much left to lose." She faced him across the small table, obscurely angry. "But get this, Biggo. I'm in it just for the money and that's all. Except that you're going to feed me, I wouldn't walk in the same room with you. I think of myself as the lowest creature on earth but you turn my stomach. I don't know what that makes you but I want you to get my feelings straight."

Biggo grinned. "I can see where we'll have a very average married life. Ready to go?"

CHAPTER ELEVEN

FRIDAY, SEPTEMBER 15, 3:30 P.M.

Biggo got tricky. He had a taxi take Jinny and him out near the airport, then dismissed it. Then they walked the couple of blocks to the airport and took a taxi to the hotel. That way, they appeared to have just arrived in town.

The Hotel Riviera Pacífico was a product of the late twenties. Originally the Playa de Ensenada, it had been built by its charter investors as the hub of a second Monte Carlo. According to the cabdriver, two million dollars had been sunk in it. At that time, the hotel accommodations were only a luxurious appendix to the casino. Then the bottom had dropped out of the American economy and the tourists stayed home with their dollars. When they began coming south again, the Mexican government classified Ensenada as a border town and that ended table gambling.

So the Riviera Pacífico was just a hotel now. "The casino stands empty, waiting," the driver said sadly.

Biggo was impressed with the place. It looked like two million dollars in the sunlight, creamily stuccoed and red tiled with many-angled roofs and sudden towers. The building was broad at each end, narrowest in the middle as if corseted. It loomed on a slight crest facing the beach and most of its sleeping quarters were in the south end.

The bulk of the cars in the tree-lined parking lot bore USA license plates. There were flowers and grass and mixed in the salty bay breeze was the fragrance of pine. Biggo took the suitcases out of the cab and sucked some of the pleasant air into his lungs. He felt opulent.

Jinny got out of the cab by herself and looked around and murmured, "I wish I hadn't come. I shouldn't have dared."

Biggo grunted.

She asked, "What are you looking at?"

"Not a thing, honey. Relax." He had seen a lanky figure slip out of the parking lot and around a corner of the building, a dark-skinned man in overalls who carried a rake. The man resembled Adolfo, his ex-cellmate, but Biggo couldn't be sure.

"Well," said Jinny finally, "does it suit your taste?" She had repaired her make-up so the bruises didn't show but something still seemed vaguely wrong about her face. "Or would you rather just camp out here?"

"Is that the way they do it in Scribner, Nebraska?" Biggo paid off the taxi and picked up their suitcases. "Now try smiling. Remember you're my wife."

"So that's a reason."

"Cute," he said. "Cute as all get-out. I'll bet you bowled them over with that in Scribner."

"Stop talking about Scribner," she said irritably. She switched ahead of him through the big rear entrance and along the tiles of a Moorish hallway with paintings on the walls. Biggo followed, grinning, watching her hips wag.

They went down tile steps to reach the registration desk. The huge beam-ceilinged lobby was off to the north, down more steps. Biggo registered as Mr. and Mrs. John S. Biggo, Scribner, Nebraska.

"Ah, Nebraska," commented the desk clerk. Jinny eyed him sourly.

"We'd like a nice quiet double off by ourselves somewhere," Biggo told him and winked. "We're on our honeymoon, you know."

Jinny made a strangled sound in her throat.

"Certainly," the clerk said. "Riviera Pacífico is the ideal location to enjoy a honeymoon. If there is anything which we may do to enhance your pleasure ..."

"Never called for help yet," said Bingo. "But I'll let you know."

A bellboy took them up to a large corner room that overlooked the trees of the parking lot. It was a bright airy room with twin beds.

Jinny sat down on one of them. When the bellboy had gone away, she said, "Well, thank God for these, anyway. Why the big act downstairs?"

"Business. You just let your husband worry about business matters."

"Well, I didn't know I was supposed to look like a bride. If there's anything I don't look like, it's a bride. You should have bought me a bouquet or something."

Biggo was going to kid her some more. But then he noticed that she was sitting there, stiff and uneasy, so he didn't. He said, "We can't afford it," and wandered around the room, examining the pale gleaming furniture. It appeared brand-new. He fingered the drapes and let more sun in through the venetian blinds. He thought it might make the room gayer for her. Biggo supposed that she was embarrassed at this pretense they were carrying off. Jinny knew most of what there was to know but she evidently hadn't gotten used to it.

He left her alone for a minute to see if anyone lived next door. No one did. A Mexican girl was mopping in there and the closet was empty. That suited Biggo fine. He hadn't yet seen many people in the rest of the hotel either.

When he went back to their room, Jinny had gotten up to stare fixedly at the room number. Then she sat down on her bed again, dragging nervous fingers along the bright woven stripes of the spread. Biggo sighed at her and then commenced whistling to keep his spirits up. He hung his coat in the closet, the Bible still in its pocket.

"Might as well unpack," Biggo said, just to be saying something. He went about it. He put his razor in the bathroom and hung his clothes in the closet, leaving Jinny exactly half the hangers. He worked down toward the Beretta automatic. He decided it would cheer him up to spend the rest of the afternoon cleaning it. He thought how comfortable its weight would be in his coat pocket, a balance to the Bible. It would make him feel like he was doing something besides waiting. He stuffed the rest of his clothes into a bureau drawer.

And then the suitcase was empty, completely.

Biggo gaped at the barren lining for an instant. Then he swiftly searched the pockets of the suitcase. After that he went through the clothes he had put away to see if the gun and ammunition had gotten mixed up with them.

The idea was slow taking hold but at last he looked at Jinny. He asked, "Where's the gun?"

She didn't bother to raise her head. "I threw it away."

"*You did what?*"

"I threw it away. And the bullets too."

"You're kidding." He tore into her little blue suitcase, dumped her belongings on the floor and pawed through them. "Where is it? Come on—I got to have it."

"I threw it away. Guns scare me. It's in the bay." She gazed down on him calmly. She seemed to be thinking of something else altogether. "I threw it away. That's all."

"That's all?" cried Biggo. He rose to his feet and wavered like a smoke cloud over an explosion. "Just like that? My pretty Beretta's gone?"

She nodded.

"You held on to my watch and suitcase tight enough!"

"I didn't want the gun found on me in case I got searched by customs. It's always my luck to be picked out for a shakedown." She pulled her legs up on the bed and turned away. "Oh, let's not talk about it anymore."

Biggo kicked her tiny heap of clothing and it scattered across the carpet. "No gun. Some people in this town would just as soon kill me and I got no gun to do anything about it when it happens. You see the spot you put me in? Where am I supposed to get another one in a place like this? No wonder the jefe didn't cause any fuss over it. It was gone already. Look at me!" He grabbed Jinny's face between thumb and forefinger and jerked her around so he could confront her. "I could crack in your teeth and love the sound of it."

Her mouth puckered up and was homely. Her eyes swam and she slid away to fall face down on the bed, sobbing.

Biggo stood over her perplexed. She never failed to frustrate him. He snarled and walked around the room a little. Then he kicked her strewn clothing into a neater pile. Finally he said, "Forget it. Shut up. I'm not going to hit you."

She struggled up to her elbow. There was a wet place on the spread where her face had lain. "I don't care. What makes you think it matters?"

Biggo made the big effort. He sounded almost generous. "Forget it, will you? It was just a gun."

"Oh, hell," Jinny said and began to sob again. "I don't give the first damn about your damn gun. I'm not crying about that."

Biggo just looked at her.

She said, "This is the very room. Look at the number on the door."

"What are you talking about? Or do you know?"

"I'm talking about me!" The tears kept coming and running into the sides of her mouth. "There were too many of us on the farm. I was the talented one, I could sing. You can guess how I did in Hollywood. I didn't have any voice at all. I was a carhop, usherette, worked in a dairy—all the jobs." Crying made her words come out in gasps. "Sometimes I got to sing with some little band but I was down to hostessing when this fellow said he'd give me my big chance on television. I came down here with him to meet some people. But there wasn't anybody here to meet except him in this very room. He was just kidding about me ever getting a chance at anything. He was just like everybody."

She sprawled on the bed again, hiding her face. Biggo grunted. He went over to pat her shoulder but Jinny flinched away from him. "Keep your dirty paws off me! Don't ever think I trust your big talk. Every last one of you has got the same thing in mind."

"Well, that bloody well doesn't include me!" Biggo snapped. She made him mad all over again. It made him madder still that Jinny wasn't too far from being right. "Shut up that bawling or you may squat in Ensenada the rest of your life."

He got his coat and went out, slamming the door as he left.

CHAPTER TWELVE

FRIDAY, SEPTEMBER 15, 5:00 P.M.

No Beretta. Biggo sat at the hotel bar until about five o'clock sulking over it. He couldn't think of where he could get another gun in a peaceful town like Ensenada without the transaction coming to the attention of the police. Capping everything else, the Beretta's loss seemed tragic, even deathly. Earlier this afternoon—after he'd fluked out of jail—he had felt impregnable; now, in the dark oaken and muraled taproom, he felt flayed. He began to think his powers were being stripped away from him, layer by layer, one by one. "I feel like Toevs looks," he complained. He reassured himself by flexing the thick tendons in his wrists; difficult to reach the veins even with a knife; powerful as ever.

"A little something to do would cheer you up, Biggo," he said. He picked up his coat from the next bar stool and prowled around the slender middle of the hotel, through the lobby and dining patio, hoping to meet somebody who'd start something. Nothing happened. Defeated, he bought a cigar in the shop next to the taproom. He moseyed back through the lobby to the foot of the stairs, unwrapping it. Then he dropped it and swore as he bent over. He felt eyes watching him. He looked up and then pretended he was bowing.

Pabla Ybarra stood at the bend of the staircase, a slim sheath of pale blue satin. Where the evening gown ended, a gauzy shawl was clasped around her bare shoulders. The sun came through a window behind her and through her blonde hair so that she looked like a figure in stained glass.

He grinned, feeling good all at once. But she only smiled quizzically. She couldn't quite place him. Biggo took his coat off his arm and spread it on the tile floor. "For the queen," he said.

She frowned as if baffled. She came down the stairs. At the very last minute, she avoided stepping on his coat. Then Pabla said, "Why, it's the prisoner!" and her pink smile curved deeper. "The very religious prisoner!"

Biggo picked up his coat and tapped the Bible in its pocket. "I carry it everywhere. It seems to bring on visitations."

She laughed. "I really didn't expect to see you again."

"I made sure you did. I've been waiting by this stairway for hours." He kicked the cigar to one side. He felt a little closer to her. He had made a discovery, why her dark eyes had a soft misty look. She was near-sighted. Somehow, suddenly, that brought her within his reach.

Just as suddenly, two people were standing behind her like a guard. Pabla said, "Señor Smith, may I present my duenna, Señora Garcia." Biggo nodded to Mamacita, the frosty old woman in black. "And Señor Emilio Valentin. He accompanies me." Valentin bowed nastily. He was a snaky Latin with gray sideburns and he wore tails. He appeared to have been born in tails.

There was a moment of small talk during which Biggo corrected his name to John Smith Biggo and Pabla's mouth quirked. Then Valentin flourished his wrist watch before his eyes.

Pabla's chin came up. "Please, no occasion to hurry, Emilio. Once we arrive we will be there long enough, heaven knows."

"But, señorita—"

Pabla said no without letting it sting. "Would you play us something, Emilio, while we wait?"

They were drifting toward the center of the lobby, an immense beamed room with iron chandeliers and tapestries and heavy carved furniture. Valentin accepted his exile to the distant grand piano. A second later, Pabla got rid of Mamacita with a whispered errand.

Then the two of them had the lobby almost to themselves and Pabla indicated he should sit beside her on an antique divan. Biggo did but kept his distance. He was breathing straight shots.

She said, "It's very gallant that you should want to see me again, Señor, ah, Biggo. But it's unbelievable. Don't I remind you of your past?"

He chuckled. "You remind me that luck can always get better. But, you know, I was only in that jail for one night—and that was all a mistake." He was bringing himself up to gentleman status. "Uh, why don't you call me just Biggo?"

"How odd!" She tested the name by itself. "It's so harsh."

"It fits."

"Oh, no," Pabla said gravely. "On the contrary, I find you very gentle and lamblike." She smiled then. "I hope that doesn't offend you."

"Well, no." It didn't from her. It was just as well that people like Jinny or Lew Hardesty would never hear about his being a lamb. And it occurred to Biggo suddenly that it would do him no good with Pabla if she found out about Jinny, his "wife." No explaining a setup like that. Pabla's innocence must have its limits even though she accepted his presence at the hotel solely as a tribute to her charms.

For the moment—which was all that counted—Biggo believed his own lies. They talked about Mexico City, where she would have to go home after the fiesta. Music came from the piano and he gloated over how near and pretty she was. Once, when she crossed her legs, he kept his eyes from looking there but he couldn't help imagining how slim and golden they must be, and fresh to the touch. With the music and her faint fragrance, he felt a special tender desire for her, something new. He learned that Mexico City had changed some in the twenty years since he'd been there; quite a shock to recall that he had been there before Pabla was born.

Mamacita returned but stayed in another far corner of the lobby, watching. Valentin sneered over the piano occasionally. Even surrounded like that, Biggo was having a wonderful time. He lowered his voice. "I've got a hunch why you sent the duenna back to your room."

Pabla shook her head. "No, you're wrong." Her smile was mock-melancholy. "Please don't assume I speak with every señor I release from jail."

"Nothing like that." Biggo grinned. "I think you sent her back after your glasses."

Pabla became unqueenly enough to gulp. She touched his arm. It tingled. She murmured, "Oh, never mention that again, Biggo! I never wear them except in strictest privacy and if certain of my girl friends knew—" She realized she was looking fiercely earnest and she burst out laughing.

Biggo said, "Don't worry about it going any farther." It was their secret.

They looked into each other's eyes. She met his gaze quizzically and Biggo guessed she hadn't been around enough to be afraid of him. Her hand stole up to her throat and massaged gently. She noticed and dropped it to her lap. "A nervous habit," she apologized. She confused prettily. "I find myself doing it before each—" her eyes danced "—each crisis."

He didn't know what she was talking about.

"There's something I've managed to refrain from mentioning so far," she said impulsively. "Am I to understand that you won't be seeing me tonight? You haven't said."

Biggo looked blank.

Then a hand slapped across the back of his neck and a voice said, "Biggo!" Lew Hardesty stood there, grinning down at him.

Biggo barely managed not to speak his mind.

Hardesty pretended to discover Pabla. "Oh, I'm sorry. I didn't realize I'd interrupted anything—"

Biggo thought, Like hell you didn't. Pabla gazed at the newcomer curiously. She had taken her hand off Biggo's arm. Biggo wished that Hardesty didn't look quite so young and dashing. Resignedly he lumbered to his feet and made the introductions.

"I should have realized," said Hardesty in a voice that made love. "Not only the queen of the fiesta but also the principal artiste of tonight's concert."

"Thank you, Señor Hardesty." Pabla gave Biggo an arch smile. "Apparently not every American in Ensenada has failed to read the posters."

"Señorita," Hardesty explained, "he's an old man. His eyes aren't so good."

A joke about eyes didn't go over with Pabla. Suddenly she was no longer teasing Biggo. She rose, and Valentin and Mamacita closed in from opposite ends of the lobby.

Biggo said, "Oh, you sing. Sure—I've seen the posters." Then he saw what Mamacita had returned to the room for; she carried a violin case.

Pabla told him, "I've only a little name in Mexico City. None at all here. You're forgiven for not feeding my ego."

"I'll be there tonight. The loudest clapping—that'll be me."

"I'm afraid the tickets are more than sold." She extended her hand; it was warm. "It's been good to see you again. Until the next time."

Biggo said much the same. He was glad to see Pabla hardly bother to say goodbye to Hardesty, only a cool little nod. The trio went off across the lobby, Pabla leading in her princess manner.

"Hell on fire," said Hardesty. His gaze crawled after her body. "There goes a fleshpot your buddy Lew wouldn't get bored with. That has bounce."

Biggo started to tell him to shut up. Then he realized no matter what ran through Hardesty's mind, that didn't dirty Pabla in the least. So he growled, "What bloody misfortune brought you out here?"

"I like to mix with class. This beats the motel where I'm quartered.

What's your own reason?" Hardesty was asking after his business again.

Biggo told most of the truth. "I quartered out here just to lose you."

Hardesty fingered his scar and made the gesture seem knowing. "Why all the secrecy, Biggo? Why don't you just out and tell me you need help?"

Biggo snorted.

"You know, I just paid fifteen bucks to have my distributor rewired." Hardesty punched him playfully in the stomach. "That was real cute. Right now I'm trying to think up a present for you. Of course, if you gave me a break on some deal, I might forget it."

"You can forget it."

Hardesty shrugged. Biggo said, "Goodbye, Lew," and went over to the shop and bought another cigar. Hardesty trailed after him. "Say, what happened to that other girl? The one with all the figure."

"Maybe you've got me mixed up with her mother. I wouldn't know." As an afterthought, Biggo suggested, "Say, why don't you go look for her?"

"One's as good as another. Besides I've got to dress if I expect to make the concert tonight."

Biggo laughed. "You didn't hear the lady. Tickets are sold out, she said."

"Sure they're sold out. I bought one of the things yesterday just to get rid of a kid in a bar." Hardesty thumbed in his watch pocket and actually had a ticket. He winked at it. "Third row center. I ought to learn every line and curve from there. Pity she's dressed so warmly."

"You talk a good fight," said Biggo. He eyed the ticket and hoped the sick feeling didn't show in his face. By all rights, he should be the one going to watch Pabla play. But he didn't intend to ask Hardesty for the ticket.

Hardesty made some more bright remarks, got no rise out of Biggo, and finally went away.

Biggo wandered back into the lobby. He felt lonesome until he sat down on the antique divan where Pabla had been with him. Some of her aura seemed to linger there so he didn't light his new cigar. He leaned his head back and enjoyed himself. He imagined her hand was lightly touching his arm again.

The imagination was familiar; it puzzled him. He thought back. He thought, I haven't gotten a kick out of one person so much since— when? Maybe since I was her age.

Yet the thought didn't make him feel old at all. He dreamed gently.

He felt possessive. All of a sudden it rushed into his mind how vitally important she was to him and he sat up, wondering. He said aloud, "I'm in love, by God!"

CHAPTER THIRTEEN

FRIDAY, SEPTEMBER 15, 6:00 P.M.

He whistled into his room. Jinny's face looked puffier than ever from crying. But Biggo was in good humor; even the contrast between her and the girl he was thinking about didn't depress him.

"Well, you sure feel good," Jinny commented sullenly. She sat at the dressing table, putting her stuff away. She wore a pink-checked bathrobe.

"It's not such a bad day, honey."

"You get a chance to kick a cripple or something?"

"Come on, cheer up."

"Have you noticed what my face looks like?"

"You should complain. I'm the one who has to look at it."

She pitched her hairbrush at him and missed a mile. Then she laughed. Biggo had to admit she had a pleasant laugh. "I keep forgetting we're not really married, thank God," she said. "I'm all right. I'm through bawling."

"That's the baby doll. How about getting dressed? I feel like getting around some food."

They changed their clothes. Biggo got out a clean shirt. They were both worldly people and there was no excessive modesty about dressing. Biggo missed seeing her in girdle and brassiere, anyway, because he was engrossed with himself in the mirror. He swelled his massive chest, thinking, Good a man as ever. He felt young.

Jinny laughed again. She had caught him at it. Then she said, "For crying out loud, you blushed!"

"You're out of your head." He didn't like being laughed at when he was thinking about himself and Pabla, together.

Jinny eyed the mirror critically. "I guess you really are a soldier." His upper body was a hash of scars, most of them well-worn to pale markings against the hairy tan of his body. He had no left nipple, only a white slick of tissue. She asked, "Where?"

"Anybody that's got the hire."

"No, I meant where'd you get all those souvenirs."

"Not souvenirs. Every one means I made a mistake of one kind or another. Didn't dodge a spear here. Bullet—bullet—knife—bullet, came out the back. This mess here came from a broken bottle in Johannesburg."

She wrinkled her nose. "You look kind of gross." He said nothing and put on his shirt.

Jinny said, "Not everyone gets to carry their mistakes around with them like that, I guess." She threw down the lipstick in disgust. "Biggo, I can't go downstairs with this face. You go by yourself."

"On our wedding night?" He kidded her because he was sorry for her. "What'll people think?"

"Well, I'm just not going. I've still got some feelings."

So he had dinner sent up to the room. It was nicely served by two waiters in Mexican costume and they ate by candlelight. Jinny wore the black one of her three dresses. Biggo, with Pabla in mind, practised being charming. He told stories. He answered most of Jinny's questions about Lew Hardesty but she thought Lew was a nice fellow anyway. So he told her about the first time he had mixed with Hardesty, some time ago in Port Safaga. It involved a fight and a bet and a brothel. It ended with an Egyptian sunrise and Hardesty howling, "For God's sake, sister, that's enough!" Hardesty had had a tough time living the episode down, which was how the "*Ezzy yellallah*" cry had come to be the signal for surrender between the two men. Jinny found that story gross also.

Afterwards the strolling orchestra put in an appearance under their window. Jinny dreamed, "This breathing spell is kind of a nice one." She glanced at Biggo. "Guess I should say thanks. Well, I do say it." Her voice lied away, something about "sleeping on the beach."

"Is that what you were down to?"

She muttered yes. A moment later, "I'm not a streetwalker, Biggo. I'm even worse. I'm a cheat and there's nothing lower. Times I wish I were a good honest streetwalker. I don't know."

"Buck up. Hope makes the world go round."

"Oh, maybe. When I was a kid, they told me it was love did it." The orchestra had drifted away. They could hear it on the stand in the dining patio. The night was blue, later-looking than it was. Jinny began getting ready for bed.

She said, "I don't know what you're up to, what all this funny business is for."

Biggo grunted.

She said, "No, I'm not asking to be told. I don't want to be. Don't trust me, Biggo. You'll be better off." She nodded sagely, satisfied she had done the right thing.

He already had the Bible in his hand. He had intended to shove it under his pillow. Instead, he flopped on the bed and leafed through it for appearance's sake.

"Biggo, do you really read it?"

"Sure. Say, this Abner was quite a fellow for his years."

"Who?" Jinny had gotten into her bed.

"This Abner ben Ner. He was Saul's chief of staff, then the same for Saul's son." He read to her about the engagement by the pool of Gibeon. "You see, this Asahel ben Zerubiah was a younger fellow, one of King David's bunch, cocky fellow. He thought he'd give Abner a bad time. Abner warned him off but Asahel asked for it. See, right here—'wherefore Abner with the hinder end of the spear smote him in the body, so that the spear came out behind him.'" Biggo shook his head. "That's not easy, not even with the point-end of a spear. Takes quite a jab. These are the jabbing muscles, along here." He showed her on his arm.

She looked and said, "I see."

Biggo decided she wasn't too interested. He thumbed back farther and found something with women in it. He thought Jinny perked up, hearing about Deborah the militant priestess and Jael, Heber's wife, who pounded a tent peg through the head of the fleeing Canaanite general.

Biggo said, "What it really means is that the Hebrews picked their time. The rains come in that country between September and April. The Hebrews had something like ten thousand volunteers against this big Canaanite army under Sisera. And Sisera had nine hundred iron chariots, besides all his infantry. The Hebrews picked their time, waiting in these hills to the north of the Esdraelon plain where they couldn't be gotten at by the chariots. Which put the chariots backed up against the Qishon River. So when the rains started, the chariots bogged down, just like tanks. So there you have the chariots stuck fast and nine hundred teams of horses scared and raising hell with your foot soldiers so when the Hebrews frontal-attacked it was a pushover for ..."

But Jinny had fallen asleep.

Biggo sighed and got up and turned off the light. He tucked the Bible under his pillow. He remembered the cigar he had bought and sat by the window, smoking it and looking out. He sat there for a long time. The smoke misted out the window and went north in the blue night.

His thoughts went with it, to Pabla at her concert in the town hall. He wondered. He thought maybe it was time he settled down. When he finished this peacock business he would have ten thousand dollars. "This time I'll hold onto the money," he murmured. "Make plans." Of course, Pabla was young enough to be his daughter but she was the sweetest cleanest female he'd ever seen and far stranger marriages had worked. "She likes me, I know she does." He smiled happily. "Get a rancho somewhere down here and settle down. I've done enough fighting for one man. Time I thought of myself."

At eleven o'clock, the town bells rang, just as they had for the first Grito de Dolores more than a hundred years ago. Biggo could see an edge of the parking lot from the room's rear window and he watched for Pabla to return. Presently she did. Her blue satin dress was part of the moonlight and her hair shone like a coin. Behind her walked Mamacita and Valentin, shadows. Biggo's glimpse of her was all too short.

He got the bit of white satin ribbon out of his wallet and felt it and sniffed it. It smelled like his wallet now. But it had belonged to her though it had his finger marks on it. It was getting less white.

Other cars returned to the hotel, among them Hardesty's Chevy. Hardesty swaggered past Biggo's gaze for a second. Finally, the world seemed to have quieted down for the night.

Biggo put his ribbon away and pitched his cigar butt out the window. As he undressed, he considered the matter of Hardesty. He said, "If you know what's good for you, Lew, you won't go butting in between me and her. Hell, you don't know what true love is like, anyway."

CHAPTER FOURTEEN

SATURDAY, SEPTEMBER 16, 9:00 A.M.

A decent night's sleep made Jinny look a lot better. She sang in the shower and Biggo didn't think she had such a bad voice. She came out and put on her peasant blouse and striped skirt outfit. She sniffed at the surly freshness in the air and, as Biggo began to shave, announced she'd wait for him downstairs.

There was a lucky feel to the brilliant Mexican morning. Biggo gloried in it as he took his time dressing. He slipped his coat on over his tieless shirt, put his Bible in his pocket, and ambled down to join the girl at breakfast.

His mood changed abruptly when he reached the bougainvillea patio and its carnival-colored umbrella tables. Lew Hardesty was there ahead of him. Hardesty sat with Jinny and two orange juices at a bright blue table. He was being very charming to Jinny and she was all smiles.

So Biggo got mad. Every time he turned around there was Hardesty and he was getting a bellyful of it. It had passed the funny stage. He stalked up to the pair and Hardesty was surprised and not any gladder to see him. A seersucker suit and bow-tie brought out Hardesty's tan lean romantic looks which further displeased Biggo.

They grunted at one another. Biggo settled his chair intimately by Jinny's and growled, "You might have waited for me, honey."

"I've only had orange juice."

Hardesty said, "Biggo, my stomach's always touchy at breakfast and there's a lot of other tables around."

"Nobody asked you. This is all reserved." Biggo banged for the waiter and ordered two large breakfasts without consulting Jinny. Then Hardesty ordered one for himself.

The strain tightened. Jinny put her hand on Biggo's sleeve. "Please, let's just enjoy ourselves, huh?"

"We did last night, didn't we, honey?"

Her smile went away entirely. "Biggo," she said as a plea.

Hardesty's eyes snapped from one to the other. "What's the setup?"

"Don't get personal," said Biggo. To Jinny, "You know, if we can't have our privacy down here, we ought to keep on eating in our room. That way we don't have to bother getting dressed."

Jinny said nothing. Her face whitened and showed the memory of the bruises.

Biggo looked at Hardesty. "I figure if I'm paying for it I can order it the way I want."

"You've got it all worked out?" Hardesty asked. Even he seemed somewhat offended at Biggo's crudeness. Not that Biggo exactly liked asserting himself this way but he figured he had his rights and he was fed up.

Biggo said, "Any objections?"

"To you, maybe. Some of us think it's a free country, Biggo. Every man for himself, you know, including women too."

Jinny's head was bowed and her lower lip was between her teeth. Hardesty said, "I think we'll leave it up to the lady fair."

"The hell we will. Take your turn when it comes around, Lew. Till then, stay out."

"Or what?" drawled Hardesty.

"That's right. Or what? I'm not an Arab with my hands tied behind my back."

"Well, I'll tell you. I'm getting tired of hearing about those pet Arabs. Are you just talking or do you mean it, Biggo? I think you're just getting old, babbling."

Biggo tossed the contents of his water glass in Hardesty's face and it ran down, soaking into the seersucker suit. Except that Jinny gasped, nobody spoke for a minute.

Hardesty slicked back his wet hair. "I guess we'd better settle it," he said then and got up.

Biggo got up. "I understand the north end of the hotel is empty."

"Five minutes," Hardesty promised and went away. Jinny drifted to her feet and Biggo took her wrist. "Now, you're not going to go after him."

"No," she said dully, "I just thought I'd go up to our—to the room."

"The food's yet to come."

"I'm not hungry."

"Well, don't be worried about me. Nothing's going to happen to me."

"No, I suppose not. I just want to go up to the room."

Biggo sat alone at the table when the three breakfasts came and he wasn't hungry himself. He tipped the waiter heavily and paid for the food and had it sent back. He couldn't feel very proud of himself. He had had to show the girl who was boss and he was about to show Hardesty the same thing but still he didn't get any kick out of it. "Always these bloody complications," he snarled.

Then he got an idea, a pretty fair idea, that dissipated his ugly thoughts. He jumped up and looked around for an accomplice. None of the waiters filled the bill and there was nobody handy in the lobby. He wandered out into the sunshine and circled until in the parking lot he saw a familiar figure. Adolfo had put his rake to one side and was trying the trunk of a Packard.

Biggo hailed him, "Hi!" and the Mexican jumped a foot. He snatched up his rake and burst into an explanation of just what he was doing. Then he patted his overalls where his heart was and grinned. "Don Biggo!"

They shook hands warmly. Adolfo indicated the Packard. "Truthfully, I was looking for something to steal."

"How's Rosita?"

"Fertile and loving, the Lord be thanked." Adolfo scanned him frankly, as an old friend. "I see that you have risen in the world since the time of our common residence."

"That may be or not, amigo. Perhaps I could use your help. Do you work here?"

Adolfo raised his shoulders, amused. "Don Biggo, that's a divided question. To the hotel management, I look familiar, walking around with this rake. But I'm not on their pay-list and I make no claims. It happens I found the rake and so no one questions me while I walk around seeing what else I might find."

Biggo laughed. "You're my man. Listen ..." He described Hardesty swiftly. "This fellow with the scar will be leaving the hotel shortly, I've no doubt. That's his car over there. Do you think you could encounter him like this—" he demonstrated by bumping into Adolfo "—apparently by accident?"

"I think so."

"And then to run away quickly without being captured?"

"I think so. I'm a very quick runner."

"*Bueno.*" Biggo gave him five dollars, which Adolfo made a pretense of not wishing to accept. They shook hands again and parted.

Biggo entered the corridors north of the lobby. He passed a long sunken ballroom, deserted, with scores of tables. At last he came to draperies covering a fancy iron gate. The afternoon before he had glanced inside. Now he looked around quickly and went through the draperies and the gate, closing them again. And he was in the ill-fated gambling casino.

The place was as huge as a cathedral and as hushed. To one side sprawled a cocktail lounge, ready for business—someday—but the pyramids of glasses were dim with dust. There were other rooms meant for cards and light filtered richly through the window drapes to reveal not a stick of furniture. The banking windows were closed. The gambling end of the hotel was a wealthy invalid, betrayed.

Biggo's feet strode soundlessly across the thick carpets. The hub of the deserted casino was the immense roulette room, octagonal and three stories high. Far above hung a crystal chandelier like all the glass in the world.

The room dwarfed even the two big men. Hardesty had put his folded coat on the floor in the corner. He unbuckled his goat-leather holster from around his shoulder and from it protruded the well-known pearl handle of his Mauser. He put the weapon out of sight beneath his coat and stood up and gazed at Biggo.

With one movement Biggo got out of his own coat and it plumped to the floor from the weight of the Bible.

They had nothing to say as they sized each other up and walked into each other and swung at the same instant. Then for a time their feet touched as they hammered at flesh. Biggo had the weight but Hardesty was taller and faster with as good a reach. And Hardesty was the younger.

Hardesty danced away from the hammering first. He kicked Biggo in the crotch and Biggo locked his ankle between his thighs and threw him. Hardesty rolled as Biggo jumped at him with both feet so that Biggo slipped off his hip and they were both down.

Then they both wallowed in a keen glow of pain, kneeing and gouging and butting, breaking out every dirty action they had ever used or seen. Biggo tasted the carpet dust in his nostrils. He thought of nothing but the twenty Arabs at first and then of nothing at all. He bit and grunted and groped for joints to smash. "This is what," he said hoarsely. The fierce joy of the fight was all mixed up with the flashes of agony.

In the first minute he was supremely happy; he had been born for this. And in the first minute blood was streaming into his vision from his torn eyebrow. The eye itself blazed where Hardesty's thumb had lost its hold. They broke apart and spun to their feet.

Hardesty's face was wrong, a damp mask with the jaw slipped to one side. He hadn't noticed the dislocation yet. Biggo laughed and charged, bulling the other man against the wall but he couldn't get his arms free to hit him. Biggo rammed the jaw some more with the top of his head. "I'm beating you," he growled and his breath slobbered in and out. "I'm beating you." It was a sweet sound, hearing Hardesty's head bounce against the plaster, "Maybe you'll learn to—"

Hardesty slipped aside and kicked him in the kneecap. Biggo faltered and caught a judo chop across the side of the neck that paralyzed his right arm. He fell down and felt the flame of a kick in the stomach. He grabbed Hardesty's pants cuff and twisted him down on his face. He raised a fist high and smashed it at the back of the exposed neck. He only saw his knuckles crush the carpet nap; that arm was numb. He crouched, staring stupidly at the place on the carpet. "I missed," he said, amazed.

He located Hardesty across the room. The other man's bow-tie was gone and his shirt shredded. His mustache was mixed with nose-blood. He discovered the fault with his jaw and jerked it back into place.

Biggo mumbled, "I missed." He lumbered to his feet, his mouth wide in search of breath, and charged. He cursed, knowing he was moving too slowly. His wind had disappeared. There was nothing within his huge cage of ribs but a dry ache. Hardesty stood there, grinning like a devil, and met his charge and knocked him down. He kicked his shin across Biggo's throat.

Gagging, Biggo scrambled away. But Hardesty didn't bother to follow. He stayed on his feet, secure and confident. Biggo whimpered and struggled to lift the suddenly tremendous weight of his own body. He tried to shake the tired feeling out of his head and saw the red drops spatter on the carpet and charged again.

Hardesty sauntered aside and met him with a heel of the hand. Biggo's head jolted back and he saw the chandelier swimming in the sky above and he thought his spine had come loose. From then on, it was Hardesty's fight.

Biggo saw the white grin dimly. It had bruising force which beat about him everywhere and drove him backwards across the room. He couldn't escape; he could hardly breathe. He would reach deep within his big frame for a breath to help him live and then reach deeper still, all to find nothing. He sobbed for air and fought back without really seeing and forgetting to close his fists.

Then his knees were buckled and his head was propped against the grill of a banking window. Hardesty wove an arm through the grill and levered with it against Biggo's throat. He spoke for the first time.

"Say it," Hardesty commanded.

Biggo strangled. "Not through," the words labored out. Hardesty tightened the arm and Biggo couldn't feel life in any part of his body. He forgot about everything but air and how sweet it was. He lost sight of the white-grinning face above his as the clouds rolled in.

"Say it," he heard the voice.

Biggo moved his lips a good many times. Finally, the words came in a croak. "*Ezzy yellallah.*"

Hardesty let him fall. When Biggo came to, Hardesty had buckled the holster on again and was adjusting his coat to hide his tattered shirt. He cleaned his nose and mustache and then came over.

"How you feeling, Biggo?" he said without rancor.

Biggo grunted.

"You're over the hill, that's all. You'd better stay in your own class after this." He helped Biggo to his feet. "Come on, Dad. I'll take you home."

Biggo swayed on his feet and laughed without heart. He let Hardesty wipe off his face and they shook hands as they had always done finally. "Good fight," Biggo mumbled. Leaning on Hardesty, limping, he let himself be helped out of the casino. They went out a side door and along the beach front of the hotel in the blinding sun. They managed to stay away from people.

Jinny sat mending a stocking by the window which overlooked the parking lot. She just looked at Biggo as Hardesty brought him in. Nobody said anything. Biggo slumped down on the nearest bed. Hardesty left.

Jinny got a washrag out of the bathroom. "Come on over here to the window." Biggo did. She tried to be careful of his face. "It hurt?"

"Uh-huh."

"You deserved it."

She helped him out of his coat. Even her gentlest touch was agonizing. She got her nail scissors and snipped away the rest of his shirt. She found angry marks on his body to press the cold cloth against. He began to feel like all one being again. He said thanks.

She shook her head, working on his mangled eyebrow again. "I suppose you're satisfied now, now that you've gotten yourself hurt."

Biggo grunted. He touched her arm and pointed. Across the parking lot, two figures had met suddenly, collided, and broken apart. One was Lew Hardesty on his way to his Chevy. The other was Adolfo, stepping suddenly from between two parked cars. The seeming accident over, Adolfo was hurrying away. Hardesty opened his car door, then felt hastily inside the coat. He looked around helplessly for the vanished Adolfo.

"There you are," Biggo said through swollen lips. "It all works out in the end."

"What was it? Did that Mexican pick his pocket or something?"

"What else is Lew going to think?" Biggo reached in his own hip pocket and pulled out the pearl-handled Mauser automatic. It cuddled in his hand. "I'm back in business again," he said. He chuckled proudly.

Jinny stood up and looked down on him, pitying. "Sure, sure, that's why you went and just let him beat you up. Go on, tell me," she said. "Oh, you're so damn clever." She went into the bathroom.

Biggo tried his best but he couldn't feel clever. He couldn't feel anything except a million years old.

CHAPTER FIFTEEN

SATURDAY, SEPTEMBER 16, 5:00 P.M.

He tossed around on the bed, feeling the need of rest but unable to get any. In the middle of the afternoon, Jinny said she was going out to wade and left him alone. He grumbled to himself.

Not that he hadn't been beaten before in his life. But he'd never been left without a good excuse before. All he could think of was what Hardesty had said: He was getting old. So, as if one fight a day wasn't enough, he fought that idea and later on cat-napped a little and was awakened about five by a knock.

It was Valentin, Pabla's accompanist, at the door. He sneered at Biggo's half-dressed battered appearance as if it might soil his greenish lounge suit. He said, "A message from Señorita Ybarra."

Up to then Biggo had been ready to kick him the length of the hall for waking him up. Pabla's name made the difference. "Sure. Let's have it."

"Since you did not see fit to attend the concert last night," said Valentin, "the Señorita Ybarra will play for you in her rooms." Having done his painful duty, he strolled away.

Biggo blinked, then yelled him down. "Not so fast. Say it again." Valentin gave him a reptilian look and repeated softly. Biggo asked, "Right now? Where's her room?"

"Her suite," said Valentin. He gave a second floor number in the waist of the hotel. "You will doubtless be able to find it." Obviously, he hoped Biggo would be struck dead first. Biggo let it pass. Obviously, this was Pabla's idea over the objections of her two chaperons.

Biggo gazed at himself in the mirror. "You," he said. "You she wants to see." His smile looked awful. His face wouldn't win any prizes today. But most of his aches had gone already. He dressed swiftly. He hid the stolen gun in a bureau drawer but stowed the Bible in his coat pocket. Clean clothes made some difference. He left the room briskly.

Jinny was coming down the hall, carrying her shoes. She was windblown and sunburned and cheerful again. "Oh, boy!" she said at the sight of him.

He ducked his head. "Uh, I'm going out for a walk."

"I'll hold my breath, you can bet."

He growled something and kept going. He thought about how unfair it was to contrast the two women. Pabla made him feel as big as he was and young. She had a spell about her. She was the one.

Mamacita opened the door for him. The old woman was about as friendly as Valentin. Biggo couldn't blame either of them. Their job was to watch over a young girl. To them, Biggo was just another man, without honor. They didn't know how special he felt.

The suite was the hotel's best. There was a baby grand piano and the violin lay on the piano's shawl. Pabla came in smiling; she didn't play at keeping him waiting. She had on the same pale blue satin gown and the same misty scarf around her shoulders as the night before. Her hair was brighter gold in the westering afternoon. "See, Señor Biggo? For your concert, I wore—"

She saw his face. "Biggo—you've been hurt—"

"Huh?" Admiring her, he had forgotten. He felt his bad eye. "I had a little accident."

Pabla moved her hand and Mamacita went into the bedroom obediently and closed the door. They were alone. Only then did the girl cross the room to him. She was deeply concerned. "Oh, my poor friend," she murmured. Her fingertips moved over his face, unbelieving. "It must have been a very tremendous accident."

"My own foolishness, I'm sorry to say."

"Does it pain when I touch it? Did I hurt you?"

"No." Biggo had shied away when the firm ends of her breasts encountered his chest. It embarrassed him that she didn't know what she did to him. "You make it feel better."

"Thank you," she said but she drifted across the room again and he wondered if he had done the wrong thing. She was a new sensation to him and he wanted her so badly—he meant to have her—he didn't know quite how to cope with her unworldliness.

Pabla tickled her parrot in the corner. The bird, like a gaudy Mamacita, said nothing and watched Biggo beadily. The girl turned around gravely. "I'm sorry you couldn't attend last night."

"I'm more than sorry. But the tickets were—"

"Then it wasn't another woman."

"No. No, there isn't any other." The thought of having to explain Jinny sickened him. Using her for a shield didn't seem like such a clever idea now—not if Pabla found out.

"I knew. I don't know why I said that, Biggo." She was smiling at him and things were all right. "The other American—your friend—was there. I played to him. I always have to forget the audience and play for someone in particular."

Biggo learned what the worst kind of jealousy was. But she said, with her shy candor, "You were the one I wanted to play for in particular, though."

"Why?"

"Because there is religion in music."

He grunted.

"Because I think we like one another. Because, somehow, I don't think we're so very different." The words escaped her hastily and she bit her lip. "Sending for you to come here, that was not the proper thing."

He had a hundred confessions of his own, feelings he wanted her to know about. He fumbled for them and all he said was, "Yeah, I got the idea that Mamacita and Valentin don't approve." Because he didn't have ten thousand dollars yet; nothing to offer her; not until the peacock appeared.

Pabla shrugged, glancing at the bedroom door. "We can have our privacy until I choose to summon them. Perhaps I'm headstrong because I understand more than they do. At least, I think I do. Surely, living is something more than rules, isn't it? It's not a finger exercise but a melody to enjoy for its beauty. Beauty is everything." She tossed her head and laughed suddenly. "Even if I'm wrong, I don't want to know I'm wrong."

"I'm not the man to argue with you. Especially you. Especially now."

Pabla made a sweeping curtsy and laughed again. "Now that we agree, I shall play for you. Please sit down, over there. You've stayed in that very spot ever since your arrival." She got her violin and tuned it deftly. Biggo sat and watched her movements.

She took her stance before the west windows. "Please," she murmured, "your requests must be ones I know. To read music I would have to put on my glasses and I feel foolish in them."

His musical knowledge was limited and earthy. "Uh, play what you like. I'll like it too."

He did. He recognized none of it but absorbed it into his big body so that there were moments of tingling deep in him, climaxes. Maybe it was the music or maybe it was the sight of her with the light streaming in past her. She had flung aside the scarf to make place for the violin on her bare shoulder. Her sheathed body swayed slightly with the rhythms in unconscious seduction. Biggo clenched his fingers into his palms, bitter with himself for thinking that. Yet he hadn't had much experience with evening gowns and there was always the idea that beneath the satin was not a stitch of clothing unless perhaps stockings. He did his honest best to concentrate on the soaring music but in front of his eyes was live satin over the round of her hips.

However, for a while, he forgot people like Jinny and Lew Hardesty. He forgot that he carried Jaccalone's fate in his pocket. And that Silver Magolnick's assassin waited for him somewhere away from here.

At last Pabla's pink mouth stopped dreaming over the violin. The sun was nearly down. Her hair, as she pushed it back, was the brightest thing in the room. She put the violin away and returned to the window, looking out, looking troubled.

Biggo got to his feet awkwardly. "That was about the nicest thing that ever happened to me, Pabla. That was beautiful."

"Yes, it was," she said, not boasting. "Music is beauty distilled. You want to catch hold of it, touch it." She pointed out the window. "There is more beauty."

He came over and stood slightly behind her. Together, they looked silently out across the sand and the scalloped surf. A half mile out a long white power yacht posed against the sunset.

Pabla sighed. "My father's," she said. "*La Carlota*. I only came in to the Riviera Pacífico because of the duties of the fiesta. Tonight the ceremonies will end and tomorrow I must go back to my home out there."

"You mean you're leaving town?"

"Shortly, Biggo. I am so hungry for beauty, perhaps the way I was raised or reaction against it. I don't know. I know all my life—that's not long, is it?—I've run after it. How do you catch up with it?"

"I don't know." The room was darkening. He didn't know. Her hair was not too far from his cheek but he didn't know. "Are you sure you have to go? Why?"

She shrugged gently. "Because I have always gone."

There was the matter of her fragrance; she was closer to him than she realized, he knew. When he made a gesture of anger with his helplessness, they were touching accidentally. The line of her back against his coat. His heart pounded. He wanted to tell her she couldn't go and why but he was standing too close behind her to speak at all.

He knew she was thinking of the yacht and not of their touching yet when he looked down past her naked shoulders there was the cleft deepening between her young breasts and becoming out of sight under the satin. And Biggo knew exactly what he was going to do next.

First, he would turn her around and find out what the pink mouth was like. And he would bend her back, tightening her supple body against his while his hand stroked her. The satin would pull down or up and there would be no more wondering about her breasts or her golden legs. If she wore anything at all under the dress it would only be a wisp to be torn aside. Pabla nude on the couch or on the carpet beneath this window; would she succumb because of his overwhelming passion or because she dimly realized in her innocence that she wanted to do exactly what he was about to do?

He put his hands on her warm arms. He thought she trembled and was aware of their touching then. Her hand crept up to her throat. Her nervous habit—before a crisis, she had told him.

"I'll be damned if I will!" he growled and snatched his hands away. Pabla whirled with a gasp and he stepped back so she wasn't near him. He had startled her.

He muttered something about leaving. Pabla was regarding him. Against the west sky he couldn't make out the expression on her face, fright or tenderness or what. Did she sense what had nearly passed between them? He hoped not.

She spoke softly. "Thank you for coming to hear me play." Then she called, "Mamacita!" The duenna appeared in the room by magic. She and the parrot stared balefully.

As the old woman opened the door for him, Biggo gave her an arrogant grin. Someday, when things were settled, he might tell her about the close call. He might have soiled the ribbon in his wallet but not, by God, Pabla. He was tough enough to wait for rightness.

"I'll be seeing you," Biggo said to the girl by the window. "Soon."

"Yes, Biggo. Thank you. Please do."

On the way back to his own room, he bought the daily papers at the cigar shop. They soaked up the dampness in his hands. Desire and Pabla were still with him. "I still got my chances," he whispered. "I didn't wreck anything."

Jinny had to unlock the door so he could get in. She had just finished bathing and the room was steamy. Her bathrobe showed her plump thigh, rosy-white from scrubbing, as she walked. "Where've you been, anyway?"

"Around." He stripped off his coat in the moist warmth and tossed the papers on the bed. He looked at her soft curved body. She didn't notice the indiscriminate desire in him.

"A likely story. How's the face?" Jinny padded up to him and examined it. "Um, not so bad." The robe was loose in front. He drew in his breath and his chest swelled and bumped the gentle nubs of her breasts.

Then she saw what glinted in his eyes and she tried to say, "No," but her voice wouldn't come. Biggo clamped her to him and pulled the robe down. Her mouth shrieked open just as his mouth met it, searching. Roughly his hand groped down her naked back.

Her arms were pinned and she kicked and bit uselessly. He chuckled at her sensual struggle against him, her wild writhing. The robe had fallen away, tangled around their feet as they swayed back and forth, and he discovered how smooth her skin was.

The robe tripped them both and they lurched toward the bed. He managed to throw her face-down across the spread, his hands sliding to a new grip around the swell of her hips. He threw one leg across the back of her knees to stop the flailing of her bare legs and buried his face hungrily against her neck. The curling ends of her hair were still damp from the bath. He growled against her skin, inarticulate.

But her arms had gotten free and one snaked up at him. Her fingernails closed over his eyebrow and she tore it open again. Biggo yelled and let her loose.

"Damn you, you big lummox!" She rolled off the bed and backed away, her hands clawed against him. "You hairy bum, you leave me alone! You don't touch me!" She was sobbing.

"Oh, shut up," said Biggo. All lust had fled.

"Don't tell me to shut up!" Jinny blazed. She rescued her robe and jerked it up into a tight cocoon. "I'll talk just as much or as little as I want to! You stay in your own gutter! Stay out of mine and you don't touch me ever!"

"All right, all right." He was sitting up wearily on the bed and he tried to look at the newspapers. "Let's forget it."

"I told you you make me sick at the stomach—I don't want anything from you except a plane ticket. You think, just because I have to take your bloody charity—Oh, God, I even talk like you now!" She grabbed up her clothes and slammed into the bathroom. The lock clicked.

Biggo leafed through the papers slowly, just to be doing something. Blood dripped onto the print from his eyebrow. He smeared it aside, tired and disgusted. Jinny was right, everything she'd said. It stuck in his throat to think that Pabla should ever learn what he really was. When Jinny finally emerged from the bathroom, fully dressed, he glanced shyly at her. He growled, "Hey, uh, Jinny ..."

"What now?"

"Just wanted to say I'm sorry."

She puttered at the dressing table for a while. Then she sighed. "Okay. I suppose you're only human. But that's bad enough. And from now on—"

The rest of what she was saying was lost to him. Biggo had stopped listening. He reared up straight, eyes riveted on the Ensenada evening paper in his lap.

Squeezed among the *Avisos de Oportunidad* was a small notice, only two lines of fuzzy type. "I am no longer responsible for the debts of my wife. P. R. Pavón, 22 Calle Estradura."

Just an innocent personal, small among the classified ads. But Biggo felt a slow thrill begin at the pit of his stomach. Because, in Spanish, "*pavón*" meant "peacock." And for that matter, so did "*pavo real*," which might be, undoubtedly was, what the initials P. R. stood for.

CHAPTER SIXTEEN

SATURDAY, SEPTEMBER 16, 8:00 P.M.

When they got back up from dinner, a little after eight, the phone was ringing. Biggo got in and answered it while Jinny switched on the lights.

The voice in his ear rasped, "This Biggo?" It took him a moment to realize it was Daniel Toevs.

"Well, how you doing, Dan'l, you old goat?" Biggo cried in surprise. His hopes came up strong; maybe something good had happened in Cleveland.

"I'm doing fine."

"What's new in Cleveland?"

"I'm not in Cleveland. I'm in town. Here in Ensenada."

The toothpick dropped from Biggo's mouth. "Oh, for God's sake!" he said. "What do you mean by coming here?"

"I'm here to give you a hand. I've been checking hotels ever since the bus landed. Finally tracked you down."

Biggo groaned. He could see Toevs assiduously laying bare his trail. "Well, get out here before you do any more damage. Anybody following you or anything, a red-haired fellow?"

"Hell, no," Toevs said proudly. "You think I can't take care of myself, don't you? Well—"

"You alone? Or did you drag one of your tarts down here for company?"

"Naturally I'm alone. No one with me or behind me either. Don't you worry. I been watching and I haven't even used the same name twice."

After he had hung up, Biggo mechanically wiped the sweat off the telephone receiver and ambled around helplessly. "Saddle me with that old goat," he muttered. "The last bloody straw."

Jinny watched him. "What is?"

He didn't say. "We're going to have some company, dear," he snapped. After that she kept her mouth shut. His temper was written all over his face.

It took Toevs about a half hour to get to the room. He looked even shabbier and paunchier than he had in Cleveland. The rum smell came in with him and got worse when he swore cheerfully and shook hands with Biggo. Then he saw Jinny with her black dress and buxom figure and his eyes popped. His astonishment was so comical that Biggo forgot his bad mood and laughed.

Biggo said, "This is my wife, Jinny by name."

"I didn't know," Toevs said. "When did it happen?"

"It never did. Call it a business arrangement."

"I'll call it that," said Toevs and winked. He looked Jinny over.

She soured. "Biggo, your guff is bad enough. Our agreement didn't say anything about rum-dummies like this one."

"Isn't that the prettiest voice you ever heard?" Biggo asked Toevs. "She sings, too." He didn't care what construction the old man put on the situation. Jinny was a good-looking girl, even when you knew her faults.

Toevs got a clear view of Biggo's face.

Biggo said, "Oh, I settled that Arab matter with Lew Hardesty."

"I never knew him," Toevs said. He chuckled. "But I'd hate to meet him now that you've settled him."

Biggo looked at Jinny's steady stare. He fumbled. "Oh, he doesn't look so bad, I guess." A second's silence. "He beat the living daylights out of me." Biggo laughed, more or less.

"Oh." Toevs rubbed his jaw where two days' whiskers were like frost. He cleared his throat. "Well, that's about the end of the old bunch, isn't it? Time's passed quicker than I thought, Biggo, when some kid newcomer can beat the daylights out of Biggo Venn." It might have been the biggest disappointment in his life. He looked older.

"Not that bad," Biggo said. "Besides that's not what we've got to talk about. Sit down, Dan'l, let's get to it."

"What about her?"

"She's safe enough." It made no difference now. Jinny already knew enough about him to make trouble if she felt like it. A little more wouldn't hurt.

"Thanks," said Jinny drily. She flounced into the chair by the window and crossed her legs. Toevs got an eyeful of nylon. She said, "Take a good look, Pop. No extra charge."

"Well, here we are," said Biggo. Unsmiling, he gathered up Daniel Toevs' lapels and brought their faces together. "Now, Dan'l, tell me just what the hell you are doing in Ensenada."

"Please, Biggo—I couldn't stay up there and let you take all the risk down here." Toevs squirmed in the grasp but his whiskery chin was high. "Not after what you called me on the phone."

"Figure you could do the job better? Cut me out of it?"

"Ah, you know me better than that. What's got into you, anyway? Here we been friends since God knows when. But over the phone you said I—"

"I know what I said. It still goes and if I don't break your neck it's just because I'm a sweet-tempered fellow by nature." Jinny laughed and Biggo told her, "You just sit there, honey—no noise." He gave Toevs a little shake. "You're the last person on earth I wanted to see down here. This thing's been a mess from the start and you're the last straw. Magolnick knows you so his bunch down here knows you. But they don't know me yet and I want to keep it that way."

"Nobody saw me."

"No red-headed fellow in a black suit? He belongs to Magolnick. And he'll kill. He's got that look."

"Nobody saw me, I tell you." Toevs shook his head, wanting to be understood. "Don't you see why I had to come, Biggo? There's not much left of me, I guess, but I'm not a coward like you called me. Not just because I let you come—"

Biggo released the lapels and waved a hand to shut him up. No use to argue about why Toevs had come. The old man was here and that was that. "All right, all right. Exactly what did you have in mind doing?"

"Give you a hand. You haven't made the trade yet, have you?"

"No. No way to make contact."

Toevs took a trashcan copy of the evening paper out of his coat pocket. "Have you seen this personal ad, the Pavón one?"

"Pavo Real Pavón. Peacock, Peacock. Sure, I saw it."

"Well, what about it?"

"I wouldn't touch it with a ten foot pole. It stinks like a camel."

"Ah, Biggo, no," Toevs protested. Biggo repeated. Toevs ran his tongue over his lips. "It's the signal, isn't it?"

"Yes, it is. Also it's a sure enough deadfall. Jaccalone wouldn't send up a rocket like that, not after what happened to your friend Zurico. So it must have been Silver Magolnick's people who did it. I see it that way because it's exactly what I'd do."

Toevs scowled stubbornly. "The signal's the signal. He thumped the newspaper. "That's Jaccalone begging to trade. You can't brush off twenty thousand like that."

"Just watch me if you don't think so."

"Aren't you even going to scout it?"

"No. If Magolnick's people don't get a nibble on this, they may think they've scared off the deal," Biggo plucked the Bible out of his pocket and flipped it over in his hand, intending to give Toevs confidence. Then he remembered Toevs didn't know what was in it. "After that we'll be able to go ahead on our own tack."

Toevs gazed at him for a while. "Your own tack," he said and laughed scornfully. "And what might that be? Far as I can see you been down here doing your own fighting and your own—" he and Jinny clashed eyes "—and nothing for me. What kind of partners is that? Biggo, my half of that twenty thousand means a lot to me. And if you ..." His voice trailed away, mixed up.

"And if I what?"

Toevs got up. He was taller than Biggo, facing him. He said slowly, "I gave you half of this proposition because I thought you still had the nerve I had at your age. Right now I don't think I used my head about it because it turns out you're yellow."

Biggo still held the Bible. He slapped Toevs across the face with it. Jinny whimpered as if it were she who'd been struck but neither man paid any attention to her. Biggo murmured, "Dan'l, I'll see this business out in my own way and in my own time."

Toevs didn't say anything.

Biggo said, "You asked me in yourself. I didn't beg for this business but now I'm in and I'm in charge. You either ride with me, old rummy, or you don't ride at all. Which puts you down on your backside."

Finally, Toevs sighed and blinked. His shoulders slumped. "All right."

"All right what?"

"You're in charge."

"That means I'll handle the negotiations and you'll get out of town."

"All right."

Biggo had gotten the words he wanted but he didn't like the rebellious look on the old man's face. But there was no way to get inside a man and bully him there in his soul. Biggo said, "You're broke, aren't you?" Toevs nodded; he reeked with where the original two hundred had gone. Biggo dealt him out thirty dollars more.

Toevs said, "That isn't much. Not to hole up in San Diego with."

Biggo wished he hadn't slapped the old man. He said, "All I can spare. It's costing me to wait this business out and that's nearly half of what I got."

"All right."

"Now, try not to drink with strangers, Dan'l. This Hardesty is about your size with a scar on his right cheek. He thinks I'm up to something and he'd like to cut in. Given the chance, he'd ruin things for us just so he could laugh." Biggo put a hand on Toevs' shoulder, friendly. "Watch your step, Dan'l."

Toevs slid from under his hand. He didn't look at Jinny who had witnessed his humiliation. He didn't look at Biggo who had caused it. He said, "Who's going to bother with an old rummy, anyway?"

After the door had closed, there was silence. Jinny asked finally, "Did you have to hit him?"

"I don't know. I thought so at the time." Biggo flopped on the bed. "It was for his own good. If he'd gotten his way, he'd have monkeyed around till he got hurt. Waiting's the only tactics. Look what happened to Zurico."

"Biggo—was Zurico a friend of yours?"

"I never saw him till I saw him dead. Pity because he didn't belong in this." He twisted his head to see Jinny. "Did he ever drop a hint as to what kind of a peacock he saw?"

"No," she said.

"It isn't important." Suddenly, needing sympathy, he told her what was hidden in his Bible and all about the deadlock he was waiting out. She listened somberly, not even getting mad when he said, "Bringing you out here with me—I had an idea I could send you into something like this Pavón deadfall. To test the ground, see if it was safe for me to follow. That's the truth. I'm not nice when I'm after something." He shrugged. "But I didn't send you. You're safe. I wouldn't. You're sort of a good kid and you've held up your end of the bargain."

Jinny smiled slowly and shook her head at him. "You're a dangerous guy, Biggo. And that's a lot of money. What will you ever do with it all? Settle down?"

"Me?" He snorted but a pang went through him at the thought of Pabla. "Maybe. Maybe it's about time." He riffled through the Bible, pretending to think about anything else. He saw her still smiling at him. "What's so funny?"

"Nothing. I'm just glad you told me about everything. It's always nice to be told things." Jinny said, "Would you like to read to me again?"

"So you can go to sleep on me again?" He chuckled. "There's something I don't trust you at. You told me not to trust you."

"I promise I won't even blink. But isn't there anything in there not so bloodthirsty—something pretty?"

Biggo grunted. He leafed until he found some fairly clean pages. "This looks fair. Let's see." He read. "'How beautiful are thy feet in sandals, O prince's daughter! Thy rounded thighs are like jewels, the work of the hands of a skilled workman. Thy body is like a round goblet wherein no mingled wine is wanting. Thy waist is like a heap of wheat set about with lilies. Thy two breasts are like two fawns that are twins of a doe. Thy neck is like the tower of ivory; thine eyes are the pools in Heshbon by the gate of Bath-rabbim ...'"

"That's Solomon," Jinny murmured. "Start at the beginning."

She broke in on his vision of Pabla, her young golden movements. Jinny's face was flushed, to his surprise. It embarrassed him that she should have no one. To make up for it, he said, "You know, you're a mighty pretty baby yourself. You ought to buck up, think more of yourself."

Jinny didn't say anything.

Biggo found the beginning, "'Let him kiss me with the kisses of his mouth'," he read. He paused several times. He got as far as, "'... I will rise now and go about the city. In the streets and in the broad ways I will seek him whom my soul loveth.'" He paused again. "'Uh, I sought him, but I found him not.'" He raised his head. "Jinny—"

She said, "I know. You better go look."

"I'm afraid of what he might do. He was feeling pretty low when he left here." Biggo got up off the bed. "Hell, somebody's got to worry about the old fool. Be just like him to go spring that trap."

He went over to the bureau drawer and rummaged for the Mauser automatic. He put on his coat and dropped the pistol in his pocket. He still was holding the Bible. He dropped it in Jinny's lap. "You can finish it yourself."

She didn't touch it. She gazed at him. "Aren't you afraid you might lose it?"

"No," he said. "I'm not afraid of that." He went out to look for Daniel Toevs.

CHAPTER SEVENTEEN

SATURDAY, SEPTEMBER 16, 10:00 P.M.

Biggo was nervous. He didn't know why in particular. For a Saturday night the town was lifeless. He guessed the people must be gathered inside somewhere, winding up the fiesta of Grito de Dolores.

After the taxi dropped him, he walked around the bus depot, keeping to the shadows and looking for the old man. The last bus left Ensenada at ten but it was a little late. He didn't see Toevs in the waiting room. He waited until the passengers boarded the high yellow vehicle and the engine roared before he let himself know what he had known all along: Toevs didn't intend to leave Ensenada.

"Crazy old fool," he said. But he wasn't mad, just worried.

Lights and people brightened Avenida Ruiz. Biggo avoided the main street, not consciously, but Red had last been seen there. He made for the embarcadero, for the Calle Estradura. That was where Toevs would be scouting around, proving what a fellow he was.

The Calle Estradura was not a straight street and in places not a street at all. It was a sort of intermittent loading zone, crescent shaped, which followed the outline of the bay. It commenced somewhere north of Zurico's and gradually eased around to somewhere short of the Riviera Pacífico, never more than a stone's throw from the dark water's edge. Once in a while storage shacks blanked off the view of the bay, then there would be vacant lots of sand. It was unpaved.

Biggo began at the north end. He prowled like an animal, keeping to the shadows. The moon was clouded tonight which suited him just as well.

He discovered number 15, a rundown bait house, closed. It was not too far from the fishing pier where Zurico's body had been found. Number 15 was the first indicated address. It proved that 22 Calle Estradura didn't exist because there were no structures of any kind along the west side of the street for quite a stretch. Only the granite shoring and lapping water.

Biggo stopped and listened. Nothing sounded out of place. Music from a café or bar trickled over faintly from Avenida Ruiz. A set of headlights weaved along the highway far to the north, probably the border-bound bus. In somebody's house a dog was barking.

He lifted the automatic out of his pocket, liking the weight of it in his fist. He pushed off the safety. He held the gun in a ready position, high across his chest. Slowly, he advanced on Calle Estradura. His head was thrust forward as if he could sniff out the trouble. His feet made no noise on the uneven ground.

His lips formed the words, "Come on, come on," constantly. He was begging for action.

Almost at once the request was answered. One of the shadows ahead of him moved. Biggo stopped and became just another part of the night. A quick sideward movement took him behind the rear stoop of a small warehouse where there was even deeper blackness.

Somebody was walking quietly—but not as quietly as Biggo had—across the street at an angle. The person was coming toward him. He could see the man's outline now. It wasn't Toevs and there were no other considerations in Biggo's mind. As the man walked past him, Biggo leaned out and smashed him behind the ear with the muzzle of his pistol.

The man grunted, not loudly, and folded face downwards onto the dirt. Biggo didn't touch him. He waited for a second man. But no one else appeared and there was no additional sound. Biggo then knelt by the fallen man and turned him over and made a soft clucking with his tongue.

The man, unconscious and breathing hoarsely, was Red. He wore the same black suit as when he had watched at the airport and when he had watched at the Hotel Comercial. He bled from behind the ear.

Biggo didn't waste any more time with him. Walking quickly now, he angled toward the locality Red had just quit. He still held the automatic at ready but it was only a gesture. He knew what he was going to find because it seemed inevitable.

Daniel Toevs was a crumpled shape across a block of the granite that edged the bay shore. The street was narrow here, where number 22 would be had it existed. Between the backend of Zurico's and the next building was a narrow alleyway. Somebody had waited in that black slot for Toevs the way Biggo had waited for Red. And when Toevs had come scouting, the somebody had stepped out and put a gun against Toevs' spine and shot him to death. It probably hadn't made much noise at all, the gun tight against Toevs that way.

The pockets of his shabby suit had been turned inside out. The lining of his coat had been ripped in several places. He had been searched hastily and his wallet had been tossed aside. Biggo fumbled with it. The money was still in it. He didn't take it back because it was so bad dying, much less dying broke. Toevs wasn't a bum; no reason he should look like one to anybody.

Biggo crouched there and patted the old hand helplessly. The flesh was still warm. He began to cry. He straightened Toevs' clothes a little. So this was the end of all of them, the soldiers of fortune, shot in the back on a foreign waterfront. He remembered the Daniel Toevs of only ten years ago, of Marrakech, full of strength and the joy of fighting. Biggo rocked back and forth on his heels, sick at heart.

"You old son of a bitch," he said. "Why were you such an old son of a bitch?" It was all the benediction he could think of.

There was a movement nearby. Biggo raised his gun sharply. But it was only a mongrel, coming up stiff-legged and smelling at the odor of death. Biggo's lip curled. He clawed up a rock and threw it hard. "Not yet you don't get him," he growled. The dog fell down and then scooted away into the night.

The action turned his grief into wrath. Biggo got to his feet and wiped his sleeve across his eyes. He stretched his arms as if gathering in weapons and his fists were clenched for their own power; the gun only happened to be in one of them. Daniel Toevs had been his own kind and his friend. His brother even, by virtue of the blood they had shed together.

He said, "Don't worry, Dan'l. They'll pay. Red and anybody else." He turned and, walking stiff-legged as the dog had done, went back the way he had come. He thought about the redheaded man lying there unconscious, waiting to be paid off. There was death on his face and in his mind.

He stopped. Caution came back to him. He was no longer the only person on the Calle Estradura. Down the street where he expected to find Red lying, lights danced. Flashlights, a pair of them. The beams glanced off leather belts and big buckles, off the barrels of carbines. Police.

But of Red there was no sign at all. Biggo had crouched by the body longer than he'd thought. Red had come out of it and escaped.

Biggo shook with fury but he made himself move backwards into the darkness. He found a passage and went through to the next street. He walked one block and then another. He kept saying, "Later, Dan'l, later. We can wait some more." He remembered to put the Mauser away in his coat pocket before he reached the lights. He was stumbling a little. He said, "They'll find you soon. They'll take care of you, Dan'l. They'll keep the dogs away."

A taxi took him back to the Riviera Pacífico. Somehow he got through the corridors to his room. Jinny took one look at his red eyes.

"Biggo," she said. She was ready for bed but she got up.

"I didn't make it," he said. "I didn't do anything. They shot him in the back and left him for the dogs."

She didn't say much. She didn't try to sympathize or tell him it wasn't his fault when he knew it was in a way. She just took his arm and led him over to his bed. "Try to get some sleep, Biggo. Then you can think about it." She took off his coat and hung it away in the closet. She brought the Bible from under her pillow and stuffed it under his pillow.

He watched it change places. "Red killed him. Now I got the whole thing, both halves of the twenty thousand. All I have to do is wait them out. But the money's running low. Need money to just wait."

She whispered, "That's not what you're thinking about." She unbuttoned his shirt.

"No. I guess that's love, seeing yourself in somebody else. I loved the old fool. They killed him and they killed me. I saw me lying there and that's just the way I'll die. Dan'l and I, we're the same thing. I shouldn't have talked to him like that."

"Please," said Jinny. "Try to get some sleep, Biggo." She knelt before him and started unlacing his shoes. "Wait till morning, Think about it then."

"Yeah," he said. "I guess." He lay back on the bed and shielded his eyes against the light. She finished undressing him and turned off the light. Later she heard him speaking but only caught one little part of it, "... remember, Dan'l, the time we ..."

CHAPTER EIGHTEEN

SUNDAY, SEPTEMBER 17, 11:00 A.M.

Biggo passed the night but it couldn't be called sleep. Sleep itself didn't come until the room turned gray and then he was unconscious until he heard distant clanging. He usually woke up quickly but today he drifted, not wanting to enter the world again, until he made out that the clanging was church bells and that it was Sunday morning. According to the sun, around eleven o'clock.

He rolled over to look at Jinny. Her bed was made up. She had gotten up ahead of him and he hadn't heard her movements. He stayed where he was a while, staring at the neat bed and thinking about Daniel

Toevs. He half-dreamed, willing himself to meet Red again. He had no doubt about it. He would meet Red and he would settle for Toevs. With Red and anybody else connected with him. "Old Dan'l, you're worth a lot of settling," he mumbled. "I hope there's an army of them." He expected Jinny to come out of the bathroom any minute. When Biggo realized he wasn't hearing anything he raised on his elbows and looked around.

The bathroom door was open. Jinny wasn't anywhere in sight. He threw back the sheet and got up, uneasy. Bleary-eyed, muscles stiff, he gazed around their room. Where was she? He didn't see her little blue suitcase. He threw open the closet door. Only his own clothes remained.

He went then to his pillow and found the Bible was still under it. He groped his wallet out of his pants. Inside were two tens. The five and the flock of ones were missing—approximately fifteen dollars. There was no note or explanation but there didn't have to be.

He said, "She's left me."

She had made her bed and left him. For the second time this week he had awakened in a room they shared to find himself alone once more. He looked through the wallet again and the airplane ticket was gone too. The church bells had stopped ringing by now and he could hear a plane pass over the hotel, high above. He didn't go to the window to look.

Biggo dressed slowly and shaved, trying to figure out exactly how he felt about it. He thought he ought to feel anger for the girl but he didn't. Only disappointment and a sort of sluggish sadness. Jinny had gotten out when the getting was good. She called herself a cheat but she hadn't cheated him; she'd only taken a fair share of his money and the ticket. Not his wrist watch and clothes this time—or the Bible. He guessed she had foreseen that the peacock business wouldn't ever come to anything, that he would run out of money and the thing would peter out and he would give up. He found he was wondering about that himself, decided she was wrong, decided what she thought didn't matter anyway. Toevs was about the only thing that mattered.

But he felt like a loser as he wandered from bathroom to bedroom and put on his coat with nothing in mind. "Well?" he asked himself. Well, he missed not having Jinny to talk to. Well, so he was alone again.

He said suddenly, "Pabla," wondering what had taken the idea so long. "Pabla." Today was the day she was supposed to leave the hotel for her father's yacht. But it was still early and perhaps if she hadn't left yet, she could find a way to be alone with him and talk to him. He threw his shoulders back and straightened up for the first time that morning. Pabla was the rightest answer he had ever come across.

He put the Bible in his left-hand coat pocket and Hardesty's gun in his right-hand coat pocket. From now on they would be part of his clothes. Then he was ready to go.

The hotel was quiet with a Sunday hush. As he went downstairs he passed the honeymoon couple who had flown down here in the seat ahead of him. The young fellow and his cute trick of a wife. They were cosily arm-in-arm and they even had a smile to spare for Biggo. He grunted. It almost surprised him that they were happy and that all the world wasn't concerned in his troubles.

He strode through the lobby and up a staircase to Pabla's second-floor suite. He knocked and hoped.

Mamacita answered the door. She listened to him and then shook her head distastefully.

"Well, señora, can you tell me where she is?"

She said, "The señorita is not here. I am busy with packing. Excuse me." She closed the door in Biggo's face.

He let off some of his steam by making a noise with his lips that she would hear through the door. Then he whirled and stalked down the hall. At the turn he ran smack into Valentin. The accompanist wore a silk maroon shirt and maroon slacks. He looked like part of a gypsy quartet and he smelled of cologne.

Biggo got hold of the silk shirt in front. "You'll do," he said. "Where do I find the Señorita Ybarra?"

Valentin wriggled a little but not much, so as not to ruin the shirt. "Please, señor, I don't know. I am late—"

"I think you know. You're a watchdog, aren't you? I want to see her."

"But I—we—" Valentin shook his head plaintively. Biggo's stolid stare continued. Valentin's lips twitched with nervousness. Then he managed a smile that stayed put and the longer he smiled the nastier it got. "Certainly. If you truly seek the señorita, she is bathing in the ocean. There is a cabana south on the beach, very vivid. You know how to find the ocean, I suppose."

Biggo let it pass. He was glad enough to learn that Pabla was still around. He said, "Thanks, amigo," and turned Valentin loose. He reminded himself that someday he must slap that snotty smile off the fellow's face. But not today.

With every step toward the beach, he came more to life. The death of Toevs, the grinding frustration of his mission down here, the running-out of Jinny—those were all familiar parts of a sordid life. Familiarities you never got quite used to. But Pabla was a new thing—a combination of youth and beauty and innocence. He desperately needed some of that close to him. He needed to be exposed to some of that to rub off and restore his strength. Even to watch her at a distance, playing in the breakers, that would help him. "You're the one, Pabla, angel," he murmured. She could restore him. He hurried.

In front of the hotel where a fountain gurgled, he swung past the shaded deck chairs and down onto the concrete promenade that ran the length of the hotel, stopping abruptly at the sand dunes on each end.

The tide was out. The wide white sand was clean. There weren't even any people swimming or sunbathing. Biggo stopped, scared. No Pabla. He decided if Valentin had lied to him, he would break his neck.

Then, past where the promenade ended, he saw the cabana. It was a gay tent, orange and crimson, with even a little fringed awning. "Sure, in there," Biggo said. He was suddenly positive and his heart thumped as he hastened over the dunes toward it, grinning.

He came near and heard her voice, low as if talking to herself. He hesitated, not wanting to frighten her.

Then he realized she was reliving their few moments together just as he had relived them. Pabla was murmuring, "It is beauty that is vital. The only vital thing in the wide world, I believe, and so elusive. For beauty I would ..." Her voice trailed off. Biggo smiled.

He pushed the tent flap in. He hadn't known it was fastened and a couple of snaps gave. He stepped inside where it was hot and yellow-dark.

He couldn't believe he was there. He couldn't speak.

Pabla lay on a sort of chaise longue. She wore a two-piece white swimsuit but the bandeau had been tossed aside onto the canvas floor. She lay half under a man and her golden arms were twined around the small of his back, tugging him closer, and her golden legs were tangled up with his mahogany-tan ones. The man was Hardesty and he wore bathing trunks. Each of their mouths seemed trying to swallow the other.

Biggo stood above them, a silent empty-eyed hulk, as the girl lapsed into pleasant shudders and the man dropped his head to bite her neck and shoulders. Then her eyes flicked open.

She pushed against Hardesty and he said, "What—" and then he saw Biggo too. Hardesty sat up, an idiot smile on his face, and the only noise in the tent was the faint rubbing of their skins as the pair untangled.

Biggo's head swam. Whatever was caught in his throat made a whimpering noise when he tried to say something. He had nothing to say, no formed thoughts in his head. Only the swirling.

Hardesty made an attempt to carry it off. "Didn't anybody ever teach you to knock, old man? Or I guess you can't on canvas, come to think of it."

Biggo's lips moved. He put his hands up to touch his head. When the first sanity came, it was inconsequential. It was, Why does she just sit there smiling as if she were alone with me? Pabla, why don't you even have the decency to get dressed, now that I'm here?

Then the swirling stopped in his head and he saw their shamelessness like an explosion. His eyes squinted and his lips tightened against his teeth. His hand dropped into his coat pocket onto the Mauser.

Hardesty knew. He scrambled back. "Biggo!"

Biggo grunted. He wanted to smash and destroy. He wanted to hit back and he wanted company in the agony of being hit. He could taste the hate that curdled tight in his belly.

Pabla had slipped to her feet too but she had come nearer. Except for the heated eyes her face was sweet and endearing. She held out her arms to him and her voice crooned, "Biggo ..." She was all golden flesh except for the white material banded around her loins and she was offering herself to him. To him too. "Biggo, please don't be angry with me ..."

The touch of her hands chilled him. It cured the knot in his belly and the taste in his mouth changed. He unclenched his fingers from around the gun and let it stay in his pocket. He took a step away from her. Her bandeau caught on his shoe and he kicked it away.

"No," he whispered because he didn't want her to touch him. "No," he said again because he didn't want to kill when it wasn't worth it.

Pabla couldn't understand.

He stumbled over the portal, getting out of the tent. The sunlight blinded him. He swung his head until he located the outline of the hotel and plodded toward it as if it signified home. His shoes dragged in the sand. "No," he said dully. It hadn't happened. He didn't believe it. Then the real pain of disillusion came down on him and it was the hell of all roads leading to the same place.

CHAPTER NINETEEN

SUNDAY, SEPTEMBER 17, 1:00 P.M.

All around him lay silence. Unless he moved there was no movement at all in the cloudy mirror. If he closed his eyes there was no one at all to see the dusty pyramids of glasses, the empty tables and stools, the bar itself curving off into infinite dimness. When he held his breath the heavy air didn't get breathed by anyone.

He focussed at the peacock on the wall. "So it boils down to this—do you really exist or do you just exist because I happen to be here?"

The peacock said nothing though Biggo waited. There was a lot of gold thread—like Pabla's hair—woven into the peacock and it was the central figure on a brocaded tapestry that hung to one side of the bar. The tapestry was suspended from a long wrought-iron spear.

"Oh, you exist," Biggo growled finally. He kept one hand secure around the bottle he had bought in the hotel taproom. It was already a third empty. "You'll last, when all the rest of us are dead and gone. Vanity of vanities, says the fellow." He poured some more of the bottle down his throat. In the mirror he could see the face of the squint-eyed old man who was drinking too.

He didn't like the look on the mirror's face. Biggo swung back and located the peacock again. He had found his refuge and he wanted to sink deeper into it, into being alone. There was no lonelier place than these almost forgotten gambling rooms at the north end of the hotel. "Pabla," he whispered suddenly. The sick hurt had caught up with him again. Just when he thought he had it destroyed with the bottle it would come again.

"I should've known better," he mumbled to the tapestry. "You're just like her. El Señor Pavo Real Pavón. You and her parrot, all feathers and show. I'll bet that parrot talks about beauty too. But what does it mean, huh?" He scowled, puzzled. He wanted to know. "What am I supposed to believe? You can't believe in anything. Did you ever try to hold on to anything? There's nothing there, nothing anywhere."

The gold threads in the peacock glinted a little, that was all. Biggo drank some more. He wanted to cry but he wouldn't let himself. He had cried over Toevs and he wasn't going to cry over Pabla too. That might make them the same and they weren't.

"I should've known," he said. "I'm old enough." He slumped forward, holding the bottle cool against his cheek. "Pabla ..."

Presently a new voice said, "Is this a private drunk or can just anybody get in?"

Biggo turned his head. Instead of the peacock were a woman's white shoulders and a woman's white face. "No," he said. "You're not true either." He tried to see through her to the tapestry.

Jinny said, "I knew if I hunted around long enough I'd find the hole you crawled into." She slipped up onto the stool next to him. She wore the black dress that showed off her back down to her slip. She looked out at the deserted casino and shivered. "Funny you'd bring your troubles here, though. Isn't out there where Lew knocked your ears down?"

Biggo began to believe she was actually there. "Hello, honey," he said. "Hello."

"We all get licked eventually, you know. You can't win. It's rigged." She puffed her cheeks and blew out her breath. "Boy," she murmured and put her hand on his forehead.

He struck it away. "What'd you do with your suitcase? You ran out on me. What'd you come back for—more money? You can't have any more."

"Oh, you damn dumb lummox," Jinny said. She smiled and patted his hand. "Suitcase is back in the room. I should have left you a note, shouldn't I? But I didn't think you'd wake up. You didn't sleep all night."

"How do you know?"

"Buck up, Biggo," she said and rummaged in her purse. "Look at this stuff." She laid three bills on the bar in front of him. They were twenties. He counted them with his forefinger. She asked, "Well, aren't you going to say anything? That gives us about eighty dollars again."

"Where'd you get it?"

"Remember the airplane ticket? Well, it wasn't redeemable so I went into town this morning and put on a crying act in some of the bars and showed my knees a little and I found a sucker. I got nearly forty-five dollars for it. Isn't that wonderful?"

"Yeah," said Biggo. He barely understood. "That's swell."

"Of course, it was worth fifty but I figured I'd better take what I could bloody well get. The rest of that sixty is what I took from your wallet to make change with." She waited for him to speak and when he didn't she hugged his arm impatiently. "Aren't you proud of me, though?"

"I'm proud of you."

She took out his wallet and put the three twenties in it and slid the wallet back in his pocket. She put her hand on his forehead again. "You didn't really think I had run away, did you? I didn't think you'd wake up. I had to take the suitcase to make it look good and I had to take my clothes to make the suitcase weigh something. I thought you'd see my toothbrush was still in the bathroom and my hairbrush and so forth."

"Yeah, I guess I should have."

She flared up. "Hell's bells, Biggo, I did my best! You ashamed of me?"

"No," he said and put on a grin. "No, I'm proud of you, honey. I'd have been lost without you."

Her coming anger vanished. She blinked and rubbed her nose and slid her hand over his big fist on the bar. "You're taking it pretty hard, aren't you? That's all right, Biggo. Anything you want to do, go ahead. It's tough to lose somebody. Cry if you want, get it out of your system."

He shook his head. He couldn't figure out how she knew about Pabla. Then he realized she was talking about Toevs.

She asked, "Does it make you feel any better to get drunk?"

"I don't know. Maybe."

Jinny looked around at the high empty rooms and bit her lip. She got off the bar stool and took his arm. "Come on."

"Come on where?"

"If you're going to get plastered, that's swell. I'll get that way with you. But not here."

"What's wrong with here?"

"Because it's dead and you're alive. We're alive. Come on. Let's go up to our room and do it there."

She carried the half empty bottle and held onto his arm up to their room. She had made the other bed while Biggo was out. Her blue suitcase again sat in its corner. Jinny helped him out of his coat and tie and kicked off her shoes and sat down with the bottle.

By three o'clock they were high as the sky. They were solemn about it and sat side by side on his bed, passing the bottle back and forth. They told the stories of their lives.

"I don't know what I did wrong," Jinny said. "I wish someone'd tell me."

"I don't know," he said. "No use blaming anybody but ourselves, though. If you can't take blame, you're no good."

"That's right. But who's any good?" She stood up and pulled her dress off over her head. "Too damn hot," she complained and flung it into the corner. She didn't put anything on over her slip. Through the pale rayon could be glimpsed the hint of her black girdle but no brassiere.

She huddled next to him and he told her the life story of Daniel Toevs and what a wonderful fellow he had been.

Jinny said, "I wish I'd had a chance to get to know him. I wasn't nice to him." Tears came easily to her eyes.

"Well, you didn't know, honey. It isn't your fault for everything."

"Times like this it seems like it is. I guess you're right. All you can do is try to make up for things. Isn't that what we're getting plastered for—to make up for things by being as sorry as possible? Poor Dan'l!" She kicked the empty bottle with her stocking foot.

Biggo watched it roll and shine in his eyes. "I'll settle for Dan'l," he growled. He put his arm around her and patted her reassuringly. A strap slipped. Neither of them noticed.

"I feel sorry for *us*, too. You know how to fight but I don't. You know what we are? We're outcasts." She nuzzled tipsily against his collarbone. "I don't want to be one. I don't want to fight. Oh, Biggo, who wants us? Who'll settle for *us?*"

"I don't know that anyone wants us. I don't even know how to fight anymore."

They leaned against one another and eventually he told her about Pabla, from the beginning. He told her how Pabla had appeared in the jail like an angel and how he had met her again and found out about love all at once. And how, after she had played her violin, she had stood close and desirable in the darkening room and he'd done such a noble thing, not laying hands on her. And then in the cabana tent, indecent with Hardesty and not bothering to cover herself.

His voice dragged to a finish. Jinny hadn't said anything. Once she had vaguely tried to adjust her drooping slip but had failed and forgotten it. Her cheeks were flushed, vivid above her white naked shoulders. She lay back against the headboard of the bed and gathered Biggo to her. "Oh, Biggo," she whispered. She rested his head on her breast, warm and soft. "Poor Biggo—I didn't know how it was."

"I should've known. I was the sucker."

"Yes, you should have known. You're such a big baby. Pabla—the way you thought of her—people like that just don't exist, Biggo, honey. Honey, honey, you were dreaming."

"Maybe I was. Kind of odd, I can't get mad at Hardesty. Like Hardesty didn't have anything to do with it. Just me, blind and dumb."

"You hush now and listen to me." But Jinny didn't say anything for him to listen to. He nestled there and heard her heart and sighed, toying idly with the ribbon straps that had lagged low on her plump arms. After a while she cracked their silence with a vicious, "I could kill her."

"That's all right, honey."

"I guess." She murmured. "I never had anyone to hold like this before." She sighed too. "You know, I've forgotten being here the first time. In this room—you know."

"Good. You're a good kid, Jinny."

"You're a good kid yourself. You're too rough and nothing but a big baby but you're good. You won't ever hit me again, will you?"

"No." He discovered that the hem of the slip had ridden up to her stocking-tops and he commenced to stroke the silken sides of her legs with no other thought but that they were pretty. Out of the storm had come this calm, this lingering nearness of another being, and he was grateful. He added, "Just don't ever rig the liquor or throw away a perfectly good gun again."

Fascinated, she watched his hand trail back and forth reverently over the contours of her stockings. "You can be gentle, can't you? I'm scared of guns and things like that, Biggo—violence. We're out of liquor. I'm scared of getting sober. No, don't move yet." She held him tight against her. "You know, you weren't really in love with her, I don't think. You were just all moony over her, like a school kid. You were in love with love."

He didn't answer for a while. Then his voice was muffled against the cozy flesh of her bosom. "Maybe that was it. Second childhood."

She shook him gently and the slip dislodged finally and became nothing but a twisted swath of rayon around her hips. She didn't pay any attention. "You're not that old! Quit thinking about it all the time. A man is a man until he's dead." She paused and they both thought about Daniel Toevs. Her tone was more subdued. "Well, what I mean is, look at all the big movie stars, the men. Hardly any of them less than forty and some of them fifty. You're grabbing for something you don't really want, you big ox, darling."

He grunted. Their hearts were beating the same peaceful rhythm and their breathing was the same. When he had thought about it for a long time, he said, "No. I guess what I thought was Pabla was probably something I wanted as a kid, when I ran away from home. Romance, is that what I mean? Hell, I don't need anything out of a kid's storybook. Why should I want the same thing I wanted that many years ago, huh?"

"That's right, honey baby." Jinny tousled his head and kissed the top of it. Then she pushed him upright. "It's wearing off," she said. "Go down and get us another bottle. I don't want to lose ground. I want to keep what we got so far."

Apart, they both realized suddenly how exposed she was. "So do I," Biggo said.

She reddened and began to do something about the errant garment. Then she changed her mind and met his eyes. "I guess," she said faintly, "all that people like us ever get is a moment here or there. Whenever the time and the place cross. I guess we ought to take advantage of it."

He nodded tensely. He didn't move because he was afraid to lose himself any minute and force his brutality on her. Jinny was lovely, mussed and gazing at him so seriously. Thoughtfully, she unsnapped the tops of her stockings. Her hand crept within the folds of the slip and he heard the rasp of the girdle's zipper and she squirmed, using both hands. Then she paused with a shy laugh. "Times when you could be some help, you know."

His arms went around her and he pressed down on her mouth, remembering to be gentle. A breath later he forgot all his good intentions as fast as she did. He discovered response and delirium and explosion and then a placid infinity through which they drifted, hugged close together.

Finally she opened her eyes and patted his cheek and whispered, "How about that other bottle? We want to stay drunk. What we got, we don't want it to start wearing off."

Biggo stumbled to his feet and nearly fell down. "Wearing off, hell," he said and grinned down at her foolishly. He picked up her hand and held it. "Just don't you move, that's all. Don't run away from me again or anything."

Jinny nearly purred. She tried to sit up and clutched her head. "I just thought I'd change into something."

"You look good right now, honey."

"I just got a prettier slip, that's all."

"I'll be right back," he promised. He kicked his coat aside and the Mauser skidded under the bed. He walked carefully out of the room.

He made it down to the taproom and bought another bottle and fumbled the change back into his pocket. Then he heard her speak to him.

"Biggo," said Pabla softly.

He knew she was standing in the archway between the taproom and the lobby. His muscles tensed and all he had to do was turn around to see her. She wanted to talk to him badly, wanted him badly. She'd put it all into speaking his name.

But he didn't turn around. The bartender started to say something and changed his mind, only glancing curiously toward the archway and then at Biggo. Biggo stood still and wondered, Is it over? It was fine when Jinny was talking yet how was it when Pabla called his name? He didn't stir and presently he sighed because he knew she had gone away.

He looked behind him and the archway was empty. He picked up his bottle and walked into the lobby. He wasn't sure how he felt. Confused, mostly.

But now Pabla was gone. It was a strange sort of relief and he made his way over to the French doors of the lobby because he knew she was going out to the yacht. It wouldn't spoil anything to watch her go.

The glare from the ocean hurt his eyes. Biggo squinted and saw the figures going away from him. There was Mamacita carrying the violin case and the parrot and Valentin carrying suitcases. Pabla walked in front, carrying nothing. She had on a bright blue street dress that showed how slim her body was and how shining her hair.

The trio was headed for a motorboat that waited at the stone jetty at the end of the beach. They reached the jetty and boarded, one by one. Pabla boarded last and the driver of the boat stood up to help her in.

Biggo's face creased in a horrible grimace. He shoved open the French door for a better view. He half-raised the bottle in his hand as if to strike from that distance. Because it was more than his imagination wanting it so. The driver of the motorboat was Red.

CHAPTER TWENTY

SUNDAY, SEPTEMBER 17, 4:00 P.M.

His mind was fogged with whiskey but it recorded two things clearly. One was the remembered taste of hate and the other was the white wake of the motorboat cutting away from the jetty.

Biggo followed, the bottle held clubbed at his hip. He shambled across the hotel lawn in a weaving line and his eyes were fixed on the trail of the boat. He didn't stop until the low wall that separated the promenade from the beach struck a blow across his thighs and the bottle shattered. The noise brought him closer to reason. "Can't get them now," he said and looked down stupidly at the sharp neck of the bottle still in his fist. "Got to be later."

The motorboat had curled out of sight behind the yacht. He stood staring at the yacht and, "I'll come," he promised it. And he promised Toevs.

His drunken brain had a hard time putting its pictures in order. Toevs lay dead over a chunk of granite shoring. Pabla lay writhing in a man's arms. Red had killed Toevs; and Red and Pabla had gone home to the yacht. The assassins were home now, all together out there.

Biggo dragged his forearm across his eyes. "Damn drunk," he said. "Why do I have to be drunk now? Got to get out there. Got to straighten up."

The yacht. It might have come up from Acapulco—or down from Los Angeles. What mattered was that its sleek beautiful lines enclosed in one place Silver Magolnick's people. It might be a fortress in its way but to Biggo it was a white spot on a blue bay, like a mark on a map— a destination.

"Good," said Biggo after he had stared at it a while. "Good for me." But he knew he was in no shape to start anything. The liquor wouldn't let him think very well and his limbs dragged like dead weights.

So he half-rolled over the promenade wall and lit feet first on the beach. He trudged through the dry sand until he reached the hardpack at the water's edge. The sun was getting lower but it was still hot. He began to trot along the tide line, head down. By the time he passed the first dunes that hid him from the hotel his stomach was rolling over and over. He stopped. He spread his legs and bent down and stuck his fingers into his throat.

He vomited away most of the whiskey in him and his head felt ready to float off. He pulled himself together and jogged back up the beach. He didn't peel off his shirt though it was already tight and dripping against his torso. He wanted to sweat away the whiskey, force the alcohol numbness out of his pores. Up and down he went, not looking at anything except his shoes as he ran and his footprints he had left on previous laps.

Over the noise of his own breath he heard somebody calling but he didn't look up. When he came back on his next lap Lew Hardesty was waiting for him.

Hardesty looked clean and cool in a gray sport suit. He grinned and said, "Hey, Biggo—what's up?" Then he shied away as Biggo thudded closer and a wary expression replaced the grin. Biggo realized he was still carrying the broken neck of bottle around with him and he dropped it and started back down the beach.

Hardesty fell in stride with him. "You're a little old to go in training."

"Get out of here," said Biggo. He kept running.

"I don't like to see you kill yourself off, champ. And this is a high-class beach you're stinking up." As Biggo swung around to make the return trip, Hardesty caught his arm. "Slow down, Biggo." Biggo shook loose but Hardesty blocked his path.

"Get out of my way," Biggo said.

Hardesty's face was serious. "Look, Biggo," he said and then had to stop and scratch his scar and frown at the breakers to get his words in order. "What I want to say is that I don't give a special damn about you any more than you give a special damn about me. But we've known each other a long time, here and there, and there aren't a whole lot of us who've known each other a long time. See what I mean?"

Biggo said, "I'm busy."

"Well, in that tent this morning, I didn't like the look on your face. It made me think. I didn't know I was cutting that deep. I didn't know what was going on—or is going on—with you and that Ybarra girl. I still don't. It wasn't like that little scrap of ours yesterday, nothing like that—" Hardesty flushed and hunted more words. "Whatever happened this morning, I'm sorry."

Biggo squinted at him. "I guess you must be talking about Pabla."

"Yes. What I—"

Biggo shrugged, "Oh, to hell with her."

Hardesty laughed and pretended to wipe his brow. "Well, you could have fooled me. I thought this morning maybe you were going soft."

"Not me. Don't worry about me."

"Well, good. She's just another one of those that can't get enough. I paid her a call in her room the other night after the concert. I said to myself, Lew, old man, I bet that's too good to be true and furthermore I bet that hair is dyed. And, what do you know?"

"Oh, shut up," said Biggo, "I got more important things on my mind."

"Like what?" Hardesty asked quickly.

"Like getting sobered up. Out of my way."

"Like what?" Hardesty said again.

Biggo stared at him for a few minutes. He was drenched with sweat and his breath sawed in and out. But he was beginning to lose the numbness. He was beginning to have a few ideas.

He said, "You been wanting in, haven't you, Lew?"

Hardesty grinned. "Well, well, I knew you had something."

"You're going to have to do a little work for a cut."

"Anything beats China. I'd like to get in a position where I could bargain with that blinking Egyptian. And that takes more than my present stake."

Biggo thought a minute, scowling out at the yacht. "You're going to have to trust me for what it's worth. It'll be worth something. I got a matter to settle with some people. Maybe I can do it alone and maybe I can't. But it might happen easier if I had some help. You still interested?"

It sounded like money to Hardesty; he had that gleam in his eye. "Keep talking."

"One of us got killed last night, Lew. A fellow you didn't even know. An old fellow named Dan'l Toevs and he was a good friend of mine since—well, from way back. They shot him from behind and left him for the dogs to get." Biggo sucked in his breath. "It isn't right, Lew, not right at all. We're tough fellows, that's what we're paid for. But they haven't any right to shoot Dan'l in the back and leave him. Somebody's got to care."

Their eyes met. Hardesty said softly, "Yeah. You wonder about that once in a while."

"Something's going to be done this time."

"Who shot him, Biggo?"

"I don't know his name. The man who hired it done was named Magolnick but he isn't here. He's far away, like the Egyptian. But the people who worked it out and set it up are on that ship." Biggo drank in the sight of the yacht again. He was feeling better, more like it. "Those are the wallahs I want. And am going to get. How about it, Lew?"

"With you," said Hardesty as if accepting a drink. "I never passed up a fight yet."

"I'll handle the execution end. That's my matter. Toevs was my friend. I want you to back me up, that's all."

"What about a boat to get out there?"

"What about it?"

"Tonight?"

"After dark. Say, after eight. Along here somewhere."

Except for the handshake, that was all there was to it. They had worked together before. They parted and Biggo went into the hotel and had some black coffee in the bougainvillea patio.

When he felt the stuff coming out his ears he returned to the room.

He walked steadily now. He was tired but his mind and body belonged to him again.

Jinny was curled up on the bed, passed out. She hadn't changed into the prettier slip. Biggo pulled the coverlet over her and went into the bathroom and took a long shower, hot and cold alternately. He felt more ready by the moment—not feeling good but keyed up and purposeful.

"Tonight, Dan'l," he said. "Breach for breach."

Jinny was still asleep when he came out of the bathroom. He hunted out the Mauser automatic from under the bed and sat down by the window to clean it.

After a while, Jinny said drowsily, "What you doing, Biggo?"

He held up the gun to show her.

"I guess I dozed off," she said and smiled dreamily. Then she sat up quickly. "What are you doing with the gun, Biggo?"

"I found out who killed Dan'l and where they're holed up." He went on with his work.

It sank in. She said faintly, "You're going after them."

He nodded.

"When?" she whispered. He told her. "Biggo, I don't want you to go. You'll get hurt, I know you will, or something terrible—"

"One of those things, honey." Biggo made a helpless gesture, reaching for the right way to explain. "Dan'l was my kind. If I don't go—well, then nobody would ever go." He said, "Somebody's got to care."

She sank back and stared at the ceiling. Then she rolled her head to look at him and her eyes were scared and wet. "I guess you're right, Biggo. Somebody's got to care."

CHAPTER TWENTY-ONE

SUNDAY, SEPTEMBER 17, 8:00 P.M.

A little before eight, Biggo got ready for bed and had Jinny do the same. Then he called room service for a boy to bring up a nightcap for them. He made sure the boy got inside the room and saw they were about to retire. Which covered the trail as best he could.

After that Biggo put on his dark suit and a dark blue sport shirt. He slid the Mauser between his belt and the flat of his belly and told Jinny, "In a half hour, call the switchboard and tell them to wake us up at eight in the morning. Then wait a couple minutes longer and turn out the light. Leave it out. Get dressed now but put on your bathrobe if you have to answer the door." He tried to think out possibilities, squinting at the Bible in his hand. "Plan on anything happening."

Jinny was nervous. "I'll be praying every minute, Biggo."

"Good," He smiled tightly. "I never learned, myself." He tossed the Bible to her. "This might help you. It won't do me any good where I'm going."

She said, "Honey ..." as he started out. He paused, looking the question. "Nothing. Just take care of yourself."

He nodded and winked at her, though he didn't feel like it. He took his time getting out of the hotel, making sure no one saw him. The moon was thin again tonight and the night was dark on the beach. He didn't expect trouble yet but he unbuttoned his coat so the automatic was quick to either hand.

Lew Hardesty was waiting at the stone jetty. A rowboat wallowed beside him.

Biggo said, "Is that your best?"

"Didn't know you were expecting the *Queen Mary*. This'll be quiet." The stink of oil rose from the rags tied around the shafts of the oars. Hardesty hadn't changed clothes since the afternoon. He wore a tie as if he were going to a party.

"Let's go," said Biggo. He could just make out the pale shape of the yacht, about a half mile out. The waves on the bay weren't big enough to give them any trouble. Off to the north the lights of Ensenada twinkled merrily, a promise of life. In the rowboat there was only death.

They pulled straightaway, since no deception but silence could be used in approaching the ship over a naked waste of water. They had to depend on luck and dark not to be sighted. Biggo took the first spell at the oars, so he could rest before the actual boarding.

When they changed positions, halfway, Biggo sketched tactics. "The gangway, whatever they use, is on the other side of the ship. I'll board from this side. You hold against her and wait for me. I won't take long."

"What've you got, by way of arms?"

"Nice little Mauser. Yours."

Hardesty chuckled after a minute. "Well, I fell for that. Neat."

"I'll give it back to you. Afterwards."

"My pal," Hardesty said and chuckled again. "I wouldn't take it on a silver platter—after tonight. The police in this town may have heard of ballistics. Besides I got its mate." He sighed, "They were a pretty set. Hate to break them up after all of these years."

"Yeah, nice guns," Biggo said.

Then they shut up because they were pulling within earshot of the vessel. Carefully, Hardesty eased the rowboat alongside the hull of the yacht. She was a lovely craft, designed for long and comfortable hauls. The water was bright here from the reflection of her sloping sides. Racing lines, probably diesel power. The ports and windows of the superstructure were shrouded and no light escaped.

With their hands, they fended the rowboat from stern to bow of the yacht. All was shipshape; no ropes dangled and the deck edge was above leaping distance. Finally they slipped between the anchor chain and the hull.

Biggo held onto the chain. Hardesty steadied the boat and held up a clenched fist for luck. Biggo dragged himself up, hand over hand. It was a short climb and a moment later he was peering over the gunwales. The deck was deserted. He vaulted lightly over the rail and in the same motion snatched the Mauser free from his belt. There was no sound but his own labored breathing. He was tense with excitement. This was battle and the automatic was another part of his own right hand.

He prowled aft, reached the stern and crossed it. There he stopped. Here, on the starboard side, lounged a man-shadow. He was about where Biggo imagined the gangway was. He was smoking a cigarette. It gave off a rank smell and the glowing butt limned the merest indication of the man's profile. He had something slung over his shoulder. A rifle.

Biggo crept toward the unsuspecting sentry. He advanced like a stalking cat, bent almost to the deck, his head as low as his knees. The sentry continued to puff the cigarette and gaze out at the open sea. Biggo paused. The yacht had broken her silence. From somewhere in the superstructure came the trill of a piano as hands commenced playing. It served to cover any noise his shoes might make on the decking and he advanced faster.

He was ten yards away, five, three. The sentry dreamed his dreams. Biggo sprang, his arm lashing out with the barrel of the Mauser while his other arm was already catching the man's suddenly limp body.

"One down," Biggo breathed. There had been scarcely a sound for anyone to hear, only the clip of steel on bone. Biggo crouched over the sprawled sentry a second, getting an idea. He slipped the rifle from around the man's shoulder and stuffed the automatic back in his waistband. "Make Lew happier," he said. Then he went in search of the piano he could hear.

The rifle was a Garand. It felt even better than the pistol as he carried it ready at his hip. Its weight of power lifted him up like a drug; with a rifle he was master of any situation. He scorned caution now. He moved into the passageway and began trying the doors of the superstructure. The second door was the right one. It widened into a view of the yacht's salon, a luxurious low-ceilinged room, white and gold. And there were four people present.

Valentin sat idling the keys of the baby grand against the far wall. Nearby, Mamacita was crocheting close to her eyes. Red, a gauze taped behind his ear, was sunk in a low leather divan against the starboard wall. He was dealing out solitaire on a hassock in front of him. And Pabla sat at an ornate writing desk, reading a lavender-tinted letter. A small pile of mail lay before her. With her rimless glasses across her nose she looked more like a secretary than a queen.

It was Valentin who saw Biggo first and his hands dropped off the keyboard and he began trembling. Then the other three looked up and saw. They all stopped what they were doing, frozen. None of them could decide whether to stare at the rifle or the look on Biggo's face.

Biggo kicked the door shut behind him and leaned his back against it. He grinned like a skull and all their eyes got more frightened. The rifle swung lazily back and forth. "Finish reading, Pabla," he said finally. "That's your last love letter."

"Biggo," she choked. She eased around at the desk to face him and he let her. "Why are—what are you doing here?"

"Paying off a debt."

Red shifted slightly on the divan but his weight was trapped by its softness and the rifle snout suddenly stared in his direction, "Just sit still," Biggo said.

He looked his prizes over again, joy in him. Red was big but a slow thinker and he wore the sick face of a gunman caught unarmed. It was impossible to tell about Mamacita; her beady eyes didn't show anything and her crocheting didn't quiver in her hands. Valentin was about to dissolve into senselessness.

The white and gold room was taut with fear and Biggo relished it.

The next movement was the drifting of the lavender letter from Pabla's hand. She arched her back a little against the desk. The wall behind her was hung with a collection of fans, from one end to the other. She was a blue and gold figure against a background of delicate art and she seemed to coil a little within her bright blue dress. She crossed her legs silkily, without care.

"Biggo," she said, "I'm actually glad that you chose to come, even like this." A smile worked onto the pink mouth. "We have so much to be explained between us."

"Yes."

"I don't quite understand, Biggo." She wasn't fool enough to try to rise and get closer to him. She tried to put it across from the desk chair, with her silk knees and her dress cut low across her impudent breasts. "If it is because of our mishap this morning, you're being a little foolish and wild. Delightfully wild. But we can mend what was torn of ours. Lew means nothing to me, believe that, nothing."

"Who does?"

She kept at it, working with all of herself, an imperceptible squirming. "If you only would realize what it is to be bored and disappointed. I dreamed of—but you wouldn't pay any attention to me. I was weak with—" She stopped.

Biggo was staring straight through her glasses into her eyes. He licked his lip as if he'd just spit on her. He said, "Save your wind, Pabla. That was this morning, long ago. I'm here tonight for an accounting." Hungrily, the rifle kept track of them all. "It didn't touch me when Zurico was killed. It didn't touch me when I was being hunted, myself. But when a fumbling old man—when he got killed by a carrion dog that didn't have the guts to face him out at his own death—then's when I got it too. Got it deep. I'm here to settle, all you scum."

Pabla couldn't quite follow it but Red's slow brain began to catch up. He shoved out his hands in protest. He spoke for the first time that Biggo had heard and his voice was a blustering rasp despite his fear. "Hey, you're talking cockeyed, buddy—"

Biggo grunted and his finger sweated eagerly on the trigger. It was sheer pleasure, watching them break down.

Valentin's voice shrilled up, "*Ay de mi!* He is going to kill us! He is going to murder us all!" His eyes bulged after he had put it into words.

"Not murder," said Biggo softly, "Execute."

Mamacita racked out a gasp.

Biggo gazed implacably at the natty semi-conscious lump named Valentin, at the tears on his face. "I hate to spend a good man's bullet on you. You ought to be stepped on, you greasy pimp. You sent me down to walk in on this tramp during her romp this morning. You knew what she was doing. I guess she doesn't feed you enough leavings."

Pabla's face had gone chalk-white. Her hand crept up to her throat, almost strangling herself. Nervous habit—crisis nearing. The greatest crisis of all. The pink lips had dried up. "Biggo, Biggo, you've gone mad!

Why should you—you can't—you can't—"

She was the last to break and she broke harder than the rest. Her eyes rolled wildly around the room. They fastened on Red, begging him to do something. Red's heavy shoulders had sagged. His lips formed a word. "Magolnick."

Biggo smiled and readied the rifle. Red would be first. Biggo said to him, "Magolnick. It's an ugly word but it connects us all together, even the dead. I wish he could be here. Not that he could help you now though—"

"Biggo!" Pabla's eyes flared wide as if they had screamed at him. "In God's name, Biggo, please listen to me—"

The rifle swinging around hushed her. Biggo squinted, listening to the footsteps in the passageway outside. He sidled away from the door, clearing it, moving to where its opening would shield him. He watched the four people and the door.

The footsteps stopped outside. The handle turned, the door swung in, a man entered. He didn't see Biggo, pressed against the wall. He didn't notice the strained faces of the four. He closed the door and, in turning, found himself in the presence of Biggo Venn.

They just stood there silently, eyeing one another. The man had never seen Biggo before. He didn't recognize him. But Biggo recognized the newcomer in front of his rifle. He knew him from a picture torn out of a newspaper, a picture still folded in his wallet. The bald white-fringed head, the hook nose and red-veined face belonged to Tom Jaccalone.

CHAPTER TWENTY-TWO

SUNDAY, SEPTEMBER 17, 9:00 P.M.

There was a lot of talking to be done. They did it at gunpoint but the rifle was largely ignored, even by Mamacita and Valentin who wept softly with relief. Biggo kept the Garand ready because he still didn't like the group he faced. But there was no more question of shooting.

"I'm beginning to see how we got our wires crossed," Tom Jaccalone summed up a few minutes later. He was canted in an easy chair, one leg slung over its arm. "I was worried of something like this when that old fool insisted on all those funny arrangements."

"That old fool went and got himself killed trying to deliver you the Noon confession," Biggo snapped. "Let's not run down the dead."

Jaccalone's eyes glittered and the veins in his face darkened. He wasn't the kind to have a very good grip on his temper. But he shrugged. "It doesn't matter, anyway,"

"It does to me. I want the man who killed him."

Red—his name was Ussher and he was the yacht's first mate—said, "I am casing that phony address on Calle Estradura last night. I heard the shot, what there was to hear. But by the time I found the old man he was already dead and frisked. I didn't see anybody."

"You're lucky twice. I came back looking for you."

Red flexed his fingers. "You're a strong man with that rifle."

"Or without it," said Biggo.

Jaccalone waved his hands impatiently. "This is no time for fooling around. Venn, I want that paper. I've been waiting out here long enough. I want to get this tub back to Pabla's papa and get back to business up north. Where's the paper?"

"Not with me. I can get it."

"How soon? Tonight?"

"Soon enough."

"Damn it, when?"

"When you help me locate the Magolnick people. When I've settled with them."

Pabla said slowly, "You can't keep it for yourself, Tom. You'll have to tell him."

"Tell me what?" Biggo asked.

Jaccalone shrugged again. It was his reaction to anything meaningful. "We've got a Magolnick man. We've got the fingerman. Red picked him up this morning. He's below in the kitchen—the galley, I guess it's called."

Biggo began to smile, even at Pabla. "Well, thanks, honey, and I mean it. You just did something for me."

She perked up. She pointed behind her, at the wall of fans. There was the white satin-bow fan from the fiesta. "That is the one you may remember from the parade. This other is the fan I was supposed to carry." The other was a dozen feather eyes, shading from blue through green to bronze—peacock feathers, a widespread wedge of them. "It was supposed that I could display it all through town during the parade. But the Magolnick agent, by means of Zurico, let us know we had better not. Strange, Biggo, that you should have been so close to me the whole crucial time." And Pabla stretched lazily for his benefit.

In return, Biggo grunted. "I want the fellow who killed Toevs."

"Oh, you can have him," Jaccalone said negligently. "You won't find out much. We haven't."

"We'll see."

"But he's the man. He put the Pavón ad in yesterday night's paper. You can have him," Jaccalone promised again. "One of Silver's boys more or less isn't anything to me. He's only a beginning, what's going to happen to Silver and his boys."

He got out of his chair. He was pudgy with easy living, not healthy. His breath came short but Biggo knew it wasn't because he was scared. He said about the rifle, "Point that thing down. You're frightening me." To the others he said, "You stay here."

Pabla began, "Why can't I—" and Jaccalone only glanced at her and she said, "All right, Tom." Biggo left the rifle leaning against the wall. He still had Hardesty's automatic behind his belt and he knew Jaccalone wouldn't try anything as long as the Noon confession was hidden.

Jaccalone led the way down. He didn't say anything and he didn't look around to see if Biggo was following. He was used to leading and big men with guns were nothing new at his heels. His whole attitude was one of faint contempt. Biggo had something he wanted; money would buy it; that was all there was to it.

They went down steps into the interior of the vessel, opened doors, passed along companionways, reached the galley.

Jaccalone said then, "Red worked on him a trifle, just out of curiosity, but he's a stubborn boy. It didn't matter much to us." He threw open the door to the galley which was already lighted and gleaming. Biggo stepped over the threshold, hands clenched in anticipation.

The man was strapped over a meat block, spread-eagled under the light like a patient in an operating theater. He was wearing faded overalls and no shoes. He rolled his head to sneer as the two men came in. He and Biggo stared at each other for a long moment.

Biggo swore in Spanish. "In the name of a thousand saints, how did you get out here?"

Adolfo parted his swollen lips in a grin. His tongue was big with thirst. "A misunderstanding, Don Biggo. Please explain to these hounds that it is a misunderstanding." There were cigarette burns on his face and body and occasional small open cuts.

"You know him?" Jaccalone asked Biggo.

"Sure I do. Let him up. He doesn't belong to Magolnick."

"He put the ad in the paper."

"Is this the truth, Adolfo?"

Adolfo bumped his head against the meat block in agreement. "It is the truth, as he says. But why has this followed? Abducted virtually from the arms of my Rosita and given my taste of hell." He thrust hopelessly against his ropes. "I was better off in the *calabozo.*"

Biggo knelt and began to free the Mexican from his improvised rack. Jaccalone didn't protest. Adolfo sat up, swayed and rubbed his limbs painfully. Biggo brought him a short drink of water. "Not too much— take it easy, amigo," Then he perched on one edge of the meat block and suggested to Adolfo, "Tell me about this business, this Pavón ad."

Jaccalone murmured, "He won't talk about is."

Adolfo raked him with a scornful look. "This foreigner—" he didn't include Biggo in the deprecation "—will never understand. I am a man, a Mexican of honor. I cannot be bullied, Don Biggo. I have loyalty. I have faithfulness to my hire."

"Certainly, amigo. But I beg that your pride end for my sake. A lifelong friend of mine has been murdered. I want to do justice."

Adolfo gazed at him and nodded quickly. "But you are my friend— there's the difference. You ask and I tell. I was hired to carry the announcement to the newspaper office. I didn't understand, I still don't. But, in its way, it was a matter of self-preservation."

"I don't understand."

"Do you remember what I did for you in the parking lot behind the hotel? The scarred man I bumped into by accident, according to your instructions? To my sorrow, that American came across me in town shortly afterwards and accused me of stealing a pistol of his. I told him I had already sold it. Rather than return to the *calabozo* I did this other simple job for him. I placed the advertisement with the newspaper, pretending that I was Señor Pavón."

A pounding in Biggo's ears and a searing fire in his chest as he sprang off the meat block. He shook his heavy head, feeling the import of Adolfo's statement sink in. The word, "Hardesty!" hissed between his teeth. Then he roared it like a battle-yell. "Hardesty!" The pans shook along the racks in the galley. Both the other men gaped at his frenzy.

But he didn't explain; it wasn't for them. It was for him, Biggo Venn, the picture that was suddenly clear before his eyes, the wrath of excitement. Lew Hardesty was in Ensenada because he was the Magolnick agent, a job between jobs. Hardesty had killed Toevs, and before that Zurico. It had been a game of who-makes-the-first-slip— and Biggo had made it that afternoon. Since Hardesty knew his own identity, it had been easy for him to see that Biggo's enemies aboard the yacht must be the Jaccalone faction. So he had gladly brought

Biggo out here to wreak a wrong vengeance.

"He's gone now," Biggo whispered. "He's gone back." There would be no rowboat waiting beneath the anchor chain. Hardesty would have started back to the hotel to find the Noon confession and destroy it. Biggo dead aboard the yacht or Biggo a murderer aboard the yacht; it didn't matter to Hardesty. Either way, the yacht was supposed to be a trap to hold Biggo.

He clamped his fists against his head and made himself come to the present, where sanity was. It was still to be settled. "For Dan'l," he growled. "For me." This transcended twenty Arabs in a long-ago desert. This was himself to be settled. By blood; only blood could cool this passion.

He held tight to the sanity of the pistol butt at his waist and swung toward Jaccalone. "Get me back to shore. Otherwise you can kiss your paper goodbye."

Jaccalone caught some of the passion. "I'll get you there if I got to fire you out of a gun." He stormed out of the galley.

The three of them went up and the people in the salon sprang to their feet as Jaccalone plunged into the room. Then he was gasping so hard for breath that he couldn't get his commands out. Biggo did it for him. "Red—you're going to take me to shore in the putt-putt."

Red looked at Jaccalone for confirmation, got it and rushed out of the salon. Biggo told Jaccalone, "He'll put me and Adolfo ashore on the jetty. I'll settle my business, get your paper and meet anyone you want to send back there in a half hour. Send the money with them—cash."

Jaccalone said, "You know, I'm not a guy who likes to be disappointed—"

"Me neither," said Biggo and went out on deck. The sentry was still an unconscious heap by the gangway. Adolfo was going through the man's pockets.

"I'm owed something for my troubles," he told Biggo apologetically. "Isn't that true?"

"I'm going to need you for a job when we reach the hotel, amigo. But not unless you feel strong enough for it." Adolfo's swollen smile made him stop. "All right, that's fine,"

Behind him, Pabla said softly, "Biggo."

This time he turned. In the gloom of the superstructure her blonde hair glowed of its own. In the water below them, Red was fighting to make the boat engine come to life. Biggo said, "If you're still hunting beauty you won't find it on me. I've had a bloody bad day and the night doesn't look any better."

The lens of her glasses glimmered as she shook her head gently. "You are still very angry with me, aren't you? I'm sorry, truly I'm sorry, Biggo. I was so drawn to you—and you to me—that morning in the *calabozo*. You were the—" she made a little hunching movement with her shoulders "—the ideal of virility and strength. My breath went out of my body, I was that impressed." She chuckled. "The jefe was quite disturbed by my choice."

Adolfo had drifted away discreetly. Biggo said, "What matters about it?"

"When I saw how it was with you—that great innocent love of yours—it tormented me, Biggo." She put her hand on her hip and stroked up across her dress until her hand lay beneath her breasts, lifting them slightly. "You are such a rare combination of strength and innocence."

"You bet I'm rare. Rare as hell. I'm out of my time. You don't find them like me anymore."

"No. That is true." She brought her fragrance nearer. "You're going tonight. Will you miss me? Tomorrow, when you've completed your mission for Tom, when there'll be no excitement to anticipate—will you miss me?"

"Not at all."

"I think you must be lying. And there's no need." A step closer and her breasts rested against his chest as they had once before; her thighs brushed expertly against his legs. "You could come with me. When you've finished with tonight. A ship like this needs men, strong men, and you are the strongest. Oh, I know how strong you must be!"

He was looking down at the flower of her upturned face, he was breathing her and he was feeling her delicate movements against him. But he was thinking of the girl back in his room at the Riviera Pacífico. Jinny, who had gotten nothing but a kicking around from life and from Biggo Venn and who was still waiting back there, standing guard over the Bible like a good soldier. Loyalty, and she had even said she'd pray for him. He ached with impotence when he thought what might happen to her because of loyalty like that.

Pabla had her eyes lidded. She slid up a hand to adjust her glasses, whispering, "Can't you imagine it? We could cruise for weeks, perhaps months. Days to stretch in the sun. Nights like this, but with moonlight. We could follow the full moon ..."

Below them, the motorboat kicked over, spluttered, set up a roar. Biggo's whole body answered to it. He put his two fingers against the lens of her glasses and his thumb against her soft mouth and straight-armed. Pabla flew backwards and lit in a sprawl. The glasses broke in fragments on the deck beside her. She was suddenly a shocked awkward sight of exposed flesh and ungraceful limbs.

Biggo scarcely glanced at the sight he had created. He yelled at Adolfo, "Let's go get 'em, amigo," and went down the gangway to the waiting boat.

CHAPTER TWENTY-THREE

SUNDAY, SEPTEMBER 17, 9:30 P.M.

Hardesty's Chevy coupé still sat in the parking lot behind the hotel. Biggo stationed Adolfo among the skinny pine trees nearby and made him repeat his instructions.

Adolfo said, "A cockcrow. If that doesn't stop him, any kind of noise my frightened throat can make."

"Make it loud. Can't let him reach the car. I got nothing to follow in." Biggo left him, strode north a few paces to where he could see the windows of his room on the second floor. They were lighted. He expected that. One was raised partway, along with the venetian blind. By Jinny, probably, for night air. No figures passed before the half-open window or threw shadows on the blinded one.

Biggo went into the hotel. As usual the lobby was deserted. He closed himself in the phone booth. He could see the switchboard girl, a few yards away behind the registration desk, answer his dialing. He asked for his room number. He waited while the phone rang and rang. He sweated and ground his teeth.

At last Jinny answered. Her voice was cautious and shaky.

Biggo said, "You all right, honey?"

"I'm just fine," she got out.

"Don't say much. I know Hardesty's up there. I'm coming after him so be ready to duck fast. Understand?"

Jinny said, "Yes ..."

"Try to make him think this is anyone but me. Say good night."

Her breath fluttered. "Good night," The connection clicked off.

The honeymoon couple came through the lobby, heading for their room. They didn't see Biggo. He watched them pass and when they had gone, he slipped out of the phone booth and took the stairs two at a time. He didn't make any noise and he held the Mauser by his hip, his coat masking his hand.

He reached the corridor. Then he stopped.

The door to his room was wide open. Light from inside spilled out on the carpet with Jinny's awkward shadow. She stood in the doorway, her body sideways but her face twisted in his direction. Her bathrobe was draped over her green suit and Biggo could see finger marks on her throat.

Then Lew Hardesty said, "Come on, Biggo, take it slow." He was out of sight, behind her somewhere. Biggo couldn't locate the gun muzzle he knew was pointed at him.

Jinny whimpered, "He was listening. He made me answer." Her head jerked back as she winced with pain. Hardesty was holding her by an arm doubled against her spine.

Biggo uncovered his Mauser. A chill shook him. He flattened against the wall so Hardesty couldn't lean around the girl and find him. He called, "Lew, you're boxed. You better step out and get it over with."

Hardesty laughed.

"Come out and face me. Or I'm coming in to get you."

"I doubt it," said Hardesty. His voice was tense but not really worried. "Not you. Not with people in the line of fire. They might not be ready to duck fast enough. Understand?" He was mimicking Biggo's words on the telephone. Jinny whimpered and winced again, face bloodless.

"I didn't tell him, Biggo!" she moaned, "I didn't!"

Biggo couldn't meet her eyes, her eyes that begged to be taken out of this somehow. She was caught between them and she had reached the final point of fear. She was ready to die if only that meant escape.

Hardesty said, "She means she wouldn't tell me where to find the Noon confession. If I had a little longer, she would. Shall I close the door and have her tell me or do you want to tell me?"

Jinny sobbed as Hardesty worked on her arm.

Biggo sucked in his breath with hers. The length of the corridor lay between them, but they breathed together again. His right hand hung straight down, tired with the weight of the automatic. All the bones in his big frame seemed to sag with weariness. Nothing seemed important enough to have Jinny's eyes beg him like that.

He said, "Let her go, Lew. Don't hurt her anymore."

"But I haven't all the time in the world, you know." Hardesty's voice sounded as if he was enjoying himself; Biggo knew his vicious streak. "She'll tell me in a minute or so."

"She doesn't have to, I'll tell you. Let her go."

"You quitting?"

"I'm quitting. You win."

"Let's hear it,"

"Let her go. I want her out of this. Let her go first."

Silence except for a choked cry from Jinny that sounded like, "No, no!" but Biggo couldn't be sure. Then Hardesty said, "If you mean that, kick your gun down the hall where I can see it. But be careful, Biggo."

Biggo put the Mauser on safety. He skidded it along the carpeting so that it stopped near Jinny's feet. She was shoved out into the corridor and Hardesty's hand pounced on the gun. Then he stood in the doorway, his white teeth gleaming, a pearl-handled weapon in each fist. "Come in, Biggo," he said.

Jinny was as far away from Hardesty as she could get, crammed against the opposite doorway. Biggo trudged past her. He pulled out his wallet and shoved its money into the pocket of her bathrobe. Hardesty watched the transaction like a cat, making certain nothing else passed between them.

Biggo told her, "You tell them all hello back in Scribner."

"Biggo ..."

"Get away from here, kid. Get away fast. I'm a jinx. I never did a thing for you."

"Biggo ..."

He cursed at her softly, "Get out of here, I tell you."

Jinny whimpered and shifted dazedly against the doorframe. She turned away, her hand trailing along the wall.

Hardesty said, "That's the smart little lady. Do what he says." He followed Biggo into the room. Drawers had been dumped out and the beds were torn up. Hardesty closed the door, dropped the left-hand pistol in his coat pocket and reached behind him to twist the lock.

"Okay, Biggo. Show me."

Biggo crossed to the dressing table. The raped room—his and Jinny's—hurt his eyes. "It's in the Bible," he said dully.

"Show me."

He picked up the Bible from the dressing table and thumb-nailed open a corner of the binding so that Hardesty could see an edge of the hidden paper.

Hardesty grinned harder, excited. "Aren't you the fancy one, though? I was beginning to think you had it on you. But I couldn't believe you'd carry it out to the yacht."

Biggo grunted.

"Toss it over."

Biggo tossed it and Hardesty plucked it off the bed and slipped it in his other coat pocket. Biggo grimaced. "Why?" he asked. "Even remembering that Arab business, I never thought this was your style."

But he should have known. It was written in black letters across Hardesty's career that this was his style; he didn't know right from wrong.

"Well, hell," said Hardesty. "I didn't expect you'd be the one dealing with that gangster Jaccalone, either. You know, when you're on the beach a lot of things look good that you wouldn't touch other times. You know how it is. I had an old friend close to Magolnick and Magolnick knew that one of his regular boys could be spotted mile off ..."

Biggo was shaking his head, "No, I don't know how that is. Dan'l Toevs wouldn't have touched the job you took, not even broke and rummed up he wouldn't have touched it. Neither would I. I guess only you would touch it."

Hardesty flushed darkly, not ashamed but knowing he was supposed to be ashamed. "Pay is pay," he said and his mouth bleakened. He raised the Mauser. "I guess you'd never let me get a night's sleep, would you?"

"No."

"What I thought. I'm not worried about police but I know you. Police don't cross the water much but you—I don't want to be looking for you to turn up in every town in the world, every night."

"That's right. I'd follow you. You'd never sleep. I could follow anywhere."

Hardesty said, "Well?"

"You want me to turn my back, Lew, so it'll feel natural to you?"

It was ready to end. Biggo was ready to have it end. Hardesty's mouth was open to say the last thing but he didn't. Jinny's voice knifed through the locked door. "Biggo, say something. Are you all right?"

Both men jumped. They were keyed high. Hardesty swiveled so he could watch Biggo across the room and the door behind him too. He said harshly, "Get away from here!"

"I won't!" Jinny quavered. "I want to know if Biggo's all right."

Biggo said, "I'm all right, honey. You do as I told you. Get out of here before you're hurt some more."

"I won't!" she cried. "I'm not going till you come with me. He's got the paper, hasn't he? What more does he want?"

Biggo smiled stiffly. It got no answering smile from Hardesty. The younger man's nerves were coiling tight; they showed in his suddenly taut mouth. He didn't like having Biggo on one side and the invisible girl raising a fuss on the other. "Look, Jinny!" he snapped. "Get away from that door. Get going!"

"Not till Biggo comes with me. Why are you keeping him in there?"

"Get away!" Hardesty said.

"You don't tell me what to do!" The door bumped as she kicked it. "You want me to count to ten? Till you let Biggo come out there I'm going to scream and yell and you'll see what—"

Hardesty swore edgily. Her voice began to rise and he snapped his gun over and fired through the door. There was a black hole in the panel and a silence. The gun was on Biggo again.

Then Jinny laughed. It was a peculiar easy laugh as if she had been engrossed with fear and now it was put aside.

She said, "That's twice as good as a scream, Lew—"

Hardesty snapped around and laid three more holes across the door. And Biggo spun and dove headlong for the partly-open window. His shoulders tore off the lower edge of the sash and he took the screen down with him. Hardesty's fire ripped over his head, inches late. He hit on his left shoulder in the flower beds below, somersaulted like a paratrooper in the springy earth and rolled into darkness.

He got up and ran. At first he ran blind, just getting out of range of the window. Hardesty would have to follow through the window rather than chance getting stopped in the hotel. Biggo hoped that Jinny had sense enough to stay with the crowd the shots would bring, not wander out alone where she might block Hardesty's path again.

Then, with the thought of the danger she had taunted, his mind began to cool into solid formed purpose. "Got to get a gun," he muttered. But that was impossible.

A weapon, then.

He dodged into a doorway, heard the voices coming past him, footsteps hurrying. When they had gone by, he ran down the hallway, up some steps toward the north end of the hotel. He had remembered the peacock.

He found the draperies that covered the iron gate to the empty gambling casino. He burst into the gloom of the bar.

The peacock tapestry with its threads of gold still hung from the wrought-iron spear. He grabbed it with both hands and jerked it down. He caught the spear and tilted it so that the iron rings sewn to the tapestry clanked off on the floor. The spear was heavy and nearly as tall as he was. The ornamental spear head rattled loosely on the square rod. There was a bolt that he tightened with his fingers so that the spear head was secure. Then it was a weapon.

He trotted to the rear of the bar and kicked a window open into the night. And from the parking lot sounded a high shivering cockcrow.

CHAPTER TWENTY-FOUR

SUNDAY, SEPTEMBER 17, 10:00 P.M.

After the cockcrow rose an eerie scream. Spanish words Biggo couldn't quite make out but it held the thrill of some old bandit yell. "Good boy, Adolfo," growled Biggo and leaped into the bushes under the window.

A shot racketed, also from the direction of the parking lot. Biggo charged along the back of the hotel at a dead run, the spear in lance position helping feel his way. No more shots. He crossed the edge of the parking lot toward the pine grove. "Don Biggo!" Adolfo called weakly. "Don Biggo!"

He was staring, his face a muddy color, at the slim bole of a pine where a bullet had cut whiteness through the bark.

"Where is he?" Biggo panted.

The Mexican was vibrating with fright. But he had done his job. Hardesty's car still sat in its place, empty. Adolfo pointed south, "There! Around the hotel—toward the water!"

"Stay with it," Biggo said and slapped Adolfo's shoulder and ran again. Biggo laughed aloud. He had the trail. Hardesty was badly rattled. He had let a scared yell keep him away from the car, the one escape; the bullet mark on the tree was too high for good shooting. "Afraid of me," Biggo chortled as he rounded the south bulge of the hotel. "He's afraid of me!" And there was a fleeting violent satisfaction that the younger man's inexperience had betrayed him.

His feet slapped onto the concrete promenade along the ocean front. At the far end he saw the figure of darkness, limbs spread in running. Hardesty—trying to make Ensenada. Biggo raced after him. The figure turned and there was a wink of light and then the sound of the shot. "Keep at it," Biggo muttered. "Come on." He hadn't even felt the wind of the bullet. The range was too great for Hardesty's weapon and Hardesty was on the run.

It was a hunt, a pursuit, a charge. Biggo's left shoulder ached from his dive through the window despite his professional landing. The night air burnt like acid deep in his lungs and he had to claw down after every breath to feed his ravening body. But he had inevitable purpose to goad him and Dan'l thought he had guts and Jinny didn't think he was getting old. "Dan'l," he said, "Jinny." They put animal strength in him and the distance between him and the quarry began to close. Because Hardesty was carrying a load of fear.

Hardesty sprang over the wall into the dunes, stopped to fire again. "Use 'em up," Biggo grunted. He had a vague notion of making Hardesty waste all his ammunition. He didn't think Hardesty had enough rounds to stop him, the pace he was going. But he had no idea of how many shots had been fired. He shouted and Hardesty obligingly wasted still another bullet.

They were both in the dunes now. At first there was only the sound of their feet on the soft sand, punctuated by the pistol fire. Then Biggo heard something else, the liquid chug-chug of an engine. His face split in a hideous grin. Red and possibly others were returning from the Ybarra yacht. They were behind Hardesty. Hardesty would either run into a pocket or he would have to stand and fight it out. Biggo thanked Red's timing; the spear was getting heavy.

Hardesty saw his position. He stopped at the top of the next gray dune and spun about. Biggo slowed down. He faced Hardesty from one crest to another, across the gentle chasm between the two sand mounds. They looked at each other silently. They had returned to the desert.

Finally Biggo said, "Got you, Lew."

"The hell you have." Hardesty had to suck for breath. "Come and get me. If you're man enough. I'll finish what I started in the casino." He tossed the automatic away. It was empty.

"I'm coming," Biggo said. He started. He still lugged the drapery spear. But when he shifted it to advance he saw that the point had fallen off somewhere during the chase. All he held was a long iron rod, blunt-ended, not a spear at all.

But it was part of his right arm now so he kept hold of it as he slid down the side of the dune. Hardesty waited for him on the crest of the next ridge, feet braced apart, in the position of advantage against the sky. He waited for Biggo to come within reach.

Biggo struggled upwards in the slipping sand. He watched Hardesty's feet for the kick that would launch the hand-to-hand struggle. He was nearly up to him. Hardesty's feet moved—but not to kick. Biggo's eyes jerked up and he saw too late what he should never have forgotten; the second Mauser. Hardesty had tricked him.

The younger man had tempted his blood-lust and had lured him into point-blank range.

Even in the gloom he glimpsed the flash of Hardesty's grin. His hand came from inside his coat with the automatic. The hand shook slightly but Hardesty raised his other arm to level the barrel over it and he had all the target in the world.

Timelessness at the point of death. Biggo didn't know that he moved or thought. He did something he had never done before. He prayed. Not to the twentieth century God of the churches and Sunday schools. He prayed to the war god of the Old Testament, to Yahweh, the storm god of Sinai. And he prayed as Moses and Joshua and Gideon prayed. Not for mercy and forgiveness but for strength to invoke the ancient law against the evildoer. Eye for eye, tooth for tooth, breach for breach.

The words thundered in his ears or it might have been the blood pounding. But he heard them plain and strong:

... wherefore Abner with the hinder end of the spear smote him in the body, so that the spear came out behind ...

All was a part of the same instant, the aiming pistol, the cruel white grin of Hardesty and Biggo Venn lunging. He lunged uphill with a blunt useless rod on uncertain footing—and he struck with all his strength and more. He struck Hardesty as Saul's aging captain had once struck Asahel, his tormentor, in the long-ago mists of history.

And that was all. Lew Hardesty was no longer a dangerous man in the prime of his manhood. He was only a writhing shape on the gray sand. The sand slowly darkened, blotting up the blood as it crept past the iron rod which had skewered him.

Biggo knelt by him and raised Hardesty's head. All his hatred had passed into the spear thrust and now it was gone forever. He would not have changed the outcome if he could but the act was done and over. Hardesty, beaten, was another reflection of Biggo. Once they had fought together.

He said softly, "Sorry, Lew."

Hardesty's eyes, glazed with dying, cleared for a moment. He didn't know right from wrong but he understood this. His grin was still contorted on his face and his lips formed words. Biggo bent closer although he knew what they would be. *"Ezzy yellallah,"* said Hardesty. He said no more.

He put Hardesty's car keys in his pocket and he took the Bible from Hardesty's coat. He picked up the pearl-handled Mauser from where it had fallen. Out by the jetty Biggo could see the motorboat rocking there gently. He got to his feet and crunched down the dunes to it.

Pabla and Red were the only ones in the boat, watching him as he approached. It came to Biggo that they had watched through the whole fight without interfering. It hadn't mattered to them who won. They were waiting to deal, one way or another, with the victor.

Biggo growled to Red, "You're a big strong man. Go up there and get him. He's the Magolnick agent—outsider, not what you were looking for. Let your boss figure out how to get rid of him without trouble to any of us."

Red looked at Pabla. She nodded. He climbed out of the boat and went to get Hardesty's body.

She said, "Do you have the paper, Tom's paper?"

"Yeah." He showed her the Mauser. "Also this. Let's see the money."

"Biggo, I feel how harshly you are thinking of me. Perhaps you are justified in a way. But on the yacht when you struck me—struck me through love, not hate—I understood. I could feel your—"

"The money," he said. "Give me Dan'l's money."

"Dan'l's money?" She was puzzled.

"Oh, forget it," he said wearily. He split the Bible's binding open the rest of the way and pulled the deathbed confession of George G. Noon from its hiding place. He flipped it at her, not much caring whether it fell in the water or not.

She caught it. She pressed on a flashlight to inspect it. The beam played over her legs. Her skirt was hoisted above her knees. Her legs still looked good but Biggo wondered why he had ever expected them—or her—to be anything special.

Red came back, carrying Hardesty's body. It was a difficult task because Lew had been a big man and then there was the iron rod like a spit. But he got the dead man into the boat. Pabla barely gave him a glance. Biggo made sure that Red saw he was armed.

She passed him up a long full envelope. Biggo opened it and riffled through the hundred-dollar bills. It looked like enough to be twenty thousand dollars but he didn't bother to count it. He just wanted to get away from all of them and what they reminded him of.

Pabla said softly, so Red couldn't hear, "Now you have the money you earned, Biggo."

"That's right, isn't it? Paid in full."

"Perhaps, in money. I must sail south with Tom, of course. After that, when Tom leaves ... You'll be traveling with your money, seeking beauty. But it is nothing alone."

"No," said Biggo. "It's nothing alone." He wasn't thinking of Pabla but she didn't know that and would never be made to believe it. She was so certain.

She whispered, "I'll wait to hear from you." Then Red had started the motorboat and she was gone into the dark, blonde hair blowing but with her regal assurance whole and perfect. Biggo stood and stared at where she had disappeared. Nothing he said could ever crack that barrier of vanity. Only time could do that, when she finally realized that he wanted no part of her.

He laughed. He stuffed the Bible in one coat pocket, the Mauser in the other. He put the envelope of money in the pocket inside his coat. He began to run again, tired as he was. Jinny would be waiting to hear, worried about him, praying.

As he entered the lobby of the hotel, he almost collided with the desk clerk. The Mexican pounced on him. "Señor Biggo, *por Díos*, you've returned! A moment more and it might well have been too late—"

Biggo grabbed his coat. "What do you mean? What're you talking about?"

"The tragedy. A prowler in your room during your absence. Your wife has been shot—"

Biggo cast him aside and sprinted across the lobby, up the stairs. A knot of guests and employees crowded around the open door of their room. He shoved through them. Jinny was lying on her bed, lips pale and suffering.

"Jinny!" he cried and thrust aside the maid who hovered over her. He crouched beside her, groping for her wrist, "Jinny, honey ..." But the pulse beat was strong and regular. She opened her eyes slightly and then winked so that the others couldn't see. Biggo said, "What—" and she frowned. She whispered and he put his head close to hers.

She said, "Play up till the doctor comes. This is my big scene. I always thought I had talent. I thought if I keep them busy here while you— but what'll we say when the cops arrive?"

A grin spread over his face. He touched her cheek with his. "Good girl." He was on top of the world again. Then he saw the right side of her dress, wet and stained. Blood, her blood, against the green wool. He said, "You're not acting, honey. How bad is it?"

"Not so bad. I just got one of your kind of souvenirs, Biggo. That's all."

He shook his head at her, wonderingly. Scared to death, she had still refused to leave him alone with Hardesty. She'd wanted Biggo safe. She'd taunted Hardesty into firing and then, wounded, had laughed and pretended he had missed. She had maddened Hardesty. Just to give Biggo his chance.

To cover his emotions, he swung around and roared at the staring faces. "Well, where the hell's that doctor? My wife is hurt."

There was confusion.

Biggo's eyes gleamed at the crowded doorway. "My wife can't wait all night. These injuries might be serious." Trying to be gentle, he lifted Jinny up off the bed.

"Biggo," she hissed, "it's only a scratch on my arm No need to—"

"Shut up," he muttered. She did. The crowd let him through. He strode down the corridor with her across his arms.

She cuddled. "This is a hell of a way to duck a hotel bill. What about our clothes? Every other stitch I own is—"

He said, "Shut up or you'll really need a doctor." He glared back at the people trailing and they stopped at the back entrance of the Riviera Pacífico, not following into the parking lot. He put Jinny in Hardesty's car.

Adolfo appeared out of the darkness. "Is it done?"

Biggo shook his hand gravely. "It's done, amigo. It could not have been done without a friend of your courage."

"You're leaving Ensenada, Don Biggo?" Adolfo sounded sad about it.

Biggo glanced at the people watching, out of earshot, "Leaving quickly," he said. "My best to the fortunate Rosita. And this." He fingered some bills out of the envelope inside his coat and slipped them into Adolfo's hand. "There are also certain belongings in my room which might be sold to your profit."

Formally, Adolfo bowed. "The departure of Don Biggo empties this heart. But I'll see that the police are misled. *Vaya con Díos!*"

Biggo got in beside Jinny and fitted the key in the ignition. The last thing he saw as they quitted the Riviera Pacífico was Adolfo's face, mournful but grinning too.

CHAPTER TWENTY-FIVE

SUNDAY, SEPTEMBER 17, 12:00 MIDNIGHT

They reached Tijuana by midnight, a midnight there that glared with neon and the headlights of cars packed bumper to bumper, oozing through the border gates into the United States. They joined a line and then just sat, grinding ahead a little at a time while the immigration men asked cursory questions of cars ahead.

They hadn't said much, speeding up from Ensenada. Biggo had told Jinny the barest details of the finish and the rest had been the darkness roaring against the windshield as they raced along the desolate highway. They didn't even sit close together because of Jinny's arm. All Biggo could think was that the job was done, another week ended during which men had died, and this was aftermath, hangover.

So they sat in Tijuana, waiting to be passed through out of Mexico.

Jinny said suddenly, "I guess you don't need to have any more worries."

"I don't get you."

"I mean about getting old and losing your grip. Not after today. Not after tonight."

He grunted. "I guess. Still plenty of fight left."

"I imagine you'll be going to China now—really, not just talking. With that much money, you can pick your side. Be a general, even."

Biggo rested his head against the back of the seat. "Easy. I can even pick my war." He couldn't get worked up about it. After a while, as they crawled forward a few more feet, he said, "Uh, you going back to Scribner now?"

"I don't think so. Oh, I know I won't. It's too far past. I'll do something."

He said, "You know this money is part yours."

"Oh, don't be silly!" she snapped at him. Then they argued, stubbornly and pointlessly, about whether Jinny would or wouldn't share the money. The car behind them honked and the line had moved ahead without Biggo noticing. He closed the gap. An open convertible pulled alongside of them in the other line, the couple occupying less than half of its front seat. The radio was playing Mexican music, too loud for Biggo and Jinny to argue without shouting.

The music stopped just when Biggo was ready to tell the fellow to turn it down. A Mexican announcer spoke. "X-E-R-B in the Rosarito Beach Hotel, Baja California. We bring to you a late news flash. Ensenada ..."

Jinny had something more to say but Biggo gripped her arm.

"... death was reported tonight of the well-known American gambler, Thomas Jaccalone. Mr. Jaccalone, lately a resident of Mexico City, succumbed to a heart-attack aboard a friend's pleasure yacht in Todos Santos Bay ..."

The convertible moved on. Biggo looked at Jinny. Then he laughed, "By God! The excitement was too much for him. He got what he'd been wanting and it was too much for him." He laughed again.

She asked, "What strikes you so funny about it?"

He chuckled harshly. "The way it is funny, that's all. The war's over and it might as well never been fought." He wrenched his head away from her gaze and stared out through the windshield of Hardesty's car, not seeing anything ahead. "It's never been different, wherever I went, that's the joke." Toevs, Zurico, even Hardesty—all wasted for nothing. He began to laugh again.

Jinny got scared. She grabbed his shoulder, trying to pull his head around. "Don't laugh like that, please, Biggo. Don't!" Then she was saying, "Don't go to China, Biggo. Please don't go to China or anywhere. Not after this afternoon. Can't you go somewhere where we can get drunk once in a while, where I can hold you? I like holding you and you like being held, tell me you do. Oh, honey, you don't want to go to China, do you?"

He looked at her close pleading face. He said the words before he really knew he meant them. "No, I don't want to go to China."

"You've done so much fighting, honey. You've got a right to stop. Don't go away and get hurt again."

"No, I don't want to," he said and this time he knew what he was saying. "I've done enough. My time's past. There's not much use for animals like me anymore. Where'll we go? Scribner?"

"No, no," she said and patted his leg excitedly, "Some place that's new to both of us. Say, a farm somewhere. Apple farm. I love apples."

"Oregon," said Biggo. They were both a little lightheaded, both wanting to laugh now, at themselves and for themselves. A horn blared behind them uselessly. "We can pick up a pretty little farm up there—hear it's wonderful country. We got a good beginning, twenty thousand dollars and a family Bible and us ..."

He hugged her and she kissed back hard but she was wincing when they came out of it. She said happily, "You big ox, we've got a long time to do that in. How about getting me and my souvenir to the doctor?"

The gate was clear ahead. Behind them the honking started again and Biggo leaned out and yelled back, "Keep your bloody shirt on, you son of a dog!" He drove into the customs gate and they answered the questions about where they were born and said they hadn't bought anything in Mexico. Then they were passed through.

THE END

SINNER TAKE ALL
······················
WADE MILLER

DAY FOUR

At the moment that Hernando Sotomayor became the late Señor Sotomayor, only four persons knew that he had been murdered. The dead man was not acquainted with any of them, and he would have been hard put to guess the reason why they had chosen to kill him.

Neither the time nor the place seemed appropriate for murder. It was an occasion that pulsed with life, a sultry August Sunday afternoon. The breeze that usually swept from the Pacific across the Mexican border town of Tijuana was absent, and the thousands who filled the grandstand at the Caliente race track sweltered good-naturedly in the hope that fortune would repay them for their discomfort. The fourth race had been run; the horses were wending their way postward for the fifth.

Hernando Sotomayor was perhaps happier than most of the throng, since he was money ahead for the afternoon. His contentment rested on a solid foundation of well-being: his export-import business thrived, his marriage was happy, his children were full-grown and responsible. And though his heart was not the vigorous organ it had once been, his physician assured him that this was no more than to be expected of a man in his late fifties. Sotomayor knew that he was in the prime of life.

Even the heat did not bother him, although it caused sweat to glisten on his bald scalp and to dampen his heavy mustache. His dark suit coat hung over the back of his chair, leaving his tight vest to corset his solid girth of good living. He gestured as he conversed with his wife and the other members of his party, alternately flashing quick grins of merriment and scowls of black ferocity; whatever his expression, it disappeared within the second. His deep voice rose often above the cacophony of the crowd to cheer on a favorite or call to a friend or summon the waiter to replenish his highball.

Because of his exuberance, no one paid any particular attention when Sotomayor suddenly stumbled to his feet and clutched with both hands at his chest. Most eyes were fixed on the horses skittering nervously about the starting gate. It was only when Sotomayor fell headlong across the chairs in front of him that those nearby realized that anything was wrong. And then they heard Señora Sotomayor's piercing scream. Heads turned and eyes peered, seeking the reason for the commotion.

The two men and the woman who sat in the comfortable box in the clubhouse above the grandstand did not require Sotomayor's fall or his wife's scream to focus their attention upon the stricken man. They had been watching him intently for some time, and their expressions were expectant rather than curious.

The younger of the two men, a slender, curlyheaded Latin, said softly, "Well done." He might have been commenting on an interesting sporting event.

The other man did not reply. He sat as motionless as a chunk of mahogany, which he resembled in build and hue, and kept his binoculars pressed against the lenses of his smoky sunglasses. All about the Sotomayor box, people were standing, crowding in so closely that it was impossible to see the man who had fallen. He came into view momentarily as hands lifted him up, like a cork bobbing to the surface, only to disappear again as he was deposited gently on the concrete floor. A pair of track attendants pushed roughly through the mob, pausing to consult with the white-jacketed waiter who hovered nearby. One rushed off, apparently in search of a doctor.

"Look at him run," the young woman said amusedly; she was auburn-haired and doll-like, with a doll's fixed smile. "Someone should tell him that it's already too late."

"Close your mouth," the man with the binoculars murmured. The girl made a petulant *moue* with her lips, but he did not pay any attention to her, so she began to scan the track program, no longer interested in the events below.

Nor was the man with the binoculars watching the frantic first-aid being administered to the stricken man or the attempts of friends to comfort his wife. To himself, he whispered, "The drink, you fool." His magnified gaze was fastened on Sotomayor's highball glass which stood forgotten on the box railing. As if moved by telepathy, a white-jacketed waiter sidled into his field of vision. Seemingly by accident, his elbow encountered the glass, knocking it to the floor. The plastic glass did not shatter, but its contents spilled and were soaked up immediately by the warm concrete. The man watching above lowered his binoculars and, for the first time, smiled.

There was a roar from the crowd as the horses broke from the starting gate and the flat voice of the public address system began to describe the race. The horses thundered by the grandstand, and only those vitally concerned were still paying attention to Sotomayor. Not waiting for the doctor, some were carrying away his limp figure, while others supported his widow, who appeared on the point of collapse.

The girl complained, "Now that that's over, can't we have a little fun? I want to place some bets on the next race. I feel very lucky today."

"We're leaving," the man with the binoculars informed her, "Have you forgotten that we're to have a guest for the evening? I want you well-rested, Odilia, in case our North American friend needs a trifle more persuasion."

"I thought he had already agreed to terms."

"In principle, yes. But having come this far, I don't intend that our assassin should back out on the bargain."

The younger man said dubiously, "General, is it quite wise to make these arrangements so far in advance? If Lazar fails to rise to the bait …"

"Are you questioning my tactics?" the man he had called General demanded sharply. "I am a student of character, Balbin, which is the reason I have been entrusted with this mission. I say that Bruno Lazar will rise to the bait. I say that what has been accomplished here today will lure him out of hiding and to Tijuana as nothing else would. Do you disagree?"

Balbin shook his head. "I'm sure you understand these matters far better than I, General."

"Bruno Lazar will come, mournfully and without suspicion, to the funeral. Do you appreciate the irony, that it will be his own funeral as well?" The General smiled again. "Perhaps you are still too young to deal in ironies. For myself, I find it very amusing."

The mansion that stood on the Paseo de la Reforma seemed, on first inspection, to differ little from the homes of other wealthy Mexico City families. Old and rather graceless, it was two stories of weathered gray stone capped by a red-tiled roof, set amid four acres of lawn and vegetation, and surrounded by a high wall of stuccoed adobe bricks. A second glance revealed certain differences, however. The top of the wall was studded with shards of broken glass to make scaling it perilous; the massive gate was operated electrically by controls within the house, and the windows of the house itself were sheltered by steel latticework. Noteworthy also was the absence of trees, or shrubbery more than ankle-high; anyone approaching the house across the grounds would be clearly visible long before he reached it. Floodlamps on the roof made certain that darkness would be a perpetual stranger.

The house resembled, in total, less a home than a fortress—or a prison. To those who lived within its walls it was both. The name on the mailbox was Pedro Palacios Ramirez, but this was a fiction. Only the initials had significance: they stood for Partido de Principios Radicales, or Party of Radical Principles. And this, in turn, was merely another way of saying Bruno Lazar.

Bruno Lazar was not a man who by nature preferred to hide behind an alias or a high wall. But circumstances demanded it. An army coup, so common to the southern hemisphere, had driven him from his homeland five years earlier, together with a number of others who were unable to countenance the aims and methods of the new regime. Lazar, a former senator, newspaper owner and cabinet officer, had become the focal point for these expatriates and the symbol of hope for those of like mind who had remained behind. The Mexican government, in addition to providing him with a refuge, had licensed him as a publisher, tolerantly closing its eyes to the knowledge that Lazar's publications were intended solely for his former country. Smuggled across the border, passed covertly from hand to hand, his tracts and pamphlets nourished the underground, although they had not yet succeeded in bringing it to the point where it could seriously challenge its masters. But water, continuously applied, will wear away a rock, and Bruno Lazar was content to be the water. Unfortunately, in this case the rock was capable of striking back.

On this particular Sunday evening, he stood in the basement of his fortress abode and read the first copy, its ink still wet, of his latest attack upon his enemies. Nearby, an ancient flat-bed press was spewing out additional thousands that would tomorrow begin their tortuous journey to the south. The tract dealt with the corrupt manner in which the military government had appropriated communal lands for oil speculation while posing as the champion of the poor. Lazar smiled a bit as he read his words.

He spoke to the man operating the press, although he knew beforehand that he could not be heard over the clatter of machinery. "It has come to me, Mintegui, that I have reached the position for which every publisher yearns—to be able to print the entire truth with no fear of the consequences."

Mintegui merely nodded as he continued to feed paper into the press. It was unlikely he would have done more even if he had heard. He was a short and bushy-browed man of stolid Indian stock, the sort who can be fiercely loyal to a man while only dimly comprehending an ideal. His earlobes were pierced, but he'd long ago had to sell the tiny jewels that had been the pride of his life. Yet he held tenaciously to his faith in Lazar, who referred to him fondly as "my will of iron," because his given name was Guillermo.

Lazar possessed little physical strength of his own; his force was largely intellectual. No longer young, he limped badly from ancient bullet wounds, supporting himself on two ebony walking sticks with tarnished silver heads. His body, formerly spare and commanding, was bent now in a perpetual arc that gave him a little potbelly. Deep-shadowed lines gullied his calm face, and his eyes, once piercing, were watery. His only personal vanity was the jet dye he used on his hair and mustache, which fooled no one; otherwise, he had the untidiness of age. Dandruff speckled the shoulders of the bathrobe he wore most of the time, and his nails were chewed down to the pink quick. Still, old or young, healthy or infirm, Bruno Lazar carried about him an air of dedication that scorned the calendar.

On the far wall, the red light above the telephone began to flash on and off. Due to the noisy surroundings, the bell had been replaced by a bulb. Mintegui saw it first and pointed without breaking the methodical rhythm of his work. Lazar moved to answer it with his spidery gait.

"Yes, yes, of course I remember you," he said. "What's that? I'm not sure I understand you—your father, you say?" He motioned at Mintegui to halt the machinery and listened with fierce concentration. When he replaced the receiver at last, his face was contorted in pain.

Mintegui, watching him as intently as a dog watches its master, asked, "Bad news, Jefe?" His voice was a grating monotone, like the grinding together of rocks.

"Extremely bad. The death of an old friend." Lazar unashamedly wiped away the tears that were trickling down his cheeks; like most Latins, he did not consider it unseemly for a man to cry. "Hernando Sotomayor—you've heard me speak of him often. We were together at the university many years ago."

Mintegui crossed himself automatically. "An accident, perhaps?"

"His heart. Quite unexpected, although his son tells me that there had been some previous concern I hadn't known about." Lazar shook his head sadly. "I must tell the others."

As he hobbled toward the stairs, Mintegui moved to assist him, but Lazar waved him away. "No, no—go on with your work. It must be finished tonight. The plane leaves at dawn." He ascended the steps slowly, reflecting somberly that this was the way of the world: men died, but life went on, regardless. It was a measure of man's ego that death, the ultimate end of all, should nevertheless be unexpected, should still come as a shock. Perhaps it was because everyone secretly believed in his own immortality. Thus, the passing of a contemporary served as a jarring reminder that no one was exempt. Lazar had reached the age when he felt the loss of a friend keenly, as if in some manner part of himself had died also.

He paused at the head of the stairs to recapture his breath. For a moment, the two men in the huge, high-ceilinged study were unaware of his approach, the tapping of his canes drowned in the thunderous finale of Beethoven's Ninth issuing from the record player. Then the younger of the two noticed him and hastened across the room. "Jefe— are you ill?" His name was Vicario, a plump young man, well-built and well-groomed from his sleek black hair to his polished pointed shoes. Like Mintegui, he referred to Lazar as the Chief, the mark of respect due age and position.

"My health is unchanged," Lazar told him. "No, no, Doctor—don't bother to get up. I don't require your professional services tonight."

Dr. Neve came to meet him anyway, his gaze sharply appraising. "Better let me be the judge of that, Bruno." He was Lazar's age, a small man with an old dark face, dried up by life, plumed with white hair. Whitely sprouting from his jaws and chin was a spade beard, the token of the medical profession in his homeland. Rimless glasses perched on his nose and hooked over his ears; the sidepieces, for safety's sake, were tied to a braided leather cord that drooped around the back of his neck.

Lazar waved aside Neve's attempt to take his pulse. "My anguish is mental, not physical." He limped to the high wing-backed chair that was by custom his, and seated himself with a sigh.

Behind him, the other two men exchanged significant glances, and Neve went to the sideboard. He sloshed some brandy into a goblet and offered it to his chief. Lazar did not drink it but held the glass cupped in his hands while he regarded the contents pensively. When he showed no signs of speaking, Neve suggested, "Something to do with the telephone call ...?"

"It was Felipe Sotomayor. You may recall him; he came here once to see me. His father, my old friend, died this afternoon in Tijuana."

Neve pursed his lips regretfully, and Vicario turned off the record player with a vicious movement of his wrist, the music dying away as if strangled. It was the way Vicario did everything, with barely suppressed fury. His body seemed scarcely able to contain his constant anger, his constant excitement; yet the springs of his vehemence never ran down. He was always making fists though there was nothing to strike at. He ate spasmodically and slept worse, even after doses of sleeping medicine that would have stunned a tiger.

He asked, "Was he one of us?"

"Hernando? Not really, except in sympathy. But I never had a better friend, or one I will miss more." Lazar raised his head. "I must send a telegram of condolence to his widow immediately for whatever comfort it might be to her. Where is Dorlisa?"

"I'm here, Jefe," a woman's voice said. She was midway down the stairs that led to the upper floor, a tall full-figured woman in a powder-blue dress that, though modestly cut, showed glowing flesh well-allotted. She carried in her hand a notebook and pencil.

"You heard?" asked Lazar. Then, remembering, "Of course. You monitored the call."

Dorlisa von Ritter came to join them. Though big-boned and square-shouldered, she carried herself delicately, as if bearing treasure. Her blonde straight hair, cut evenly all around just above her collar, was gold that swung gently with each step, setting off the caramel color of her complexion, the same tint as a healthy suntan. Her eyes were shifting shades of blue, like turquoises glimpsed through flowing water, and she had a broad mouth with wide pink lips, soft-looking; they protruded slightly in a quizzical expression. She put her hand lightly on Lazar's shoulder. "I am very sorry, Jefe." Despite her Nordic appearance and name, she was as Latin as the others, the daughter of a German family that had migrated, three generations before, to the new world. Nominally, she was Lazar's social secretary, but due to the complete absence of any social functions, Dorlisa's job consisted of running the huge house and whatever else that might require a woman's touch.

Lazar acknowledged her sympathy with a nod. He mused to himself, "The telegram—and flowers, of course—but it hardly seems enough. I wonder ..."

Neve, seeking information, asked Dorlisa quietly, "How did it occur?"

"A heart attack. He was attending the races and apparently the excitement ... It was very sudden and unexpected, the son said. The funeral's Thursday."

Vicario said bitterly, "Why must it always be the good men who die before their time while the bastards linger on forever?"

"That is a question that has plagued men down through the ages. The obvious answer seems to be that this is a world more attuned to evil than to good."

"I refuse to accept such a cynical theory, Doctor," Vicario said heatedly. "The world is neither good nor evil, and to believe it is means that you are attempting to shift the responsibility from society where it belongs."

Dorlisa didn't listen to the argument; they were all great arguers, she knew from long experience. Instead, she watched Bruno Lazar. He sat abstracted, pondering. Occasionally, his lips moved silently as if he were testing what he would say. From her knowledge of the man, she felt certain that she knew what he was thinking. She could almost predict the manner in which he would put his thoughts into words. First would come the little apologetic cough which prefaced every important decision, followed by a quick tug on the mustache, and then he would say ...

Lazar coughed and his hand strayed to his mustache. "My dear friends," he said, "I have been doing some thinking. I have decided to attend Hernando's funeral."

Dorlisa nearly smiled, so completely had her intuition been borne out. The other men were taken by surprise, however. "Why?" Vicario demanded. "Surely, there's no need of it. A telegram and flowers should suffice."

"I disagree. I must pay last respects to my old friend."

Neve bounced up from his chair; despite his age, he was still a limber and indefatigable man. "No!" he objected loudly. "Absolutely not, Bruno. I forbid it entirely."

Lazar asked quietly, "Is that your medical advice, Doctor?"

"It is merely common sense. It's foolish of you even to consider going out into the open, giving your enemies a chance to trap you. I'm surprised at you."

"And I," Vicario added, "am surprised to find you a victim of sentimentality, Jefe. A dead man doesn't care who attends his funeral."

"Nor can he smell flowers or read telegrams," Lazar said. "Following your logic, I should rightly ignore the whole affair."

"Ridicule doesn't change the facts. You would be running a great risk for reasons that do not warrant it."

Lazar looked at Dorlisa. "Haven't you anything to add, my dear? Surely, you must consider me an old fool also."

Dorlisa said, "I understand your feelings, Jefe. In your position, I'd probably feel the same. But the others are right. A trip of such a great distance would give the enemy a perfect opportunity to ambush you. In fact, it occurs to me to wonder if this isn't already an ambush." She smiled slightly. "But perhaps the past few years have made me over-suspicious."

"And they have made me weary of hiding," Lazar said. "So you are all against me?" He saw in their faces that it was so. He set the brandy snifter aside carefully. "You mention the risk. Let me refresh your memory. When I came to Mexico, a refugee, who interceded with the government on my behalf? Who loaned me money until my own funds became available? Who succeeded in getting me licensed as a publisher so that I could continue our fight for freedom? I believe that Hernando Sotomayor ran considerable risk himself, yet I never heard him mention it." His voice, asthmatically hoarse, could still rise to a bellow in a dispute. "You call me sentimental, Vicario. I say thank God I still have sentiment left, that the years have not squeezed it out of me."

Vicario muttered, "I say merely that the danger is too great."

"I understand that you are concerned for my safety," Lazar told him, his voice softening with affection. "And you may be right. But dangers exist to be overcome. A free man who spends his life cowering in a hole is not truly free."

There was a momentary silence broken by the thud of Neve's fist upon the library table. "Fine phrases never stopped a bullet and never will! Think of your responsibility, man, the loss to the cause if—"

Dorlisa slipped quietly away to the desk beneath the plaque bearing the twin lions, rampant, that was the coat-of-arms of their lost homeland. The men did not notice her departure, and she, in turn, ceased to listen to the argument that continued to rage. She knew, as she had from the beginning, who would win. Quickly and surely, she wrote the telegram to Señora Sotomayor that would express Lazar's feelings exactly. Then she took out the airline schedule and began to scan it for available flights to Tijuana.

Although it lies close to the Pacific, Tijuana (the name itself is a Spanish corruption of an Indian word meaning "by the sea") possesses no harbor of its own. The La Playa jetty will accommodate small craft, but larger ships must seek the deeper waters of Ensenada fifty miles to the south, or anchor a considerable distance offshore, a prey to wind and currents. In August, however, there is little danger in either, and this is what the yacht had chosen to do. It was a large vessel and bore Panamanian registry, but this was as noncommittal of its true ownership as its name, *La Polilla*, "The Moth." Ostensibly a pleasure craft, it carried hidden armament worthy of a warship—and this was actually what it had once been.

General Gayoso lounged at the quarterdeck railing. The evening was clear and fogless, and the lights of the Mexican border town cast a glow over the coastal hills like a false sunrise. It was cool now, following the heat of the day, and Gayoso was experiencing a gratifying sense of well-being. Most of this was mental; he was buoyed up by the daring coup at the race track, the feeling that events were marching according to plan. Gayoso was no stranger to success or to daring. His career had consisted of gambling hugely and generally winning, from the day he had left his native swamp country as an illiterate Indian *mozo* to begin the steady climb that had brought him to his present position as head of his government's Political Advisory Bureau, a euphemism for counter-intelligence.

Gayoso was a big man, in age somewhere between forty and fifty; he himself did not know precisely. The only clue to advancing years was his hair which had commenced to thin. What remained was shot with metallic gray and worn long onto his massive neck. He kept it in place with a perfumed pomade that scented his surroundings. His cheeks were hairless, as were his arms; his mahogany-colored flesh was as smooth as planed wood and nearly as hard to the touch. A flat humped nose with cavernous nostrils dominated his face. Behind his smoky sunglasses were black pools of eyes, always agleam with a zest for living. Gayoso wore the glasses constantly, night as well as day. His intimates suspected that it was the same vanity that prompted the matched diamond rings he wore on either hand. They were mistaken; Gayoso was fiercely proud of his hawklike vision and fearful of its diminishing. It was his only real fear, and one that he kept carefully concealed.

So far, his gaze had lost none of its sharpness. Though it was a mile distant, he was able to make out the yacht's launch tied up at the jetty, and knew the moment it cast off and turned its prow in his direction. He could nearly distinguish the passengers, the boatswain Domingo and the other man, the tall North American. Since this was what he had been waiting for, Gayoso turned away from the railing with a pleased smile and strolled into the ship's salon.

It was a long, low-ceilinged room, luxuriously appointed but carrying a quasi-military air. Crossed cavalry sabers were racked on one wall near a furled regimental pennant, and there was a tinted picture of a fleshy-faced man in an over-decorated field marshal's cap on the other. Yet the only person in the lounge who wore a uniform was the ship's captain, a weathered sailor, who stood watching two younger men playing cards.

One of these was Balbin, the young lieutenant who was Gayoso's aide. He was classic-featured and curlyheaded, with slanted eyes and brows plucked into shape. He had the body of an athlete and would have been handsome but for bad teeth and the white scar under his chin. Presumably it was a saber scar, a mark of honor, yet he generally sat with his chin cupped in his hand as if to hide it. He looked up quickly at Gayoso's entrance. "Yes, General?"

"The launch is coming. Our honored guest will be here in a few moments."

Balbin threw down his cards with a gesture of relief, glad for the interruption since he was losing. "It's about time."

His opponent didn't share his satisfaction. He growled, "Another half-hour, and I'd have made a real killing." His name was Procope, a sallow and sinewy man with an arrogant, dangerous gaze as if daring anyone to look directly at the scattering of pockmarks across the arch of his nose. He had the long slender fingers of a pianist or a pickpocket. They were constantly in movement, playing in turn with the sharp point of his nose and the equally sharp tip of his chin, varying this with an occasional tug at the wet droop of his lower lip.

Gayoso spoke to the captain. "I'm expecting a radio message from our embassy in Mexico City. I'd be obliged if you'd bring it to me the instant it arrives."

The captain touched his visor respectfully and hastened away. Though the titular head of the yacht, his duties were limited to its mechanical operation; in all else, Gayoso was the unquestioned authority.

Gayoso turned his attention to the woman coiled like a kitten in the big leather chair in front of the television screen. It was tuned to an American channel from nearby San Diego; a pair of jugglers were tossing torches back and forth. Gayoso spoke her name twice before she heard him. He said, "Odilia, turn that damned thing off immediately. We don't have much time."

Odilia moved reluctantly to obey him. Her mood, which varied with the needle, was indolent. "I don't know why you're in such a sweat," she complained. "He's only a North American, after all."

"But a very special North American. Get into something provocative and be ready when I call you."

Odilia examined the sheath cocktail dress she wore. "Don't you like this? I think it's very chic." She was a small young woman, petite in every feature, with a fashionable pallor. Auburn hair was piled thick and velvety atop her head and, beneath it, her glossy forehead was like a fabled pearl. Bared shoulders were two lesser pearls; then began her intimately-fitting gown that covered while inviting to attention further jewels. There was an air about her that smacked of aristocracy—though now somewhat tarnished—that set her apart from the men. Her smile was bright and red but a bit *triste*, like the best of Latin love songs, another mark of her breeding. There was a beauty mark alongside her mouth, as if to serve as a guide.

"I had in mind a negligée," Gayoso said bluntly. "Something that suggests easy removal. You're not dealing with one of your poetry-spouting *aristos* now."

Odilia sighed. "Why does it have to be a North American? They're such a gross and clumsy race." She drifted away toward the staterooms below, her movements as delicate as a butterfly's.

When she had gone, Gayoso spat out an epithet, a swamp-country term which made the other two men laugh. Balbin said, "Nevertheless, General, there's something in what she says. I don't enjoy being associated with the Yankee, either."

"Well, no one expects you to sleep with him, at least," said Procope.

"That's true. I'm afraid I'd have to draw the line at a horse trainer, no matter how much depended on it." Balbin grimaced, bringing the scar on his chin prominently into view like a second lopsided mouth. "Poor Odilia. I hope she can stand the fragrance of manure."

Gayoso had been staring out the porthole, seeking a glimpse of the launch. He wheeled around. "Listen to me, both of you. No matter how much you may detest North Americans in general or this one in particular, I'll horsewhip the first man who makes it obvious. Is that clear?"

Both men stiffened to attention and their assent was nearly simultaneous. Gayoso said, "For the time being, the North American is our weapon, and our personal opinions are of no consequence. It has taken me a long time to find the ideal assassin. I don't intend to have my efforts jeopardized at this late stage."

Balbin ventured, "General, you know that any one of us would have gladly sacrificed himself to silence Lazar."

"Oh, I know you're brave enough. But you're shortsighted. The North American is the perfect monkey to shake down our coconuts. If he succeeds, splendid. If he fails, the United States gets the blame, not the motherland." Gayoso paused, and in the silence they could hear the chug-chug of the launch engine, nearing the yacht. "One thing further. Procope, I want no mention made of your connection with the racetrack incident. I prefer that our assassin not know that part of our campaign."

"Does he have a weak stomach?"

"Worse, he comes from a nation of sentimentalists. He comes from a people who consider us of Latin descent to be the hotheaded creatures of passion and sensibility. Well, perhaps we qualify in the boudoir, but even there we keep one hand on our purse and the other on the whip. Our coldblooded neighbor from the north is a childishly sensitive soul even though he'd never admit it. He will do anything for us with his fists or with firearms, but I fear he would draw the line at poison." Gayoso snorted. "It makes for a rather patchwork philosophy, but they don't regard poison as *manly*. So we shall have to lie about Sotomayor."

"For that matter," said Procope, "I have no desire to brag about being a waiter."

"Is it possible he could have seen you at the track already?"

"Not very likely. The trainers seldom come near the grandstand. They know their horses too well to risk money gambling on them."

The yacht shivered slightly as the launch ground to a halt against its side. Gayoso said briskly, "Very well. Now let's put on welcoming smiles for our monkey."

He came into the saloon a moment later, preceded by Domingo the boatswain, and stood looking about warily, a bony loose-jointed man who seemed too tall for the low-ceilinged room. Gayoso went to meet him with hand outstretched. "Welcome aboard *La Polilla*, Mr. Cox. We've been waiting for you."

"I couldn't get away any sooner. Had a mare with a pulled tendon who needed me." His voice was soft, used to gentling animals, but buried in it was a middle western twang. "You weren't specific about the time."

"That's true. Let's see—you've already met Balbin, my aide. This gentleman here is Procope, a representative of our labor movement. Mr. Jack Cox."

Cox's big-knuckled hand engulfed Procope's slender fingers. "Glad to know you." He told Gayoso, "I speak pretty fair Spanish if you prefer."

"On the contrary, this gives us all a chance to practice your language, which seems these days to be the international tongue. May I offer you a drink?"

"Never turned one down yet. Straight bourbon if you've got it."

Gayoso snapped his fingers at Balbin who hastened to prepare the liquor. Gayoso suggested that Cox sit down and indicated the chair of honor under the rampant-lions coat-of-arms. Cox lowered himself into it cautiously as if afraid he might soil it. He had come direct from the race track and still wore his working clothes, gray gabardine trousers tucked into low-cut boots and a faded khaki shirt with the sleeves rolled up. His exposed forearms were so lean as to show prominently every vein and ligament; from them jutted knobs of bone at wrist and elbow. Cox's face, beneath coarse brown hair combed straight back, was long and hollow-cheeked, quite average and placid. There was nothing about the man to suggest that he was anything out of the ordinary. Except, perhaps, his eyes, darting and suspicious, that were amber and somewhat opaque like tinted glass, revealing little of what went on behind them. Not a handsome man, but Gayoso, whose perception in such matters was almost feminine, thought that women generally would find Jack Cox intriguing. Which was all to the good in this particular job.

He seated himself opposite the American and raised his highball glass in a toast. "To a successful conclusion."

Cox said noncommittally, "I didn't know we'd begun yet."

"I see no reason why we can't come to terms. You must feel the same, or otherwise you wouldn't be here."

"I could have come along for the ride, General. It's just as easy to say no as it is to say yes."

"Not when you consider the rewards for saying yes. When I talked to you before, I mentioned money, a good deal of money. Perhaps you think that it was merely conversation." From his wallet, Gayoso extracted a crisp bill and placed it on Cox's knee. "To seal our bargain, Mr. Cox."

Cox picked it up slowly. It was American currency, one thousand dollars' worth. He didn't say anything.

Gayoso, watching his fingers stroke the bill, said, "The other forty-nine thousand will be paid over to you when you have finished the job."

"Fifty thousand bucks," Cox said. "You must want this fellow dead pretty bad. Are you sure he's worth it?"

"That's not a question which concerns either you or me. Men have often been killed for much less, it's true, but my government believes in paying well those who serve her well. And there are other rewards to this job, perhaps even more important to a man like you." Gayoso paused.

"I'm listening."

"I know something of your background. I made it my business to find out before I approached you. You're not welcome in the United States—or perhaps I should say that you're too welcome there for your comfort. Mexico has refused to extradite you, but your status here is, well, uneasy. You're a man without a country. Very well, I offer you a country—mine. Citizenship, a new life, a new name if you prefer ... all these can be yours. Fifty thousand dollars could enable you to live quite comfortably. Or perhaps a commission in the army might be arranged. I believe you were a soldier once."

Cox nodded. "First Cavalry. Korea. I was a sergeant."

Balbin winced perceptibly but Gayoso said, "I came up from the ranks myself. We're a young and vigorous nation. There's no limit to where a man might rise, or how fast. Do I tempt you, Mr. Cox? I'm trying to, I admit."

"Sure you tempt me," Cox said. "When I was a kid my mom used to hide castor oil in my orange juice. But I could still taste it. And to this day I can't drink orange juice."

Gayoso shrugged. "When I look at you, I see a man, not a child. But if I'm mistaken ..."

"I didn't say that. But I've never murdered anyone before."

"Murder." Gayoso pursed his lips thoughtfully. "It's an ugly word. I prefer execute."

"It adds up to the same thing. A man dies."

"You were a soldier, a rifleman. In battle, when you encountered an enemy, you shot him. You had no personal animosity for the man, yet you killed him and thought nothing about it. Was this murder? Yes, of course it was. The justification is that you were acting under orders and protecting your country from someone who would harm her. Do you understand what I'm trying to say?"

Cox said quietly, "I don't like people standing in back of me." Procope, who had drifted behind his chair, moved hastily away.

Gayoso said, "Bruno Lazar is an enemy of my country, far more deadly than a common soldier. We are actually at war with him. To remove him is not murder but good military tactics."

"Then why don't you get one of your own people to do the job?"

"We've tried. Lazar is cunning and well-protected. My men have failed. That's why I am trying to enlist you. Lazar might not suspect an outsider."

Cox considered. "How do you figure it could be handled?"

Gayoso gestured at Procope. "The weapon." Procope fetched a guitar case that stood in one corner of the salon. Gayoso opened it and removed the guitar. When he turned it over, Cox saw that it had no back and was the hiding place of a rifle, disassembled. "You know something about guns. Do you recognize this one?"

Cox studied it a moment and shook his head.

"It's a Krag 25, custom-made, perhaps the finest big-game rifle in the world. It uses a 300 magnum shell and will stop an elephant in his tracks at four hundred yards. The scope is nitrogen-filled for very long-range shooting."

Gayoso stroked the polished walnut stock sensuously. "A beautiful toy, don't you agree?"

Cox took the guitar from him and examined the rifle minutely, section by section. He said, almost to himself, "When I was a kid on the farm, I used to dream about owning a gun like this."

"Take it," Gayoso suggested. "A rifle is like a woman. It needs an understanding master."

Cox smiled faintly. "You're sure trying your best to fence me in."

"You know the target. You know the weapon. You know the rewards." Gayoso spread his arms in an expansive gesture. "I have nothing more to say. The rest, Mr. Cox, is up to you."

Cox got to his feet. Still holding the false guitar in his big hands, he walked to the nearest porthole and stood staring out at the night. The other men watched him in silence. Balbin glanced nervously at Gayoso who nodded confidently. Finally, Cox said without turning, "It'd have to be in writing. No offense, General, but I don't trust anybody anymore."

"If you prefer." Gayoso had no objections; unlike Cox, he understood that a written agreement would be serviceable to both sides, not only in the present matter but also in the future. "Balbin can draw up the necessary document tonight. Why not stay and have supper with me? Better still, spend the night aboard. There's no reason you shouldn't begin to enjoy the benefits of our association immediately."

Cox came slowly back to where Gayoso sat. He shook his head. "Thanks, but I've got some packing to do if I'm going to Mexico City. I want to get started on the job right away." He held out the guitar. "And you'd better arrange to have this shipped to me down there. Too risky to carry it with me. The customs men shake down foreigners pretty thoroughly."

Gayoso cleared his throat. "Since our first conversation the situation has changed. It won't be necessary for you to go to Mexico City, after all. Bruno Lazar will be coming here instead."

"To Tijuana?"

"It happens that a close friend of his has died here, poor fellow—though it's a stroke of luck for us. The funeral, I have learned, is Thursday. If I know Lazar, and I have made a close study of him, he will attend it. I'm waiting now for confirmation from our embassy in

Mexico City."

"I didn't think Lazar was the kind of man who walks into traps."

"He doesn't know that it is to be a trap. It is your responsibility to see to it that he doesn't find out until it is too late. To a large extent, you're on your own."

"I'm used to it."

Balbin said, "It occurs to me, General, that a situation might arise where it would be impossible to use the rifle. Don't you think that Procope or myself should be available—"

"I don't want help," Cox said flatly. "Put that in the document, too."

Balbin couldn't quite repress his hostility. "No one man is invincible. If other weapons, other techniques should be called for ..."

Cox looked at him, sensing that for some reason the younger man disliked him intensely. He said, "You name the weapon, and I'll handle it."

Gayoso started to intervene but decided to let the quarrel run its course. The two man must find their positions in respect to each other. So he said calmly, "Well, Balbin, do you care to meet the challenge?"

In reply, Balbin removed the two cavalry sabers from their rack on the wall and presented one to Cox. He said, "For your edification only, Mr. Cox. I won't draw your blood."

"Thanks," Cox murmured. He hefted the blade tentatively, like a riding crop.

"Whenever you're ready," Balbin said, coming to *garde* position.

Cox nodded. In the same movement, he kicked Balbin sharply on the kneecap. As his adversary doubled forward in pain, Cox used the flat of his hand against the back of Balbin's neck to send him pitching to the carpet. He put the tip of the saber against the young man's Adam's apple. "Say uncle," he commanded pleasantly.

Procope started forward angrily, but Gayoso waved him back. Balbin glared up at his conqueror, unable to move against the blade without having his throat cut. Cox repeated his order and, when Balbin had grudgingly complied, he said, "There's more than one way to skin a cat. That's what we say back in Indiana. There's probably something in Spanish that means the same thing." He removed the saber from Balbin's throat, and the young man scrambled to his feet.

Gayoso laughed. "You've made your point, Mr. Cox. I think even Balbin respects your resourcefulness. May Bruno Lazar do likewise." He rose briskly to his feet and in a gesture of exuberance clapped both hands to his waist where customarily he wore a broad military belt. "And now, perhaps you'd care to wash before supper. I can even provide a change of clothing if you'd like. We're well-supplied here, as you can see."

Cox regarded his stained apparel. "I guess it wouldn't hurt any at that."

"Procope will take you below. Don't bother to hurry. We have considerable time—until Thursday, in fact."

When Procope had led Cox out of the salon, Balbin said furiously, "The slimy bastard! Next time I'll slice off his ears."

"Calm yourself," Gayoso advised. "You heard what Cox said, regarding the ways of skinning a cat? We have a proverb also—to clean a cesspool, a wise man wears gloves." He smiled thinly. "But after the cesspool is cleaned, the gloves can be discarded."

Dorlisa von Ritter stayed in the shower until the water began to run cool. The small bathroom was fogged with steam. As she toweled her body slowly, she occasionally caught a glimpse of her reflection in the clouded mirror suggesting a nymph rising from a pool. How pleasant that sort of existence would be, to live perpetually in a misty world without intrigue and fear and violence. Yet she knew that, for her at least, it was out of the question. Reality had to be faced.

It confronted her in the shape of her suitcase which lay open on her bed. A slightly musty odor clung to the case, like a room that hadn't been used in a long time. Dorlisa had scarcely left the mansion, except for necessary shopping or an occasional solitary concert, since the day she had come to share Bruno Lazar's exile. Now, suddenly, she was to be uprooted, hurled several hundred miles to a city she had never seen, there to face unknown people and possible dangers. She had not realized until this evening how seclusion had become her normal way of life. She felt like a nun who had been abruptly ordered to leave the convent.

As Dorlisa had foreseen, Lazar had won the argument. He would attend the Sotomayor funeral in Tijuana four days hence. Yet the others had wrung certain concessions from him. Instead of public transportation, where he could not avoid notice, he would travel to the border city in the armored sedan they kept for those occasions when it was necessary to leave the fortress. Vicario and Dr. Neve would accompany him. Dorlisa had drawn the assignment of scout as the person least likely to attract the attention of enemy agents. Her plane reservation had been made; tomorrow morning she would be in Tijuana, long enough before the Lazar party to make necessary security arrangements and to scent traps, if any existed.

For traveling, she donned a two-piece suit of gray wool, innocent of any adornment, and a felt cloche which concealed her golden hair. She looked, she thought, like an American tourist returning home after a vacation in Mexico City. Even the name under which she had reserved her ticket—Mrs. Weber—sounded American. It was not, but neither was it an alias; it had been her husband's name, and she was entitled to use it, though she preferred not to.

There was a knock on the door, and Vicario came in. He said, "I've phoned for the taxi. It should be here in a few minutes."

"I'm nearly ready. I just have to put a few things in the suitcase."

He sat on the bed and watched her transfer her belongings from the dresser to the valise. He said moodily, "I wish you weren't going."

"It's part of my job. Who knows? I might even enjoy the change."

He knotted his fists angrily. "The whole thing is idiotic. I can't understand why the Jefe can't see it as we do. Dorlisa, do you think he's becoming senile?"

"No. Quixotic, perhaps, but he's always been like that."

"It may amount to the same thing," Vicario muttered. "I can't help loving the old fool but when you consider the risk he's running—"

Dorlisa rumpled his hair affectionately. "Quit fretting so. If there's anything wrong in Tijuana, I'll find out in plenty of time to warn the rest of you off."

"You know what we heard last month. Gayoso himself has been given the job of silencing the Jefe. Perhaps we're making it easy for him."

"Gayoso isn't omnipotent, despite his reputation. I know his agents."

"They also know you," Vicario pointed out. "This affair may be as dangerous for you as it is for Lazar. Even more so, since you'll be alone."

"I'm hardly important enough for Gayoso to bother with."

"Please promise me that you'll be careful," Vicario said earnestly. "I can't stand the thought of anything happening to you, Dorlisa."

She smiled at him. "I promise." She knew what Vicario was leading up to, so she went quickly to the dresser to forestall it. She was fond of the young man in a motherly fashion, but nothing more. Nor was she convinced that Vicario's emotion toward her ran any deeper; propinquity could sometimes be mistaken for love. In any case, she desired nothing beyond his friendship. Dorlisa believed she had put passion behind her.

Vicario followed her to the dresser and slipped his arm around her waist. "Dorlisa ..."

"Please, Vicario—now is no time for that."

"When in heaven's name is the time, then?" he burst out. "When are you going to start taking me seriously?"

Dorlisa sighed. "What's wrong with the way things are now? Why must they be changed? You know I'm fonder of you than anyone. Won't you let that be enough?"

"Marry me," he urged. "I'll make you love me."

She had no wish to be cruel, only to make him understand, and chance supplied her with a tool. Her packing had disclosed it, lying hidden at the bottom of a drawer. She showed it to him, the framed photograph of a man with handsome, haughty features. "Did you know my husband?"

Vicario's arm slid away from her waist. "Only by reputation."

"Then you know the story." The photograph was signed in a dashing hand: *Eternally, Mertel*. "Perhaps you can understand why I don't want to become—well, involved again."

"Don't judge my love by his. I'm no traitor."

"Vicario, I'm not judging you. It's just that I don't feel anything anymore. I have nothing left to give you or any man."

"Do you still love him?" Vicario demanded. She shook her head. "You've kept his picture."

"I'd forgotten it was there. It has no significance for me." It was only partly true, but she didn't care to explain the reason she had retained the portrait. Not through love, certainly; that had died long before the man himself, with the revelation that he had been secretly working with the military junta that symbolized everything Dorlisa abhorred. Rather, the picture was a warning that she had kept at first to remind her of her lost innocence. It had long since outlived her need of it. She laid it aside. "Poor Mertel. Eternity was such a short time for him."

Vicario said, "It's time you stopped doing penance for his treachery."

There was a core of truth to what he said, and Dorlisa was angered that he should have uncovered it. She said shortly, "I'm happy with my life."

"How could you be? You're a young and beautiful woman and meant to be loved. You may have locked away your desire, but some man will find the key." Vicario regarded her wistfully. "I wish to God that I could be the man."

She was touched, her momentary anger vanished. After all, he was paying her the highest compliment in his power. "The trouble with you is that you're a romantic and, like all romantics, don't really understand women. There's no lock, Vicario—and no key."

"I understand you better than you do, Dorlisa."

"Then when I return from Tijuana I must ask for a complete character reading. I might learn something."

"Don't laugh at me," he grumbled.

She put her hands on his arms. "I don't mean to. You're my dearest friend. And perhaps someday ..." She paused, then shook her head. "No, that's not fair. I won't bind you with half-promises. You deserve so much more."

He moved to embrace her, and she would have permitted it but the telephone rang. Reluctantly, Vicario answered it. "Neve says that the taxi has arrived."

Dorlisa closed her suitcase decisively. "I'm ready."

"Do you have a gun?"

"You know the Jefe's principles. And I have no knowledge of weapons."

"I hope it doesn't become necessary for you to learn," Vicario muttered. He picked up the photograph. "What about this?"

Dorlisa's hesitation was only fractional. She said, "Burn it."

Procope came back to the salon with the news that Odilia was not in her stateroom, so Gayoso impatiently went in search of her. He found her aft, huddled in a deck chair. "Just thinking," she said defensively, in answer to his question.

"You shouldn't waste your time on things for which you have no aptitude," Gayoso told her. She had not changed into the negligée as he had commanded, and Gayoso knew that she had probably forgotten all about it. Every slack line of her body told him that she was in a depressive state, and this was confirmed by the slight blurring of her voice. Gayoso felt contempt for her addiction while at the same time using it as the whip to drive her. He said, "Go below and begin your work. The North American, Cox, is showering in your quarters."

"I saw him come aboard. He walks like a plowman."

"He's agreed to terms. I want you to demonstrate to him that he hasn't made a mistake." With the toe of his boot, Gayoso nudged the girl's thigh. "Give yourself a shot if you have to, but do the job as I expect it done, full of charm and aristocratic graces. That is, if you haven't forgotten how a lady behaves."

Odilia got to her feet. "There's no need to be coarse," she said sulkily. Gayoso merely snorted and walked away. Odilia watched him depart with dull resentment. He had no right to talk to her as he did, merely because he held a higher rank; they were both in the same service. And her blood, Spanish all the way back to the conquest, was infinitely superior to his, a peasant Indian. When they got back home she would have to complain to someone.

But for now she knew that she must obey Gayoso's orders, so she went below slowly to the carpeted deck where the passengers' staterooms were located. Male clothing lay strewn carelessly on her bed. The bathroom door was open, and she could hear the sound of running water. She paid no attention but from the bedside table got out a small leather kit. It contained several vials of stimulants, a syringe and an array of fine needles that would not mar her lovely skin. With the skill of long practice, she assembled the hypodermic and withdrew some colorless liquid from one of the bottles. She injected the drug in the soft flesh of her upper left arm close to the armpit and sat with eyes half-closed in anticipation.

She felt the effect of the stimulant almost immediately, responding to it like a flower opening its petals to the sun. Color crept into her cheeks; she sat up straighter on the bed, and her lips parted in a satisfied smile. She put away the leather kit carefully and turned to look in the direction of the bathroom. The shower was still running. Through the frosted glass door, Odilia could dimly make out the figure of Jack Cox. She speculated lazily on what kind of lover he would make. Inept, no doubt, and always in a hurry; that, she knew, was the North Americans' national character, and there was no reason to believe that it did not extend into bed, too. Yet, they were vigorous, driving; a race that usually clawed its way to the top of whatever heap it found itself in. Odilia's original distaste began to give way to thoughtful interest. If Jack Cox were that kind of man …

Her dark eyes began to sparkle, not wholly the result of the stimulant. Gayoso intended her merely to be the North American's plaything, part of the bait that would set the hook firmly. But Odilia could recognize opportunity. The assassin of Bruno Lazar would be an important man, and rich besides. He might conceivably rise to great heights. If she played her cards right, there was no reason why she could not rise with him. What a joke on Gayoso that would be!

Hastily, Odilia removed her outer garments and selected a negligée from the closet, one virginal in its whiteness but impudent in its cut. She seated herself at the dressing table and pinched her cheeks for added color. Deftly she painted her mouth and brushed a faint film of powder across her exposed throat and shoulders.

She heard the shower halt, followed by the sounds of a man drying himself. She remained where she was, her back to the doorway, and pretended to use a hand mirror to examine her hair. Then there was the pad of bare feet, a sound that stopped abruptly as their owner entered the bedroom and discovered her for the first time.

Odilia turned slowly and gracefully on the bench. The movement allowed the negligée to slide away from one slender leg. "Hello," she said simply.

A towel knotted around his waist was his only garment. He stared at her in surprise. "Where'd you come from?"

"This is my stateroom. The fools must have made a mistake when they brought you here."

"I'm sorry. You should have said something earlier."

Odilia smiled. "I could hardly come in the shower to tell you, could I?"

"I guess not. Well, if I can use your bathroom for another few minutes, I'll put on my clothes and get out of here."

"There's no hurry." She regarded him, pleasantly surprised at his appearance. Out of his stained work clothes, his big body ruddy from the vigorous toweling, Jack Cox looked younger and more presentable than she had imagined. "I seldom get an opportunity to talk alone with a stranger." She lowered her eyes demurely. "A custom of my society."

He looked down at his nakedness and chuckled. "I'll bet you don't at that. I don't think any kind of society would exactly understand this setup."

Odilia adopted a haughty air. "Would you please explain what you mean by that remark?"

"No offense. But you'll admit that neither one of us is dressed for company."

"That depends on the company," she said and regretted it immediately; the retort did not jibe with her pose of ladylike reserve.

He was sizing her up, too, but she couldn't read the amber eyes. "I guess we should introduce ourselves." He put out his hand. "I'm Jack Cox."

"My name is too long for anyone to remember, even myself. My friends call me Odilia." She trembled slightly at the contact with his flesh. He had the powerful shoulders of a horseman, ridged with muscle, and beneath the prominent rib cage she could detect the faint pulse of his heart. She felt her own pick up speed as his manhood stirred her. Even when she rose to her feet, he continued to tower over her, stallion-like, and the image this presented to her mind caused her to breathe faster. She stammered slightly. "You're a North American, aren't you?" He nodded. "I've never known a North American before."

"Are you part of this Lazar business? I guess you must be, or you wouldn't be here."

"I'm an agent of my country," she said, trying to make it sound like a boast rather than a confession.

He was standing so close to her that she could feel his breath, warm and scented with whiskey. He murmured, "Gayoso said there'd be compensations."

Odilia knew that she should move away from him before he touched her again. Her intention was to be flirtatious but not forward, to invite pursuit but avoid surrender. Yet she was not her own mistress. The drug, fanning her desire while it crumbled her resolve, was causing her to fall once again into the old behavior pattern. "You'd better go now," she whispered, almost pleading.

"You said there was no hurry."

"Please—I didn't mean ..." But she felt, without willing it, her lips part softly and her body sway forward toward him.

"We both know what you meant." His hands touched her bare shoulders, slid lightly down her arms, pushing the filmy negligée before them. A warm tingling sensation invaded her thighs, and her legs began to quiver. She had only one thought, more of an excuse: Perhaps it doesn't matter, perhaps this is the best way, after all ...

A buzzer sounded sharply in the cabin. Cox dropped his hands, startled. "What the hell is that?"

The sudden interruption was, to Odilia, like a wet towel slapped across her face. It broke the spell of sexuality which had enfolded her, and she was able to step away from him. Inside, she was shaking but she couldn't be sure whether it was due to relief or disappointment. With some difficulty, she said, "It's a summons. I'm wanted above."

"Tell them you're wanted below." He reached for her again.

She evaded him and gathered the negligée modestly about her. The buzzer erupted again like an angry rattlesnake. "I must go." She managed a smile that she hoped was provocative. "After all, this is not good-by. We'll be working together in this enterprise."

"You're right. It isn't good-by." He regarded her across the bed, and this time she could read his gaze without difficulty. "As a matter of fact, it isn't even good-night."

Supper was a lavish affair in the Latin manner, with both a fish and a meat course. The quantity of food was far beyond the capacity of the three people before whom it was placed. Gayoso ate heartily, but Cox, unaccustomed to more than three meals a day, made only a token effort. Odilia, opposite him, made none at all, merely sipping occasionally from her wine goblet.

The conversation followed the same pattern. Gayoso did most of the talking. He prided himself on being an excellent host, and his range of interest was great. Anecdote followed anecdote, and not until the brandy was served did he mention the job that lay before them.

As he offered Cox a cigar, he said, "You'll be pleased to learn that events are moving exactly along the lines that I predicted."

"How's that?"

"Bruno Lazar is coming to Tijuana to attend the funeral."

Cox raised his eyebrows. "You positive? Seems kind of soon."

"I'm always sure of my facts." Gayoso spoke pleasantly to Odilia, "My dear, why don't you return to your stateroom until you're needed? I know how political details bore you."

Odilia looked quickly at Cox, not wishing to be dismissed like a menial. "Perhaps, this time, if I remained I could be of some service, assist in the planning—"

"I think not." Gayoso's voice, though still pleasant, had a knife-edge to it. "I'm fully aware of your great talents and the setting in which they are best put to use. You will wait below." He turned quickly to Cox. "I haven't apologized yet for summoning Odilia away earlier. I hope it didn't inconvenience you too greatly. But I felt that you should have your supper before you had your dessert. I believe that's the North American custom, correct?"

Odilia rose hastily and fled from the salon without another glance in Cox's direction, but not in time to escape Gayoso's bellow of laughter which pursued her out the door. Cox asked quietly, "You that rough on all your people, General?"

"Different tools require different methods. Odilia is a toy, for all of her dreams of lost aristocratic grandeur. She has her uses, like all toys, but they do not necessarily command respect. I have not made Odilia what she is, but I see no reason to pretend she is something she is not."

"I guess we're all tools when it comes down to it."

"But of varying degrees of worth. You, Mr. Cox, are a weapon and deserve to be treated with deference. I, too, am a weapon, which is why I deal with you as an equal."

Cox eyed the sabers on the wall. "Speaking of weapons, where's the kid with the sword? I didn't hurt him, did I?"

"Balbin? No, only his pride. I sent him ashore with Procope, an errand to keep him busy. Our discussion tonight really concerns only the two of us."

"And Bruno Lazar," Cox added.

"Well-taken. Let me tell you what I have learned. I received a radio message from our embassy in Mexico City." Gayoso consulted his watch. "At this moment, one of Lazar's agents is boarding an airplane bound for Tijuana."

"That doesn't mean Lazar himself is coming. It might mean just the opposite."

"I disagree. This is precisely the move I expected. Even the agent is the person I would have selected." Gayoso drew deeply on his cigar. "It should make your work easier, Mr. Cox—or, at any rate, more pleasant."

"Why?"

"Because the Lazar agent is a young woman."

Cox frowned. "A woman? Is Lazar loco?"

"Not at all. The woman is the most capable of the entire Lazar gang, which is why I expected that she would be given the assignment of making the security arrangements prior to Lazar's arrival. I see that you have managed to dazzle Odilia. Do you think you can do the same with this other woman?"

"I'm no lady-killer. In both senses. Why do I have to bother with the woman?"

"I'll make a further prediction. Lazar will slip into Tijuana in a surreptitious manner, pay his respects to the deceased and be gone again before his presence is generally known. That gives you very little opportunity to perform your job. But if you could ingratiate yourself with the woman, learn Lazar's timetable ..." Gayoso shrugged. "You'd be able to set up the assassination to your convenience."

Cox considered the ash of his cigar. He said finally, "How much do you know about her?"

"Her name is Dorlisa Weber, though she prefers to use her maiden name which is von Ritter. Her husband is dead. She is twenty-nine years old, is five feet, six inches tall, weighs one hundred thirty pounds, has blonde hair and blue eyes and is in general quite well-formed."

Cox grinned crookedly. "No birthmarks?"

"That is up to you to discover for yourself," Gayoso said blandly. "But I advise you to proceed with circumspection."

"I always do."

"Mrs. Weber is a dangerous woman. I don't mean violent. But she is very intelligent and, what's worse, she possesses a full measure of what other women usually only think they have—intuition, the ability to see behind the mask. In fact; if she weren't on the wrong side, I'd admire her exceedingly."

"What makes you think I'll be able to fool her?"

"For one thing, your nationality places you above suspicion. Secondly, you're an attractive male. Thirdly, and most important, Mrs. Weber has already been betrayed once by a man, her husband."

Cox frowned. "That last part just doesn't make sense, General."

"Very little in this world does. In matters of this sort, innocence is a better defense than experience. Haven't you noticed that it's easier to seduce a married woman than a maiden? The married woman will, unconsciously at least, assist the seducer simply by being familiar with the game. The maiden has to be led every step of the way. In the same manner, Mrs. Weber—who has been betrayed before—will assist you to betray her again."

"You're too damned sophisticated for me," Cox said. "I never found women that easy, married or otherwise."

"It's merely a matter of technique, and that comes with practice. First, I'll outline to you the way in which you are to become acquainted with Dorlisa Weber. After that"—Gayoso looked significantly at the door through which Odilia had vanished—"you'll have the balance of the evening to practice technique."

Jack Cox lay in the darkness of the stateroom and stared upward at the ceiling he could not see. Beside him, the girl slept fitfully. Occasionally, her body jerked convulsively and she whimpered, a prey to nightmares. Around them the yacht was quiet except for the faraway creak of the anchor chain. The sea, as placid as a pond, caused no movement of the ship that he could detect.

Cox estimated that it was after midnight. He was not sleepy in the least. His pulse had slowed but his mind continued to fret, trying to assemble in one neat package all that had happened and was to happen. Bruno Lazar ... the Weber woman ... the zero hour on Thursday ... they all seemed unreal, the figments of someone's imagination, not his.

Yet the thousand dollars was not imaginary, nor the rifle in the guitar case beside the bed. And, certainly, Odilia was real enough.

She had been cold and haughty when he had finally come to her, fiercely determined to prove herself a lady, if for no other reason than she had been branded otherwise. Bedding her without the use of force hadn't been easy. Cox wondered if this wasn't what Gayoso expected, with his talk of practicing technique, just as he obviously expected that

Cox would succeed. Cox suspected uneasily that Gayoso regarded them all, Cox included, as marionettes moved by invisible strings that he manipulated as he pleased.

For the moment, at least, he had no complaint about Gayoso's string-pulling. The present held luxury he'd nearly forgotten existed, and the future—beyond Thursday—promised even more. If the price for all this seemed a trifle steep, well, there was a Mexican proverb which covered the situation. *No hay rows sin espinas.* There are no roses without thorns.

He'd had a bellyful of thorns for the past three years, and with no roses attached. Sleeping in stables, scrounging for work, the barely-tolerated guest of a country not his own ... it was a life he could abandon without regret. To join up with Gayoso meant closing the door on his past, but it was not the first such door that Jack Cox had closed. He had left the farm for the army—that had been one door. And then the army for the job with Magolnick—another door. Never one to worry about consequences, he supposed now that he had ridden his luck to the limit. The war had been a dangerous business, but he'd come through it with no holes in him. Running Magolnick's security squad had been dangerous too, but he'd never had to kill anybody nor had he taken any really bad beatings. And certainly the work had been more rewarding than GI pay and issue clothes and mud. Until his luck died in the home stretch.

The crackdown, always expected but never actually believed in, had hit hard. The handbook operation folded, Magolnick and company were scooped up for a tangled series of court trials and mistrials, and Cox fled into Mexico, one jump ahead of a subpoena.

He had no criminal record. The state wanted him as a material witness, cooperative type. But he had refused the terms; he couldn't bring himself to turn on his friends, any more than he could detect the fine difference between on-track and off-track betting. So the state withdrew its deal and tried to extradite him as a criminal, conspiring to obstruct justice, and a dozen other longwinded items. All of which might have succeeded, except for election year. The administration fell into the hands of the other party. The prosecution continued amid the general housecleaning, but now the Magolnick case had become inextricably bound up in politics. Through no doing of his own, Cox had become, technically, a political refugee. Until the wind changed, he was now nonextraditable, temporarily safe in Mexico.

With the closing of this door, however, he found that he had entered an empty room. His bank account in the States had been impounded, and it was difficult for a foreigner to find employment. His youth on the farm had taught him how to manage animals; he scratched up work of a sort at the race track, as a sweeper, a handler and—more recently—as a trainer for horses whose owners couldn't afford a permanent staff. He told himself it was a living, but secretly he wondered. Gayoso's offer had burst through the clouds with the glory of a rainbow.

Yet how would it feel to shoot down a stranger, deliberately and in cold blood? In war, there was a weird kinship with your enemy, even though he was no more than a blur in your sights. No such bond or purpose linked him with Lazar, and the very word "assassin" had a snake sound to it.

Even so, Cox couldn't work up the repugnance the idea seemed to call for. Just as the farm had taught him about horses, the army had taught him about killing. It was another kind of work for which he had a proven capacity. As Gayoso had pointed out, this was merely a different sort of battlefield; he was once again a soldier under orders. And there was nothing in the bargain which demanded that he enjoy it, any more than he had enjoyed Korea. Bruno Lazar was nothing to him. From all he could gather, the fellow was a dangerous radical whom the world could very well get along without.

His thoughts swept past the faceless figure of Lazar to the woman, Dorlisa Weber. He tried to picture her, somewhere in the midnight sky between Tijuana and the capital, rushing unwittingly to meet him. Beautiful but dangerous, Gayoso had termed her. And vulnerable; yet Cox suspected that her seduction—which didn't necessarily have anything to do with sex—would be the hardest part of his job. Far more difficult, certainly, than this evening's purely physical encounter with Odilia. She had teased and withdrawn, she had been alternately cold and fiery, even in the moment of surrender she had fought him like a wildcat ... but they had both known that she would ultimately do his will. With Dorlisa Weber, there was no such guarantee.

He had four days to master her and, through his mastery, to destroy Bruno Lazar. Could he do it?

Beside him, Odilia stirred, reminding him of her presence. With this woman, also young, also beautiful, it had taken him less than four hours. Hours, not days. He felt a surge of confidence, and thought with a grin that this was probably just what Gayoso, the puppet master, intended. He stroked his hand down her bare back, and she turned lazily toward him, like a cat awakening.

"Yes?" she whispered huskily.

"That's the right word," Cox told her. His arms enfolded the softness of her body. "Say it again. I want to get used to hearing it."

"Yes," she repeated obediently and then, a moment later, almost a gasp, "Oh, yes!"

The door swung open on squeaking hinges. Procope replaced the lock-pick in his pocket and, with a mock bow, invited Balbin to enter. Balbin pulled down the tattered shade over the single window before he turned on the light. Procope closed the door behind them, and they stood gazing about for a moment at Jack Cox's home.

There wasn't much to see. The room, which occupied one corner of the huge stable, had apparently been added as an afterthought. The floor was concrete and the walls and ceiling were unpainted plywood. The furniture consisted of a metal-frame bed, a rickety table that held an electric hotplate and a shadeless lamp, a small refrigerator and a canvas folding chair. A native rug covered a portion of the floor. The other door opened onto a bathroom so tiny it might have been a closet, yet a tub, toilet and washbowl had somehow been crowded into it. Cox's clothes hung on nails driven into the plywood walls and even on the receiver of the wall telephone. And, although the room was clean enough, it was permeated by the odor of the barn beyond.

Procope murmured, "To lock the door on this demands a colossal egotism."

Balbin bounced experimentally on the bed. The springs sagged. "I hope he enjoys his taste of luxury. It should make returning to his hog wallow even more unbearable."

"Perhaps we should hurry," Procope suggested uneasily. "Someone might see the light and come to investigate."

"Our presence is easily explained. We're waiting for our friend to return. After all, you work here yourself."

"The General wishes me to avoid suspicion, not create it. That's why I'm continuing to play the waiter for another week."

Balbin shrugged. He opened the box he carried and removed the small tape recorder. Attached to it by a considerable length of wire was a microphone the size of a button. He asked Procope, "What's on the other side of this wall?"

"A harness room, I believe."

"That should do nicely." Balbin pulled the bed away from the wall and, with Procope's knife, dug a small hole through the plywood. Following his instructions, Procope took the recorder into the harness room by the barn entrance. A few moments later, he passed the microphone and its trailing wire through the hole where Balbin seized it. Balbin attached the button to the hollow base of the table lamp, a central location, and covered the wire with the rug. He experimented by speaking from all sections of the room, with varying degrees of volume. Each time, Procope knocked immediately on the wall, indicating that the sensitive microphone had picked up his voice. Balbin smiled with satisfaction. The recorder, though small, was sophisticated, containing an electronic stop-and-go regulator that was actuated by a minimum sound level. The tape moved only when there was something to record. Gayoso was willing to use Cox, but he was not willing to trust him. And in this Balbin heartily concurred.

He inspected the American's meager belongings while waiting for Procope to return. Cox owned nothing of value with the possible exception of a well-cut tropic-weight suit, beige in color. This alone, of all his clothes, reposed upon a hanger. Balbin, with slow deliberateness, worked a clot of saliva into his mouth and spit upon the coat. It made a dark blot on the light cloth, almost like a wound.

Procope came in quickly. "Are you finished?"

"Did you find a good hiding place for the recorder?"

"It's on a shelf, above eye level, behind a stack of bridles. No one will find it. Now let's get out of here before someone finds us."

Balbin was in no hurry. He stood regarding Cox's coat for a moment longer and then, regretfully, wiped away the saliva with his handkerchief. Procope, watching him, said, "I have no love for him myself. But one would almost conclude that you wish him to fail in his task."

Balbin shook his head. "That would be unpatriotic. I wish very much for him to succeed. But I have a further wish." He showed his bad teeth in a grin. "That he meets with an accident immediately afterward."

DAY THREE

The bumpiness of the air awakened her. The sky outside the small window was no longer black but gray. It was dawn. On the forward bulkhead, the illuminated sign was just flashing on, advising passengers in two languages to fasten their seat belts and to cease smoking.

Dorlisa looked at her seat companion. "We must be nearly there."

"Yes," the girl agreed with obvious thankfulness. She was a chic young Mexican who had boarded the plane at Guadalajara. Her fingers appeared bloodless from gripping tensely to the seat arms. "I never spent such a long night in my life."

"I must have dozed off. I don't remember a thing."

"I know. I've been envying you every minute of the way. My nerves just wouldn't let me sleep."

Dorlisa said, "I gave up having nerves a long time ago. I had to. But I'm not sure I'm to be envied."

The airplane began a gradual bank, and the countryside below slid into her vision. Barren foothills gave way to patches of cultivation, farmland, and shortly afterward the outskirts of the city which she supposed was Tijuana. They passed over the huge oval that was the race track and then a smaller circle, the bull-ring. Close by were the rolling greens of a golf course and a cluster of buildings whose purpose didn't seem readily identifiable. Prominent among them was a tall Moorish tower, like a minaret. Dorlisa questioned her neighbor about them.

"Agua Caliente," the girl explained. "Long ago, it was a gambling casino. Now it's an industrial school, run by the government. I don't think the tower is used for anything at all."

"And that large building over there? Is that the cathedral? I see a cemetery."

The girl craned her neck to look. "Yes, that's the new one, Nuestra Señora de los Remedios." She giggled. "Some people call it the rich man's church because it's beyond walking distance for most."

Dorlisa wondered if Sotomayor had been a member of this parish. It seemed likely and, if true, she would come to know Remedios Cathedral well during the next four days. But for the moment it was gone, vanished behind them, and so she studied other features of the panorama below, trying to orient herself. To the south stretched mountains, the interior of Baja California. To the north, beyond a line impossible to detect from this height, lay the United States, a country she had never seen. Dorlisa could barely make out the shape of the port city of San Diego, obscured by an early morning fog bank.

The girl mistook her intense gaze. "I suppose you're glad to be going home. Have you been away a long time?"

She assumed that Dorlisa was an American; considering the blonde hair and blue eyes, it was a natural error. For an instant, Dorlisa thought of correcting her. But then caution intervened. "Yes, a very long time."

"I thought so. Do you know why? Because your Spanish is so fluent, no trace of accent at all."

Dorlisa accepted the compliment with a nod, wondering if the girl would have said the same thing if they had been speaking English. Probably not; she was proficient enough, but her English was hardly on a par with her German, which she had learned at home, or her Spanish, which she had learned at school. It hardly mattered. She wasn't expecting to have any dealings with Americans, anyway.

The haphazard streets and cluttered residential districts of Tijuana passed beneath, scarcely any activity visible at this hour. The coastal hills fell away and they soared above the placid ocean as if intending to head for the forlorn islands on the horizon. A sleek yacht, looking like a toy, lay anchored a mile or so offshore.

The airplane shuddered as its landing gear was lowered, and they turned onto the final leg of their approach to the airfield. Dorlisa put her head back against the seat rest with a sense of regret. Unlike her companion, she was sorry to see the journey come to an end. For a brief while she had been detached from the earth and its problems. Now they were rushing up to meet her again.

The wheels touched, the plane sped down the runway past the terminal building, turned and trundled back. They came to a rocking halt; the engines died. With the other passengers, Dorlisa filed past the professional smiles of the stewardesses and, in the first yellow sunlight of the day, entered Mexican customs. While her suitcase was being checked, she said good-by to the girl who had been her neighbor, agreeing that they should see each other again, but evading any definite arrangements. A moment later, the girl had forgotten her as she was swallowed up in the embrace of her large and affectionate family. Dorlisa watched with a pang of envy.

The formalities at customs completed, she carried her suitcase out into the terminal—to find that her arrival was of importance to someone, after all. A man in shirtsleeves appeared suddenly in her path. He was sallow and sinewy with a pockmarked face. He bounced toward her on white crepe-soled shoes, his lips parted in a grin. "Taxi, señora?" he inquired. "Very good. Very cheap."

Dorlisa hesitated. "I'm not sure yet exactly where—"

"I'll take you any place you want to go. This way, please."

He seized her suitcase and darted for the door. Dorlisa had no choice except to follow him. She had no real objection, anyway. It would be easier to get information regarding Tijuana from the taxi driver than from a travel folder.

The taxi, parked close to the terminal steps, was indistinguishable from other dark-colored sedans nearby except for a printed Libre sign on the windshield. The driver, hastening ahead of her as if afraid she would change her mind, opened the rear door for Dorlisa to enter.

As she bent her head to do so, she saw that the taxi was already occupied. A man was crouching on the floor between the seats. He held a pistol in his hand.

Dorlisa's surprise changed to understanding in a flash. She flung herself backward in an attempt to escape the trap. The driver was behind her. He seized her shoulders and hurled her into the waiting arms of the man with the pistol. Her head struck the back of the seat. She fell forward on hands and knees, overcome with dizziness. She heard the door slam, the engine roar. Before she could scream or resist further, they had left the possibility of outside help behind, and she was alone with her abductors.

The man seated on the track railing called impatiently, "Hey, Cox! Let's get this show on the road."

Cox pretended not to hear. He patted the sleek flanks of the horse, a chestnut gelding that fidgeted on the track beside him. He said to the exercise boy, "Now I want you to watch him real close on the turns. He's been trying to drift out on us."

"All right, all right," the boy agreed. "You've already told me that four times this morning."

"I'll tell you a dozen times if I feel like it." Another horse on an early morning time-trial thundered by, close enough to pelt them with soft clods of earth. Cox bent to examine the saddle girth. "Who cinched this thing up so tight, anyway?"

"I did," the boy snapped. "The same as I do every morning. What the hell's the matter with you today, Jack? You're as jittery as a yearling."

"Nothing's the matter with me," Cox lied. "I just want to see things done right around here for a change."

"Tell it to the boss," the boy suggested, jerking his thumb at the man sitting on the railing. "He's calling for you. Can I mount up now?"

"Hold it a minute." Cox trudged across the chewed-up ground toward the rail. As he did so, he glanced quickly at his wrist watch. It was nearly time. "What is it, Mr. Kramer?"

"What is it?" Kramer was the horse's owner, a fleshy red-faced American. He operated a chain of supermarkets in San Diego. "I came down here to see Harem Guard run, that's what-is-it. Why are you stalling, Cox?"

"Just going over some instructions with the exercise boy."

"You could have read him the Sermon on the Mount by now. Look, I want to get a clocking on this horse—today, not next week. Maybe you got nothing better to do with your time, but I have. I got a meeting at nine, and part of it's got to do with Harem Guard. If he can't do the mile in one forty-nine, there's no use us entering him in ... Hey, Cox, are you even listening to me?"

Cox wasn't. He had been watching the dirt road that ran past the race track grounds on the south side, beyond the backstretch. He brought his attention back to Kramer with an effort. "Sure, I'm listening."

"You hiding something?" Kramer demanded, his red face screwing up suspiciously. "Something wrong with Harem Guard you aren't telling me? By God, Cox, if you've let anything—"

"There's nothing wrong with the horse. He'll run when I'm ready for him to run." He was finding it difficult to be subservient this morning, what with a thousand dollars in his pocket. He didn't like Kramer, anyway.

Kramer's pudgy body seemed to expand with anger, like a balloon filling with air. "Well, I'm ready for him to run right now. I hired you because I wanted to help out an American down on his luck. But if you think you can't be replaced—"

He broke off in bewilderment as Cox suddenly turned his back on him and stood staring off across the infield. "Hey," Kramer said uncertainly but Cox had forgotten his existence. His attention was entirely for the black sedan that had turned onto the road behind the track. He could not make out the sedan's occupants, but he knew who they must be.

He ran toward Harem Guard. The exercise boy was a puzzled obstacle in his path. Cox brushed him aside and seized the reins. He vaulted onto the gelding's back and kicked his heels into the ribs.

"Come on, boy!" he urged. "Let's not keep the lady waiting."

"Feeling better?" asked the man with the gun.

Dorlisa shook her head, not in reply but in an attempt to drive away the dizziness caused by her collision with the seat back. As soon as they left the airport parking lot, the man in the rear had assisted her to a sitting position beside him. His attitude was one of casual concern but he still held the pistol in his lap.

"Sorry we had to play rough," he said. "But you didn't give us any choice."

Her vision cleared, and she could see him distinctly. He was a young man with curly hair and slanted eyes, kept from being handsome by the white scar under his chin. He was neatly dressed, almost foppish, in contrast to his confederate. Dorlisa could see only the back of the driver's head, plus the slash of countenance visible in the rear-view mirror. She studied both men in turn, committing their appearances to memory.

Curlyhead didn't seem to mind. He showed bad teeth in a grin. "You don't have to talk if you don't want to. I find it helps relieve the tedium of the journey."

"Where are you taking me?"

"To view the countryside." They had descended from the plateau on which the airfield stood and were crossing the dry bed of the Tijuana River. The sandy wasteland was host to a swarm of squatters' shacks, one-room dwellings constructed of tarpaper and flattened gasoline tins, the city's most squalid slum. He added, "The scenery improves later."

They were heading roughly east, toward the rising sun. Dorlisa, whose sense of direction was good, recalled that Agua Caliente, the border playground, was there. Beyond that lay farmland, and the rugged sierras. She wondered if they intended to kill her. She said carefully, "I believe you're making a bad mistake."

"Oh, I hope not. We can't afford to make mistakes."

"Don't you see that if anything happens to me, Lazar will know that it's a trap? Or perhaps you believe that in some manner you can force me to betray him. If that's the case, you're very much mistaken."

Curlyhead looked puzzled. He said to the driver, "What's she talking about? Do you know anybody named Lazar?" The driver shrugged.

Dorlisa said impatiently, "Oh, stop pretending. I'm not a fool."

"You'd never prove it by your conversation. Perhaps I should explain exactly what it is you've gotten into. My friend and I are in the greeting business. We meet incoming airplanes, trains and buses for the sole purpose of welcoming rich American tourists to Tijuana."

"I'm not an American, as you know very well."

"Well, at least I hope you're rich," Curlyhead said philosophically. "Your suit is expensively cut. It should bring twenty-five dollars in some quarters. And there's probably something of value in your suitcase, pearls perhaps—you look the sort of woman who wears pearls."

"Are you trying to make me believe that you merely intend to rob me?"

"It's of no interest to me what you believe. Oh, I would like you to know that we don't intend to harm you. Unless, of course, you do something foolish." He gestured negligently with the pistol.

For the first time, Dorlisa felt uncertain. From the moment of her capture, she had assumed that Bruno Lazar was in some way involved. But the kidnapping made no sense, since it was certain to scare Lazar back into hiding. Could Curlyhead be telling the truth—that their interest lay solely in her material possessions? She did not recognize either of the pair from her file of Gayoso's agents, and they had been careful not to identify themselves by name. Yes, it was possible ... yet the whole affair was so fortuitous, that she alone of all the passengers on the flight should be singled out for their attention, that she couldn't quench her suspicions completely.

Whatever the answer, it was imperative that she escape. Being stripped and abandoned on some lonely mountain road was merely the lesser of two evils. She looked covertly about her. The door was within easy grasping distance. But to attempt to leap from the car while it sped along the boulevard was out of the question. If they should stop for some reason, or even slow down ...

For the moment, the car showed no signs of doing either. They were still heading east. Dorlisa recognized landmarks she had spied from the air: the bull-ring, the cathedral, the looming grandstand of the race track. All appeared deserted; she would find no help here.

Abruptly, the car slowed, and the driver swung off to the south on a dirt road that appeared to veer close to the track's backstretch. Curlyhead sat up quickly. "Where are you taking us?"

"Short cut," the driver explained tersely. "Much faster this way."

"I hope you know what you're doing," Curlyhead grumbled.

They came abreast of the track, drove parallel to it, separated from it by fifty yards of weed-choked ground and a wooden railing. A horse thundered by, gradually outdistancing the automobile. The rider, bent close to his mount's neck, did not glance in their direction. If he had, he wouldn't have seen anything to interest him, Dorlisa thought with a sense of hopelessness. Perhaps she should have screamed, tried to attract …

The sedan came to a halt with a suddenness that sent her pitching forward. Directly in front of them, the road was barred by a huge mound of earth and a sign that warned, unnecessarily, CAUTION—SEWER EXCAVATION.

The driver stared at the barrier incredulously. "That wasn't here last week."

Curlyhead cursed. "Well, it's here now, you jackass, you and your precious short cuts." He leaned forward to berate the other man. "Are you just going to sit there and gape? Turn the car around."

Dorlisa saw her opportunity. With her purse, she struck at the hand that held the pistol, knocking it to the floor. In the same motion, she flung open the door and leaped from the sedan. She began to run across the uneven ground toward the distant fence. In that direction lay other human beings—and rescue.

Curlyhead yelled at her to stop. An instant later, she heard his footsteps in pursuit. She didn't look back. Thorns clawed at her calves; she felt a heel snap off her shoe; she nearly fell. The fence was still as far away as heaven. Sobbing with despair, Dorlisa knew that she would never make it. Curlyhead was too close, she could imagine she heard his panting breath at her back.

She heard another sound, a drumming sound that grew in intensity, the sound of a horse galloping. She saw it, careening along the backstretch, coming closer, its tall rider sitting erect in the saddle. She tried to shout at him to save her, but her breath was gone. She knew that he would pass by, unaware. She had lost.

It seemed like a miracle, then, when the rider saw her. And seeing, understood her need. He reined the horse sharply toward the rail without checking its speed. The chestnut vaulted the barrier like a jackrabbit and came bounding across the field toward her. She heard Curlyhead yell in alarm as he began a frenzied retreat toward the sedan.

Horse and rider loomed above her, giant-sized. He didn't speak. He bent in the saddle and scooped her up. She welcomed his strong grip even while it bruised her flesh. She tried to thank him for saving her. But the exertion and the fright, compounded by the bump she had received earlier, were too much for her. She fainted.

Cox rode back to the stable area with the woman in his arms. She hadn't regained consciousness, and he wondered if Balbin had accidentally injured her in some fashion. He decided not. There was a slight redness to her forehead but, as far as he could tell, her clothing had suffered more than she from the wild race across the weed patch. Her skirt was ripped partway up one thigh, one of her pumps had lost its heel, and her nylon hose were in shreds. They had contrived to make him appear a rescuing knight; she had cooperated by becoming the picture of a lady in distress.

He was glad of the opportunity to study her without her knowledge. Dorlisa Weber was both more and less than he had expected. Gayoso had called her beautiful but Cox had discounted this, knowing the Latin tendency toward gallantry where women were concerned. He saw now that Gayoso had not exaggerated. Dorlisa's hat had fallen off, and her hair swirled about her head like molten gold. Her flesh was a deeper gold from which were carved the classic features of her face and the statuesque column of her throat.

Yet, by the same token, she didn't appear in the least dangerous, the other word Gayoso had used to describe her. She lay in his arms as soft and defenseless as a dove. And younger than the calendar age attributed to her, twenty-nine. Cox had pictured her a tough and shrewd woman; at this first encounter she seemed more an innocent child. He reminded himself that a young tigress, asleep, might appear to a stranger to be gentle and cuddly—and still be a tigress.

A small crowd was awaiting his arrival at the stable. Kramer was among them, and the exercise boy, and the balance were other track employees drawn by the excitement. Cox paid no attention to them. He dismounted in front of his quarters and carried the woman inside and placed her on the bed. She was beginning to stir, her eyelids fluttering.

Someone pounded on the door. Cox opened it to face Kramer. Harem Guard's owner was shaking with anger. "You're fired!"

"Okay," Cox said calmly. "If that's the way you want it."

"What the hell do you mean, taking my horse out like that, making him jump fences like a steeplechaser? You could have broken his leg or maybe even his neck. I thought you had more brains than to pull a fool stunt like—"

"Why don't you save your breath, Mr. Kramer? You already fired me."

His indifference bewildered the other man. "What's got into you, Cox? I'm just trying to understand what makes a good horse trainer break all the rules in the book without even an explanation. You better talk to me, because you're going to have to talk to someone, that's for damn sure. When I tell the management what happened …" He peered past Cox. "Who is that girl, anyway? Where'd she come from?"

"When I find out," Cox said, "I'll write you a letter." He closed the door in Kramer's face.

Kramer had the last word. He yelled through the door, "If I catch you within a hundred yards of Harem Guard, I'll have you arrested, you hear me?"

When Cox turned, he saw that the woman was sitting up on the bed, staring at him. He said, "Hello, you all right?"

She said slowly, "I think so. Are you the man on the horse?"

"Yeah. My name's Cox, Jack Cox. The horse is named Harem Guard but I can't introduce you to him. Maybe you heard."

"I did hear. Does it mean you've lost your job because of me?"

"Kramer was looking for an excuse to fire me, and I was looking for an excuse to quit. So it doesn't matter. Anyway, I'm more interested in hearing about you. Exactly what sort of party did I crash?"

Dorlisa massaged her forehead. "I have a rotten headache. Do you happen to have any aspirin?"

"I can probably scare up a couple." He went into the bathroom and rummaged in the tiny medicine cabinet. Dorlisa studied his back, speculating how much she should tell him. Her training made her wary of strangers, even this one in whose debt she stood. He came back to her, carrying a pair of white tablets on his palm, and a tumbler of tepid water. She thanked him, and he shrugged. "I've got some horse liniment too if you need it. But that's about the limit of my medical supplies."

"The aspirin will do nicely." She surveyed her ruined clothing and was thankful that the damage was no greater. If Curlyhead had caught her … "What happened to the men, the ones in the taxi?"

"They didn't wait around. Last I saw, they were heading for Tijuana."

"I wish you could have stopped them. They have my suitcase." She hesitated. "You see, they intended to rob me."

He raised his eyebrows but didn't comment.

"I just came in on the plane from Mexico City. They forced me into the taxi. They said they were going to take me out into the mountains and leave me there."

"How'd they happen to pick on you?"

"Well, I was traveling alone. They said they prey on rich Americans and I suppose I looked like an ideal victim. I told them they were making a mistake but—"

"Where you from, anyway?"

"I've been living the past few years in Mexico City." She smiled. "I'm very rude. I haven't even introduced myself. I'm Dorlisa Weber. Mrs. Weber."

He acknowledged the introduction with a nod. "I guess you'll want to call the police. If they work fast, you might get your suitcase back."

"No," Dorlisa said quickly. To involve herself with the authorities would mean explanations of the reason for her presence in Tijuana, possible publicity that she didn't dare risk for Lazar's sake. "I don't want to call the police. There was nothing of value in the suitcase anyway, just a few clothes."

Cox looked skeptical. "They shouldn't be allowed to get away with this sort of thing. I'll phone the police myself if you'd rather."

"Please—I really don't want to bother." She knew her refusal sounded peculiar so she changed the subject. "But I would appreciate using your telephone if you have one, to call my friends in Mexico City. I'll pay the toll, of course."

He revealed the instrument by removing the sweater that hung over it. "Help yourself."

The call was put through quickly to the big house on the Paseo de la Reforma. Mintegui answered, his voice thick with sleep. Because Cox was listening, Dorlisa made her conversation guarded. "Are you alone?"

"Yes," Mintegui told her. "The others left several hours ago."

"That's too bad. I was hoping to catch them."

Mintegui understood. "Is something wrong?"

"I'm not sure yet. I might have to change our plans. There's no way to get in touch with them?"

"Only in the manner that was agreed upon, the newspapers."

"I suppose that will do. I'll call you again later." She hung up and stood for a moment, considering. She had been too late to intercept Lazar and abort his journey. There was nothing to do but proceed according to plan, though with greater caution than before. And, despite the bizarre events of the morning, it was possible that there was no real cause for alarm. She turned around and discovered that Cox had dumped the contents of her purse upon the bed and was examining them. She said indignantly. "What are you doing?"

"Snooping. I'm trying to find out why a woman gets herself kidnapped and robbed and still doesn't want to call the cops." He read her driver's license. "Dorlisa von Ritter."

"Von Ritter was my maiden name. I still use it. My husband's dead."

He held up her cigarette lighter, embossed with the crest of rampant lions. "You're not American at all, are you?"

"Did I claim to be?"

"You gave me that impression."

"I'm not responsible for your imagination, Mr. Cox."

"Matter of fact, I'm wondering how much of this whole deal is my imagination. Maybe I just imagined you needed help out there on the backstretch."

She softened, remembering her debt to him. "That was real, I swear. It occurs to me that I haven't even thanked you for rescuing me. I did need your help very greatly. I can't explain the circumstances as fully as you might like, but I am grateful."

His lips formed a grin that lightened his hollow-cheeked face. "In that case, I'll apologize for going through your things." He restored her belongings to the purse. "As you were just about to say, it's none of my business who or what you are."

She smiled too. "I'm seldom that rude."

"Then maybe you won't turn me down if I offer you some coffee. It'll only take a minute to make it. I think we both could use a cup."

"I'm sorry. I must leave. If you'll phone for a taxi ..."

"I promise not to ask any more nosy questions. I don't get a chance to entertain a pretty woman every morning."

She was shaking her head regretfully. "I have some very important matters to take care of and I'm already late. Please forgive me."

"Some other time, then. Where are you going to be staying?"

"That's one of the matters I—" She paused, staring at him oddly. After a moment, she murmured, "But if you believed I was an American, why did you speak in Spanish?"

He hesitated. "I guess I'm just in the habit."

"You spoke in English to the man, Kramer."

"Does it matter? One language is as good as another. I'll call your cab now."

"Never mind. Perhaps it would be better if I make my own arrangements." Her attitude had shifted subtly to wariness. Her turquoise eyes calculated him, again a stranger. "Thank you once more for your assistance, Mr. Cox. And good-by."

He let her depart without further argument and stood watching her limp away toward the grandstand. So far so good, he thought. The meeting had worked according to plan; the ice had been broken. But Gayoso had been right on all counts: the woman was as sharp as a razor. She had caught him in his one mistake, the natural error of speaking her language instead of his own. Cox didn't consider the blunder fatal, but it was a warning. He would have to do better next time. Next time ... when he returned the cigarette lighter that reposed in his pocket.

There was a bank of telephone booths behind the grandstand. No one was around to eavesdrop but Dorlisa closed herself into one of them. However, she did not telephone for a taxi. She again put in a call to the Lazar headquarters in Mexico City.

She was on the phone for a long time, most of it waiting while Mintegui checked the files. There was no Jack Cox listened among Gayoso's operatives, or indeed any North American at all. The descriptions of the two men who had kidnapped her did not tally with those on file.

Dorlisa hung up with a feeling of relief. Perhaps the whole affair had been genuine, after all, and she was seeing phantoms where none existed. Certainly, there was no real reason to suspect Jack Cox of being anything more than he appeared, her accidental benefactor. Dorlisa was surprised to find she didn't want to think of Cox as a possible enemy. Why?

"You're being foolish," she told herself aloud. "Either way, you're not going to see him again." This decided, she dialed for a taxicab to take her into Tijuana.

Gayoso came into the yacht's salon, tugging a bathrobe around his bare chest. He began to grin when he discovered the suitcase that Balbin was carrying. "It worked, then."

"As smooth as butter. We picked the Weber woman up at the airport. We let her believe that we intended to rob her and then allowed her to escape at the proper moment."

"Did she seem to accept your story?"

"It's hard to know," Balbin confessed. "She's not simple-minded. She mentioned Lazar but Procope and I pretended ignorance. We showed no interest in anything except her money." He smiled. "It called for a bit of acting. She's damned attractive."

Gayoso glanced at Odilia. She was seated at the grand piano in negligée, moodily reading through the lyrics of the sheet music. He said. "Hear that, Odilia? You have competition." She shrugged without looking up. Gayoso asked, "And what about the North American? How did he perform?"

"Well enough," Balbin said grudgingly. "At least, he arrived on schedule. I can't answer for what happened after that. I left Procope to observe from a discreet distance."

Gayoso rubbed his hands together. "Well, we've made a good beginning. What happens next is up to Mr. Cox."

"I hope your trust isn't misplaced, General."

"I trust no one. Neither, apparently, does Mrs. Weber. But this morning's adventure was just audacious enough to dazzle even a suspicious woman. If she has doubts, she will argue them away. After all, Cox is her knight errant, complete with charger, the epitome of romance." He indicated the suitcase. "And now, since we have become thieves, let's examine the loot."

Balbin opened the valise on the coffee table and watched while Gayoso scrutinized the contents. Odilia, her curiosity aroused, came to stand beside him. Balbin asked, "Just what are you looking for, General?"

"Nothing significant. Lazar is too wise a fox to commit anything to paper. But I find that personal belongings are indicative of their owner's character. For instance, there are no firearms here or weapons of any kind. Mrs. Weber doesn't believe in violence, you see."

"That box ..." Balbin suggested.

"A tool-kit, suitable for installing locks on doors. Very practical and very functional, also characteristic of the woman."

"I don't believe she's a woman at all," Odilia said spitefully. She snatched up a handful of Dorlisa's lingerie and regarded it with scorn. Though expensive, the undergarments were plain, unadorned by frilly lace or fancy embroidery. "Are you sure she isn't homosexual?"

Gayoso roared with laughter. "In that case, we should have sent you to rescue her. No, Odilia, despite the tools and the lack of the usual feminine plumage, Dorlisa Weber is very much a woman. Before Thursday, you'll discover how much of a woman she is. And so, I suspect, will Jack Cox."

Cox completed his duties at the track before noon. Despite Kramer's shouted warning, he spent a good deal of time with Harem Guard, going over the animal carefully to make sure that the morning's escapade hadn't done any damage. He was fond of the gelding, as he was of most horses. He felt sure that he hadn't asked more of Harem Guard than the animal could deliver safely, no matter what Kramer thought. He was relieved to learn he had been right; the chestnut was in good shape.

He told the exercise boy, who watched him dourly, "You can tell Mr.

Kramer that Harem Guard will do one forty-nine easy. He's ready."

"I'll tell him, Jack. But it won't get your job back."

"So there's other jobs."

"You sure act worried. Somebody die and leave you a lot of money?"

"Not yet."

One job had ended; his new one was just beginning. After lunch, he put on his beige suit. He noted for the first time a discoloration on the lapel and wondered about it. He had no choice but to wear it, anyway; it was his only suit. The guitar case with its hidden rifle reposed under his bed. From it, Cox removed the telescopic sight and concealed it under his coat. The bulge was scarcely noticeable.

His first stop was the automobile rental agency in Tijuana. He had some difficulty in selecting precisely the right car for his purpose. There were plenty of brand-new vehicles available, but Cox felt that such ostentation would not be in keeping with his supposed station. Dorlisa noticed details. Finally, he persuaded the dubious management to rent him a middle-aged Ford generally used for company business.

He drove about aimlessly for a while, getting the feel of the car, and then proceeded to the Cathedral de Nuestra Señora de los Remedios. There was no one about. He parked directly in front of the imposing Gothic structure. With his trainer's stopwatch in his hand, he got out and trudged up the broad steps to the entrance, walking slowly as an elderly cripple might walk. It took thirty-seven seconds.

"Figure thirty," he muttered. "Still plenty of time."

Cox did not enter the cathedral, although the doors were invitingly open. What went on inside did not concern him. He lighted a cigarette and studied the surrounding terrain. The cathedral sat quite alone on level ground that had been cleared for subdividing, but the nearest house was over a mile distant. Its only neighbor was the former casino, now an industrial school, its tiled tower rearing up above ancient palm trees like a periscope. Its summit offered a clear view of the church steps and afforded the only spot where a rifleman might lie in ambush. But was it close enough?

Cox paced off the distance, hoping that he didn't appear too conspicuous. In Tijuana no one paid much attention to the behavior of others; it was nearly an unwritten law.

He was pleased to discover that the base of the tower was less than two hundred yards removed from the cathedral steps, well within the range of the rifle. Gayoso had assured him it was effective at twice that distance. There was a door, bolted shut, which presumably gave access to the top. Cox examined the barrier, wondering if it were as stout as it looked.

A sound made him turn, and he found that he had an audience. A half dozen boys from the school, the oldest not over twelve, were regarding him soberly. One of them held a soccer ball; his appearance had interrupted their game.

Cox adopted a stern tone. "I'm the government building inspector. Why is this door locked?"

The largest of the boys said, "It's not really locked, señor inspector. All that is required is to kick the bolt very hard."

"And how do you happen to know this?" Cox demanded. The boys glanced uneasily at each other, and he guessed that the tower was off-limits to them. He put on a scowl. "Very well. Run along about your business, and I may forget to report your trespassing."

The boys vanished into the surrounding shrubbery, noisy with relief, and Cox opened the door in the manner they had in indicated. The tower was a hollow shell, and any purpose other than decoration was hard to imagine. A circular steel ladder led upward. Cox ascended, emerging at last into a small high-ceilinged room at the very top. A huge bronze bell hung there, but its clapper had been removed. The plaster walls were inscribed by countless scribbled names, and the floor was littered with cigarette butts and other trash, proof that he was not the belfry's first visitor. It was also reassuring proof that the tower suffered from official neglect.

A wide embrasure, waist-high, pierced each wall of the belfry. One of them faced squarely toward the front of the cathedral. Cox put the telescopic sight to his eye. The cathedral leaped toward him; he could read the Latin inscription carved above the doors. He focussed on his rented automobile, then let his gaze travel slowly up the steps to the wide threshold. He imagined his target's back filling the scope, he could almost feel the stock against his cheek, his finger closing on the trigger.

"Bang!" he said softly and smiled. For a marksman it was scarcely a challenge. Bruno Lazar was as good as dead.

Cox had little fear of capture. At first, as Lazar collapsed, there would be only the usual confusion when someone faints in the public place. Then, when the blood was noticed and memories began to recall the quick sound of a shot, the natural assumption would arise that the victim had been struck down by a pistol bullet from the funeral crowd. Probably not until the police arrived would anyone consider the possibility of a long-range rifle shot, and notice the familiar commanding eminence of the tower. By then, Cox intended to be a good distance across town.

He was about to put the scope away when he saw a man saunter around the corner of the church. Even at a distance, he looked familiar so Cox studied him through the glass. It was Procope, Gayoso's rat-faced henchman. Procope paused to give the Ford a covert inspection and then strolled on. Cox smiled again, more grimly. Despite his insistence that he have a free hand, Gayoso was keeping him under surveillance. A man who didn't trust others usually couldn't be trusted himself. It was a good thing to remember.

The rental agent swung the beam of his flashlight around the big living room. "Well, there you are, Mrs. Weber. I think you'll admit that this is an outstanding value." He spoke without real hope. They had been looking at houses all afternoon, continuing into the early evening, and he had come to the conclusion that there was little chance of pleasing the blonde woman. He wasn't even sure what she was looking for or her reasons for refusing the others he had shown her. In every case, the routine had been the same: a minute inspection of the house and grounds, followed by a murmured, "I'm sorry, but this won't do." At first, he had believed price to be the stumbling block, but his attempts to bargain had met with disinterest. He was puzzled and he was tired. Nevertheless, he continued doggedly, "Of course, it's hardly fair to judge a house without lights, but I can assure you that you won't find anything finer in all of Tijuana."

Dorlisa said, "I'm sure of that, and I want to thank you for your patience in showing it to me." The rental agent sighed, sensing another rejection. Dorlisa added, "It's exactly what I've been looking for. What did you say the rental was?"

"Two hundred dollars a month," the man stammered, unable to believe his ears. "But perhaps something could be arranged—"

"Two hundred is satisfactory." The price wasn't important, as long as the house met her requirements. This one did. It sat on a small hill, elevated above its neighbors, so that no one could look down upon it. The garage was beneath the house, enabling the occupant to enter or leave without unduly exposing himself. The patio was enclosed on all four sides, open only to the sky. The grounds were surrounded by a tall iron fence with a stout gate. It was, in fact, a smaller version of the fortress in Mexico City. "I'd like to arrange to take immediate possession. Tonight."

"Of course. I'll arrange to have the utilities turned on in the morning."

"And I'll want telephone service as soon as possible."

"That may take a little while," the agent said timorously, afraid that any obstacle might upset the deal. "I'll do the best I can. Why don't we return to my office and draw up the necessary papers?"

"I'll give you a check now, and you can bring the papers around tomorrow. I've already ruined most of your evening, I'm afraid."

"Not in the least," the agent lied gallantly. "The motto of our firm is: Every Client a Friend. It's been a pleasure, Mrs. Weber."

Dorlisa smiled. "In that case, I'll ask that you drop me off somewhere downtown. I have some shopping to do."

As they drove back to the business district, the agent suggested, "If you intend to be in Tijuana on a permanent basis, perhaps we should consider a lease arrangement. It would be to your advantage financially."

"My plans are indefinite at the moment." After all the trouble she had put him to, Dorlisa didn't have the heart to tell the man that she only required the house for three days. "Perhaps later."

She exchanged the first month's rent for the house key, and they parted with mutual satisfaction on Tijuana's main street. Avenida Revolución was the only section of the city that most tourists ever saw, and it was bedecked accordingly. Row after row of colored lights were strung across it like artificial stars, but they were dimmed by the brighter neon of countless bars, restaurants, burlesque shows and curio shops. Automobiles honked their way along the broad boulevard and pedestrians swarmed the narrow sidewalks. Most of the wanderers were Americans—whole families of them, including babies in strollers; also servicemen on liberty, and groups of thrill-seeking teenagers. They fingered the exotic goods displayed by the sidewalk shops or peered curiously into the tawdry nightclubs or examined with embarrassed grins the photographs of nearly nude women displayed outside. Among them prowled the natives—shills for the bars, taxi drivers offering rides to the jai alai games, children with trays of chewing gum and cheap jewelry ... surveying each passerby with eyes of shrewd opportunism, hardened to refusal and impossible to discourage, quick to note the hesitation that might mean a customer. Sound ran rampant—brassy music pouring out of open nightclub doors, taco vendors hawking their wares, automobile horns blaring, mariachis strumming their guitars, all mingling together in a frenetic cacophony, both weird and compelling. Glare and noise were the twin components of Avenida Revolución, and the dollar was king. It was neither Mexican nor American. It was, simply, the Border.

Dorlisa viewed the frenzy with detachment. It interested her only as another manifestation of human behavior of which she already had a rather low opinion, anyway. She was not a tourist and, even if she had been, Avenida Revolución would have held no attraction for her. Her presence there now was occasioned by the fact that it was the only section of Tijuana in which the shops remained open at night. She chose an establishment that appeared more reputable than most and made her purchases. Earlier in the day, she had bought sandals to replace her broken pumps and paid a seamstress to mend her ripped skirt. But now it was necessary to duplicate the items stolen with her suitcase, at least the more vital ones. She bought pajamas, toothbrush, a flashlight and enough candles to last until the utilities were turned on. A new tool-kit was more difficult to come by, but she took what she could find and also secured a pair of night latches for the front and rear doors of the rented house.

Her shopping complete, Dorlisa hired a cab to carry her back to her new home. By contrast with Avenida Revolución, the rest of Tijuana was somnolent. She welcomed the stillness; it had been a long and taxing day.

But the day was not yet over. An automobile was parked in front of the house, and when Dorlisa mounted the steps, her packages under her arm, she discovered a man was sitting on the porch. Apprehensively, she put the flashlight beam on him, poised to run if need be.

"Evening," said Jack Cox. "I was about ready to give you up."

"What are you doing here?"

He grinned. "Isn't it obvious?"

Suspicion flared up in her again. "And how did you know where to find me?"

"A little bribery here and there. Your taxi driver told me he'd taken you to the rental office. So I hung around there until the man came back. He got the impression somehow that we were old friends, and he gave me the address. So here I am."

"I'm afraid I'll have to ask you to leave."

"I had a hunch you might. That's why I brought this with me." He held up her cigarette lighter. Until this moment she had not been aware of the loss. "I figure one good turn deserves another."

"Did you go to all this trouble simply to return my lighter?"

"Sure. That's why I swiped it in the first place. With a lady, a guy needs a good excuse to ask her to dinner." He stood up and Dorlisa noted that he didn't much resemble the rugged horseman of the morning. Cox wore a neat beige suit with a conservative tie; his hair had been cut and his boots polished. He looked so normal, so without guile, that her suspicion melted away. She was glad to see him.

She said, "Thanks for being such a trustworthy thief. But I can't have dinner with you, Mr. Cox. I can't spare the time."

"If that's your problem, then I have the solution. Wait here." He strode past her down the steps toward his car. She waited, wondering, until he returned, carrying a paper bag. He offered it to her. "Dinner."

She peered into the bag. It contained a bottle of champagne, still cold, and two goblets. She chuckled. "I must say you're well-organized."

"If you mean I know what I want. Now it's your move."

"I'm not trying to be inhospitable. But I do have work to do here, and it's not fair to ask you in when—"

"Maybe I can help. I'm unemployed at the moment, remember?"

She did remember, and that she was responsible for it. She said, "If you insist on continually putting me in your debt, how am I ever going to repay you?"

"You be thinking about that. I've worked on speculation before."

"In that case ..." Dorlisa used the key to open the front door, and he followed her into the dark living room. She lighted a half dozen of the candles she had purchased and placed them about at strategic locations.

Cox was inspecting the premises. "Very nice, but kind of large for one person. You expecting company?"

"What makes you think that?" she asked warily.

"Your phone call to Mexico City, I guess."

"It's possible that friends will join me here later. By the way, I'm complimented that you had your suit cleaned for my benefit." He looked puzzled. "You forgot to remove the tag from the sleeve."

He regarded it with chagrin. "It was just the coat that was soiled. I can see I'm going to watch my step with you. You're damned observant."

"It's the result of the sort of life I've led, I'm afraid."

"Let's hear about your life, Dorlisa. Sit down, and I'll open the champagne. No good talking with a dry throat."

"Have you forgotten the conditions of your employment? The work comes first."

"Okay." Cox set the bottle aside. "But champagne's a lot better cold." He removed his coat and hung it on a chair. "No use getting it dirty again."

As he rolled up his shirt sleeves, Dorlisa noted his lean, powerful forearms, muscular from horsemanship, and she recalled how easily they had held her this morning at the race track. She said, a little more hastily than necessary, "In those bags on the couch you'll find some safety latches and a screwdriver."

"Sure thing." He rummaged in the bags and came across the cotton pajamas she had purchased. He raised his eyebrows. "Somehow I didn't picture you as the pajama type."

The remark, with its tinge of disparagement, piqued her. "I really don't care to be thought of as any type at all."

"No offense. It's just that these don't have much git-up-and-go. Beautiful clothes and beautiful women ought to go together."

"The latch," she suggested coldly. "It's in the other bag."

He found it and began to install it on the front door. As he worked, he inquired, "You afraid the boys from this morning are going to come back after the rest of your stuff?"

The idea hadn't occurred to her but she replied, "Something of the sort."

"Well, I wouldn't worry too much about that if I were you. I think they got as big a scare as you did."

"Just the same, I'll feel more secure this way."

"Remember what happened to the Trojans, the wooden horse bit? After all, you let me in without a struggle."

Her earlier suspicions, when voiced by him, sounded so ridiculous now that Dorlisa smiled. "You don't look in the least like a wooden horse, Jack."

"Blame the candlelight." He finished the task and viewed the results. "That should keep out the whole Mexican army." The safety latch, added to the door's lock and bolt, presented a formidable barrier.

Cox repeated the operation on the house's rear door while Dorlisa held the flashlight. She admired his easy competence; it had been a long time since she had known a man as skillful with his hands as with words. Cox's presence, more than bolts and chains, gave her reassurance. It was pleasant to have other strength to draw on for a change, masculine strength.

He asked, "What are you going to do about the windows?"

They were double-hung in the American fashion, screened but not barred. "I don't know. Keep them locked shut, I suppose."

"You'll suffocate in this heat. Come on and I'll show you a trick." He led the way back to the living room and took one of the goblets he had brought with him. "And I'll need a pencil if you've got one."

Dorlisa supplied it, puzzled. He lowered the top half of one of the windows about six inches. "This gives you the air you need," he explained. He placed the goblet on top of the bottom half of the window, resting one corner of the base on the pencil so that it resembled a leaning tower. "Now try to open the window. Be as gentle as you can."

She obeyed. But at the first hint of movement, the goblet lost its precarious balance and toppled toward the floor. Cox caught it in midair. He grinned at her. "See how simple it is? The cheapest burglar alarm ever invented."

She was impressed. "Where did you ever learn a trick like that?"

"The fruits of misspent youth. You can do the same thing with a grenade and a piece of string but the breakage is greater. Of course, in Korea it didn't matter."

"Were you a soldier?"

"Who wasn't? Don't encourage me or I'll tell you how I won the war."

"I think I'd like to hear it—after dinner."

"You mean we're finished? That's the kind of working hours I appreciate."

"It would have taken me half the evening alone. Thank you for helping me."

Cox hefted the champagne bottle. "Ever see anyone knock out the cork with one blow?"

"You're joking. It's not possible."

"Don't bet on it. I used to make a lot of sucker money that way." With the flat of his hand, he struck the bottom of the bottle sharply. The cork flew across the room and he poured the foaming wine into the goblet Dorlisa held.

"There must be a trick involved."

"No, I just have a big hand." He took one of hers and examined it soberly. "I wouldn't advise you try it, Dorlisa."

She withdrew her hand. He had given her no real cause to doubt him but, the safety of Lazar quite aside, they were still a man and a woman, alone in a darkened house. She knew almost nothing about him except his name. She sipped at the champagne and made a face. "It is much better when it's cold. I should have let you open it earlier." She had a vague sense of having spoiled something. Had it been so important that the latches be installed first? For the first time in years, Dorlisa felt resentful toward the obligations she had assumed and wished to be free of them, if only for a moment. She held out her empty glass. "Please."

He refilled it. "Not too fast on an empty stomach. You'll regret it later."

"Perhaps I'll regret it more if I don't." The wine was not merely warm, it was hot; she could feel it in her stomach, radiating heat like a furnace. "I don't have to be afraid of a little champagne, certainly."

"That's what people generally say just before they fall flat on their faces."

"I'm quite all right and nearly ready to hear the story of your life that you promised me." To her surprise, she giggled. "Excuse me."

He was watching her closely. The wine hadn't affected him in the least. "Maybe we'd be better off sitting down."

"Of course," she said with dignity and turned toward the couch. The liquor hit her abruptly. No dinner, very little lunch, and she was not a drinker, anyway. The walls reeled dizzily and for the second time that day she fell into Cox's arms.

The strength of his grasp was like an electric shock. Perhaps even more of a shock was the realization that she enjoyed the feel of him close to her. She thought in amazement, *What's happened to me to permit this?* Her distrust, not only of Cox, but of all men, rushed back. With frantic movements, she struggled to free herself of this enemy who sought to take advantage of her weakness.

It wasn't necessary. Cox released her immediately, retaining only a grip on her elbow so that she wouldn't fall. "Easy now," he cautioned as if speaking to a child. "Take a deep breath."

She was bewildered by her easy victory, and the words she had ready to hurl at him died on her lips. It had all been her imagination; he had done nothing but save her from falling. Dorlisa felt ashamed of herself and her suspicion. She murmured, "I didn't mean to..."

"My fault. I should have stopped you at one." He dropped her elbow. "If you're feeling all right, I think I'd better say good-night."

Once again, she was surprised. She didn't want him to leave on this note. "Please don't think badly of me, Jack. I generally behave much better than this."

"You had a hard day." He patted her shoulder. "Goodnight, Dorlisa." He added, "And don't forget to lock the door after me."

When he had gone, she lingered by the door, wondering if he might return. But he did not, and Dorlisa turned slowly toward the bedroom. Her principal sensation was confusion, both about Jack Cox and about herself.

She picked up the austere pajamas and regarded them distastefully, although they were the type she always wore. "No get-up-and-go," she said finally. "No get-up-and-go at all."

Cox paused at the curb to light a cigar. It was a luxury he hadn't been able to afford recently. But it looked as if his luck had changed. He was satisfied with the way the evening had gone. Little by little, Dorlisa was lowering her guard. He had been tempted mightily to pursue his advantage when she had toppled into his arms but some instinct had saved him. It would have been a mistake. She had showed him that by the way she began to struggle. By playing the gentleman, he had put her just that much deeper in his debt.

Nothing, Cox knew, disconcerted a woman more than a man's refusal to make a pass when the opportunity was presented him. This amused him, as it had amused him to install the safety latches, knowing how futile they were. All the locks in the world weren't going to save Bruno Lazar.

He was enjoying the game and, in a way, would be sorry to see it end. Dorlisa made a worthy opponent. In different circumstances he might even ... but Cox remembered the lesson of his boyhood. Don't grow too fond of the livestock, because the spring slaughtering inevitably rolled around. Today was only Monday—but Thursday would come.

A dark-colored sedan was parked down the block, where it had been all evening. Cox regarded it for a moment and then grinned. He sauntered down the sidewalk and, when he had drawn abreast of the automobile, turned suddenly and thrust his head into the open window. He asked pleasantly, "Do you happen to know what time it is?"

Balbin glared at him from the driver's seat. "Eight minutes past eleven," he muttered.

"Thank you. Then at nine minutes past eleven, I'll expect you to be gone. Because if you're not, at ten minutes past eleven, I'll be kicking you all the way down the hill."

"Don't push me too far, Yankee. I might forget your exalted position."

"Just remember your position the last time we tangled, sonny. Flat on your back, wasn't it?" Cox was still smiling. "Stay off my tail, you and your ugly buddy. I'm running the show, and I don't like kibitzers."

"I'll inform the General. He'll be delighted to hear it."

"Not half as delighted as he'd be if Mrs. Weber sees you again and puts two and two together. She's very good at addition." Cox blew a stream of smoke at the other man. "Your minute's up."

Balbin started the engine with a violent movement. Cox barely had time to withdraw his head from the window before the sedan shot off down the street. He watched it out of sight and then walked slowly back to his own vehicle. It was a peculiar setup, he thought. He didn't know whom he had to fear the most, his enemies or his allies.

Dr. Neve awoke with a start and glanced out the window. The dark landscape, slipping silently by on either side of the armored sedan, gave no clue as to their whereabouts. He didn't know if he had slept for a moment or an hour. He asked Vicario, who was driving, "What time is it?"

"Nearly midnight."

Neve yawned. "Then it's almost Tuesday. You must be tired. I'll be glad to take the wheel for a while."

"I'm accustomed to little sleep. Don't worry, Doctor—your turn will come. We still have a great distance to travel."

"Where are we now?"

"Somewhere between Guadalajara and Mazatlán. I haven't consulted the map recently."

There was little need to. Only one all-weather highway ran between the capital and the California border. As long as they remained upon it, they would eventually reach their destination. Their rate of speed was calculated to deliver them to Tijuana early Thursday morning, the day of Sotomayor's funeral.

Neve glanced into the rear seat where Bruno Lazar slumbered, snoring softly. "At least, Bruno seems to be enjoying the journey. I've seldom seen him so relaxed."

"It's difficult to understand the reason, considering the risk."

"Bruno is different from you and me, Vicario. We're bookkeepers, always adding up columns of figures, balancing the profit against the loss. Bruno is a poet. To live dangerously is merely a form of self-expression."

"How about the rest of us who don't happen to be poets?"

Neve shrugged. "Perhaps we're overestimating the danger. Soon we'll be able to procure a Tijuana newspaper. If there's anything suspicious, Dorlisa will smell it out and warn us off in time."

They slowed to pass through a village. No light showed in any of the adobe huts and the only sign of life was a mongrel dog who bristled sleepily at their passage. Vicario said moodily, "I have another theory about the Jefe. I believe he doesn't care to live any longer and that is the real reason for this morbid pilgrimage."

Their headlights swept across the crude headstones of the village cemetery. Neve shivered but he spoke lightly. "That's your imagination speaking."

"Call it anything you like—but there is death in Tijuana."

"Of course. We are going to a funeral."

"Yes," Vicario agreed. "But whose?"

DAY TWO

Dorlisa awoke Tuesday morning without the sensation of having rested. She had slept poorly, unusual for her. It could be blamed on a number of things, a strange house, an unfamiliar bed, the champagne. Whatever the cause, she felt jittery and depressed, although the sunshine outside her windows promised another beautiful day.

The breakfast she was able to prepare didn't lift her spirits any. Without gas or electricity, she could not boil an egg, toast bread or brew coffee. She ended by eating half of a grapefruit and a few graham crackers. She consoled herself by thinking that such a diet was good for her figure, and then was surprised that such a thought should occur to her. Who really cared what her figure looked like? Women dieted for the sake of either vanity or a man, and she had neither.

Or was she being quite honest on both scores? Once she had taken great pains with her appearance and had enjoyed the result. That had been in the days before her exile when she had conceived that her sole ambition was to create the pleasant climate in which marriage flourished. In the gray years since, she had submerged her sex in duty. She thought of herself primarily as a soldier rather than a woman. But since coming to Tijuana she felt nearly forgotten desires stirring in her again, the female chafing at the drab uniform of the soldier. Perhaps it was due to the hedonistic ferment of the border city, perhaps to the danger of her mission ... or perhaps Jack Cox was to blame.

In the living room sat the bottle of champagne, flat now, and the goblets he had brought. Dorlisa fancied that he had left something more behind him, a certain atmosphere of masculinity. For a moment, she recalled how he had held her against him. She put the memory aside. Facts had to be faced. Primary among them was that she was not a free agent. Her commitment to Bruno Lazar was total, and by her own choice. Last night she had come close to outright disloyalty, but it mustn't happen again. Cox had no place in her life.

She emptied the balance of the champagne in the sink and placed the bottle in the trash. This symbolic act performed, she felt more resolute and began to busy herself arranging the house to her liking.

It had stood vacant for several months and dust was everywhere. While awaiting the arrival of the utility men, she attacked the floors with broom and mop. Like a good soldier should, she thought, and felt her life fall once again into its familiar pattern.

When at midmorning the doorbell rang, she had ceased to think of anything beyond her responsibilities. She went briskly to admit the crew that would restore the gas and electricity.

Jack Cox stood smiling on the porch. He wore a flowered sport shirt and a hat of gay straw and carried a wicker basket on his left arm. "Good morning," he said. "Are you ready?"

"Ready for what?"

"To start enjoying life. I thought we'd go to the beach. The swimming is great this time of year. I even packed a lunch." He tapped the wicker basket. "No champagne, though, just beer. On ice."

Dorlisa was annoyed to discover how her heart had quickened at his appearance. "I'm sorry. I have other plans."

"Well, I'm flexible. I'll bend mine to suit yours."

"I'm afraid it's not possible." She was acutely conscious of how she looked, minus lipstick, her hair bound up in a scarf. It occurred to her that Cox had never seen her except in disarray. "My schedule leaves no room for play."

"What are you—a train? Beautiful women shouldn't have schedules." He gave a mock sigh. "Okay, hand me the broom, and we'll get to work."

Dorlisa had forgotten she still carried it. "Oh, no—I don't want you to do that. Just because I have obligations is no reason to spoil your day."

"It's my day. Let me spoil it if I want to."

"You must have something better to do with your leisure."

"No, I'll just sit around and watch you work. What could be more leisurely than that?"

"All right, if it's what you really wish." As a sop to her conscience, she added, "But only for a little while."

Despite his promise, Cox didn't sit down. He wandered about the living room, examining the bric-a-brac on the book shelves. "Reminds me of home. Every year the folks came back from the county fair loaded down with junk. Never threw any of it away."

"Where is your home, Jack?"

"Indiana. A little place named Garrett on the B & O line." He shook his head. "A long, long way from here, you can bet."

"Rather strange to find you in Tijuana, isn't it?"

"I guess you could say that about a lot of people. Half the population here came from some other place. It's a city of drifters." He was studying her curiously. "Where do you fit in, Dorlisa? You're not American and you're not Mexican. Von Ritter. That's German, isn't it? But you're not German, either."

"Oh, I guess I'm just a drifter too," she replied lightly.

"No, I think you're an international spy. Woman of Mystery, like the newspapers say. Only thing I haven't figured out is who you're spying for."

She laughed. "Do you intend to denounce me to the authorities?"

"Of course not. I don't get a chance to meet a spy every day. I intend to keep you all to myself."

"I'd better finish my sweeping." She felt that to continue in this vein would be dangerous.

"I'll keep my word. I won't lift a finger to help you." He went to stand at the French doors that opened onto the central patio. "How about that? That's Cupid in the fountain there. I wonder where the water comes out?"

In the darkness, she had not examined the patio. The fountain was dry and the basin choked with leaves. "That's not Cupid. It's one of the Aztec deities—Tonantzin, I believe. As a matter of fact, it's not even supposed to be a male figure. Tonantzin was a goddess of fertility."

Cox looked closer. "You're right. And here I always thought I could tell a woman when I saw one. Especially with her clothes off."

"Appearances can be deceiving."

"I guess I'd better stick to the touch system." He put his hand experimentally on her waist; it hovered there, able to move in either direction. "Can't go around making mistakes all the time—"

She slid away from him and held the broom between them like a barrier. "I've changed my mind. I'll allow you to clean the leaves out of the fountain. The water will be turned on shortly."

He took the broom with an amused expression. Dorlisa was able to watch him as she worked in the rooms that surrounded the patio. And to hear him; Cox hummed and occasionally spoke softly to himself—the result, she supposed, of working with horses. Once she heard him mutter, "She doesn't look so damn fertile. Hips are too narrow." It took her a startled moment to realize that he was speaking of the goddess. She smiled, glad that she had allowed him to remain. Perhaps duty and pleasure did not necessarily have to collide, after all.

And his presence was comforting when the utility men finally arrived shortly before noon. They seemed to be typical laborers, nothing to alarm her, but Dorlisa remembered her experience at the airport and was happy not to be alone in the house with strangers. They bustled about, turning valves and lighting pilots with professional ease, and were gone again within fifteen minutes.

Her own tasks finished, Dorlisa attended to her personal grooming before joining Cox in the patio. He had discovered the spigot that allowed water to flow into the fountain and was viewing the result with satisfaction. A thin stream of water, amber with rust, gushed from the idol's mouth.

Cox was equally pleased with Dorlisa's appearance. "Nice," he complimented her. "Soon as I wash up I'll be right with you."

She didn't understand.

"Our picnic," he explained. "I figure we can have it right here in the patio. If you want, we can even go wading in the fountain."

She shook her head regretfully. "I can't."

"Then forget the wading. We'll just eat." He saw she was still shaking her head. "All right, so it's the company you object to."

"That's not it, Jack." She was anxious that he not misunderstand. "I enjoy being with you. But I have to go out. I'm already behind in my schedule."

He blew out his breath in relief. "I was beginning to think I had spotted fever or something. There's no problem. I can drive you any place you have to go."

She started to refuse again and then didn't. He obviously wished to be with her and she—admit it—wished the same. "I'm afraid I can't promise you a very exciting journey."

"That remains to be seen. Where are we going?"

Dorlisa smiled. "To church."

General Gayoso was a methodical man and his life, either afloat or ashore, was lived within the framework of a rigid discipline. In the morning, he exercised. During the afternoon, he slept, resting his precious eyes. His evenings, and most of the night, were devoted to the duties of his office. Gayoso's subordinates and his mistresses usually found it difficult to adjust to this reversal of the customary order, but it was a routine he deviated from only in emergencies.

The launch brought Procope out to *La Polilla* a few minutes before noon. He was in time to see the conclusion of a fencing match between Gayoso and his aide on the quarterdeck. The weapons were sabers, and both men wore the prescribed uniform of glove, plastron and wire-mesh mask. Balbin was always careful to allow his superior officer to win these bouts but perhaps his consideration was unnecessary since

Gayoso was a strong swordsman. Rather than a slashing attack, his tactics consisted of a series of parries and disengagements calculated to lure his opponent into a mistake; in boxing, he would have been called a counterpuncher.

Procope watched the match come to its predictable conclusion. Balbin, following an engagement *in quarte*, left himself momentarily exposed to Gayoso's riposte. Gayoso lunged, his blade passing over that of his opponent, the blunt point stabbing into Balbin's chest. He stepped back immediately, and the two men bowed to each other. Gayoso removed his mask, grinning.

"Well fought," he told Balbin. "You're beginning to extend me."

"I still have a great deal to learn, General."

"Be careful. When the pupil exceeds the teacher, then it is time to get another pupil." He glanced at Procope. "Perhaps you would care to learn."

Procope shrugged. "It's too fancy for me. I prefer my knife."

"And a turned back," Gayoso agreed. "Well, a jackal is as important as a lion in the balance of nature. Did you bring the tape?"

"Yes, there was no difficulty. I replaced it with another."

The two men followed Gayoso into the yacht's salon. Procope put the spool of recording tape on the player. While they waited for the machine to warm up, he said, "The waiters' union has called a meeting at the track for tomorrow afternoon. To discuss a jurisdictional matter, I believe. Ordinarily, I wouldn't bother with it but, under the circumstances, perhaps it would be wise if I—"

"Attend by all means," Gayoso said impatiently. "Now be still so that I may hear."

They listened as the tape spewed out the record of all that had happened in Cox's quarters during the past twenty-four hours. There was little of interest save the conversation between the American and Dorlisa Weber the previous morning. Gayoso sat expressionless through it, his saber across his knees. Only when Dorlisa challenged Cox's use of Spanish did he grimace slightly like a man watching an error in a sporting event.

Balbin seized on the blunder eagerly. "The clod will spoil everything."

"Perhaps. But Cox is resourceful—as you should know. My feeling is that Cox will vanquish the Weber woman just as he vanquished you."

"That bout isn't over, General."

"You do indeed have a great deal yet to learn, Balbin, and one thing is that there are other weapons besides sabers. We must be sure to save the tapes. In fact, I think I'll make that your responsibility."

Balbin was puzzled. "Certainly, sir, but I don't see—"

"I'm doing you a favor. In the years to come, those little spools might turn out to be a great source of satisfaction to you. If Cox succeeds in seducing her, we may value having proof of the affair that a court-martial would accept." Behind his smoky sunglasses, Gayoso's eyes observed Balbin with amusement. "Or have you forgotten, Lieutenant, the penalty for consorting with an enemy of our country— which, by then, will be Cox's country also?"

"Death," said Balbin slowly. "Yes, General, I'll guard the tapes. Very, very carefully."

As they drove downtown, Cox asked, "Now isn't this better than a taxi? Cheaper, too."

"And safer," Dorlisa added with a smile.

"Well, I can't guarantee that. I don't care for any woman to feel too safe with me. A little uncertainty makes life interesting."

Dorlisa was silent for a few moments. At last, she said soberly, "I'm afraid I'm not being very fair to you, Jack. This isn't the pleasant excursion you planned. Worst of all, I'm not even at liberty to tell you the reasons for what I have to do."

"Okay, we'll make a deal. You don't tell me any international secrets and I don't give you any tips on the horses. Fair enough?"

She regarded him wryly. "Do you always drive such hard bargains?"

"Part of my system. I figure to make myself indispensable to you— then you'll be in my power."

She started to reply to this, then thought better of it, and directed him instead to find the office of the Tijuana newspaper. He parked at the curb while Dorlisa went inside alone. He watched her through the glass as she conversed with a clerk and filled out a form which he supplied. Money changed hands. Cox thought he knew her purpose, to place a coded message which Bruno Lazar would understand. The Tijuana papers circulated at least as far south as Mazatlán, which meant that a notice printed today would be in Lazar's hands no later than tomorrow. It could be a warning or an all-clear; with what he knew of Dorlisa, Cox guessed that it would fall somewhere in the middle. Proceed with caution.

It was advice he would do well to keep in mind himself. Dorlisa might trust him with her person, but she still didn't trust him with her secrets. Under ordinary circumstances, he would have been content to settle for one without the other—there was no denying her attractiveness—but not now. However, the initiative would have to come from her, despite his natural impatience. All he could do was to grease the slide.

So he made no attempt to question her actions when she returned to the car. Nor was she disposed to explain. She sat quietly for a while, eyes indrawn, and he pretended to be interested in the pedestrian traffic, wholly Mexican at this hour, which coursed up and down the sidewalk. Dorlisa seemed to be debating something with herself, because she finally murmured, "Well, there's still time to change my mind later on."

He surmised that he had been right, and that she hadn't warned Lazar off. But he said innocently, "If you're worried about our picnic, we can have it anytime you say. I brought the hamper with us."

"No, that's not what I meant." She sat up straighter and said briskly, "I think we'd better go to the cathedral now."

He nearly made the natural error of turning toward Los Remedios without further directions, but he caught himself in time. "Which one? There's two or three around town."

"The new one, near the race track. Nuestra Señora de los Remedios."

He drove there and parked in the same spot he had occupied on the previous day. Dorlisa did not enter the church. She wandered about the broad steps, studying the building and its surroundings as he had done. Like a couple of baseball teams, Cox thought: both of us taking batting practice before the game starts.

He saw that Dorlisa was staring at the tower of the industrial school. He said casually, in an attempt to divert her attention, "That used to be a gambling casino with a hotel and swimming pool and everything. They've made it into a boys' school. Pretty, isn't it?"

"Yes," she replied dubiously. "That tower—what is its use?"

"None that I know of. There seems to be a bell in it."

"How far away would you say it is, Jack?"

He knew the distance precisely but he exaggerated a trifle. "At least two hundred yards, probably farther."

"I think I'd like a closer look," Dorlisa said and started off across the fields toward it. He had no choice except to trail along. It seemed to Cox that he was reliving a dream, repeating exactly his actions of yesterday, except that this time he was not alone. He hoped that they would not encounter the boys again. If Dorlisa learned that he had been there before ...

That much of his apprehension was baseless. They met no one, and when they arrived at the wooden door he had carefully bolted behind him, he said, "Well, here you are. Just a deserted tower and locked up tight, besides."

She was examining the bolt. "The door's been tampered with. Recently, too. Those are fresh splinters."

"Probably the boys from the school. You know how kids are, always looking for a place to hide."

"A place to hide," she repeated and craned her neck to stare at the belfry high above them. "Yes, it would make a very good place to hide."

"I remember when I was a kid back home—" Cox continued a trifle desperately. But she was not listening. She turned and started abruptly back the way they had come. He caught up with her. "What's the rush?"

"Oh, I'm sorry." She seemed momentarily to have forgotten his presence. "I was thinking of something important. Forgive me, Jack."

"Sure. Well, where shall we go now?"

"To the cathedral. There are arrangements to be made."

He accompanied her, wondering. They entered the church by the front door. Cox had been reared as a Baptist, but it had been several years since he had entered any house of worship. The last time he had attended divine services had been in Korea, shortly before the Pusan breakout. And then it had not been through a sense of piety but rather like a gambler hedging a bet. Yet a residue of awe remained and that, plus the knowledge of his mission, made him uneasy in the brooding silence of the cathedral.

Dorlisa had no qualms, however. She observed the customary ritual with easy familiarity and beckoned Cox to follow her down the long, carpeted aisle toward the altar. She knocked on a door to one side of it.

"How do you know your way around?" he whispered. "You been here before?"

"No, but I have attended the original Remedios in Cholula. This appears to be an exact copy. I believe this door leads to the vestry."

She was right, and repeated knocking finally produced an answer. A priest, a young man in a black robe, greeted them quietly. Dorlisa inquired for the bishop and was informed that he had been called away to Mexicali and would not return for several days.

"Then perhaps you might assist me, Reverend Father. It's in regard to the Sotomayor funeral on Thursday."

The priest inclined his head. "Yes, a very great loss to our parish. In the bishop's absence, I will conduct the Mass."

"One of the mourners—my uncle—was an old friend of Señor

Sotomayor. He wishes very greatly to attend the services. However, he is quite infirm, and I'm afraid that he'll find it impossible to negotiate the front steps." Dorlisa paused. "I wonder if there is another way that he might enter the sanctuary, a side door perhaps ..."

"I see." The priest pursed his lips, considering. "Yes, I think something of the sort could be arranged. Please follow me."

He led them through the vestry into a long refectory and opened a door there. They peered out at a driveway under a massive porte-cochere. "Would this do?" he asked Dorlisa. "Your uncle could be brought directly here by automobile. The door is wide enough to admit a wheelchair if need be."

"This will do splendidly," she told him. "Thank you very much, Father." As they walked slowly down the driveway toward the street, Dorlisa said with satisfaction, "Things are working out very nicely, Jack. I'm sure that Uncle Bruno will be pleased with this arrangement."

Uncle Bruno might be pleased, Dorlisa might be pleased—but Jack Cox was far from sharing their satisfaction. The porte-cochere was on the opposite side of the cathedral from the tower, completely hidden from its sight. His scheme, so confidently constructed, lay tumbled into ruins by this woman who smiled brightly at him. He felt like swearing. But she was expecting him to return her smile. With a great effort, he somehow managed it.

They had passed through Mazatlán in early morning. The highway turned almost directly north, skirting the shores of the Pacific which shortly became transformed into the Gulf of California. Only two cities of any size lay between them and the American border. By afternoon they had reached the first of these, Culiacan, a sprawling community of more than twenty-five thousand people. Lazar directed them to stop so that he might purchase a Tijuana newspaper.

Vicario objected. "It's still too early, Jefe. We can't expect a message before Hermosillo at the earliest and probably not until we reach Mexicali."

"I know that as well as you do. But I desire to read Hernando Sotomayor's obituary. That is, if neither of you considers that it may be dangerous to do so."

His tone was petulant, and Neve regarded him with professional eyes. "You look pale, Bruno. Are you feeling all right?"

"A bit liverish. And a bit tired of our present relationship. I am not a madman, and you are not my keepers."

Neve chuckled. "I can prescribe for the former, at least. You'll find a bottle of yellow pills in my bag on the floor at your feet. Take two of them immediately and repeat in four hours."

Lazar continued to grumble as he rummaged in the doctor's satchel. "If I had been allowed to follow my first inclination and take the plane, we would have all been spared—" His voice sharpened with surprise. "What is this doing here?"

He plucked an object from the bottom of the bag. It was a Beretta automatic pistol, smaller than a man's hand. Lazar stared at it as if it were a poisonous reptile. Neither of the other men spoke. "Well? Does anyone care to offer an explanation?"

Vicario spoke but he addressed Neve. "You fool—why did you hide it there, of all places?"

"It slipped my mind," Neve confessed.

Lazar said coldly, "My feeling toward firearms is no secret. Why was this thing brought with us?"

"Blame me," Vicario said. "I suggested it."

"The responsibility is equally mine," Neve argued, "since I agreed with him. We know your attitude regarding violence, Bruno, and we hid the pistol out of respect for you. But be realistic for once. We must have the means to protect ourselves. It's nature's law. Even the scorpion carries a stinger."

"I'm not an insect. Neither am I a bandit, and I don't intend that you reduce me to that level."

"Carrying a gun is the surest way to guarantee you won't have to use one."

"I know a better way." Lazar rolled down the bullet-proof window and hurled the pistol into a culvert.

Vicario jammed on the brakes, halting the armored car in the middle of the roadway. "Jefe, I protest. You have no right to throw away the pistol simply because you wish to become a martyr."

"Is that what you think of me? Neve calls me unrealistic, you call me a thanatophile—in love with death. Perhaps you'd be interested in my own appraisal." He bent his head, eyes closed, while the other two men glanced uncomfortably at each other. "I consider that we are a handful of human beings, chosen for a specific mission, needing no weapon except the truth. I don't want to die, but merely to live is nothing. Victory for my ideals is what counts. Death is incidental. If I am the target for assassination, then I am victorious, because that means that my ideals have grown so strong that my enemies are sick with fear. And my task is finished."

"Your mission is not that limited, Jefe, and that is why we wish to guard you. Once the junta is overthrown, the people will look to you as a messiah."

"When the junta is overthrown, the democratic government will be formed by younger and more vigorous leaders. People like you, Vicario, and Dorlisa. I'm not your messiah. If anything, I am merely John the Baptist, preparing the way for him."

"John the Baptist's head was served to Herod on a platter," Neve murmured.

"True, but he had accomplished his purpose." Lazar raised his face and regarded them with piercing eyes. "If either of you finds it impossible to adapt yourself to such a role, we'll part here in Culiacan, and I'll continue the journey alone. If you stay with me, I'll hear no more talk of meeting violence with violence."

There was a moment of silence, and then Vicario started the armored sedan rolling forward again. After a while, Lazar murmured, "You're an excellent physician, Neve. I haven't taken the pills, and already I feel much better."

"Where are you going now?" Cox demanded.

Dorlisa didn't notice the crossness in his voice. In her mind, she was busily checking off all the danger points. Lazar's arrival and departure from the cathedral had been taken care of and there was nothing to fear during the Mass but ... She continued on around the side of the building toward the graveyard. Cox tagged along at her heels like a surly dog.

The cemetery was as new as the church it served. Few headstones dotted the flat ground and grass had not yet come to cover the brown adobe. At one side, a pair of bare-chested laborers were apathetically digging a grave. They had succeeded in excavating to the depth of only a foot or so, apparently feeling that there was still plenty of time before Thursday.

Dorlisa didn't approach the gravediggers but looked about alertly for possible ambushes. She couldn't find any. The burial grounds were surrounded by a high stucco wall and were hidden from view of the tower by the cathedral. Two eminences overlooked the cemetery, but both were rather distant: the summit of a wooded hill and the grandstand of the bull-ring. She sought Cox's opinion. "Have you done much shooting, Jack?"

"I told you I was in the army."

"In your opinion, how far away is the plaza de toros?"

He scrutinized it. "Hard to say. Four hundred, five hundred yards."

"And that hilltop?"

"Maybe a little closer than that. Why?"

"Idle curiosity." Dorlisa took his arm. "Well, I think I've seen enough."

"Are you sure you don't want to take some pictures?" he muttered.

She glanced at him, startled at his tone which was so unlike his usual banter. She put it down to the surroundings. Few people cared for cemeteries; they were an all too tangible reminder of mortality. And Cox knew nothing of the reason for her presence here. In his place, she would probably react in the same somber fashion.

As they drove back to the city, Dorlisa expected that he would question her about what happened, despite his promise. She couldn't blame him for being curious. And she began to prepare a story to tell him, a story that contained enough truth to satisfy him but minus details which might endanger Lazar.

However, it was not needed. Cox did not bring up the subject. In fact, he made little effort to carry on any sort of conversation. Dorlisa attempted to tease him out of his sullen mood. "I warned you that you might find our excursion a trifle unusual, didn't I? I think I lived up to my promise admirably."

"Yeah, you're full of surprises."

"You say that as if it displeases you."

"No, I like a woman with hidden depths." But he didn't smile, and the compliment sounded wooden. "Where to now?"

"Downtown. I have another surprise up my sleeve, one more to your liking."

Following her directions, he parked on Avenida Revolución in the center of the business district, and she left him to enter the local outlet of Maya de Mexico. She had occasionally shopped in the Mexico City branch and was confident of the quality of the merchandise. She asked the clerk to show her their bathing suits.

The style, Dorlisa discovered, ran to abbreviated costumes far more daring than the last suit she had owned. With a start, she realized that this had been nearly ten years ago; she'd had no reason to buy one since. And for just a moment she wondered why she was buying one now. She argued this feeling away. Her duties for this day were completed, and there was no reason she couldn't devote at least a few hours to her own pleasure.

However, her abandon did not extend to purchasing the bikini type she was shown at first. She inquired after something cut along more conservative lines and finally settled for a simple one-piece suit of black nylon. It still exposed more of her body than she would have preferred, but it was the best she could do. The clerk showed obvious disapproval of Dorlisa's choice; this particular suit, she explained, was usually bought by middle-aged matrons or by fathers for their daughters. It was too plain, too austere—if the señorita wished to appear truly chic ...

Dorlisa stuck to her decision. But the remark rankled. Was that what Cox would think too when he saw her in the suit, that she lacked the youthful daring necessary for the current mode? Her gaze fastened on a headless dummy garbed in panties and brassiere. The garments were of white lace, gossamer thin, about as practical as a cobweb.

As the salesgirl approached her again, the wrapped bathing suit in her hands, Dorlisa said impulsively, "The lingerie—do you have it in my size?"

"Of course." The clerk couldn't suppress a look of surprise. "But this is our bridal design. Perhaps something more substantial would be to your liking."

Dorlisa felt herself blush but she said doggedly, "I wish to buy these. Will you wrap them separately, please?" After all, she reasoned, she needed to replace the lingerie stolen with her suitcase; she owned nothing beyond what she wore. And if the lacy garments were not her usual style, no one would ever know it except her mirror.

Nevertheless, her cheeks were still warm when she rejoined Cox in the automobile, and the lingerie was hidden in her purse. He was staring out the window. He seemed almost to have forgotten about her. His greeting was abstracted. "Did you get what you were looking for?"

"I believe so." She waited for him to question her about the surprise she had promised. When he didn't, she finally asked, "Would you like to see what I bought?"

"Didn't seem to me that you were gone long enough to buy anything."

"You're certainly not very complimentary. It's been thirty-five minutes. Perhaps I won't show you, after all, if that's going to be your attitude."

His smile flickered briefly. "You know you're dying to."

"And you know entirely too much about women. All right, then—I will show you." She withdrew the bathing suit from the paper bag and held it up shyly. "Do you like it?"

He inspected it quizzically. "Looks interesting."

"You should have seen what they tried to sell me. Interesting is hardly the word for them. I hope you won't mind that I chose one a little less revealing."

"My theory is that a woman should leave something to the imagination."

"Then we agree." She put the suit away. "Well, Jack, do you approve more of this surprise than the first one?"

"I'm not sure I understand it yet."

"What are bathing suits for? I'm accepting your invitation to spend the afternoon at the beach. I suppose there's some place where I can change."

"Oh, the picnic. Dorlisa, I'm afraid I'm going to have to back out on you."

It was the last thing she had expected, "Oh, really?"

"While I was waiting for you, I happened to remember that I've got to be at the track this afternoon. Tuesday's the day the American horses come out of quarantine."

She listened to his explanation, how race horses whose owners wished to return them to the United States must undergo an examination by the port veterinarian, and how he as a trainer must be present to sign the certificates. The excuse was reasonable enough but she was conscious of an aching disappointment, both in him and in herself that she had put herself in the position to be brushed aside like this. She cut across his apologies, "I understand perfectly. Your work must come first."

"Yeah, I guess that's it, all right. Don't think I'm not sorry."

There was a lesson here, and she hoped she had learned it. If his job came first, then so did hers—to the exclusion of everything and everyone. She said coldly, "It's probably just as well, anyway. I have a thousand things to do at the house." She couldn't think of one, but not for all the world would she have let him know it.

After he had deposited Dorlisa at her rented house, Cox wondered if he had acted rashly. Her farewell had been formal and chilly; he knew her pride was hurt. But that wasn't the worst of it. Casting about for an excuse to detach himself for the balance of the afternoon, he had been forced to concoct a lie. The American horses came out of quarantine on Mondays, not Tuesdays. A simple phone call would reveal the falsehood. He felt sure he could sweet-talk Dorlisa into forgiving the brush-off. But once she conceived him to be a liar there would be little chance of ever regaining her trust.

He had to gamble on the assumption that checking on him, at least in this particular matter, wouldn't occur to her. In his favor was the fact that the rented house contained no telephone as yet. Cox couldn't picture Dorlisa going elsewhere to find a telephone merely for this purpose, since the affair concerned her personally and not her employer, Lazar. It was much more in her character to retreat into a pretended indifference.

On the other hand, as he had admitted before, she was full of surprises.

He felt the gamble worth it. For the first time, he sensed the inexorable ticking of the clock, chopping away the minutes until Thursday. Yesterday, with all his plans made, he had believed he possessed all the time in the world. Now, thwarted by her damned foresight, he had to start over again and every hour of daylight was vital.

He returned again to Los Remedios. This time he did not stop but drove around the cathedral slowly, studying the terrain. There was no possible way to attack Lazar upon his arrival, save for a point-blank ambush. Cox had no intention of participating in a scheme of that sort. He would be seen and identified, making his apprehension certain— if he were able to escape at all. No thanks.

The only point at which Lazar would be exposed was during the graveside rites in the cemetery behind the cathedral. The surrounding wall was high but a man standing, say, on the roof of an automobile might mount it. Yet the same objections held here. The deed, if it were accomplished at all, must be done minus witnesses.

But how? With the tower of the industrial school now out of the question, what hiding place was left? For a moment, Cox considered ditching the whole thing, returning the advance payment to Gayoso with regrets. But the alternative—reverting to his stateless, purposeless existence—was so bleak that he couldn't stomach it. There had to be another solution.

With determination, Cox studied the two eminences that commanded a view of the cemetery. Neither the bull-ring nor the wooded hillock was as ideal as the tower had been in terms of distance or concealment. Dorlisa, in fact, had dismissed them as danger points. An average marksman with an average rifle would agree with her. But the Krag was an exceptional weapon, and in Cox's trunk was a medal for sharp-shooting. With a little luck, it might be possible.

He drove back to his quarters at the track and dug out the telescopic sight. He returned to reconnoiter the sites more closely. The elevation was roughly the same for both, so he chose the hillock since it was a trifle closer to the cemetery. There was no road to the summit, but a winding path led upward through the brush to a cluster of scrubby live oaks. Cox sat down in their shade and gazed around. From the absence of trash, it could be deduced that no one frequented the spot except an occasional child seeking adventure in this tiny patch of wilderness. Children presented no difficulty; they could be frightened away by a bluster of adult authority. Picnickers might be a different matter. This reminded him of Dorlisa and he smiled thinly. If she could only see him now ...

Satisfied that he was not observed, Cox took out the telescopic sight. Sitting cross-legged on the ground, his back against the bole of an oak, he focussed on the target area. The diggers were still lazily at work on Sotomayor's grave. He was able to make out their features clearly. Seeing the target was not the same thing as hitting it, of course, but if the rifle was all that Gayoso claimed the rest depended squarely on his skill.

Cox's spirits began to rebound. In some ways, the hill might prove to be a better blind than even the tower, despite the greater distance involved. The opportunity for shooting down Lazar on the church steps had been measured in seconds. Anything might have intervened to spoil his shot, another mourner stepping unwittingly into the line of fire, for instance. In the cemetery, he would have several minutes at his disposal, minutes in which Lazar would be standing reverently motionless while the casket was lowered into the earth. Perhaps Dorlisa, by forcing him to change his plans, had actually done him a favor, after all.

One task remained: to make sure that, in the less than forty-eight hours left, Dorlisa did not force him to change his plans again.

Cox descended the hill to where he had left his automobile. He moved as rapidly as he was able on the broken ground—an accident would be fatal to his escape—and clocked the result on his stop-watch. The retreat occupied a mere twenty-four seconds. It would probably take longer than that for Bruno Lazar to die.

Dorlisa sat in the dark patio and listened to the burbling of the fountain. She debated again turning off the water and decided again not to bother. It was the only sound in the house not of her own making. This evening even a poor companion was better than none.

It had been a long afternoon. As Cox had foreseen, she had spent most of it convincing herself that she really preferred solitude, anyway. The coming of darkness revealed this for the fraud it was. From the living-room window she could see the lights of other dwellings, homes where families gathered and friends were made welcome. They served to emphasize her isolation. It was a sensation she had not experienced in years, not since the first frightened days at convent school. She had believed Dorlisa von Ritter to be completely self-contained. Now she knew otherwise. Jack Cox had acted on her system like an hors d'oeuvre, awakening a thirst for companionship that she had forgotten existed.

She knew that it was a thirst not likely to be satisfied. She tried to hate him for making her aware of it. It was easier to blame herself. If he had not lived up to her expectations, the real fault lay with the expectations rather than the man. What an idiot she'd been, buying the lacy lingerie as if for a trousseau or a hope chest! At twenty-nine, she was still acting like a convent girl.

She drifted about the big empty house like a ghost, seeking diversion. Finding none that suited her, she came to sit in the darkened patio. One conclusion was inescapable: she would see no more of Jack Cox. Only in that manner could she regain her former detachment. She had been contented before; she would be again. The decision was made easier by the fact that Cox had given her no reason to believe he intended to see her again, either.

The doorbell rang. Dorlisa knew, surely and instinctively, who must be. She stalked through the living room toward the front door. She inquired coldly through the panel, "Who is it?"

"Special Delivery," Cox's voice replied. "Got a package for you."

She opened the door as far as the night-latch which he had installed permitted and viewed him through the aperture. "I don't see any package."

"It's me," he said. "I'm the package."

"I don't recall ordering you."

"Wouldn't you like a free home demonstration, lady? Absolutely no obligation to buy."

All the proud intentions in the world weren't proof against the surge of pleasure she felt in meeting him again and hearing his amiable drawl. Intelligence demanded that she send him away, but stronger than logic was the simple fact that she didn't want to. She found her fingers were trembling as she undid the latch to admit him.

Cox came in with one arm held behind his back. With a flourish, he produced a bouquet of long-stemmed roses. "For you. By way of apology."

She accepted the flowers numbly. The crimson buds glistened with moisture from the florist's refrigerator. "Thank you," she murmured. "They're beautiful. But it wasn't necessary."

"It makes me feel better. For what happened this afternoon."

"You had work to do."

"No," he said calmly. "That's what's bothering me. I lied to you."

She could only gaze at him with startled eyes.

"I didn't really have to be at the track. It was just an excuse. I don't know what happened to me out there at the graveyard. The whole thing got under my skin somehow. I felt like I wasn't fit company for anybody. I had to get away by myself for a while until I got over my black mood. I guess the whole thing sounds pretty ridiculous, doesn't it?"

It did, and she believed him for that reason; it would have been so easy to invent a better story. "No, it's not really ridiculous. I have moods, too."

"But that's a woman's prerogative. Men are supposed to know better." He shook his head in disgust. "Believe it or not, I spent my afternoon sitting under an oak tree, wondering if you'd forgive me."

She bent her head over the flowers. "I wondered, too."

"I wouldn't blame you a bit if you didn't. But if you've got a mind to, the picnic basket is still in the car. The beach is better at night than in the daytime, anyway." He watched het anxiously. "You can say no if you want. I'll go quietly."

She said softly, "If I'd been able to say no, I wouldn't have opened the door."

"Well," he said with relief. "I feel a hundred per cent better."

"So do I," she admitted, not looking at him. "Please wait for me while I change. I won't be long, Jack."

She escaped into her bedroom before he could discern the tears in her eyes. When, she wondered, was the last time she'd cried? And when was the last time that anyone had given her roses?

She retrieved the black bathing suit from the corner where she'd thrown it. As she dressed, she caught a glimpse of herself in the mirror. Or was it a stranger in the glass, some unknown virginal creature with flushed cheeks and trembling expectant body? *You fool*, reason whispered. But the woman in the mirror wasn't listening. *Please*, she was entreating, *please make me as beautiful as I feel.*

Odilia was pleased with what she saw. The reflection in her mirror was exactly what she had intended it to be an hour before when she had set out to create it, demure yet inviting. To that end, she had swept her auburn hair above her tiny ears and had donned a gray suit, modestly cut, undecorated save for a small jeweled pin in the shape of a sea horse worn over her left breast. Spike-heeled pumps gave her added height and, she believed, a certain regal bearing.

She hoped that Jack Cox would find her appearance exciting. Men generally—and particularly those not gentlemen born—derived a perverse satisfaction that went beyond mere lust in possessing a woman who also appeared to be a lady. It fed their egos as well as their appetites. Virgins were prized for the same reason. And while Cox could scarcely be expected to consider her the latter, there was no reason that he might not be convinced that she was, regardless, still the former.

Odilia had spent the day doing what was, for her, a great deal of thinking. The notion conceived at their first meeting, that Cox might prove to be the instrument that would restore her to her former privileged position, had become an obsession with her. In the two days since their parting, she had waited hopefully for him to return. He had not done so, nor had he sent any message which would indicate he remembered her as anything except a convenient bed partner. She could feel opportunity slipping through her fingers until, this evening, she had decided to seize the initiative. If Cox was too engrossed with his assignment to think of her, then he needed to be reminded of what he was missing.

That she faced competition in the person of Dorlisa Weber simply didn't occur to Odilia. If it had, she would have laughed at the idea. Who should know better than she what kind of woman a man like Cox preferred?

Earlier, when she had made her decision, she had instructed Domingo the boatswain to have the launch ready to take her ashore. When she went on deck, carrying her overnight case, she thought she spied him lounging at the gangway. As she approached, she discovered it was Gayoso instead.

"Good evening, my dear," he greeted her. "Going for a little stroll?"

It had been her intention to slip away from the yacht without informing the General. But his presence, as well as his faintly mocking tone, told her that he was already aware of her plans. She said defiantly, "I'm going ashore for a little while."

"A little while," he repeated, surveying the overnight case. "Of course. You're taking a few things to be laundered."

As always, she was no match for him at repartée. "Think what you like," she muttered.

"Thank you. Well, if laundry is not the reason, what can it be? Perhaps you're tired of shipboard life and yearn to stretch your legs.

Or perhaps this is a shopping expedition to buy souvenirs of Tijuana for your family. Have I hit upon it yet? It's really not kind of you to keep me guessing this way, Odilia."

Odilia was silent. Gayoso pretended to be struck by a sudden thought. "I know!" he exclaimed, snapping his fingers. "You're lonely. You wish to visit a friend, isn't that it?"

Odilia blurted, "Why do you bait me like this? You already know where I'm going."

"I do," Gayoso said coldly. "Back to your stateroom where you belong. Your North American will have to get along without your charming company tonight."

"You don't have any right to stop me. I'm not harming the cause."

"Whose cause—yours or mine? I believe I know what you have in mind, Odilia, and I don't intend to let you interfere with my plans."

"That isn't the real reason. You enjoy oppressing me."

Gayoso pursed his lips. "You may be right. If so, I agree that I have no real reason to stop you." He considered. "I have no wish to be a tyrant. I pride myself on my fairness. You may go."

His sudden reversal bewildered her. She stammered, "Thank you, General—I am very grateful." She hastened by him, fearful that he would change his mind again. At the head of the gangway she halted, staring down.

"Unfortunately," Gayoso said, "I was forced to dispatch the launch on another errand. But it's not a long swim, scarcely a mile. And look!" He pointed toward the beach where a bonfire glowed. "Someone has kindly built a fire where you can dry yourself afterward."

"You bastard." Odilia spit the epithet at him. "Swamp Indian!"

"Don't derange yourself, my dear. Life consists of bowing gracefully to circumstances. I understand your disappointment but if it's merely a matter of male companionship, perhaps I—"

She flung herself away from his grasp with a shudder of disgust. "Keep your hands off me! I'm not one of your cadets at the military academy." In the throbbing silence that followed, the accusation hung in the air like a sword, pointed at her. Frightened, she whispered, "I didn't mean what I said. Please believe me. I'm overwrought."

At last, Gayoso said, "Of course, you didn't mean it. You know how such a slander might provoke me. You know how I might retaliate, don't you, Odilia?"

"I know," she said humbly, all fight gone. "Please don't punish me that way. I can't live without my medicine."

"There's no reason you should have to as long as we understand each other. I suggest that you go below now and refresh yourself with your medicine. And leave your door unlocked." Gayoso stroked his hand slowly down her arm. "Should I decide later to remove any doubts concerning me that may still be troubling you."

They ran, laughing, from the surf and flung themselves down upon their blanket. Dorlisa removed the bathing cap and shook her head so that her hair swirled about her face. The flickering light from their fire made it gleam like polished gold. "Oh, that was wonderful!" she said, still gasping from the exertion. "It's been years since I felt so young and reckless."

Cox lay on his back, watching her as she stretched like a tawny cat. He said, "Being young is all in the mind. The years don't matter much."

"I suppose. But I think it's really a question of happiness."

"Have you been unhappy a long time, Dorlisa?"

She pondered the question. "Not unhappy—just not happy."

"That's too fine a line for me."

"I don't know if I can explain. It's as if my emotions have been—well, frozen, so that I couldn't feel anything."

He touched her gravely with his forefinger. "Feel that?"

"Oh, you know what I mean. You must—because it's your doing. You've brought me back to life again, Jack."

"I didn't know I was so talented." He dropped his bantering tone in the face of her seriousness. "Don't give me all the credit. You were ready to rejoin the living. I was just lucky enough to be around when it happened."

"I don't believe that. You really don't know anything about me, the kind of existence I've led. I'm not exactly the woman you might suppose."

"You're young and beautiful and unattached. That's enough for me."

"But I want you to know everything about me." She knelt above him. "It's important that you understand. Because, in a way, I'm not unattached. Have you ever heard of Bruno Lazar?"

"No, I don't think so. Wait a minute—you mentioned an Uncle Bruno ..."

"I have no uncle. That was just a story, a lie if you like. Bruno Lazar is my leader, the finest, kindest, most honorable man in the world."

"Sounds like quite a guy. I'm jealous already."

"Please don't be. Oh, how can I explain? It's all so foreign to you." She paused, frowning. "You guessed that I am not Mexican, and you were right. My home is farther south, but I haven't seen it in five years.

There was a revolution, a dictator took over, and some of us were forced to run away. Bruno Lazar was one of these. I was another. Since then, we've worked night and day to bring back honor and justice to our country."

Cox listened quietly, not interrupting her halting story. Gayoso had already made him familiar with the outline of it, although now he was hearing the other side. He had no idea which version was the truth, perhaps neither. It scarcely mattered, anyway; he had already chosen his side. Or, more precisely, the side had chosen him. They had bought his trigger finger, not his political sympathies. And democracy, he had learned, was a much-abused word.

"I swore to devote my life to the Jefe's ideals," Dorlisa told him, "hopeless though the cause sometimes seems. That's why I said I am not really unattached."

"There's more to life than causes," he reminded her. "Particularly for a woman."

"Not this woman." She hesitated and her eyes slid away from his. "At least, that's what I believed."

The way lay open for his advance but Cox sensed that he'd better proceed slowly. In telling him what she had, Dorlisa was actually arguing with herself. It was wiser not to rush her to a conclusion but let her reach it in her own time. His goal, Cox reminded himself, was not to become her lover but to remain her confidant—and never mind how sensual she looked in the fire glow. He said, "You promised to tell me everything about yourself. But you haven't."

"I suppose you mean the reason I'm here in Tijuana." She was drawing aimless patterns in the sand with her fingers. "An old friend of the Jefe's died unexpectedly, and he's coming here for the funeral Thursday. I flew ahead to make arrangements for his safety. There's always the danger his enemies may try to kill him, you know. They'd greatly like to see him silenced. So now you understand my mysterious comings and goings."

"Aren't you afraid for your own safety?"

"I'm not important enough for them to bother with. Lazar is their target. If there really is danger here." Dorlisa shrugged. "So far I'm not sure. The newspaper ad I placed, which he will see before he arrives in Tijuana, advised the Jefe to use caution. And, of course, I still have another means to warn him off even at the last moment."

Cox longed to ask what this final signal might be but he knew better. "Thanks for trusting me with all this, Dorlisa."

She turned her head to look at him. "I don't know why I have. I swore

I'd never trust another man."

"When I said you hadn't told me everything, I really wasn't thinking of your job. I was thinking of your husband."

"I was married when I was nineteen and widowed when I was twenty-four. I loved him very much, and he turned out to be a traitor." Her voice was flat. "Now you can stop thinking about my husband."

"Suits me—as long as I don't have to stop thinking about you. Hasn't there been anybody since?"

"No, not really. Oh, there's Vicario, of course. He's a young man who also works for Lazar. He has the unhinged notion that he loves me."

"I don't see anything so unhinged about that."

"Isn't it senseless to love anyone?" Her tone was shy, as if she were pleading with him to convince her otherwise. In answer, Cox polled her down against his chest. Her lips were soft, her kiss childlike. She whispered, "I don't want to be hurt again."

He knew that she was defenseless, and for the first time guilt stabbed him. Until this moment it had been an amusing game. But suddenly it was not so damn funny, after all. Was it possible that the joke was actually on him?

His silence didn't bother Dorlisa. She rested her cheek on his bare chest. She murmured, "How strange life is! I fell into your arms the first time we met. Now I never want to be anywhere else."

"Maybe you wouldn't feel that way if you knew more about me."

"But I know everything about you, Jack." Despite himself, Cox stiffened. Dorlisa didn't seem to notice. She went on lazily, "I know that you were born, and that you were once a little boy, and that you grew up to be a man with strong arms. What else is there to know?"

Now was the opportunity to push her away, to blunt the moment with humor. To continue in the present vein was dangerous to both of them. It was not right that he should desire her; he didn't dare feel compassion or tenderness. She was his enemy.

Yet he could not bring himself to make the necessary move. Passion he was well acquainted with, but sweetness had been rare in his life. So he allowed her to cuddle against his chest while his resolution crumbled. *What the hell*, he thought, *might as well enjoy what I can— it'll be over soon enough, anyway*. He began to stroke the curves of her body.

Dorlisa sat up suddenly. He thought at first that she was offended, but then he saw that her head was cocked, listening "What's that noise?" she asked.

He heard it too, the chugging of an engine. "Sounds like a motorboat."

"That's exactly what it is." She pointed toward the jetty two hundred yards distant. They watched the dark shape of a launch, its wake faintly phosphorescent, as it headed toward the lights of the vessel anchored offshore. "That must be the yacht I saw from the air. I wonder who it belongs to."

"Maybe it's a pirate ship."

"It looks so beautiful." She hugged her knees pensively. "I wish it were ours, Jack. Wouldn't it be wonderful if you and I were able to sail away together, any place we pleased?"

For an instant, it did sound wonderful. But *La Polilla's* lights, Gayoso's headquarters, brought him back to reality. He couldn't have everything. "Maybe we could arrange it—after Thursday, I mean."

"Thursday," she mused. "Yes, there will be an afterward, won't there? I'd nearly forgotten there was anything except tonight." She shivered. "I think you'd better take me home now."

"If you're cold, I can build up the fire."

"No, suddenly I'm very frightened. I feel as if my whole life has changed, and I need time to adjust to the idea." She hesitated. "But if you want me to stay, I will."

He shook his head. "I don't want to rush you into anything, Dorlisa."

"Thank you for being strong. I'll make it up to you, I promise." She brushed a quick kiss across his lips and sprang to her feet. "Come on— I'll race you to the car."

Cox let her win. His victory was still to come.

DAY ONE

The sound of birds awakened her. Dorlisa lay for a while in the blissful state between sleep and awareness, listening to their chirping blend with the cheerful gurgling of the patio fountain. At last, she raised herself lazily on one elbow until she could gaze out the window of her bedroom. A half-dozen sparrows strutted about the Aztec idol, hopping in and out of the spray, ruffling their feathers to dry them. Their pleasure was obvious; the long-dormant fountain was flowing again.

Dorlisa felt a kinship with the sparrows. Her life for the past five years resembled the fountain, dry and dusty. Now all at once, a hidden tap had been turned on and her emotions allowed to pour forth. And if, like the fountain water, they had grown a bit rusty with disuse, only a little time was necessary to make them flow clear and strong once more.

A little time ... That was what she had asked of Cox the night before. Time to adjust to her changed status as woman rather than soldier. Time to catch her breath and to think. But Dorlisa admitted to herself that she was feeling, not thinking, and that she was guided by sensation instead of logic. She couldn't be intellectual about love.

She drew back a little from the word. Was she being premature, imagining something that didn't exist? A man could conjure up a mirage of water simply because he thirsted for it. She might be guilty of the same sort of thing; no binding words had actually passed between them. Dorlisa couldn't believe it. Her feeling was too strong to be an illusion. But did Cox share it, or was he merely the basin into which her awakened passion flowed? She conjured up the precious evening, moment by moment. Yes, unmistakably there was a communication between them that went beyond language. And beyond simple physical desire. His forbearance on the beach proved that he sought something from her besides her body. He could have taken that without a struggle. Yet, though aroused, he had not taken advantage of her fleshly weakness.

"I love him." She was amazed at how fresh the words sounded. She had said them before, and sometimes meant them, but now they had the ring of being invented for this moment. Tonight she would tell him. Tonight, and every night afterward.

With a wrench, Dorlisa remembered that tomorrow was Thursday. The future was not merely a long succession of idyllic evenings on a deserted beach. It was cluttered with responsibilities and crowded by outsiders. Her dreamy isolation was unreal; it would not continue. Tomorrow her past would collide with her present—and what would happen to the future then? She tried to picture her friends, Bruno Lazar and Vicario and Dr. Neve, somewhere on the road to Tijuana. They were drawing closer every moment, bringing with them another passenger, Decision. She knew that her life with them and the life she imagined with Cox were not homogeneous. Try as she might, she was not able to fit him into the framework of her existence as it had been. She would have to make a choice.

But not today, and perhaps not even tomorrow. Time had a way of solving problems, or at least presenting new ones, that made it foolish to worry. Whatever Thursday held, Wednesday was surely hers.

Dorlisa slid out of bed and stretched luxuriously. And for a moment she could not comprehend what was different from her usual arising. It was only when she saw the cotton pajamas still hanging in the closet that she remembered. With a guilty smile, she thought that was somehow symbolic. For the first time in her life she had slept in the nude.

Gayoso opened the Tijuana newspaper to the classified advertising and spread it out upon the coffee table. Jack Cox, seated opposite him in the yacht's salon, said, "It's in the personals. I marked the spot."

Gayoso read the notice and then passed it to Balbin who stood stiffly behind his chair. "Innocuous enough on the surface. Do you understand the code?"

"The address is the house she's rented. The color—yellow—is to warn Lazar to use caution."

"But not to turn back," Gayoso said with satisfaction. "Fortune remains our beloved."

"Fortune and us are still not out of the woods. There's a final signal Mrs. Weber can use if things go wrong. I haven't found out what it is yet."

"You will," Gayoso complimented him. "You seem to be in complete command of the situation."

"Yeah," Cox agreed without enthusiasm. "I'm doing great."

Gayoso studied the American thoughtfully. His training had made him acutely aware of nuances, and it seemed to him that Cox was a bit remote this morning. Something appeared to be bothering him. Did Cox, after all, have a soft spot? In a job like this, softness of any kind could be dangerous. He said, "I'm sure I don't have to emphasize how important the next twenty-four hours are to the success of our mission."

"I'm sure you don't, General."

"Everything hinges on the woman. You've made a splendid beginning, but she still has the power to destroy everything. You must, by all means, retain her confidence. Find out the final signal if you can, but not at the risk of jeopardizing your position."

"I'll do my best."

"Of course you will. You stand to lose more than any of us if the scheme fails." Gayoso thought Cox needed a glimpse of the carrot. "There are no consolation prizes in this business."

Cox got the hint. His eyes gleamed angrily. "I remember the deal."

"Personally, I will be delighted when this is all behind us and I can return to my true trade, which is soldiering," Gayoso said blandly. "No one detests this infernal cloak-and-dagger work more than I. Balbin can tell you."

"That is certainly true, General," Balbin said with a straight face.

"But we must all swallow our natural aversion to it, eh?" Gayoso leaned forward to punch Cox lightly on the knee. "Think past Thursday, my friend—a more normal life is in store for you also. Look at it this way: Lazar must die in order that you may live."

Cox said, "I'm not chickening out, if that's what you're worried about. I went into this thing for the money, and I still want it. But there's nothing in our bargain that says I have to enjoy the work, is there?"

"On the contrary, this is an affair in which personal feelings don't matter in the slightest. Hate it as much as you like—I respect you for it. No sane man enjoys war. We endure it simply for the victory."

Cox chewed his lip moodily. "Yeah, you're right about that. You've got to keep your eye on the ball."

The salon door opened, and Odilia swept in. She wore a cherry-colored sun dress, strapless to demonstrate the whiteness of her shoulders, and her face glowed with beauty. She saw Cox, and her eyes widened. "Jack!" she cried. "What a delightful surprise!"

It was all pretense, Gayoso knew. Odilia had been aware of Cox's arrival aboard the yacht and had scurried below to repair her appearance. It amused him to permit the deception, however. At the moment, Odilia might have some therapeutic value.

Cox rose to greet the girl but his "Good morning" lacked warmth. He made no effort to hold onto the hand she offered him. Odilia pretended to pout. "You've stayed away from us all this time, and now you don't even attempt to apologize. I don't believe I'll forgive you."

"I'm sorry," Cox muttered. "I've been busy."

"In that case, I'll relent," Odilia said gaily. "I forgive you. But only on the condition that you are very, very nice to me for the rest of the day."

Cox didn't appear to have heard. He looked at Gayoso. "I'd better go. I have a date for lunch in an hour."

Odilia couldn't believe she was being ignored. She grasped Cox's arm. "Surely, you don't have to leave so quickly. I want you to stay here. Oh, you're trying to tease me."

"Some other time," Cox said. He freed his arm.

"But if I coax you a little you'll reconsider, won't you?" Odilia was begging now. "Have you forgotten how persuasive I can be, Jack? Jack?"

Gayoso, watching the byplay, thought he saw an expression of distaste cross Cox's face. Cox said, "I've got a lot of things to do. Sorry." He turned away from her.

Odilia took his brusqueness like a slap in the face. But for pride's sake she fought to maintain her previous gaiety. "Certainly, Jack, I understand. Your business must come first. I'm not offended, don't worry about that, and when you're able to ..." She trailed off uncertainly. Cox was already on his way out the door.

Gayoso murmured, "Perhaps you should have taken that swim, after all." He followed Cox onto the deck and caught up with him at the head of the gangway. He said, "A final word before you go." Cox waited. "Don't think too much. It clouds the shooting eye."

"You just be sure to have the money ready," Cox told him. He went down the steps to the waiting launch without a farewell.

Gayoso leaned on the rail and watched the small boat pull away. Balbin joined him. After a while, Gayoso said, "As a shrewd judge of character, did you notice anything different about our monkey?"

"I merely find him more repugnant with each meeting."

"He shows signs of developing a conscience. And he was exceedingly cool toward our fair Odilia. I wonder if Mrs. Weber is responsible on both counts."

"Would you like me to find out? I'll be happy to keep an eye on him."

"No, the best thing to do is to leave him alone. I was careful to point out where his interests lie."

"If he is truly under the influence of the Weber woman, he may decide to double-cross us. After all, he is a Yankee and therefore without honor."

Gayoso stared thoughtfully across the blue water toward the receding launch. Cox was seated in the stem, erect and aloof; he had not glanced back once at the yacht. "There is always that possibility," Gayoso agreed. "But, in that case, I have a suitable checkmate in mind."

Those aboard *La Polilla* were not the only ones who studied the Tijuana *Heraldo* that morning. The armored sedan which bore Bruno Lazar and his party had halted for refueling in Hermosillo. This capital city of Sonora, most northern and western of all the Mexican states save only Baja California Norte itself, was large enough to carry a supply of out-of-town newspapers.

Rolling northward once more, they discussed the cryptic message that Dorlisa had placed in the personals column.

"It merely bears out what I've been trying to say all along," Vicario argued. "Things are not as they should be in Tijuana."

Lazar sighed. "Whatever became of the impetuousness of youth?

Considering the difference in our ages, I should be the one who trembles at shadows, not you."

"If I tremble," Vicario said hotly, "it is not for my own safety."

"Why tremble at all? It's a poor way to live. Bear this in mind, Vicario. Between the cradle and the grave, nothing is sure."

"All right then, Jefe, I'm a coward and not worth listening to. But Dorlisa, who is on the scene, feels the same as I. You've read the notice yourself."

"If Dorlisa had found tangible danger, the word would have been red, not yellow," Lazar pointed out. "Furthermore, I don't consider you a coward."

"Then do me the honor of paying some attention to what I say." Vicario's lips were thin with exasperation.

Dr. Neve, the eternal mediator, intervened with his dry voice. "Why are we arguing since we are all in agreement, anyway? We will proceed—but with caution, as Dorlisa has indicated. There's always time to turn back later when we see the final signal."

Vicario muttered, "Ask him if that's really his intention, Neve."

Neve glanced at Lazar, who was silent. Neve raised his eyebrows. "Well, Bruno?"

"I'm not sure." Lazar gave a wry chuckle.

"You see?" Vicario said with weary triumph. "I was right."

"But why?" Neve demanded. "Surely, you trust Dorlisa. If not, why bother sending her ahead? It makes no sense not to be guided by her recommendations now. If that's your intention, it would be far simpler to write General Gayoso a letter and tell him where you intend to be, and when."

"Don't you think it possible to trust a person without necessarily trusting in his judgment?" Lazar inquired. "You should, since that is the attitude you both have adopted toward me. Very well, I feel the same about Dorlisa."

Vicario was stung by the criticism, mild as it was. "That's an unfair thing to say, Jefe. I'd put my life in Dorlisa's hands."

"I know," Lazar said gently. "But we are looking at her with different sets of eyes. Say that she is intelligent, shrewd and loyal, and I'll agree that she is all these things and more. But I also know that she is capable of certain blind responses that, under the right circumstances, might mislead her. This is not an accusation, Vicario, so don't bristle at me. It is merely another way of saying that she is a woman."

"Then why did you allow her to go?"

"I'm afraid that was your idea, yours and Neve's. I merely agreed to it to please you. Therefore, I reserve the right to make my own decisions."

Neve was shaking his head so vigorously that his spade beard seemed to quiver. "You're changing the rules after the game has begun. I'm shocked, Bruno. Such unilateral behavior isn't worthy of you. All I can conclude is that Vicario was right yesterday, and that you do yearn to become a martyr."

Lazar was silent for a long while. At last, he said grudgingly, "I find I am still vain enough to value your good opinion of me. I'll play the game according to your rules."

"And you agree to turn back if the final signal warrants it?" Vicario pressed.

"That's what I said," Lazar snapped. He turned away from his companions pettishly and stared out the window. "And now kindly permit me to enjoy the scenery. It may be my last opportunity."

Cox drove slowly back into the city. He felt somewhat relieved. Gayoso had hardened his resolve again, reminding him of where he stood. For a while last night, he had nearly forgotten. The line that separated him from Dorlisa Weber had become blurred by emotion. Sympathy—or something—had caused him to lose sight momentarily of his objective, which was a new and better life for Jack Cox. He'd have to be more careful in the future.

It wasn't going to be easy. Her trust was disarming. Somehow he must play the lover to her satisfaction but without committing himself. He must walk a tight-rope across a dark, unsounded pit. If he allowed himself to fall, there was no telling where he might land.

Compared to this, the actual assassination of Bruno Lazar seemed the simplest part of his task.

Within five minutes, he discovered how wrong he could be. He was heading for his quarters at the track to change his clothes prior to his luncheon engagement with Dorlisa. His route took him close by the cathedral. His glance went automatically to the nearby hillock that tomorrow would serve as his sniper's nest. What he saw made him forget about his emotional tangle.

The hill, deserted yesterday, was swarming with activity today. Surveyors with transits were directing the placing of elevation stakes around the summit, and when Cox drove closer he discovered that a bulldozer was already chewing away the sagebrush on the slopes.

Stunned, Cox stopped a workman and inquired what was going on. He learned that this was part of the subdivision whose houses would eventually march right up to the cathedral walls. Because of the view, the hill offered particularly choice homesites, show-places that would be used to sell less desirable locations in the flat below.

"Are you going to clear the whole thing?" Cox asked, clinging to a faint hope.

The workman laughed. "By next week, it will be as bald as my father-in-law." He pointed upward at the live oaks under which Cox had sat. "The trees are being leveled already. Makes you think, eh? It took them twenty years to grow but in twenty minutes they are destroyed."

Cox was in no mood for philosophy. The trees weren't the only thing that faced destruction. The success of his whole plan was in jeopardy, and for the second time. He had rebounded from the first setback, but now he had a bare twenty-four hours left.

There was another deadline, though comparatively minor. In fifteen minutes he was due to meet Dorlisa for lunch. He didn't much care to make her wait, particularly not today when it was imperative that he remain in her good graces. But keeping Dorlisa content and unsuspicious would count for nothing unless he could come up with a solution for this new problem.

He rushed back to his quarters and, once again, plucked the telescopic sight from its hiding place. It was, he thought, becoming a daily ritual, but one he'd prefer to give up. He hesitated a moment, debating whether to change clothes, then decided it might save time later on. He threw on the tropical slacks and flowered shirt he'd bought yesterday, jammed the straw hat on his head and ran for his automobile.

There was no opportunity now for a leisurely survey of the terrain. Nor was one needed. Only one vantage point remained, and even that might prove to be unsatisfactory. Cox parked in the shadow of the steel bull-ring and trotted around its base, seeking an entrance.

He found one door open into a shadowy passageway that brought him out into the sunlight once more on a level with the arena. He was not the only trespasser. On the sandy floor a group of boys were playing at bullfighting. One of them held two sticks to his temples and, with head lowered, charged the would-be matadors who taunted him with their ragged shirts. Their screams of delight and mock terror made the huge amphitheater echo. They paid no attention to Cox's arrival.

He climbed swiftly up past the rows of empty seats to the top of the stadium and then along the rim to the point closest to the cathedral. It was, he realized bleakly, still a considerable distance. The shot would strain the ability of both the rifle and himself. Was it possible at all?

With a glance around to see that he wasn't observed, he dug out the telescopic sight. He squinted through it toward the cemetery. Sotomayor's grave had been completed and the diggers had departed, leaving the mound of fresh earth covered by a tarpaulin. Beside it stood the young priest he'd met yesterday, his head bent in meditation.

Cox focussed the cross-hairs on the black-robed figure in grim speculation, his own attitude prayerful. After a moment, the priest turned and walked away toward the rear of the cathedral, and Cox lowered the sight. He didn't know whose prayer was going to be answered, if either, but Cox was relieved to learn that his own still had a fighting chance.

In the arena below, the boys were shouting *"Heh, toro!"* and stamping their feet while one of them, armed with a curtain rod, prepared to administer the *coup de grace* to the make-believe bull.

Yes, he could do it. He could still reach out across the intervening distance, formidable as it was, and strike down Bruno Lazar according to plan. Not as easily as from the tower, nor as safely as from the hilltop—but Lazar would be just as dead.

"If nothing else goes wrong," he said aloud. As late as yesterday afternoon, he'd been confident that nothing would. Now he was not so sure. In this affair, which had seemed almost cut-and-dried at the beginning, everything appeared subject to change without notice, himself included.

As he left the stadium, the boys were yelling *"Olé!"* at the top of their lungs. The one with the curtain-rod sword pranced back and forth, bowing to the non-existent crowd. Although he was already late, Cox paused to watch their antics thoughtfully. For the boys, the game had ended predictably and happily. He wondered how his own game would end.

"Are you certain that you would not prefer to be seated?" the waiter inquired for the third time.

"Thank you, but I'll wait here," Dorlisa told him firmly. "My husband will arrive at any moment." The waiter, drifting away, looked doubtful. She couldn't blame him; she was becoming doubtful herself. Cox was already a half-hour late. Dorlisa was tired of hovering at the mouth of the little café, continually in the way of other patrons entering or leaving. She fancied everyone was staring at her. Her neck ached from craning to look at each passing pedestrian.

Above all, she was puzzled. She couldn't understand Cox's behavior, so considerate one moment, so unconcerned the next. When they had made the luncheon date, he had offered to pick her up at the house to save her inconvenience. She had refused; she had some shopping to do and hadn't wished to drag him from store to store, something a man didn't usually enjoy. She had cut her shopping short in order not to keep him waiting. Then he hadn't even bothered to be on time, or to leave a message explaining why. Didn't he really care, after all? Countering her irritation was the formless worry that something might have happened to him.

At last, irritation overcame worry and Dorlisa picked up her shopping bag. It contained, in addition to a small black funeral wreath, her gray wool traveling suit. In its place, she wore the crisp summery frock she had purchased an hour before. Now she wished she hadn't bothered. With an independent toss of her head, she left the café. She ran squarely into Cox on the sidewalk outside.

He grasped her elbows. "Skipping out on me?" he asked with a grin.

"I don't think that's very funny. I've been waiting since noon."

"Hit me," he invited, indicating the point of his chin. "Right about here."

As before, Dorlisa found it difficult to remain angry with him. But her pride demanded that she not forgive him too quickly. "I'd prefer an explanation instead, if you don't mind."

"I had car trouble. The fool thing died on me out by the bull-ring."

"You could have telephoned the café."

"Well, there wasn't a phone handy—and I kept thinking I'd get it fixed in a hurry." He looked contrite. "I'm sorry I made you wait, Dorlisa."

The excuse bore a well-worn air, yet it could be true. Grudgingly, she said, "I was worried that something terrible might have happened to you."

"The only terrible thing that can happen to me is if you don't forgive me."

"Oh, I don't think you're worried about that at all." She permitted him a small smile. "You know very well that I'll forgive you."

"Serve me right if you didn't."

"Yes," she agreed. "But I prefer to have you in my debt. It's a lesson I learned from you."

He raised his eyebrows. "Go to the head of the class."

"I'd rather go to lunch. All this waiting has given me an enormous appetite." But when he turned toward the café she had left, Dorlisa held back. "Please, let's not eat there."

"Why not? It's the best food in town."

"But everyone saw me leave. If I go back now, they'll think that I picked up the first man I met, just to get lunch."

Amused, Cox said, "You sure got a devious mind, Dorlisa. Don't you know that other people don't give a hoot what you do?"

"I suppose it's the result of my training," she admitted. "You see, this sort of thing is new to me. In my country, a woman never meets a man alone in a public place—unless he is her husband. That must sound antiquated to you, but I find the habit hard to break."

"No problem. I'll try to act like your husband. It shouldn't be too hard to pretend—I've already kept you waiting."

She looked away so that he wouldn't see the wistful expression that crossed her face. She murmured, "No, it won't be hard to pretend."

There was a momentary awkward silence, then he took her arm and said, "Well ..." She nodded, and they started off down the sidewalk together. After a few steps, he asked, "What's your country like, anyway?"

"You've never been there? Oh, it's very beautiful. Much greener than Mexico because we get more rain." Her voice gained enthusiasm. "You'd love it, I think. Much of it is farmland, like your own home. Someday I'll show it to you—" She hesitated and forced a chuckle. "Someday. It's a very hollow word, isn't it?"

"Oh, I don't know. Maybe I'll see it sooner than you think."

"My family's estates were in the highlands. I was born there. It's all been confiscated, of course, but I still have hopes—" She stopped in the middle of the sidewalk, so suddenly that Cox was thrown off-balance. "Jack! Look over there!"

He followed her pointing finger. "What is it?"

"That man across the street, the little one wearing the raincoat. That's one of the men who kidnapped me at the airport!"

"Are you sure?" Cox demanded. "He looks pretty ordinary to me."

"Of course I'm sure—I got a good look at him. Please, he mustn't get away!"

"I'll get the police."

"There's no time for that." Across the street, the little man had seen them also. He was hastening away along the sidewalk, not quite running. "You can catch him yourself. You're much bigger than he is."

To her surprise, Cox hesitated. "Why bother with him? Not much chance of getting your suitcase back now."

"I don't care about my suitcase! I want to question him, find out the real reason I was kidnapped. Don't you see? It might be a matter of life and death."

"Yeah," said Cox and his expression was so odd that she wondered if he were afraid. "It might at that. Okay, I'll get him for you."

"I'm coming with you," she called. But he didn't seem to have heard. He sprinted away across the pavement after the fugitive without waiting for her.

Procope had spotted the other two a moment or so before Dorlisa became aware of him. The encounter was accidental; he was on his way to the meeting at the race track called by the waiters' union. But curiosity had impelled him to linger long enough to observe how Cox was getting along with the blonde woman. He had not counted on being recognized.

It was not the only surprise in store for him. He guessed that the woman would send Cox chasing after him. But he did not suppose that Cox would actually try to catch him. Yet, as he glanced back over his shoulder, Procope noted with dismay that the tall American was gaining on him. He didn't know what to make of this. Procope's background, which consisted principally of doing Gayoso's dirty work in the trade unions, had prepared him for nearly anything. But never before had he been pursued by an ally.

However, he didn't intend that Cox, whether friend or foe, should lay hands on him. As he ran along the sidewalk, dodging nimbly through the pedestrian traffic, he looked for some sanctuary. And found it—the mouth of an alley into which he slipped. He discovered his mistake immediately: it was a dead end, terminating at the rear of a butcher shop. Procope made the best of it. He wriggled between two enormous sides of beef that were suspended on steel hooks and hoped that he couldn't be seen at first glance.

He heard Cox's footsteps pound close, then stop. An instant later, Cox's arm grabbed his shoulder and plucked him out of his hiding place. Cox, panting, asked, "Is this the best you could do?"

Procope tried to wriggle free. "What are you doing? I don't understand you at all."

"I warned Gayoso not to have me tailed. I knew it would cause trouble. And now it has."

"But I wasn't following you! I didn't even know you were in the city. Anyway, you didn't have to catch me."

"The hell I didn't. How do you think it'd have looked if I'd refused?" Cox glanced quickly back over his shoulder at the mouth of the alley. "She'll be here any second."

"In that case, I'd better leave. I can slip into the back door of one of the shops."

Cox didn't release him. "You're staying here. You're my token of good faith, and I'm not about to lose you. You'll talk to the lady like a good little so-and-so."

"I absolutely refuse!" Procope declared vehemently. "Why, she's likely to have me arrested and then the police will ask for my papers—and before you know it everything will be ruined. Gayoso would kill me!"

"I'll make sure you get a chance to escape before the police get you."

Procope opened his mouth to voice further objection. Behind him, Cox heard the clatter of Dorlisa's high heels on the pavement. He drove his fist into Procope's stomach to end the argument and turned to face the woman as she arrived, her cheeks flushed with excitement. "This the man you meant, Dorlisa?"

"I think so." She examined Procope more closely. "Yes, I'm sure of it. Jack, I don't know how to thank you."

"Shall I call the cops now?"

"No, I want to question him first." She looked around. "We can't talk here. Where does that door lead to?"

Cox opened it. "Somebody's storeroom. It's empty." He hustled Procope roughly inside and Dorlisa followed. The room, the storage area for one of the many souvenir shops, was crowded with merchandise. Stacks of straw sombreros sat atop crates that purported to hold flagons of Chanel Number 5, near cartons of clay dolls and Mexican jumping beans. Close by the door was an opened box of machetes, made in Connecticut, big chopping knives whose blades bore the inscription, "Souvenir of Tijuana, B. C."

However, Cox had been mistaken; the storeroom was not deserted. In one corner, a teen-aged clerk slumbered on a canvas folding cot. He was snoring softly, enjoying his siesta. Dorlisa said, "You can start by telling me your name."

"Jose Gonzalez," Procope managed. He was still gasping for breath from Cox's blow to the stomach.

Dorlisa looked disgusted. "The Mexican equivalent for John Smith. Surely, you have more imagination than that. Where are you from?"

Procope hesitated. "Vera Cruz."

"You're lying. I doubt if you're even Mexican at all. I know Vera Cruz fairly well. What is San Juan de Ulua?"

"A church," Procope said readily.

"It's a prison. If you were from Vera Cruz, you'd be sure to know the jails." Dorlisa's voice was as crisp as a prosecuting attorney's. "Why did you and your friend kidnap me at the airport?"

"My family was starving, and I could not find work," Procope whined. "You rich Americans have so much money, and it seemed no great crime to take a little, when I had none."

Cox thought it was a creditable acting job but Dorlisa wasn't impressed. She said, "If you insist on lying to me, I'll have to turn you over to the authorities. Would you prefer that?"

"On the grave of my mother, señora, I am telling you the truth. You must believe me. If you will only show mercy for the sake of my children, I will promise that your belongings will be restored to you."

Dorlisa said to Cox, "Would you mind opening his coat? He must have some identification."

Cox unbuttoned Procope's raincoat. He was surprised to discover that the other man was wearing a white mess jacket beneath it, like a uniform. He recognized it immediately without even reading the lettering above the breast pocket.

Dorlisa was equally surprised. "Agua Caliente Racetrack," she read aloud. She shifted her gaze to Cox. "Isn't that where you work, Jack?"

"Yeah, but I'm in another section. This man's a waiter in the clubhouse. That is, if he didn't steal the jacket from somebody."

They were momentarily off-guard. Procope saw the opportunity. He seized one of the machetes from the packing case at his elbow. Using the flat of the blade, he struck Dorlisa a vicious blow on the temple. She sagged against the perfume crates, stunned, and Cox caught her before she could slip to the floor. He yelled at Procope, "What did you do that for, damn you?"

Procope was finding no end to surprises. "What else could I do? You promised me an opportunity to escape."

"You didn't have to hit her so bloody hard."

"I used the flat of the blade." Procope shrugged. "Considering she's an enemy, I would have been justified in using the edge, it seems to me."

Cox glared at him over Dorlisa's limp body. "And I'd have cut you up for gopher bait. If you've hurt her, I still may."

Procope retreated a couple of paces, his eyes narrowed. "Perhaps she's not the only enemy in this room. Gayoso will be interested in learning what's happened here."

"You be sure to tell him."

"I will," Procope promised. He backed out into the alley, still holding the machete. From the look in Cox's eyes, he wasn't sure that the big man wouldn't follow him. It wasn't until he reached the street that he felt safe enough to drop the long knife into the nearest trash container.

Dorlisa had not seen the blow coming and therefore had no recollection of it. One instant she was standing talking to Cox, the next she found herself drifting in a foggy world that lacked dimensions. As her mind groped back to full consciousness, she heard Cox's voice close by her ear. "My wife has fainted. Too much sun. Would you mind getting her a drink of water?"

Another male voice, more youthful in timbre, said, "Of course, just a moment ..."

Dorlisa opened her eyes. She was lying on the canvas folding cot where the clerk had been taking his siesta; it was apparently he whom Cox had asked to fetch water. She began to remember the rest of it.

Cox was kneeling beside her. His face wore an anxious expression. "How you feeling, Dorlisa?"

"All right," she said slowly. "What happened to me?"

"The little fellow hit you with one of the machetes, the flat side. I don't see any blood but—"

She sat up in alarm. "Where is he?" She realized with dismay that they were alone in the storeroom. "You let him get away?"

Before he could reply, the clerk came hustling back with a glass of water. He was relieved to see Dorlisa sitting up but offered to summon a doctor, remarking on the danger of exposure to the sun, particularly for women in a delicate condition. Apparently, he believed she was pregnant. She was too disappointed with the way things had turned out to be amused at the misapprehension. She murmured, "Please, Jack, I'd like to leave."

"My car's down the block. Sure you feel like walking that far?" He saw that she did. He thanked the clerk for his courtesy and slipped a five-dollar bill into his hand. As he helped Dorlisa out the rear door, Cox whispered, "That should cover the cost of the machete and then some. Our friend took it with him."

She faced him accusingly. "Why did you allow him to escape?"

"I had the choice of chasing after him or taking care of you. I couldn't tell how bad you were hurt."

"You made the wrong choice."

"I don't see it that way. I figure you're more important than some sneak thief. At least, as far as I'm concerned." At another time, she would have been pleased with what he said. Right now, her mind was wrestling with other implications. As they walked slowly back to where Cox's automobile was parked, she said, "He's more than a sneak thief."

"I don't see why you're so worked up about him."

"Oh, don't you? Here is a man who posed as a taxi driver in order to kidnap me. Now he appears to be a waiter at the race track. I'm wondering if this could be another pose—for another purpose."

"I told you he might have stolen the uniform."

"It fit him. And it's not something he'd be likely to wear if it didn't belong to him. No, I think it's safe to assume that he actually works at the track." She paused. "Hernando Sotomayor died at the track last Sunday of a heart attack—or so they say."

Cox's head jerked around. "What in thunder are you getting at?"

"Suddenly it seems all too coincidental. Is it possible that Sotomayor didn't die of natural causes, after all? Could he have been poisoned? It would be easy for a waiter to slip something in his drink. No one pays any attention to what a waiter does."

"There still has to be a profit, especially for murder."

"Bringing Bruno Lazar out into the open would be profit enough for a number of men I know. They'd expect him to attend the funeral of his oldest friend. But it was necessary that the friend die first."

"No," Cox said, "that's too damn farfetched. Human beings just don't operate that way."

She eyed him soberly. "Perhaps I am more experienced than you in the dark side of human nature. I can assure you that some men don't care whom they hurt as long as their own ends are served."

He started to retort to this, then thought better of it and was silent. They reached his automobile, and he assisted her to enter. He didn't start the engine but sat for a while behind the wheel in frowning concentration. Finally, he shook his head fiercely. "I can't believe it's the way you say, Dorlisa."

There seemed to be a tinge of worry to his voice, as if he had personal reasons for doubting her theory. Surely, she thought, such vehemence couldn't spring from any belief in the basic goodness of man. Her original doubts about him began to seep back. She remembered his peculiar reluctance to pursue Gonzalez or whatever his real name was, and how he had allowed him to escape. Why had the little man struck her, the woman, instead of the man, the more dangerous of the pair? And Cox worked at the race track, too. Both her kidnapper and her rescuer ... Guardedly, she said, "Perhaps you'd better take me home now, Jack."

"I thought we had a date for lunch."

"I'm no longer hungry." She wanted time to think, to sort out the ugly notions rising like mist in her mind. "I'm afraid the blow on the head has made me rather ill." It was only a half-lie; she felt suddenly sick. Yet it could not be blamed on the machete. Her head ached, but not as much as her heart.

Cox lounged in the Tijuana saloon that claimed to have "The Longest Bar in the World" and ordered another beer. He wasn't much of a drinking man; he didn't gravitate naturally to a bar when he had time to kill. But tonight he didn't care to be alone with his thoughts. The noisy, jostling crowd that thronged the establishments along Avenida Revolución suited him just fine.

Neither the beer nor the noise could keep his mind from returning to the events and discoveries of the afternoon. After parting from Dorlisa, he had gone directly to confront Gayoso. He had to admit that Gayoso had answered his accusation forcefully and candidly.

"Ridiculous!" he'd snorted, his eyes flashing behind his tinted spectacles. "As a soldier, I resent the slur. I don't mind using Sotomayor's timely death to advantage, but I'd certainly never cause an innocent bystander to be murdered. What sort of cannibal do you conceive me to be?"

"I really don't know much about any of you, General."

"You seem more willing to believe an enemy than your friends. Consider a moment. Mrs. Weber may have had her own reasons for putting this foul idea in your head. As you already know, she's a devious woman. Could she suspect your true identity?"

"I don't think so," Cox said dubiously. He remembered noticing a subtle shift in Dorlisa's attitude toward him, a withdrawal. At the time, he had accepted her explanation of illness.

"She may have some doubts regarding the manner in which you handled Procope," Gayoso mused. "I suggest you spend some hours this afternoon conducting an investigation, the results of which you can report to the lady later. Visit the waiters' union, the track stewards ... You'll learn nothing but it will make you look good."

"Then you believe that Sotomayor's death was an accident?"

"No," Gayoso said, surprising him. "On the contrary, I believe that nothing that happens here on earth is an accident. It's merely a word a man uses because he is unable to see the Divine purpose. You see, Mr. Cox, I consider that we are all instruments of Providence."

There was nothing in what Gayoso had said—or not said—to cause any doubt to remain in Cox's mind. Yet remain it did, despite his efforts to argue it away. Timely was what Gayoso had called Sotomayor's heart attack. Was it just too damn well-timed?

He left the bar and wandered uneasily along the sidewalk, ignoring the clutching hands of peddlers and taxi drivers. He had no evidence, past or present, to convict Gayoso as a liar. Nothing except intuition, the same intuition that made him able to distinguish a stake horse from a plater without ever seeing them run, a feeling for potential. Cox was sure that Gayoso was by nature a dissembler, just as he was equally sure that Dorlisa was not.

But what if he were right and Dorlisa were right—and Gayoso was lying in his teeth? What difference did it make? Cox was less than twenty-four hours away from being an assassin himself. He had contracted to deliver the corpse of a man he did not know. So, perhaps, had Procope. Only the weapons were different. He had no right to throw stones at anybody.

Seeing himself in that light didn't clear his head, however. The light was too merciless. He saw revealed a castoff drifter at the end of the line, a man who would shoot down a stranger if the price were worthwhile. All the time telling himself, *I don't have to like the job— the important thing is to profit by it.* It wasn't supposed to matter if a man had been poisoned, an innocent man dying like vermin so his body could be used to bait a trap for Lazar. What kind of soldiering was that? Gayoso's kind, Procope's kind, a proud and noble profession—if your blood ran cold enough.

He walked without any conscious goal. But when he looked up and read the sign he realized that his feet had led him to where his mind had been heading all along. He stood across the street from Hernando Sotomayor's curio shop.

Cox loitered on the curb, staring at the unlighted façade. The store was closed, but through its unshuttered windows he could see clerks bustling back and forth. They appeared to be taking inventory, probably to facilitate the probate of the late owner's will. Finally, he crossed the boulevard and rapped on the door. He didn't know precisely why but it was somehow important that he find out the truth.

Damn it to hell, there was a difference between him and Procope!

A young man with a black mourning band around his shirt sleeve opened the door a few inches. "I'm sorry, señor, but the shop is closed."

"I have to talk to somebody. Any of the Sotomayor family around?"

The clerk hesitated. "Señora Sotomayor is in the office. But I doubt if she would agree to see you. Perhaps after the funeral tomorrow ..."

"After the funeral will be too late." Cox pushed into the shop. "Which way?"

The clerk continued to bar his path. "I must have some notion of your business to tell the señora. Then if she decides to see you—"

"Okay, you can tell her it concerns her husband and the way he died." Cox snapped, "That sound like important enough business to you?"

The young man gave a startled nod and hastened away. He was gone for a long while. Cox spent the time examining the glass showcases. The items displayed were several cuts above the usual Tijuana merchandise, mainly native work in silver and semiprecious stones, intricately fashioned. Sotomayor had been considerably more than just another border sharpster.

The clerk came back. "The señora will talk to you. The stairs are at the rear of the shop."

Cox went up alone. The office door stood open but he knocked on the jamb before entering. "Señora Sotomayor?"

"Yes." She was seated before an old-fashioned rolltop desk, a middle-aged woman, as lean and fierce as a bird of prey. The blackness of her mourning garb was relieved only by the taut pale skin of her face and hands, the gold of her wedding band, and the threads of gray in her hair which was drawn back so severely it was painful to see. It was held in place by an undecorated comb of onyx. "You're the American who wished to talk to me?"

The second level was not properly another story but more of a mezzanine. Small windows that he hadn't noticed from below overlooked the shop floor. Cox realized that he had been fully scrutinized before he had been allowed to come upstairs. "I have to apologize for bothering you, particularly at this time."

She inclined her head. "Then you will do me the kindness of being brief. Were you a friend of Hernando's?"

"No. My name is Cox, and as far as I know I never had the honor of meeting your husband. But I would like to know more about his death."

"It was fully reported by the newspapers."

"I'm not sure that it was. That's why I'm here. Are you really satisfied with the doctor's diagnosis?"

"Satisfied?" She gave a short bark of a laugh. "It's an odd word. If you mean do I accept it, then my answer is yes. But I will never be satisfied."

"You're sure it was a heart attack?"

"I have no reason to doubt it. Hernando had a heart condition for years."

Cox hesitated, but he could see no way to phrase the matter delicately. "I believe there's a possibility that your husband may have been poisoned."

"Poisoned?" She stared at him. "By whom? And for what reason?"

"Because he was the friend of a man named Bruno Lazar and Lazar's enemies may have wished to lure him to Tijuana."

Señora Sotomayor shook her head. "You have a fantastic imagination, Mr. Cox."

"I'll admit it's only a guess. But there's a way to find out—with your cooperation. It's not too late to demand an autopsy. I know that Mexican law doesn't require one in cases where the doctor certifies—"

She rose to her feet, confronting him. "No," she replied, breathing heavily. "I refuse absolutely to have Hernando's body violated simply to please your curiosity. It won't change anything for him or for me. I have already told this to the young woman, and now I insist that you go away and leave us all in peace, both of you."

"Young woman?"

Señora Sotomayor was looking past him. He turned. Dorlisa was standing in the doorway.

When Odilia peeked into the salon, Gayoso was playing chess with Balbin. She guessed that he was winning, as usual. He didn't see her, which was as she intended.

Since early afternoon she had been making her plans. She had to find Cox, remind him of her importance in the only way she knew. Tonight was her last opportunity. Tomorrow he would be too busy with his job and after that—who knew? Their paths might separate permanently unless she was able to show him that they shouldn't.

His casual disdain this morning had shaken her badly for a time. But reflection, with the help of the needle, had restored her morale. Cox, being a man, naturally tended to wrap himself up in his work to the exclusion of all else. But, being a man, he could be diverted by a woman … if the woman were given time and opportunity. Cox hadn't been exactly cold toward her the other evening. The spell woven before could be woven again. This time, however, she intended to wangle certain guarantees for the future.

So she made a pretense of retiring immediately after dinner. She dressed quickly in clothes she had selected earlier and, as soon as she thought it safe, stole topside again. On the previous evening, she had allowed her plans to become known ahead of time, giving Gayoso the chance to stop her. Tonight she didn't make that mistake.

Domingo the boatswain was squatting at the head of the gangway, puffing on a twisted black cheroot. He was a powerfully muscled Indian, as stolid as a bulldog, only a generation removed from head-hunting. He was Gayoso's man and could not be bribed or bought. But he could be fooled.

"Oh, I'm glad I found you, Domingo." Odilia spoke quietly but tried to avoid the appearance that she was whispering. "You're to take me ashore in the launch immediately."

Domingo shook his head. "Not possible. Orders."

"I have new orders for you. From the General himself. He's sending me on business."

"I've heard nothing from the General."

"You're hearing right now—through me. Something important's come up. We have to hurry." She tried to slide by him.

Domingo didn't stir, his body blocking the gangway. "The General must tell me so himself."

"Oh, very well then. You'd better go ask him." Odilia spoke indifferently. "I believe he's in the radio room."

She thought that was a stroke of genius. Gayoso demanded strict privacy while transmitting the coded messages to the Mexico City embassy, and any subordinate who intruded on him was likely to regret it. Domingo knew this, too, and she saw him hesitate. She said, "Please don't waste time. I don't want the General angry with me also."

Domingo rose slowly to his feet, but he didn't head for the bridge. He turned toward the launch instead. He muttered, "Well, if the General has given orders ..."

Odilia followed him down the steps, smiling. Men believed that they were so clever, masters of the word, running everything. But already tonight she had flaunted one and outwitted another. She expected to have equally good luck with the third.

They sat on a bench in the little park off Calle Allende and listened to the band play *La Golondrina*. In the darkness surrounding the lighted bandstand, other lovers listened, too, and families sat together on the grass and children dashed about in impromptu games of tag.

Dorlisa sat very close to him and said, "I have a confession to make, Jack, an apology."

"Let's make a deal. No more apologies, no matter what happens."

"I won't feel right until I get this off my conscience. This afternoon I doubted you. I even wondered if you were on the other side." She shuddered. "I feel so ashamed of myself."

"Don't. There's no reason to trust me."

"I should have known that you couldn't be anything dishonorable."

Harshly, he said, "Dorlisa, you don't know a damn thing about me."

"I know you better than I've ever known anyone before."

"Better than your husband?"

"Much, much better." She turned her head to look at him. "Does it bother you that I was married before?"

"Don't talk a bunch of junk. It isn't important at all."

"I was so happy when you came to see Señora Sotomayor and proved to me what a dunce I'd been."

"I didn't have any idea you were there."

"That's what made it so wonderful, your trying to help me without my knowledge. Only a true friend does that. It was like an answer to my prayers."

The band was playing *Adios, Muchachos*. Cox said moodily, "You ever stop to think how many prayers get said every day? They can't all be answered. There's got to be a choice made someplace."

"You mean between good prayers and evil ones?"

"I guess. But who makes the decision about which is which?" He shook his head angrily. "Hell, I don't know what I'm talking about. We make our own choices when it comes right down to it."

Her choice was to kiss him lingeringly.

"That still doesn't settle tomorrow, Dorlisa. You didn't learn anything definite about Sotomayor, whether his death was an accident or on purpose."

"That's true. And neither of us was able to trace the waiter, if that's what he was. What do you think I should do?"

He hesitated. "I don't want the decision to come from me. I can't explain why, but I don't."

"You're right. It's my responsibility. I'm afraid I find it extremely easy to lean on you. I imagine I could become a very dependent woman if given the chance." She sighed. "Oh, there'll still be time tomorrow to make a decision."

"The final signal?" he suggested.

"Yes." She didn't elaborate. "Look, the band's putting away their instruments. The concert's over. Will there be another one tomorrow, do you know?"

"Maybe. But this is our last evening."

"You sound so gloomy. Tomorrow isn't judgment day." She stroked the bony outline of his face. "Think of it as Genesis, instead."

This time he kissed her, hungrily. God, he thought, I wonder which one of us is right.

Around them the crowd was slowly dispersing, heading homeward. Dorlisa whispered against his cheek, "Let me prove it to you. I promised you I would—last night on the beach. I have no modesty where you're concerned."

"I'm acting like a damn fool, letting you do all the asking." She rose, holding his hand. "Would you think it odd if I asked to come to your quarters? My house is just that, nothing but a house, no part of me. I have a great longing to lie with you in your own bed, not merely furniture rented from strangers."

"Okay, but my place is pretty tacky. I really ought to redd it up a bit for you."

"Then why don't you go on ahead, and I'll meet you there later? It occurs to me that I really should go home first, anyway." She chuckled. "I just remembered that I bought some new clothes for this occasion, though I didn't know it then. It would be a shame not to let you see them."

Cox left Dorlisa at the house on the hill and drove back to his own place at the track. His mind was in a turmoil. Looming largest in his thoughts was the night ahead, his desire for Dorlisa. But beyond this lurked the dark shape of tomorrow, now only hours away. Then, at last, he would have to face the truth of what he had been telling himself all along: he couldn't have everything.

He parked his automobile near the stables and walked across the moonlit earth to his room. He had a half hour to prepare for Dorlisa's arrival, perhaps light a few candles and dig out the bottle of tequila from his suitcase. There was no reason that the night, even though it was their last, could not be something to remember always. He opened the door and switched on the overhead light.

"I thought you were never coming home," Odilia said, blinking in the brightness. She lay on his bed, curled up kittenlike, her shoes off.

Cox gaped at her. "How'd you get here?"

"I just walked in. The General has copies of your keys."

"That isn't what I meant. Why in hell did you come?"

"To be with you," Odilia said simply. "I wouldn't have traveled this far for any other reason. Aren't you glad to see me, Jack?"

Cox swallowed the obvious answer. Odilia would have been an unwelcome visitor at any time, and now, with Dorlisa due to arrive at any moment ... He had to get rid of her as diplomatically as possible.

With a sudden suspicion, he asked, "Did Gayoso send you?"

"That Indian bastard?" She laughed scornfully. "On the contrary, he'd be furious if he found out."

"Doesn't that frighten you?"

"Why should it? I know you'll protect me. I remember how strong you are, Jack." Odilia wriggled her body provocatively. "Why are you standing there staring at me? There's room enough here for two."

"Odilia, you'd better go back to the yacht before you're missed."

She sat up, eyes wide. "But I don't want to go, not for a long long while, perhaps never. You were certainly in no hurry to get rid of me the other night." She smiled with understanding. "You're nervous about tomorrow. Come here and let me comfort you. That's what a woman is for."

Only a few evenings before, he had found her infinitely exciting. But that had been before Dorlisa. He tried to keep the repugnance out of his voice. "Yeah, that's it. I'm too keyed up."

She took his no to mean yes. Still smiling, she unzipped her dress and slid it up over her head in a languorous movement. She whispered, "I'll need help with the rest. I'm sure you haven't forgotten how."

"Look," he said, "you made a mistake coming here tonight. I don't want to hurt your feelings—"

"You are hurting them," she told him, pouting. "Why are you so different in your bedroom than you were in mine? There's no need to worry."

"You don't know a damn thing about it."

"I know everything about it," she said proudly. "Just because I'm a woman you mustn't think that I have no importance. Why, in my own fashion I'm fully as important as that stupid Gayoso. I helped arrange this whole thing from the beginning. I was right here at the track when Procope took care of that fat Mexican. And then—"

"Say that again," Cox demanded sharply. "Procope killed Sotomayor?"

"You knew that already, didn't you? It was all part of the plan to entice Lazar here to Tijuana. It worked perfectly just as everything is going to work perfectly tomorrow, wait and see."

"I didn't know," Cox murmured. "I guess I should have."

"Anyway, what difference does it make to us?" Odilia said with a shrug of bare shoulders. "You didn't know Sotomayor any more than you know Lazar. They're just names, aren't they? Let's talk about us instead." Her voice took on a wheedling tone. "In your new life, you'll need a woman like me, someone with family and position. I'll be a source of great pleasure to you, I promise. Not only in bed but in every way, Jack. With me as your wife—"

He moved swiftly toward her and she held out her arms to receive him. Instead, he seized her discarded dress and hurled it onto her lap. "Put on your clothes and get out of here."

She let out of yelp off astonishment. "Jack!"

"And make it snappy. I've got to air the place out before Dorlisa gets here."

There was a stunned expression on her delicate face. "Dorlisa," she repeated blankly. "You mean Mrs. Weber? Why on earth would she ..." Then she reddened. "She's spending the night with you? You prefer that blonde bitch to me?"

"Read it any way you like—but get out of here fast."

"No," she breathed and the long pointed nails of her hands curved into claws. "No, I'm not going. I'll be right here on your bed—when she arrives. And I'll still be here after she's finished cursing you. Then we'll see which one of us you prefer."

Cox, conscious of the minutes ticking away, was tempted to throw her out bodily. "Okay. Stick around and kick over the applecart. Tell Dorlisa who you are and who I am. Then you can go back and brag to Gayoso how you ruined his precious plan. Only I hope I'm not around to see what he does to you."

Odilia had claimed not to be frightened of Gayoso, but involuntarily she glanced at her forearm. A shudder racked her body. "I don't care," she muttered with half-hearted defiance, but the fire had gone out of her.

"Put up or shut up." Cox said inexorably. "It's your move."

Without looking at him, she slid off the bed and put on her dress and thrust her feet into her shoes. He watched her from beside the door. When she raised her head, he saw the despair in her eyes. "Please forget what I said, Jack. I didn't mean to threaten you. You won't tell the General, will you?"

"I won't tell the General."

"I understand how it is." She clutched at the self-deceiving explanation. "You have to make love to her, it's part of your job. But afterward, when it's all over, couldn't we—"

"Good-night, Odilia." He held the door open for her.

Her lips tried to form a tender smile of parting. It was only a grimace of pain. Head lowered, she fled into the darkness. It occurred to him to wonder if she had walked all the way from the jetty but then he heard an engine roar from behind the stable and realized that she had driven Gayoso's car. The sound faded, and all that remained behind was the faint fragrance of her perfume. And the memory of her words, echoing in his mind. *Procope took care of that fat Mexican ... it was all part of the plan ...*

Cox dug the tequila bottle out of his suitcase. He poured himself a drink with shaking fingers.

Dorlisa saw the automobile leave. In the darkness, she couldn't make out the driver. She didn't even bother to wonder who it had been. She was too engrossed in herself, the strange sensation she felt at going to a man's quarters at night, the wonder that she was actually doing such a thing. It was a feeling compounded of both fear and anticipation with a seasoning of perverse delight at venturing the forbidden. During the taxi ride out to the track she twice had nearly ordered her driver to turn back. Now as she glimpsed the lighted window behind which her lover waited, she knew that she had gone too far not to go farther. She marched up to the door and rapped on it boldly.

Cox flung it open, and they stood staring at each other. She said hello and he replied, and then they were alone together with the darkness locked out on the other side of the door. Yet they remained apart, not touching, strangers. Dorlisa summoned up a smile. "Was I too long, Jack?"

"No." He made no attempt at gallantry.

She gazed about to bridge the silence. Despite his announced intention, the room showed no evidence of having been tidied. The bed was rumpled, his work clothes lay over the chair and the table bore a miscellaneous clutter. Beside a pair of sharp-pointed harness shears stood a bottle of tequila and a single glass, partly full. She said, "It wasn't fair of you to start without me."

"I'm sorry. I needed a drink. I'll get another glass."

"No, don't bother. I already feel lightheaded."

He shrugged. Dorlisa didn't know what to think. The setting was scarcely conducive to romance, nor did Cox behave like a lover. She had expected to be met with passion; instead she felt like an intruder. Cox appeared aloof and almost angry, as if he resented her presence. Timidly, she asked, "Is something wrong?"

"Of course not. Why do you say that?"

"You seem—well, not yourself."

"It's the same old me, for better or for worse."

"I thought that perhaps I had done something to displease you. I'm not sure that I know the proper moves. I need you to instruct me, Jack."

"That's what I'm here for." He seemed to throw off his dark preoccupation with an effort. "You look nice, Dorlisa. Those the new clothes you mentioned?"

"You know they're not. They're underneath where you can't see them."

"What do I have to do to get the privilege?"

"You're the instructor," she reminded him. "But it seems to me that in a situation like this, it's indicated that you should kiss me. Even I know that much."

"Sounds sensible." He put his arms around her. But there was no urgency in his grasp, and his kiss lacked conviction, too. It was almost as if he were thinking of something else.

Dorlisa broke away from him. "Something is wrong," she said, staring at him. "Please tell me what's happened."

He didn't answer her question. He turned toward the table and picked up the glass and drank off the remainder of the tequila. His back to her, he asked, "Can you ride a horse?"

"I knew how once, years ago."

"Then let's get out of this place."

"But why?"

"Because I don't want to stay here." From the wall he seized a wool shirt and a pair of levis. "These ought to do. You can change in the bathroom. That dress of yours is all right for a party but it's not worth a damn for riding."

Bewildered, Dorlisa accepted the trousers and shirt. Without another word, Cox slammed out into the night, presumably to saddle the horses. Dorlisa stood for a while where he had left her. Pride demanded that she walk out, and she would have done so had she not sensed that Cox, despite his strange behavior, somehow needed her to stay. Loving him, she could not desert him; loving him, she had surrendered the right to complete independence. She went into the bathroom and did his bidding. But as she put on the rough wool shirt and coarse denim trousers, hiding the fragile lace lingerie so expectantly donned, she felt close to tears.

When she emerged, Cox was waiting for her and outside the door two horses were waiting also. They were exercise horses, working mounts, used to rough handling.

Cox said brusquely, "You don't have to do this if you don't want to."

"I want to be with you."

"Okay." He flung her the reins. "If I go too fast, shout out and I'll slow down."

By the time she had mounted, he was already trotting off across the yard without waiting. Dorlisa spurred her horse to follow. They circled the race track, passed through a gate and entered the open fields beyond. Cox kicked his horse into full gallop, and Dorlisa followed suit. The moonlight was sufficient to make out the terrain but she didn't attempt to guide her horse, allowing him to pick his own path. Tonight she would accept what came. Cox did not glance back to see if she needed help, and she did not call to him.

They crossed a paved highway and ascended a winding canyon to a long sagebrush plateau, sweeping through the night like vengeful spirits, the only sound the thud of their horses' hoofs on the sunbaked adobe soil. Eventually the earth sloped downward again and moonbeams glinted off the placid bosom of the Pacific. They had come to the beach.

Cox reined in. Below them the shoreline arced away to the north and the south. Waves broke against it with a shimmering glow, making it appear a giant scimitar edged in jewels. Nowhere, as far as they could see, was there any evidence of man's existence; they might have been the first ever to view the scene. Dorlisa drew in her breath at the sight. The beauty alone made the wild ride worthwhile.

"Back in school," Cox said abruptly, "there was a poem I had to memorize. I still remember some of it, something about 'where every prospect pleases—'"

"'And only man is vile,'" she finished. "I learned it, too."

"I never knew what it meant before." Then, as if regretting the lapse into conversation, he sent his horse plunging down the shallow bluff to the soft sand beneath, the animal skidding on its haunches, nearly falling.

Dorlisa, her teeth clamped together in dread, duplicated his reckless descent, hanging on tightly to the saddle horn without shame. She expected to fall but did not. Horse and rider arrived safely at the bottom and plodded across to the hardpack at the water's edge where Cox was waiting.

He said shortly, "There's a cove a mile or two down the beach. I'll wait for you there."

He turned his horse south and booted it into a furious gallop. Dorlisa had no choice except to do the same. They stormed down the beach, the salt wind beating at their faces, their horses' feet kicking up a fine spray that drenched them. Despite this, despite the strain on arm and leg muscles, Dorlisa experienced a feeling of gradual exhilaration, a wild and primitive emotion that blotted out her apprehensions. It was a night like none she had ever known, but she was part of it. She knew what awaited them at the cove that she had never seen, and she was not afraid. No longer was she content to trail obediently behind the man; now she tried to pass him. But his horse was faster or his skill was greater. Gradually, he drew away, and she nearly lost sight of him in the darkness. Then suddenly he pulled up, and the race was over. The shoreline folded in upon itself, dipping behind a rocky outcrop to form a miniature harbor.

She flung herself off her horse and ran toward him. He met her halfway, wrapping her body in a fierce embrace. His lips were salty. When she finally opened her eyes, he was grinning at her, his familiar self once more. He said, "You ride pretty good. I didn't think any woman could keep up with me."

"You weren't really trying to lose me, Jack."

"I had to clear my mind. It's the only way I know how, riding hard, taking damfool chances. But I didn't have any right putting you through the wringer."

"Tell me what's troubling you. I can help."

"Remember what we were talking about earlier? How everybody had to make his own choice?"

She studied his face. "It has something to do with you and me, doesn't it? I know—it must be another woman. Was it she I saw leaving the race track tonight? Had she come to plead with you to give me up?"

He was startled and, after a moment, chuckled. "Funny—how the facts can be right and the picture all wrong. There was another woman, Dorlisa, but she doesn't matter a hill of beans."

"She can't have you, you know." She pushed away from him and yanked open the wool shirt and discarded it. The levis followed it to the sand and she stood before him in the lacy undergarments, the bridal lingerie. "I made myself beautiful for you."

"I don't deserve you to be so beautiful."

"I'll make you earn me," she promised. "I'll let you chase me as I have chased you tonight." When he reached for her, she eluded him and scampered for the ocean, pausing to glance back invitingly before plunging into the foaming water. Cox threw his own garments aside and hastened after her.

The chase was not long, nor did she mean it to be. But it pleased her to tease him, and so she pretended to struggle while the warm waves rolled over them. Until at last he grew impatient and used his strength to subdue her, whereupon she surrendered and allowed him to carry her from the noisy surf to the quiet of the little cove. They lay in the shelter of a huge boulder and, though nude and dripping, were not cold. Like some sea creatures emerging to mate upon the shore, they spoke not at all, but drew closer and closer together with the sinuous movements of a ritual as old as time. His hands explored her flesh, his mouth moved against hers until she impatiently tugged him closer still. Her softness enfolded him; they became one, fused in agonized ecstasy.

Their horses, grazing nearby, pricked up their ears at the tremulous cry of mingled delight and savage fulfilment that seemed wrenched from the night itself. Silence returned; the horses continued to munch placidly on the wild pickleweed that grew among the rocks.

Later, they talked like lovers. He told her what he had not told her before, how much he loved her, and she made him repeat it in a dozen different ways while she caressed him lightly. This, too, was ritualistic, but neither recognized it; the moment was newly sculptured, and they both confessed that there had been no other experience in their lives to equal it.

Only when she wished to talk about the future did he fall silent. She noticed.

"I don't want to think of anything except right now, this exact minute," he told her. "I wish I could get my hands on it and never let it get away."

"It's only our first time. Tomorrow will be better still. It seems to me I've wasted my entire life looking backward. I'll never do it again."

"Tomorrow. It's almost here."

"Yes, the sky is lightening." She drew him to her. "But it will still be night for a little while longer."

He made an inarticulate sound, almost a moan, and kissed her fiercely. She arched her body to press against him; sleeping desire awoke again. And though this time his need was greater than hers, since her fulfilment was already complete, she accepted him eagerly and exulted in his fury that now belonged to her as well as to him. Locked in their private world, they did not notice the coming of the dawn.

DAY ZERO

Dorlisa pulled out the stopper and let the water drain away. It left behind a fine residue of sand on the floor of the bathtub, like gold in a sluice pan. She regarded it as fondly as if it were truly precious, visible remembrance of their wild abandon on the beach.

They had ridden back to the race track in the first pale sunlight of the day, side by side this time, yet saying little. Now she stood in his tiny bathroom and toweled her body until it tingled. It was the same body which she had bathed on the previous evening, yet Dorlisa sensed that it was somehow altered, made complete as never before, even in her marriage. It was a strange alchemy, this mating of a woman with the right man in which, through giving of herself, she became not less but more. Science might explain it in terms of hormones, but it was as much spiritual as physical. Whatever the cause, she was supremely content and hoped that Cox was, too. Not even the realization that today was Thursday, with all it implied, could dissipate her serenity. Draping herself in the folds of the bath towel, she went to join her lover.

He was lying on his bed, hands behind his head, staring at the ceiling. She bent to kiss him on the lips. "I tried not to use all the hot water."

"Okay." His tone was somber, and he did not move immediately to leave the bed. Dorlisa gazed at him and finally asked if anything was wrong. "Just thinking."

"About us?"

"In a way." He heaved himself off the bed and began unbuttoning his shirt. As he moved toward the bathroom, he added morosely, "The scales are perfectly balanced. That's the hell of it."

The cryptic remark puzzled Dorlisa, jarring her contentment slightly. For some reason she didn't comprehend, Cox had reverted to his black mood of last night. Had he already forgotten the exquisite hours on the beach? She was aware that the man, more easily aroused and more easily satisfied, never committed himself as deeply as the woman. Yet she could not believe that Cox hadn't given almost as much as he had taken; certain emotions couldn't be counterfeited. There had to be another, less disturbing, reason for his dejection. And so Dorlisa brushed away the small cloud of worry and, humming softly to herself, began to dress.

One of her earrings dropped to the floor and bounced under the bed. She knelt to retrieve it and saw for the first time a guitar case concealed there. She was surprised; Cox had never given any hint of being talented musically. Curiously, she drew the case into the open and raised the lid. The instrument looked new but it was badly out of tune. When she plucked the strings without removing the guitar from its nest, the result was an unharmonious jangle.

She called to Cox, "If I'd known you played, I would have insisted you serenade me."

"What'd you say?" he asked through the door which stood slightly ajar. The water gurgling into the tub prevented his hearing her.

"Never mind. I'll tell you later."

She was about to close the guitar case when she discovered the wire. It emerged from a small hole in the wall behind the bed and disappeared beneath the rug. Her first dismissing thought was that it was the telephone connection but she realized immediately that this could not be so; the wire ran in the opposite direction. Hesitantly, she pulled the rug aside and followed the exposed wire across the room on hands and knees until it reached the table. There it twined itself around the thicker cord of the table lamp, like a vine about a tree trunk, until it vanished under the base of the lamp itself. Her heart thudding with premonition, Dorlisa turned the lamp over and saw the tiny button-shaped instrument fastened there.

"A microphone," she said in a whisper. "What does it mean?"

Her mind was fastening on the fact, more than a premonition now, like the jaws of a trap. There was no earthly reason why anyone would desire to put a plain horse trainer under surveillance. Unless he was not really a plain horse trainer ... Suspicion, hammered into the core of her being by the years, burst the bonds she had lately put upon it. It couldn't be, she wasn't willing to accept it—but she could not ignore it. She had to know.

In the bathroom a few paces away, she could hear Cox splashing in the tub, oblivious of her discovery. With desperate haste, she rushed outside and ran for the nearby entrance to the stable. It was still early; no one was present to observe her except the few horses in their stalls.

A tack room stood between her and the wall of Cox's living quarters. She entered it and for a moment poised squinting until her eyes became accustomed to the gloom. Then, because she knew it must be there, she spied the wire where it emerged through its freshly-made hole and traced it to a shelf above eye level. She found a box she could stand on. The tape recorder squatted in concealment behind a stack of bridles.

With trembling fingers, she rewound a portion of the tape and pressed the playback button. She heard her own voice, innocently carefree, say, "If I'd known you played, I would have insisted you serenade me ..."

"Not far enough," she muttered and rewound the tape again She turned the volume down to a mere whisper and pressed the playback button once more.

She had come in upon a conversation already begun. A woman, a voice Dorlisa didn't recognize, was saying, "In your new life, you'll need a woman like me, someone with family and position. I'll be a source of great pleasure to you, I promise. Not only in bed but in every way, Jack. With me as your wife—"

Cox's voice interrupted harshly. "Put on your clothes and get out of here."

"Jack!"

"And make it snappy. I've got to air the place out before Dorlisa gets here."

"Dorlisa. You mean Mrs. Weber? Why on earth would she ... She's spending the night with you? You prefer that blonde bitch to me?"

"Read it any way you like—but get out of here."

"No. No, I'm not going. I'll be right here—on your bed—when she arrives. And I'll still be here after she's finished cursing you. Then we'll see which one of us you prefer."

Dorlisa drew a deep breath. If it were merely that there was another woman, something she'd already halfway guessed ... Hope, reviving, received its death blow when Cox spoke again. "Okay," his voice rasped. "Stick around and kick over the applecart. Tell Dorlisa who you are and who I am. Then you can go back and brag to Gayoso how you ruined his precious plan. Only I hope I'm not around to see what he does to you."

Mechanically, Dorlisa turned off the recorder. There was more but she had no need to hear it. The one name—Gayoso—had been enough. Cox belonged to the enemy. He was the assassin of Bruno Lazar. She should have known it from the beginning, through all the fortuitous circumstances and odd discrepancies. Her mistake had been in not wanting to see what was plain before her. With a bitterness she could taste, Dorlisa realized that this was what her enemies—Cox among them—had expected of her. She was to be the Judas goat that would lead Bruno Lazar to slaughter.

She was blind no longer. Her mind, congealed by the horror of her discovery, could not sort out alternatives. All she knew was that she had to get away quickly, warn Lazar while there was still time. Beyond this goal, her thoughts held nothing but despair.

She left the tape recorder in its hiding place and ran, stumbling, out of the stable into the sunlight. And there she hesitated. Her purse still remained in Cox's quarters, and without the money it contained she would be unable to telephone for a taxi or pay the fare when one arrived. Perhaps she still had time to retrieve it without Cox's knowledge.

Creeping to his door, she listened. From the sounds within, she judged that he was still in the bath. She tiptoed inside and to the bed where her purse lay. As she clutched it, the bathroom door opened and Cox came out, a towel tied around his waist.

If she had been an actress, she might have carried off a successful deception, buying time until she could accomplish her escape. But Dorlisa was no actress. She cringed away from him like a terrified animal.

Cox saw her expression and knew. His glance went to the open guitar case on the floor and back again to her face, reading there the fear and loathing she was unable to hide. He said huskily, "You found out."

"Don't touch me," she whispered.

"You've got to listen to me. You've got to know what I decided." He came toward her, holding out his arms to seize her. "Dorlisa, I love you."

The words infuriated her as nothing else could. She had been schooled in pacificism, violence was a cardinal sin … but at his incredible protestation, primitive emotion shattered the shell of conscience. She felt nothing but a rage to punish this man who had ravished and betrayed her. She screamed at him. "Assassin!" From the table she snatched up the harness shears and drove the twin blades into his chest with all her strength.

Cox reeled backward. The shears, torn from her grasp, remained imbedded in his bare chest as he fell heavily to the floor. He moaned once and was silent.

Dorlisa stared down at him, dazed by her savagery and its results. Slowly, her eyes fixed on the motionless figure of her lover, she backed away, shaking her head as if to deny it had happened. She put out her hand in an ineffectual gesture of bewilderment and entreaty. Cox did not stir.

A shudder racked her body, a quick intake of breath like a soundless scream. She groped for the door and, holding onto it, staggered out into the stable yard. A man had just alighted from a sedan, and she collided squarely with him. He was a young man with curly hair and bad teeth.

Dorlisa stared at him but did not recognize him, seeing only the pain-contorted face of the man who lay in the room she had left. She murmured, not to the stranger but to herself, "I killed him." With unseeing eyes and uncertain steps, she walked off across the grounds, not knowing where she was going, not caring.

Balbin watched Dorlisa until she disappeared beyond the race track pavilion. He was nearly as stunned as she, both at the surprise encounter and at the words she had used. "I killed him ..."

There was no doubt whom she meant. Through the doorway, he could see Cox lying on the floor beside the open guitar case. Balbin could guess the rest. Dorlisa Weber had discovered Cox's true identity and had struck first. It seemed equally apparent that she, in her dazed state, had not recognized Balbin as her kidnapper. Thus, there was no point in pursuing her. The police could do that later; an anonymous telephone call would set them on the right track, without involving the Gayoso party in the least.

But when Balbin entered the tiny quarters, he discovered that there was no need for the police, after all. Despite Dorlisa's intention and belief, Cox was alive. The shears, driven high on the left side of Cox's chest, had missed the heart and, apparently, the lung as well; there was no bloody froth on his lips and his breathing appeared regular. When Balbin removed the shears the wound began to bleed freely.

He closed the door and sat on the bed and lit a cigarette while he contemplated the unconscious man at his feet. "Not so swaggering now, are you, compatriot?" he murmured. Familiar with bloodshed, Balbin didn't consider Cox's wound to be serious. Unless the hemorrhaging was not checked ...

The temptation was great simply to walk away and allow the Yankee to bleed to death. Reluctantly, Balbin put his personal enmity aside. Cox was still valuable for a few hours more.

He rummaged about in Cox's belongings until he found a roll of wide tape used for strengthening a race horse's ankles. With this and a wadded-up undershirt, he constructed a pressure bandage which seemed to halt the flow of blood. Then, with considerable effort, he succeeded in forcing a pair of trousers up Cox's legs and in covering Cox's upper torso with a blanket from the bed. Cox was beginning to grumble and struggle weakly against the manipulations, his eyes still shut.

"Kindly cooperate," Balbin told him with a mocking grin. "I'm saving your life."

Cox's reply was indistinct. Balbin carried him outside and deposited him, not gently, in the rear seat of the sedan. Then, more leisurely, he went about collecting items of immediate value that remained in the quarters—the rifle, the tape recorder, and the rest of Cox's clothes, including his boots.

When he returned, burdened, to the automobile, Cox was sitting up. His eyes were foggy. "Where we going?" he asked thickly. Balbin laughed. "To keep your rendezvous with destiny." He started the engine and turned the sedan in the direction of the ocean.

Gayoso switched off the tape recorder and stood regarding it thoughtfully. "Well," he said finally, "that seems to be the complete story. What we don't know we can readily guess. You're certain that Mrs. Weber believes him dead?"

"Her words were, 'I killed him'," Balbin said. "There's no doubt that's what she intended. Unfortunately, her aim was poor."

"But she doesn't know that," Gayoso mused. "I believe we can profit from her ignorance." At the far end of the yacht's saloon, Procope was crouched before the radio, listening intently to its low-pitched voice. Gayoso called to him, "Anything yet?"

Procope shook his head. "Nothing beyond the routine police calls."

"Good. If Mrs. Weber had informed the Tijuana authorities of her escapade, the airwaves would be full of it by now. So we're safe in assuming she intends to do nothing pending the arrival of Lazar."

Balbin objected, "Don't you think it more likely that she will warn Lazar off, now that she's aware of our plot?"

"On the contrary, she believes that she has disposed of the plot by disposing of the assassin. And there's the small matter of human nature. At this moment, Mrs. Weber, being a woman, urgently needs a shoulder to cry upon. She won't send Lazar away now." Gayoso nodded vigorously. "Actually, it works out very well. We'll proceed according to plan."

"Lazar may arrive in Tijuana and still not choose to attend the funeral services," Balbin pointed out. "An ambush upon his arrival at the house would be less open to chance, it seems to me."

"Where we would have an excellent view of our bullets bouncing off the sides of his armored automobile, as they have done in the past. This is to be an execution, not a battle. You understand me, Balbin?"

"Of course, General. I only wish I had more confidence in the executioner."

"Cox will do what is required, never fear." Gayoso broke off and swung around as Odilia entered the saloon. "But there's no need to accept my opinion. We'll put it up to an expert, a recognized authority. Good morning, Odilia."

She said, "I came as soon as I heard the buzzer." She wore a gauzy peignoir over her nightgown and her face was puffy with sleep.

"A dispute has arisen which we'd appreciate your settling, a question of how we should proceed in the Lazar matter."

"Me?" Odilia asked, blinking in surprise.

"But naturally," Gayoso said smoothly. "I understand that you have helped arrange this affair from the beginning. How did you put it?" He pretended to consider. "Oh, yes—I believe your exact words were, 'I'm fully as important as that stupid Gayoso.'"

Odilia's eyes were wide awake now. "I don't understand you, General. Surely you know I'd never say anything as fantastic as that. Who has been lying about me?"

"You have, last night when you went to Cox's quarters against my orders." He viewed her fright with amazement. "Surely, you're not afraid of a poor Indian bastard, are you? Or is that a lie, also?"

Odilia stammered, "He promised he wouldn't tell."

"And he kept his word. But you should know that I am not easily deceived." Gayoso paused, waiting. "Well, my dear? No explanation whatever for your treachery?"

A faint hope crept into Odilia's expression at this hint that forgiveness might, after all, be extended to her. "It's true that I went ashore last night," she said lamely, trying to construct a mitigating account as she went along. "And it's true that I visited Cox's rooms. But I was serving our cause. There was no thought of disloyalty to you in my actions, quite the contrary. I was worried that the Yankee might betray us, and I wished to see that everything was all right and to report to you if—"

She stopped abruptly, interrupted by the sound of her own voice from the tape recorder. Gayoso had pressed the playback button. "Oh, sweet Jesus, no!" Odilia choked. "It isn't true!"

"Please listen to all of it. You may find it instructive, as I did."

"I don't want to hear it!" She backed away but Balbin barred her path. He held her easily as she struggled. Gayoso didn't move except to turn up the volume until the recorded voices filled the saloon like thunder. He let the sordid exchange drag on to its conclusion although Odilia had dissolved into broken sobs long before the end. When he finally turned off the machine the only sound in the room was her piteous whimpering.

"What are you going to do with me?" she asked at last.

Gayoso regarded her gravely. "I've been thinking about that. You've flouted my authority, slandered me and disobeyed me. Your blunder concerning Sotomayor's poisoning was imbecilic. However, none of this bothers me particularly, since I've known all along that you are witless and not to be trusted. But I find another facet of this matter quite disturbing."

"I don't understand you."

"The fact that, despite all your efforts, Cox prefers another woman to you."

"That isn't true!" The accusation struck her pride, making her momentarily forget her terror. "Jack is merely acting with the Weber woman, playing a part. He'll come back to me."

"Perhaps I should run other portions of the tape for your edification." Gayoso shrugged. "But what's the use? No, Odilia, I sadly fear that you have lost your attractiveness. And, with it, any future usefulness to me."

Odilia recognized it as a sentence. She held out hands that trembled. "Please—don't kill me."

"Don't be ridiculous. I have no intention of killing you. I won't even take away the drugs that are so precious to you. My department can't use you any longer but perhaps another bureau of the government can." He paused, toying with her. "The morale and special services division of the army, for example."

"No!" she whispered. Her voice rose in a scream. "For God's sake, no!"

"Don't worry," Gayoso assured her. "I'll see to it that the brothel you enter is reserved for officers only, as befitting your aristocratic blood." He surveyed the cringing, moaning creature before him and an expression of disgust crossed his face. "Get out of here before I change my mind and turn you over to the crew."

Odilia fled blindly out of the saloon, bumping into the bulkhead. Balbin uttered a nervous laugh. "I believe you really frightened her, General. Did you mean what you said?"

"Failure is met with punishment. Those who work for me had better remember that." Gayoso got to his feet. "And now let us discover if the male member of our love triangle intends to fail me, also."

Cox had been taken to the ship's dispensary below decks. He was sitting on the edge of the treatment table while the yacht's captain, who doubled as doctor in emergencies, put the finishing touches on his bandage. Gayoso greeted him with a smile. "Well, Mr. Cox, I hear you have been the victim of an accident."

"Something like that," Cox said.

"I'm delighted to see that it is so trifling, a mere scratch." Gayoso jerked his head at the captain. "If your duties here are complete, kindly make preparations to get under way. I intend to leave these waters the moment our business in the city is finished."

The captain saluted and left the dispensary. Cox, staring at the floor, said, "It's more than a scratch, General. Matter of fact, I'm not sure I'll be able to handle the job, after all."

"What? An old soldier like you?" asked Gayoso with elaborate surprise. "I've fought an entire engagement with a dozen wounds, each more serious than yours, and then spent the evening afterward making love."

"Maybe I'm not the man you are. I feel pretty weak."

"But not too weak to earn the balance of your pay, eh? I imagine that you are burning with a desire for revenge as well, eager to settle the score with the Weber slut for knifing you. Well, you shall have your opportunity."

"I don't blame her. She only did what she thought was right."

"I admire your generosity toward a foe. It is a mark of character to bleed without bitterness." Gayoso clasped Cox's bare shoulder in comradely fashion. "And there are still several hours before the appointed time. I suggest you rest and recover your strength until the moment of departure."

Cox hesitated. "Okay, but I don't know if resting is going to change the way I feel."

"Time is a great healer," Gayoso promised. He left the dispensary, closing the door behind him. Balbin was waiting in the passage. Quietly, Gayoso asked, "You heard?"

"As I predicted, General, the North American possesses weasel blood."

"The carrot no longer has sufficient attraction for Mr. Cox. Perhaps it is time we used the stick."

Balbin looked doubtful. "Can a man be forced to do such a thing?"

"We have employed Cox's desires to bait him into doing the job we wish. Now it appears that he has a new desire, Dorlisa Weber. If he won't kill Lazar to thwart her, perhaps he will kill Lazar to save her. Once before, Cox rescued Mrs. Weber when you had kidnapped her. Let's give him an opportunity to play the hero again." Gayoso grinned. "Interesting, isn't it? How history repeats itself?"

The final signal, which had been the subject of so much speculation in the Gayoso camp, was really quite simple. It consisted merely of a funeral wreath to be placed—or not to be placed—on the front door of the house Dorlisa Weber had rented. The presence of the wreath would indicate all clear, a positive action that required Dorlisa's knowledge and consent. Thus, Lazar could not be drawn into a trap by her failure, perhaps by enemy interference, to give him warning. No warning at all was warning enough.

As the armored sedan cruised slowly past, Dr. Neve said, "That's the house. And there's the wreath on the door."

Vicario brought the automobile to a gentle stop, and the three men regarded the dwelling that loomed above the street like a small castle. Lazar said impatiently, "What are we sitting here for? The garage door is open. I feel like stretching my legs."

Vicario said doubtfully, "The drapes are drawn. The place seems almost deserted. It impresses me badly. What do you think, Neve?"

"Honk your horn," the doctor suggested. "I share your feeling."

No one appeared at door or windows in answer to their strident summons. Lazar chuckled. "Did you expect a brass band for our arrival?"

"I have learned to trust my instincts, Jefe. They have saved my life before."

"Let me point out that it is you and not I who are not following the rules. We agreed to be guided by Dorlisa's signal. Very well, there it is. Now I order you to enter the garage."

Reluctantly, Vicario turned the armored car into the driveway and halted it in the empty garage. He said, "At least, let me reconnoiter, make sure that things are as they should be."

"My privilege," said Neve, "as the oldest and most expendable." Before they could argue, he slid nimbly out of the vehicle and trotted up the interior stairs to the door. It was unlocked; he vanished inside.

Minutes passed in slow silence disturbed only by the purr of the engine which Vicario had not turned off in case a rapid retreat were called for. The two men fidgeted and finally Vicario snapped, "What's keeping the old goat? I'd better go look for him."

Neve appeared at the top of the stairs. He came slowly down the steps to join them, his face thoughtful. "It's all right," he said. "You may come in now."

"Where's Dorlisa?" Vicario demanded. "Has something happened to her?"

Neve hesitated. "She'd rather tell you herself, I think."

Lazar had to be helped out of the automobile and assisted up the stairs. His crippled legs, cramped by the long journey, could barely support him. But when they reached the upper level and stood in the shadowy kitchen, he waved them off impatiently and hobbled forward, leaning heavily on his ebony canes.

"She's in the living room," Neve said, pointing. "That door there."

Dorlisa did not rise at their entrance. She was seated in a large over-stuffed chair facing the patio, staring numbly at the gurgling fountain. She was wearing her traveling suit of gray wool and her golden hair was hidden by the cloche hat. Beside her sat a straw shopping bag that contained the rest of her belongings.

Vicario rushed forward to kiss her forehead. "Darling—I was worried that something was wrong. Neve said—"

She hardly seemed aware of him. She looked only at Lazar. "Jefe, I waited for you. I wanted to give my report."

Lazar, studying her closely, said, "I'm listening, Dorlisa."

"The Sotomayor funeral is to begin at noon. The procession will leave the funeral parlor at that hour for Los Remedios where the services will be held. Burial will be in the cathedral cemetery. I have drawn a map which you should have no difficulty following."

Vicario said quickly, "But you'll be going with us, won't you?"

Dorlisa continued in the same flat emotionless tone, "Arrangements have been made for you to enter the side door of the cathedral. There should be no danger. As we feared, this was a trap. There was an assassin. His name was Jack Cox, an American horse trainer. This morning I killed him."

There was a stunned silence. Lazar finally croaked, "Killed him? You?"

"In his bedroom at the race track. We spent the night together." Tears were trickling down her cheeks. "I loved him and I killed him."

Both Vicario and Neve moved tentatively toward her but Lazar, despite his infirmity, was swifter. He put his arms around her, cradling her head against his stomach. "My poor child," he said softly. "What have I done to you?"

She clung to him. "Please forgive me," she begged. "I know how you must despise me for betraying all you've ever taught me. I thought only of myself—and of him."

Lazar's voice was husky with pain. "No, Dorlisa, you must forgive me. Who can blame you for being a woman? You weren't meant to squander your youth for my cause. You should hate me for keeping you from a normal life. I was selfish not to have sent you away long ago. Instead, I have brought you to this." He added bitterly, "Simply that I might attend a funeral in safety."

"I believed I had principles, Jefe, your principles. I've thought and thought about it. Now I know that I've only been doing penance for my husband's guilt. When Jack made me desire him I was ready to sacrifice everything and everybody, even you. Now he's dead, and I feel so empty. There's nothing left of me at all."

Vicario turned away with a muffled sound. "Oh, God!" he said through clenched teeth. "Why?"

"There's no answer," Neve mused. "We're all ghosts, figments of an idiot's nightmare."

"I didn't want her to come here!" Vicario raged. "I knew something terrible would happen." With impotent fury, he drove his fist against the French door, shattering the glass.

Dorlisa watched him without emotion. "Please don't, Vicario."

"Why not? Let's all break things, smash the whole stinking world." Vicario shuddered, then shook his head. "I'm sorry. I'm not helping matters, am I?"

"We must think of the future," Neve agreed. "Dorlisa, does anyone except you know of the—accident?"

"Not yet. I've been waiting for you." She rose slowly to her feet. "Now I must go to the police and tell them."

Vicario protested, "Don't be a fool! There's no reason to do that. I'll have you out of here before anybody finds out. We'll leave Mexico, they'll never catch us—"

"You've committed no crime, not in the eyes of God," Neve added. "Not in the eyes of anyone, for that matter."

"Except myself. I must do my new penance. It's the one action I'm still capable of." They were not convinced and as they continued to argue, she looked at Lazar who had said nothing. "You understand, Jefe."

He nodded reluctantly. "You must follow your conscience."

Dorlisa picked up the straw bag and stood looking at the three men for a moment. "Good-by, my friends."

Vicario blocked her departure. "I won't allow it. I won't let you throw your life away."

She sighed. "Don't you see? I have no life left." Her fingertips stroked the harsh lines of his face. "My dear, find yourself a living woman."

"I want you, Dorlisa."

"No, not me. I have an affinity only for Judases. I wonder why." She contemplated this thought for a moment before turning toward the door. "Please don't follow me. I must face the rest alone."

The front door closed softly behind her. They stood without moving, listening to the sound of her high heels descending the steps until it had faded completely away. Lazar finally spoke. "The funeral this afternoon," he murmured. "It will serve to bury more than one of our friends."

There was a clock in the dispensary; Cox could hear it ticking, louder than his heartbeat and considerably steadier. By turning his head from where he lay on the treatment table, he could see its face. The hands stood at eleven-thirty.

During the two hours since Gayoso had left him, he had been doing a great deal of thinking, though in ruts that were now well-worn with use. And he had come to the conclusion that, he now realized, he had been heading toward all along. He was not going to assassinate Bruno Lazar. He wondered how he had ever believed he could. Dorlisa had taught him something about himself. Beneath the scars and callouses infected by time and circumstances, Jack Cox was still a human being. More than that, a humane being, capable of love. Whatever sins, past or future, he might be guilty of, killing a man for money was not among them.

He did not suppose, however, that his renunciation of murder automatically placed him in a state of grace. It was merely a step in the right direction. And it was entirely possible that Dorlisa, if she ever found out about it, would assume that fright had motivated him. She couldn't be expected to understand what he didn't quite understand himself, that he had discovered his soul. He hoped that someday he would have a chance to explain it to her.

But for the moment another sort of explanation was called for. How was he going to tell Gayoso, who had made a substantial down payment on his services? Gayoso, for all his bland courtesy, was not a man to accept apostasy with a shrug. Cox was no coward but he realized his precarious position. Gayoso had casually murdered Sotomayor, who had done him no harm. There was no reason to believe he might not do the same to Cox, who had done him harm. And with perfect safety—in this little floating piece of a foreign country, Gayoso was the supreme authority. Who would ever know? In some quarters, Cox was already presumed dead. For that matter, who would care one way or another? A bullet or a knife, a quiet burial at sea ... the world would get along quite well minus Jack Cox.

Yet there had to be a way out, an excuse that Gayoso would accept, however grudgingly. Cox felt his left shoulder tentatively. Too bad it hadn't been the other arm instead, making it impossible to aim a rifle. The wound pained him but it was no real handicap. Perhaps if it could be made to bleed ... Cox sat up and carefully began to remove the bandage. But before he could do more than peel away the first strip of adhesive, he heard footsteps approaching along the passageway. It was too late; he would have to play it by ear and hope that he didn't strike a false note.

Gayoso came into the dispensary, brisk and smiling. "Well, how is the stricken warrior by now? Full of vigor once more, I'll wager."

Cox tried to look wan and weak. "I feel pretty shaky, General. I get dizzy when I try to move."

"Oh? That's unfortunate. Your mission calls for a keen eye and a steady hand."

"I know. I've been sitting here wondering what we're going to do. I can hardly see across the room." Cox squinted by way of demonstration. "Just my damn luck—to crap out at the last minute."

"Perhaps a cigarette will help." Gayoso gave him one and dug a lighter out of his tunic pocket. "I'm a great believer in the restorative effects of tobacco."

Cox bent his head to accept the light, then jerked upright again. "Where'd you get that?"

"I rather thought you'd recognize it." Gayoso turned it in his fingers, a silver cigarette lighter embossed with a crest of rampant lions. "It belongs to our new passenger. I borrowed it from her a few minutes ago."

"Dorlisa," Cox said incredulously. "You kidnapped Dorlisa."

"It was really very easy, I hear. Balbin and Procope simply picked her up as she walked along the street. She offered no resistance at all."

"But why? She's no use to you now."

"That remains to be seen." Gayoso ignited the lighter, then snuffed the flame. "I have seen men lose large sums of money, wagering on how many consecutive times a lighter of this sort will function. Myself, I prefer not to gamble unless it is absolutely necessary."

"That doesn't answer my question, General."

"Perhaps it does. To be perfectly frank, some of my subordinates have their doubts about you, Mr. Cox. They believe you are attempting to default on your part of the bargain. For myself, of course, I have no such doubts. I am sure that you will do all that is required of you."

"And if I don't?"

"My orders were plain. Someone must die today. If not Bruno Lazar, then it shall be Lazar's secretary, Mrs. Weber." Gayoso gestured negligently. "The choice of victims is entirely up to you."

Cox regarded him bitterly. It was the perfect checkmate, one he hadn't been able to foresee, and he felt like a wolf in a trap, gnawing off his own leg to get free. "You touch Dorlisa, and I'll kill you." But he knew how empty the threat was.

Gayoso knew also; his smile didn't waver. "A very proper spirit. Rest assured I have no expectation of harming her. I know that your decision will make it unnecessary." He glanced at the clock. "I regret that the pressure of time requires me to call for that decision now."

Cox said, "You like to see people squirm, don't you?"

"Yes," Gayoso admitted pleasantly, "it is a weakness of mine."

"Why should I trust you? You might kill her, anyway."

"On the contrary, I'm looking forward to your reunion afterward. It should be a tender moment, very heartwarming. I would hate to miss it."

Cox slid off the table and stood erect. "All right. Where's the rifle?"

"Balbin will give it to you at the proper time. I hope you don't mind that I've altered the arrangements a bit. Balbin will accompany you, and Procope will attend the funeral services—to make sure nothing goes wrong."

The trap held him fast; Gayoso had thought of everything. The knowledge was a sour lump in Cox's throat. "Okay," he uttered. "Like you said—somebody dies."

"Good." Gayoso opened the door into the passageway. "And now that your vision has cleared and your strength has returned, may I suggest that the launch is waiting?"

In life, Hernando Sotomayor had been a man of many friends and wide acquaintance, respected by his community. In death, those friends and acquaintances turned out to do him honor, and the community paused respectfully to observe.

The funeral procession, which began at a downtown mortuary and wended its way through the suburbs toward the cathedral, had some aspects of a pageant. First came the hearse, the traditional glass-sided black carriage in which reposed the coffin under a blanket of flowers; it was drawn by a team of black horses whose trappings were black also, even to the plumed feathers on their heads. Behind this came another horse-pulled coach containing the widow and other members of the immediate family. A second coach was reserved for close friends.

Then, a short distance behind, began a cavalcade of automobiles whose passengers represented government, business and civic groups. These cars crept forward in low gear so as neither to overtake the plodding horses nor outdistance the several score mourners who marched behind on foot.

In this heterogeneous group, with components drawn from many different levels of society and several nationalities, no one questioned the inclusion of Bruno Lazar's armored sedan. Today, thoughts were turned inward, dwelling on the majesty and awesomeness of death. Still less would anyone have questioned the presence of Procope, who trudged bareheaded at the rear of the parade. His expression fitted perfectly. He too was thinking of death.

For the first time, the stimulants had not done their work. Odilia roamed the yacht like a lost shadow, seeking some relief from the nervous hysteria which threatened to shatter her being into fragments like glass.

Her thoughts darted this way and that, as much out of control as the twitching of her body, yet always returning to the fate that Gayoso had promised her. She could not believe that he meant it, while at the same time heeding the inexorable voice of reason telling her that he did. She had been aware, when she allowed herself to think of it, that her life had been like a staircase for years, each step lower than the last. By taking one step at a time, she had not minded the gradual descent particularly, nor had she glimpsed the inevitable bottom. It had seemed wonderfully daring to defy her family and run off with the young army officer, but it had been the first step down. And when he was killed and his commanding officer had offered his protection in exchange for certain favors ... another step. And then had come the revolution in which it had been necessary to prove her loyalty—the steps were coming faster now—until at last there had been Gayoso ... and now this. Her mistake lay in believing, as late as last night, that the steps could lead up as well as down.

Gradually, Odilia's thought coalesced on the one avenue still left to her. It was not salvation but vengeance. From the depths, she might still pull her enemies down with her. But how?

To destroy—somehow—the carefully contrived plan of assassination promised the most satisfaction. But, she thought sadly, it was already too late for that. Prowling wraithlike about the ship, she had watched Cox leave in the company of Balbin and Procope, his face stony with purpose. Gayoso, who remained, was more than a match for her. And then Odilia remembered the new passenger aboard the yacht, a woman like herself, also a prisoner. Dorlisa Weber.

The inspiration seemed heaven-sent. She had watched the blonde woman brought aboard, unpleasantly surprised at her beauty, since she had conceived her so differently. Dorlisa had been lodged in an empty stateroom adjoining Gayoso's quarters. Odilia thought she knew why: Dorlisa was to be Cox's reward, the icing on his cake of success. Hate burned in her at the thought. But if Dorlisa Weber should die ... She rolled the prospect around in her imagination with growing pleasure. It would be a fitting revenge on all of them. Her rival would be gone, Cox would be punished for his callous rejection, and as for Gayoso—who could say what might happen to him when Cox, returning fresh from one slaying, discovered that he had been defrauded? The prospect made Odilia giggle delightedly.

Her decision made, she moved rapidly to put it into action. Stealthily, she crept below to the deserted dispensary. Her thoughts went automatically to poison as the weapon, almost a conditioned reflex, and she would have used her own supply of drugs had she considered them potent enough. She had no trouble finding what she sought. From the pharmacy locker, she selected a vial of aconitine nitrate and prepared a solution which she drew into a hypodermic. Odilia considered she was being kind in choosing aconite; it was quick-acting and not particularly painful, the symptoms approximating shock.

Concealing the syringe in her hand, she crept down the passageway to the door behind which Dorlisa Weber waited. To her disappointment, she discovered that Dorlisa already had a visitor. Odilia recognized Gayoso's voice. Head close to the panel, she listened.

Balbin had kept the guitar case containing the rifle in his possession but as they entered the bull-ring, he handed it to Cox. "Here—you carry it for a while."

"I didn't think you trusted me with it."

"Who said anything about trusting you? It's a long climb to the top and the case is heavy, that's all." Balbin looked scornful. "You'll behave anyhow, the way a trained monkey should. Otherwise, no peanuts."

The amphitheater was more deserted than on Cox's previous visit. No youngsters scampered about the sandy floor in make-believe bull-baiting. In the lower stands a pair of young lovers sat together, eating a picnic lunch. Engrossed in each other, they did not notice the intruders.

Cox led the way upward to the rim of the stadium and around the curve of the huge saucer to the vantage point he had selected. Balbin contemplated the view critically. "It's quite a distance to the cemetery. Do you actually believe you can make the shot?"

"I'd better make it, hadn't I?"

"I'm glad to see you understand the situation." Balbin glanced at his watch. "Nearly one o'clock. I hope that they don't make us wait too long in this sun." He produced binoculars from his pocket and began to study the cathedral for some sign that the services were nearly over.

Cox contemplated the scene also. The funeral procession had reached the church some time before, and the various vehicles clustered about it were empty. He thought he could detect a sedan parked under the porte-cochere, probably Lazar's armored car. A few of the mourners, unable to find space in the crowded church, had straggled around to the cemetery and stood in little groups, waiting. At this distance, and with the naked eye, Cox could not identify anyone. He frowned slightly as an idea crossed his mind.

Balbin lowered his glasses. "Nothing yet."

Cox dug out his cigarettes. "Care for a smoke to pass the time?"

Balbin accepted, placing the binoculars on the ledge between them while he struck a match. He watched lazily through the smoke as Cox began to open the guitar case. He said, "I hope you don't harbor any foolish notion of trying to murder me with that rifle. You might escape but Mrs. Weber wouldn't. My report to the General is the only key that will unlock her prison."

Cox smiled bleakly. "Don't be afraid."

"Oh, I'm not worried. No matter how well dressed a monkey may be, he is still a monkey."

Cox didn't reply. His head was bent over the rifle, and Balbin couldn't see his eyes. It was just as well, because they were not looking at the weapon at all. Instead, his eyes were fixed on the binoculars resting on the ledge by his elbow.

Gayoso studied the woman who sat on the edge of the four-poster bed, one wrist handcuffed to a bedpost. "You don't appear to be particularly frightened."

"I'm very frightened," Dorlisa said. "I know your reputation, General."

"Reputations can be greatly exaggerated, I find. Do I look like the bogey man your people have pictured me to be?" Gayoso knew he did not. Flushed with imminent success, he had donned full military uniform, complete with polished riding boots and holstered pistol at his waist, the epitome of suave authority.

"Do you mind telling me why I've been kidnapped?"

"For the moment, I prefer to speak of reputations. Your own, for instance. I had heard that you were Lazar's most fervent disciple, devoted to his principles. Yet this morning you, a dedicated pacifist, stabbed a man. How can this be, I wonder?"

Dorlisa lowered her head. "It was a reflex action, almost an accident. I don't know what came over me."

"The plea of every sinner," Gayoso sneered. "Admit instead that you have no principles. Be honest with yourself, Mrs. Weber. When provoked, you behaved no better than any other animal."

"Did you come here simply to gloat?"

"Of course. It's one of the fruits of victory." Gayoso hooked his thumbs in his belt. "I enjoy seeing you brought down to the level of the rest of us. Do you know why I hate Bruno Lazar? It is not that he is an enemy of my government, oh, no. A mere enemy I can respect, even sorrow somewhat at his defeat, the fall of a fellow man. But Lazar and you poor sheep who follow him consider yourselves to be so far above us—a counterfeit Christ and his tawdry apostles!"

Dorlisa stared at him wonderingly. "You don't understand us at all, do you?"

"I pride myself on my eyesight, Mrs. Weber. I see you for what you are. You bump bellies with a man and call it love. You stab him and call it an accident. Pretty words—but they don't alter the truth."

Dorlisa's eyes flashed. "You don't know what truth is. You don't know what love is. No, and you don't understand how a woman can be so badly hurt that she—" She stopped abruptly, biting her lip. "There's no use arguing with you."

"Please go on. Who knows? You might convince me, after all."

"No, I'll take my punishment, whatever it is. I'll admit I deserve it. But I'm not going to crawl for your benefit, General. I forgot my principles once. I won't again."

"Then you don't care to go on living?"

"Of course I do. But it has to be on my own terms. I don't expect you to understand that, either."

"Suppose you knew that it was your life or mine," Gayoso mused. "Would you kill me, Mrs. Weber? I think you would, and to hell with your principles. You could always rationalize that I deserve to die."

Dorlisa shook her head slowly. "No."

"How can you be sure—after what happened this morning? You've already discovered you have a breaking point." Gayoso drew his pistol from its holster. "The second time is much easier—and when you consider that your life is at stake ..." He took careful aim at a vase which stood on the bureau. It shattered into fragments under the impact of the bullet. Dorlisa watched him tensely. Gayoso said, "That was to prove to you that the pistol is loaded and in fine working order. That being established ..." He dropped the weapon in her lap and stood back.

She didn't touch it. "Pick it up," he urged. "It's very easy. You simply point it at me and squeeze the trigger. A child could do it. Here—I'll even turn my back."

Cox had accused him of liking to see people squirm, but that wasn't the whole truth of this moment. Gayoso's compulsion was to pull down, to demean; no one must possess qualities that might be deemed superior to his own—keener eyesight, higher birth, better anything. And before him sat manacled a woman who professed a stronger moral fiber, a challenge like Lazar and his entire pack of ideal-mouthing runaways.

Thus the purpose of the interview was the degradation of Dorlisa, and Gayoso had prepared his props carefully. The bullet which had destroyed the vase had been the only one in the magazine; the rest were blanks. So he posed with confident unconcern, awaiting the harmless explosion he felt sure would come. He said over his shoulder, "The key to your handcuffs is in the breast pocket of my tunic, by the way." There was no reply, and he wheeled about impatiently.

The pistol lay where he had placed it in her lap. She hadn't even picked it up. She said, "Can't you see you're wrong about me?"

"I see only that I haven't supplied the proper provocation." Gayoso slapped her viciously across the face. "Do I begin to stir your anger now?" He struck her again, then a third time.

Dorlisa didn't move. A trickle of blood ran down from her cut lip. She whispered, "You can't really touch me."

"I intend to win. You'd better understand that." He was angry now, his voice guttural, truly the swamp Indian Odilia had called him. "Perhaps you'd prefer I used Cox's methods ..." He tore open the jacket of her gray suit, ripping off buttons, and ran his hands insultingly over the curve of her breasts. "Do you need to be raped before you'll fight back?"

Dorlisa closed her eyes, and her lips moved inaudibly, as if praying. Gayoso continued to fondle her body a moment longer. Then, abruptly, he released her and stood up. "You're not a woman," he told her contemptuously. "There's no satisfaction in you. I can't understand why Cox is so anxious to save you—because you're already dead."

Her eyes flew open at the name. "Cox? He's alive?"

"Of course. You weren't even woman enough to kill him when you had the opportunity."

"Alive," Dorlisa murmured. "Oh, thank God!"

"That pleases you, eh? I suppose that you'll tell me next that, despite what he's done, you still love him."

"I don't know," Dorlisa said uncertainly. "I'm just glad that I didn't kill him. Maybe it doesn't have anything to do with ..."

Gayoso smoothed back his hair with both palms. He had regained his composure and his voice was bland again. "Would you like to see him and be sure? He'll be here within an hour, perhaps less, just as soon as he finishes his job."

Her lips trembled over the question. "His job?"

"The assassination of Bruno Lazar. It should be happening any minute now, in the little cemetery behind the cathedral." He smiled at her involuntary cry of anguish. "You should feel quite honored, Mrs. Weber. Cox is only doing it for your sake."

"For my sake!"

"An even exchange, Lazar's life for yours. You see, unlike yourself, Cox is very sure of his love." Gayoso roared with sudden laughter. "What a joke! Cox will save your life, and you will hate him for it."

He had finally achieved the effect he sought. Dorlisa's shoulders sagged hopelessly and tears began to run slowly down her cheeks. Gayoso, watching, said, "Don't bother with female performances. After all, you still have the pistol." He stopped, listening. From the passageway had come a faint sound. He moved quickly to the door but turned at the last moment for a final word. "I was about to inquire if your patchwork principles extend to suicide. If not, you might find that course preferable to living with the knowledge that your lover has murdered your Jefe."

As he went out, Gayoso saw from the corner of his eye Dorlisa's hand steal slowly toward the pistol in her lap. He grinned, knowing that the blank cartridge could do no more than singe her blonde hair. It was just one more side to the joke, the funniest he had ever invented.

He was surprised to find no one waiting for him outside the door. But the passageway was empty, containing nothing but a faint scent of perfume.

Balbin flipped away his cigarette. "What in God's name is taking them so long?" he grumbled. "They should have been able to run through even a High Mass by this time."

"Maybe Procope got religion and confessed," Cox suggested. He finished attaching the telescopic sight to the rifle and leaned it against the parapet.

Balbin snorted. "Procope? He'd be more likely to slit the priest's throat and make off with the communion silver."

"Then Sotomayor wasn't the first man he's killed?"

"Nor will he be the last, I can assure you. Procope enjoys his work. Better keep that in mind." Balbin squinted in the direction of the cathedral and his voice quickened. "I believe the service is over. I can see people coming out." He reached for the binoculars.

"Yeah? Let me look." Cox's own hand grabbed for the glasses. His arm collided with the other man's just as Balbin's fingers closed around the binoculars. They were dislodged from his grasp, skittered across the wide ledge and vanished over the side. Cox swore. "What in hell did you drop them for?"

"I didn't drop them. You knocked them out of my hand." Balbin stared at him accusingly. "Perhaps deliberately."

"You're all wet. It was an accident." Cox shrugged. "Anyway, it doesn't matter. I still have the telescopic sight."

"But I have nothing. Let me warn you that I can still observe what happens, even without the binoculars."

"You talk too much." Cox rested the rifle on the parapet and adjusted the stock against his shoulder. "Now pipe down for a while. I got work to do."

Odilia went into her stateroom and closed the door behind her. The click of the latch had a finality to it, like the last tick of a clock that has run down.

She had heard all that had passed between Gayoso and Dorlisa Weber. It had affected her deeply. Her mood, which had alternated between hysteria and elation, now resolved itself into profound melancholia. No longer did she regard Dorlisa as an enemy; rather, she equated Dorlisa with herself as a sister woman. Both helpless prisoners, pawns of fate ... what hope did either of them have in this cruel game where men made the rules and held all the trump cards?

She had no doubt that Dorlisa would accept Gayoso's suggestion and use the pistol, because she herself had accepted it. Suicide was the only avenue of escape left open to her. She knew that now. In death she could still claim victory of a sort.

But it must be done beautifully, the final grand gesture that would fill them all with awe and remorse. She pictured Gayoso, respectful of her at last. She pictured Cox, brokenhearted, kneeling beside her lifeless form, realizing—too late, too late—how great her passion had been. Tears filled Odilia's eyes at the thought. "Poor creature," she murmured, and she was not speaking of herself but of the man who would suffer forever at her memory.

From the closet, she selected with great care her favorite negligée and put it on. She repaired her makeup and arranged her auburn hair for the last time. It's like going to my wedding, she thought, and felt pity for Dorlisa who had not been granted the opportunity to make herself beautiful for this most important moment of her life.

And now she was ready. She arranged herself carefully on her bed to await the coming of her bridegroom. From the bedside table she took the hypodermic of aconitine nitrate and emptied the contents into her arm. She felt nothing, only a blissful satisfaction. Her last conscious act was to fix a tragic smile—reproach mixed with forgiveness—upon her face for the benefit of the man she knew would come to find her.

The last of the mourners had emerged from the cathedral. They stood in a large formless group around the open grave, bareheaded and unmoving, while the black-robed priest went through the ritual that would allow the coffin to complete the final six feet of its journey.

"Do you see him?" Balbin demanded tensely. "Do you see Lazar? I can't pick him out without the glasses."

"You'll see him when he falls," Cox muttered. The butt of the rifle was pressed tight against his shoulder, the scope against his eye. "Shut up and let me concentrate."

Balbin was too jittery to comply. "Don't wait forever. They'll be leaving soon."

"I've got to get him in the clear. The first shot's got to do it." Beads of perspiration coated Cox's forehead. He felt his finger wanting to tremble on the trigger. He concentrated on his target, waiting for the precise moment. A mourner, shifting restlessly, blocked his view for an instant.

"Hurry," Balbin was whispering. "What are you waiting for?"

He saw his victim again. Nothing but space stood between him and the muzzle of the rifle. It had to be now. Cox sucked in his breath, held it … and squeezed the trigger. The crack of the rifle, no louder than the snapping of a branch, seemed like an anticlimax.

"He's down!" Balbin shouted. "You hit him!"

In the distant cemetery a man had fallen. Cox, staring through the scope, could see him plainly for a moment before the mourners, milling about in bewilderment, closed him off from sight. Cox had seen enough, anyway. He turned away abruptly. "Damn right I hit him. Now help me get the rifle back in the case."

"Let me have the scope," Balbin ordered. "I want a good look."

"To hell with that. We've got to get out of here before somebody figures out what happened." Cox tore the rifle apart and flung the sections into the guitar case. He snapped at Balbin, who stood staring at the distant confusion, "You coming with me or aren't you?"

Balbin followed him as he plunged down the steps toward the exit. The young lovers, still engrossed in their conversation and their lunch, didn't even look around. If they had heard the shot, they had paid no attention to it. As they ran for their waiting automobile, Balbin panted, "Do you think you killed him?"

"I hit him right in the belly. You don't last long with that kind of a bullet in you."

They flung themselves into the limousine. Balbin sat for a moment before starting the engine. "It was so quick," he marveled. "So easy."

Cox gave him a bitter look, his face pale. "Easy for you maybe, not for me. Or for him."

"Please spare me your remorse. He deserved to die."

"Yeah," Cox agreed heavily. "That's what I've been telling myself."

"Put me down," Bruno Lazar commanded. Vicario and Dr. Neve, who were carrying him, did not obey, and he began to struggle. "I'm quite able to walk, you fools. It was not I who was shot."

"You can thank the Blessed Virgin for that," Vicario grunted. "The next shot might find the right target." They reached the armored sedan and deposited Lazar unceremoniously on the rear seat.

"You have no proof that the bullet was meant for me," Lazar objected. "That poor devil was fully ten paces away."

"He was also the same height and build as you, Jefe. That's enough proof for me. Gayoso's assassin made a mistake."

"It's not right to run away like this, Vicario. We should be doing something for the man, particularly if he fell in my place."

"There's already a priest in attendance." Vicario started the engine. He snapped at Neve, who still stood indecisively beside the car, "Well? Do you need an invitation to enter?"

Neve said, "Bruno's right. We have a responsibility, particularly me. I'm a doctor, after all."

Vicario sighed and turned off the engine again. "All right then, we'll wait for you here. But please hurry. If you can't save the fellow, at least see if you can't assist him to die quickly."

Neve seized his medical bag and darted off toward the cemetery. Lazar called after him, "Find out if he has a family. Perhaps there is something we can do ..."

Vicario muttered, "The only thing we can do is to leave this cursed city as rapidly as possible."

Lazar wasn't listening. "How strange," he mused. "That another man should die in my place, not knowing, simply because we attended a funeral together. I wonder who he is."

"From his appearance I supposed he was one of Sotomayor's employees. A sallow little man with a pockmarked face." Vicario shrugged. "I find nothing strange about dying. It's a chance we all take, simply by living. He might as easily have been struck down by an automobile in the street."

"No," Lazar murmured, "there is more than chance in all this, even though we fail to understand it."

Dr. Neve came back along the driveway to join them, frowning. In a strange voice, he said, "He's gone."

"Wasn't there anything you could do to help?"

"I didn't have the opportunity. I mean the man's disappeared, simply pushed everyone aside and staggered off. I don't understand it. I'd swear that he was mortally wounded."

"Where did he go?" Vicario demanded. "Didn't anyone follow him?"

"When the priest tried to seize him, he pulled out a knife and threatened to use it. Out of his mind with agony, I suppose." Neve shook his head in bewilderment. "They'll find him again, of course. He can't last long in that condition. It's only a question of time."

And ... A question of time, Jack Cox was thinking also, a race against the clock with Dorlisa's life as the prize. Could he succeed in buying her freedom before Gayoso discovered that the coin was counterfeit?

"Can't this thing go any faster?"

Balbin, at the wheel, gave him a scornful smile, thinking him frightened of the police. He believed, as Cox intended him to believe, that the victim in the cemetery was Bruno Lazar. He would report victory to Gayoso. He had seen the shot, he had seen the man fall—an officer could trust the evidence of his own eyes. It did not occur to him that Cox, through manipulation and suggestion, had succeeded in creating an illusion ... and that his fear was that not the police but the truth would overtake him.

He had not relished shooting down Procope. The pockmarked little man, murderer of Sotomayor and no one knew how many others, deserved to die, but Cox had not wished to become his executioner. Unfortunately, there had been little choice. It was necessary that Balbin see someone fall. At first, Cox had toyed with the notion of merely wounding Lazar. But this would not do; it was too risky a shot and, though he might fool Balbin, Procope was standing by to observe the results. So, for a double reason, it had had to be Procope. Cox wondered what the little man had thought, or if he had time to think at all.

They reached the ocean and came to a sliding halt beside the pier where the launch waited, its engine chugging. Cox flung open the door immediately but Balbin grabbed his arm. "There's no hurry now. We must wait here."

"What for?"

"For Procope to join us, of course. He'll be along shortly."

Cox repressed a grim laugh. He had no intention of waiting for a dead man, particularly now when every beat of the clock meant added danger. "You stick around if you want to. I'm going out to the yacht."

"The launch goes nowhere without my orders."

"I thought Gayoso gave the orders. I'll bet he's chewed his nails right down to the first joint already, waiting for the news."

Balbin hesitated, not wanting to give in to the American yet fearful of Gayoso's impatience. He temporized, "We'll wait five minutes for Procope."

"Take a look down there." Cox pointed south along the coast to where a sleek gray vessel hovered. "That's a Mexican coast-guard cutter. Somebody may put two and two together and send it up to pay a call. Gayoso'll be tickled to death you waited around for your buddy, I'm sure."

Fear won out. Balbin cast a last glance back at the empty highway that led to the city and followed Cox out of the automobile. The limousine, rented under a fictitious name, was simply to be abandoned at dockside. It had served its purpose. Like himself, Cox reflected and wondered if it were Gayoso's intention to discard him as quickly. The next hour would answer a lot of questions.

Domingo the boatswain was crouched in the stern of the launch. He looked up incuriously as the two men swung aboard. His world was a simple one, revolving upon the axis of Gayoso's commands, and little else concerned him. He had been dispatched to pick up the shore party, they were here, and it didn't matter to him whether they were two or three. He cast off the mooring line and pointed the launch toward the yacht.

Cox continued to clutch the guitar case that contained the rifle. He had no expectation of using the weapon again. For the battle ahead, his wits would have to suffice. His wits, and a large helping of luck.

They reached *La Polilla*, scraped against the bottom of the gangway. Cox was first up the precarious steps. Balbin lingered to speak with Domingo. As Cox reached the deck he heard the launch engine roar again. He turned to see the little vessel heading shoreward. He asked sharply, "Where's the boat going now?"

"To wait for Procope," Balbin told him. "Do you expect him to swim?"

"No." Cox could think of no good excuse for demanding that the launch remain, although it represented the only ready means of escape. Without it, he might have to do some swimming himself, he and Dorlisa. He was glad to know from experience she was a strong swimmer, perhaps even more so than he.

Gayoso was waiting for them in the lounge. He was standing in the center of the low-ceilinged room, standing rather stiffly with his hands clasped behind his back, as if braced for bad news. His keen gaze studied their faces as the two men entered and then, reading something in their expression, he began to smile. "Tell me," he ordered softly.

Balbin drew himself up. "General, I have the honor to report the success of our mission."

"Bruno Lazar is dead? You're sure?"

"I saw him fall myself. Procope, when he arrives, will confirm it."

"Splendid," Gayoso breathed. He came forward, holding out his hand to Cox. "My congratulations. I'll admit I was growing a trifle concerned. I've been listening to the radio, hoping for a news bulletin, but perhaps it is still too early."

Cox glanced at the radio from which issued the soft strains of music, seeing it as a new enemy, a time bomb that might at any moment explode in his face. He allowed his hand to be shaken. "Thanks."

"Your fingers are like ice. Did you find the experience so harrowing?"

"I don't shoot a man every day."

"Very few ever have the opportunity to shoot a man like Bruno Lazar," Gayoso exulted. "Think of it, Mr. Cox! You have made your mark in history. I envy you."

"I did my job," Cox said. "Now I'd like my pay. The woman."

"The occasion calls for celebration. Champagne, I think. Balbin, fetch the glasses while I open the bottle." As he tugged at the cork, Gayoso asked, "Were there any unforeseen difficulties?"

"None," Balbin said, setting up the goblets on the bar in a straight line. "All went according to plan, very formidable."

Cox felt his palms begin to sweat. "If it's all the same to you, I think I'll skip the drink. I'm in a hurry."

Gayoso, pouring the wine, was the essence of leisure. "I'd like to discuss the matter of the reward with you, if you don't mind."

"I don't see that there's anything to discuss."

"I think there is. For your own sake, I'd like you to consider the alternatives. It's true that I promised you Mrs. Weber. Earlier, I promised you other benefits, among them money and a new nationality. Now that the heat of battle is behind us, I will renew my first offer." Gayoso handed him the goblet, brimful. "I do so because I believe you have a future with us. My country can use a man of your talents and energy. I can use you. I know that you don't like me very much but that hardly matters. Associations founded on mutual advantage generally prosper better than those founded on affection."

"I don't think I'm cut out to be an assassin. I've learned that much."

"Of course," Gayoso agreed. "I know that sort of future would not appeal to you, any more than to me. But there are other jobs that are less demanding and equally rewarding. This is what I'm offering you. Believe me, Mr. Cox, the man who shot Bruno Lazar will command a good deal of importance in my country. The possibilities are virtually unlimited."

"Let me get this straight," Cox said slowly. "Are you welshing on the bargain we made this morning?"

"I'm merely pointing out that you still have a choice. Mrs. Weber— or an exciting career. Unfortunately, you cannot have both."

Cox took a gulp of champagne; his fingers, beginning to quiver, threatened to spill the liquid. The strain was working on him. He had to bring the conversation to a quick close without arousing Gayoso's suspicions. He said, "I appreciate your offer, General, but—"

The radio cut him short. The music ceased and an announcer's voice said, "We interrupt our program of recorded music to bring you a special news bulletin. In Tijuana this afternoon an unidentified man has been shot down while attending the funeral of—"

Cox moved quickly to shut off the machine. Gayoso, startled, asked, "Why did you do that? I should think you'd be interested in your press notices."

"I didn't want to hear it. I'm sorry, General, but I just don't much care to be the man who shot Bruno Lazar. That's why I'm going to have to turn down your offer."

Balbin, puzzled, mused, "Strange, that they should not have been able to identify Lazar by this time. What do they gain by keeping it a secret?"

It wasn't a thought Cox wished pursued. He said quickly, "So if you'll just turn Dorlisa over to me, we'll consider the account square."

Gayoso sighed. "I think you're making a mistake. She's only a woman. I can introduce you to a dozen who are younger and prettier. You'll get no pleasure from Mrs. Weber. She'll never forgive you for what you've done."

"That's a chance I'll have to take."

Balbin said, "General, I can hear the launch. Procope must be coming aboard."

"Good," Gayoso said. "We can get underway immediately. The sooner we're out of Mexican waters the better."

Cox felt a surge of hope. Whatever the reason for the launch's return—he knew it couldn't be Procope—it provided a means of escape at precisely the right moment. Luck was with him, after all. He said, "Then I guess I'd better say good-by. I'll take Dorlisa ashore with me, maybe head south, hole up in the mountains until—"

Gayoso shook his head. "I'm afraid not. You should see yourself that it's quite out of the question."

"You promised to let her go!"

"At the proper time. For the safety of all of us, I can't release her here where the police are likely to find her. I'll put her ashore somewhere to the south, Guatemala perhaps. And you, too, if you haven't changed your mind by that time."

Hope died. He saw that Gayoso's decision was irrevocable. The trap was slowly closing. He could not escape it with cunning; all that remained was to fight his way free. He adopted a false resignation. "Well, if that's the best you can do ... but I would like to see her now."

"Of course. We'll go together to unshackle her." Gayoso dug a small key out of his tunic. "She's in the stateroom adjoining mine."

Cox itched to have possession of the key that Gayoso juggled negligently between his fingers. He cautioned himself to be patient. Once Dorlisa was free, then would come the time for action. It would be him against Gayoso, man to man. He hoped he was strong enough with his injured shoulder to overcome his powerfully-built enemy.

"Okay, lead the way."

Over his shoulder, Gayoso said, "Don't be surprised if you find Mrs. Weber somewhat depressed. I had a conversation with her earlier and—" He opened the saloon door.

Procope stood there. He wore no coat and the front of his white shirt was black with crusted blood. His face was chalky; from it, his glazed eyes bulged like livid marbles. He was a walking dead man, spilling out his life with every tortured step but incredibly still on his feet. He had come for his revenge. He held his long-bladed knife in his hand.

Gayoso gaped at him. "Procope! What's happened to you?"

Procope neither saw nor heard him. His clouded gaze fastened on Cox's face. "Kill—you," he gasped and a red froth bubbled on his lips with the words. He lurched forward, the knife blade pointing.

Gayoso and Balbin were motionless with astonishment. Cox recovered first since he had less to assimilate. He seized the dying man's wrist and threw him into the other two men, knocking them to the floor in a heap. His gaze, searching the saloon for a weapon, saw only the crossed sabers on the wall. He tore them both from their mountings and leaped for the door. Balbin clutched at his ankle as he passed but he kicked the hand away and reached the safety of the deck. He slammed the door behind him and used one of the sabers to bar it. It would not hold long, it would buy only a few seconds of time, but now even a few seconds were precious.

Domingo was standing at the head of the gangway as Cox ran forward. He reached for Cox's throat with both hands. Cox hit him with the flat of the saber blade, swinging it like a bat. As the boatswain wavered, he threw the man bodily down the gangway. He heard him fall the length of the steps but did not bother to watch. Behind him, the prisoners in the saloon were battering down the door.

He found the companionway that led to the staterooms below and plunged down it. He ran along the carpeted corridor, sword in hand like a buccaneer, flinging open the doors as he passed. Until, at last, he found the one he sought.

Dorlisa was seated on the bed, head bowed disconsolately. She sprang up as Cox burst in upon her. Her first expression was of gladness and then, remembering, she shrank away from him in fright. She could not retreat far. One wrist was manacled to the bedpost.

Cox panted, "It's all right. I didn't do it. Lazar's alive."

"Thank God," she breathed, and then she was hugging him tightly with her one free arm. "I prayed for us."

"Don't stop yet. Gayoso knows. We've got to get out of here." The key to her handcuffs was somewhere in the saloon above, irretrievably out of reach. He pushed her away. "Stand as far from the post as you can."

She obeyed. He measured the post with his eyes, like a woodman with a tree, and swung the saber. The post splintered and broke; a second cut sent it toppling to the floor. The cuff still encircled Dorlisa's left wrist but she was free. The sudden release made her sway. Cox caught her, turning in the same instant toward the door.

He saw the gun first, a Sten submachine gun, pointed at his stomach. Behind it, framed in the doorway, was a chunky figure in an over-decorated officer's tunic. "Stay very motionless," Gayoso cautioned. "I don't want to kill you so quickly."

Cox held the saber but the distance was too great to permit its use. He felt the bitterness of defeat. "Okay, General. You win."

Gayoso, in the struggle in the saloon, his dark glasses had been knocked off, permitting his eyes to be seen. They glittered like polished obsidian, making him somehow more malevolent. He said, "Move away from the woman, slowly, if you please. I wish her to see you die."

Dorlisa stood as rigid as marble in his arms. She was staring at Gayoso like a hypnotized animal, unable to comprehend. Cox took his arm away from her waist reluctantly, not wanting to give up his grasp on what had become the most important part of his life. Yet there was no alternative; he had gambled and lost. He said, "There's no reason to kill her. She had nothing to do with it."

"Beg me," Gayoso suggested.

"Kill me as slowly as you like—but let Dorlisa go."

"There's merit in your proposal," Gayoso admitted, still grinning. "Perhaps we should begin with a bullet in the leg—to bring you to your knees. Then a burst in the stomach for the proper amount of pain. And later, much later, the *coup de grâce*. How does the notion strike you, Mrs. Weber?"

In a strangled whisper, Dorlisa said, "You're not fit to live."

Gayoso chuckled. "I see that you still have my pistol. Why don't you use it? But I forgot—you're a woman of principle." His gaze, which had flicked momentarily toward the woman, returned to the man. "And now, Mr. Cox, suppose we begin."

Cox cast a last glance at Dorlisa and was surprised to see that her face was contorted, not in tearful despair, but in an expression of savage fury. He had seen it once before, when she had stabbed him with the harness shears. Before he could shout at her to be careful, she snatched up the pistol that lay on the bed. Leaping forward with an inarticulate shriek, she fired it in Gayoso's face.

Even in the split-second that it was happening it occurred to Cox to wonder why Gayoso had not fired first, why he had not been more concerned about the threat of the pistol. Then, as Gayoso reeled backward but—miraculously—did not fall, his head unshattered by the bullet, Cox understood. The pistol held only blanks.

Yet the blanks were enough. They could not kill but they could disable. The fiery powder, spewing out of the pistol's muzzle, seared into Gayoso's unprotected eyes, blinding him. He screamed in pain. His fingers clawed at his face.

Cox sprang forward to disarm him but Gayoso, sightless, was still dangerous. He lurched backward along the passageway, firing the Sten wildly to keep his enemies at bay. The undirected bullets lodged in the paneled walls and overhead but Cox realized it would be sure death to attack the crazily spurting gun. He grabbed Dorlisa's arm. "Come on—there's another flight of stairs this way."

She stumbled after him, still clutching the pistol. "I had to do it," she mumbled. "He was going to kill you."

"Listen to me," he commanded. "We're going to have to make a run for the launch. God knows what we're going to meet topside. Whatever happens, keep going, understand?"

"I'm not going to leave you, Jack."

"No one's asked you to yet." He half-pulled her up the steps to the deck. At first glance, he saw no one but, as he stuck his head cautiously out of the companionway, a bullet spanged off the metal by his shoulder. Balbin was crouched aft behind a ventilator hood, and he had the Krag rifle, assembled now.

Cox considered. Balbin blocked the path to the launch. Somewhere in the other direction was Gayoso, temporarily out of action—but for how long? Both men were armed. And there was the question of the yacht's crew. He hoped fervently that they were huddled safely below somewhere but he couldn't be sure; they might enter the battle at any moment. Against this formidable opposition, he had a saber and a pistol loaded with blanks.

Dorlisa whispered, "What are we going to do?"

"I've gotten this far on bluff. Let's push it a little farther. Give me the pistol." He took it, shifting the saber to his left hand. "When I give the word, we'll run like hell for the gangway. If I start firing, maybe Balbin will think they're real bullets and keep his head in."

"And if he doesn't?"

"Well, he'll be concentrating on getting me so you ought to make it."

She shook her head. "We're going to stay together, win or lose."

"For Christ's sake!" he said roughly. "I gambled my neck to get you out of here. It's the only neck I've got so don't make me waste it for nothing."

She clung to him. "I love you, Jack."

"Sure you do. So do what I tell you, you hear?" He gathered his feet under him for the charge. "All set?"

The path to freedom was a diagonal one, cutting aft across the quarterdeck from the companionway to the top of the gangway ladder. Balbin's position behind the ventilator covered every step of it at almost point-blank range. Cox felt his mouth grow dry at the prospect. He had to force out the words. "Then let's go!"

They exploded from the companionway as if shot out of a cannon. Cox opened fire as his feet hit the deck and saw Balbin duck. He thrust Dorlisa ahead of him, yelling at her to run. They scampered across the deck toward the distant gangway. Cox continued to aim the fake fusillade in Balbin's direction. And, for a moment, he dared to hope that the bluff was going to work.

But Balbin was no coward. After his first instinctive recoil, he popped from behind the ventilator hood to return Cox's fire. And he was not firing blanks. Cox felt something hit him in the chest, an impact as great as if he had suddenly rammed into an invisible timber. It knocked the breath out of him and he fell, rolling into the shallow gutter behind the stern hatch cover. As yet, he felt no pain but he knew that it would begin soon enough.

Dorlisa had reached the gangway. She paused there, looking back, and then it seemed she intended to return for him. Cox summoned enough breath to scream at her, "Get the launch started! I'm coming!" He knew that he was not, but she believed him. She vanished down the ladder.

The Krag's bullets were chipping the hatch cover an inch above his head. He lay there, the wetness of his blood spreading across his chest, wondering how long it would take Balbin to finish him. He raised the pistol and fired in the general direction of the ventilator, trying to buy time for Dorlisa. He heard the launch's engine roar. If he could stall Balbin just a little longer ...

He heard a new sound. It was Gayoso's voice behind him—he couldn't turn his head to discover exactly where—and Gayoso was shouting at Balbin not to allow Cox to escape if he valued his hide.

Balbin called back, "I have him trapped, General! He'll be out of ammunition soon, and I'll finish him then."

"Finish him now!" Gayoso bellowed. "The pistol is loaded with blanks, you fool!"

There was an instant of silence as Balbin absorbed this knowledge, and then he laughed. "Splendid." Cox, his face against the deck, heard the sound of his footsteps approaching. Balbin was in no hurry now; he was almost strolling, relishing the moment.

Cox put aside the useless pistol and grasped the saber, his sole remaining weapon, with both hands. It was a poor match for the rifle, but it was all he had. He heard the footsteps draw closer and then stop, and he knew that Balbin stood only a few feet away from him, ready for the kill. With what strength remained, Cox struggled to his knees and threw the saber like a javelin.

The point struck Balbin in the throat just below the white scar left by another blade long ago. It passed through, emerging from the nape like a skewer. Balbin fell backward to the deck, pulling at the blade with both hands. He tried to scream but only the bubbling sound of blood emerged.

Cox could not stand. His head was spinning dizzily and the deck pitched and heaved before his eyes. He began to crawl on hands and knees for the gangway. It was a million miles distant but somehow he made it. Behind him, Gayoso was screaming, "Balbin! What's happened? Why don't you answer me?"

Domingo's body—alive or dead, he couldn't be sure—sprawled near the bottom of the gangway. Beyond that, Cox made out Dorlisa's face peering anxiously upward from the launch. He tried to wave at her but the effort unbalanced him, and he slid down the steps on his belly.

She leaped up to catch him midway. "My God, what's happened to you? You're bleeding! There's blood all over you!"

He attempted to push her away. "Get out of here. I'm finished."

"I won't leave you!" With more strength than either of them would have supposed she possessed, she seized him by the armpits and half-carried, half-dragged him the remaining distance. They fell into the launch together.

Cox no longer felt that he inhabited his own body. He was a person apart who watched a drama that did not concern him. He watched two actors, one a helpless man who was bleeding to death and the other a desperate woman who scrambled about casting off the mooring line. Was this what it was like to die?

The launch, freed of its bonds, surged away from the yacht's side. But their escape was not complete, not yet. Looking upward, Cox saw Gayoso appear at the quarterdeck railing. His sightless face was thrust in their direction. He could no longer see but he could hear. Gayoso rested the Sten gun on the rail and began to fire at the sound of the launch's engine, a blind Cyclops bent on revenge. The bullets splashed in the water and thudded against the launch's gunwhale.

Cox knew that they would not all miss. He croaked, "Get in the water—swim away."

"I'll help you."

"Not me. Too far gone." He was tasting the blood now; it was in his mouth. "You can make it alone."

"It's either together or not at all! Why won't you believe me?"

The bullets were raining all about them and he was too tired to argue any more. What difference did it make, anyway? The ocean was as good as the launch to him now. He pulled himself toward the side. She was there to help him surmount the last obstacle and together they slid into the water. The launch, pilotless, glided away from them, headed nowhere. Gayoso continued to fire at the sound of its engine but his bullets no longer threatened them.

Cox found the water surprisingly pleasant; his body seemed to lose its immense heaviness and the ocean salt mingled with the blood salt in his mouth. He closed his eyes thankfully.

Yet Dorlisa would not allow him to sink into restfulness as he longed to do. She held his head above the surface and said in his ear, "Take my shoulder, Jack. I'll swim for both of us."

"It's no use," he murmured. "I can't make it."

"You will make it," she insisted. "Look—there's a ship coming! They'll see us."

The Mexican coast-guard cutter, attracted by the firing, was barreling down on the yacht from the south, its siren blaring. Once, it would have seemed the answer to a prayer; now it no longer seemed important. "Too late," he whispered.

"You're not going to die," she told him fiercely. "All you have to do is hold onto me. Don't you want to hold onto me?" He tried to tell her it was all he wanted for the rest of his life, whether that meant years or only the next moment. But he didn't have the strength to do more than grasp her arm. It was enough; Dorlisa understood.

"That's it," she said and held him afloat, interposing both her body and her will against the black depths that wanted to engulf him. "Never let go, darling. I won't."

Neither, God help me, will I. He felt timeless, soaring, as if his soul were talking to him. He forced his eyes open so he could concentrate on their goal. It wasn't so far, after all.

He clung to her and stroked out with his free arm. They swam together, as one person sharing one body.

THE END

WADE MILLER BIBLIOGRAPHY
(Robert Wade and Bill Miller)

Novels

Max Thursday series:

Guilty Bystander (1947)
Fatal Step (1948)
Uneasy Street (1948)
Calamity Fair (1950)
Murder Charge (1950)
Shoot to Kill (1951)

Deadly Weapon (1946)
Pop Goes the Queen (1947;
  reprinted as Murder—Queen
  High, 1949)
Devil on Two Sticks (1949;
  reprinted as Killer's Choice,
  1950)
Devil May Care (1950)
Stolen Woman (1950)
The Killer (1951)
The Tiger's Wife (1951)
Branded Woman (1953)
The Big Guy (1953)
South of the Sun (1953)
Mad Baxter (1955)
Kiss Her Goodbye (1956)
Kitten With a Whip (1959)
Sinner Take All (1960)
Nightmare Cruise (1961; in the
  UK as The Sargasso People,
  1961)
The Girl from Midnight (1962)

As by Will Daemer

The Case of the Lonely Lovers
  (1951)

As by Dale Wilmer

Memo for Murder (1951)
Dead Fall (1954)
Jungle Heat (1954; reprinted as
  by Wade Miller, 1954)

As by Whit Masterson

All Through the Night (1955;
  reprinted as A Cry in the
  Night, 1956)
Dead, She Was Beautiful (1955)
Badge of Evil (1956; reprinted
  as A Touch of Evil, 1958)
A Shadow in the Wild (1957)
The Dark Fantastic (1959)
A Hammer in His Hand (1960)
Evil Come, Evil Go (1961)
[Note: all further Masterson
  books are the solo works of
  Robert Wade]
The Man on a Nylon String
  (1963)
711—Officer Needs Help (1965;
  reprinted as Warning Shot,
  1967; UK as Killer With a
  Badge, 1966)
Play Like You're Dead (1967)
The Last One Kills (1969)

The Death of Me Yet (1970)

The Gravy Train (1971; reprinted as The Great Train Robbery, 1976)

Why She Cries, I Do Not Know (1972)

The Undertaker Wind (1973)

The Man With Two Clocks (1974)

Hunter of the Blood (1977)

The Slow Gallows (1979)

As by Robert Wade

The Stroke of Seven (1965)

Knave of Eagles (1969)

Short Stories

(As Wade Miller unless otherwise noted)

"The Author Confesses" (September 1946, *Mammoth Detective*)

"This Deadly Weapon" (September 1946, *Mammoth Detective*)

"Devil on Two Sticks" (November 1949, *Famous Detective*)

"Murder Has Girl Trouble" (Spring 1950, *Mystery Book Magazine*; Max Thursday)

"The Corpse Walked Away" (January 1951, *Two Complete Detective Books*; Max Thursday)

"Invitation to an Accident" (July 1955, *Ellery Queen's Mystery Magazine*)

"A Bad Time of Day" (September 1956, *Ellery Queen's Mystery Magazine*)

"Midnight Caller" (January 1958, *Manhunt*)

"Suddenly It's Midnight" (January 1958, *Ellery Queen's Mystery Magazine*; by Whit Masterson).

"The Women in His Life" (June 1958, *Ellery Queen's Mystery Magazine*; by Whit Masterson)

"The Dark Fantastic" (February 1959, *Cosmopolitan*)

"The Memorial Hour" (March 1960, *Ellery Queen's Mystery Magazine*)

"We Were Picked as the Odd Ones" (July 1960, *The Saint Mystery Magazine*)

"Seek Him in Shadows" (April 1966, *Argosy*; aka "What Happened to Timothy Owen?"; by Whit Masterson)

"The Morning After" (*The Playboy Book of Crime and Suspense*, Playboy Press, 1966)

Movie Screenplays

Kiss Her Goodbye (1959; screenplay by Alan Marcus & Bill Miller)

Classic hardboiled fiction from the King of the Paperbacks...

Harry Whittington

A Night for Screaming / Any Woman He Wanted
$19.95 978-1-933586-08-3
"[*A Night for Screaming*] is pure Harry. The damned thing is almost on fire, it reads so fast." — Ed Gorman, *Gormania*

To Find Cora / Like Mink Like Murder / Body and Passion
$23.95 978-1-933586-25-0
"Harry Whittington was the king of plot and pace, and he could write anything well. He's 100 percent perfect entertainment." — Joe R. Lansdale

Rapture Alley / Winter Girl / Strictly for the Boys
$23.95 978-1-933586-36-6
"Whittington was an innovator, often turning archetypical characters and plots on their head, and finding wild new ways to tell stories from unusual angles." — Cullen Gallagher, *Pulp Serenade*

A Haven for the Damned
$9.99 978-1-933586-75-5
Black Gat #1. "A wild, savage romp and pure Whittington: raw noir that has the feel of a Jim Thompson novel crossed with a Russ Meyer film." — Brian Greene, *The Life Sentence.*

Trouble Rides Tall / Cross the Red Creek / Desert Stake-Out
$21.95 978-1-944520-11-3
"If these three Whittington novels are the only westerns crime fiction fans ever read, they will have experienced some of the best the genre has to offer." — Alan Cranis, *Bookgasm*

"Harry Whittington delivers every time." — Bill Crider

STARK HOUSE

Stark House Press, 1315 H Street, Eureka, CA 95501
griffinskye3@sbcglobal.net / www.StarkHousePress.com
Available from your local bookstore, or order direct or via our website.

CPSIA information can be obtained
at www.ICGtesting.com
Printed in the USA
LVHW021502031220
673319LV00017B/1580

9 781951 473068